WOLVES OF BLACK PINE

By SJ Himes

Edited by Amanda Coolong

Cover design by Kellie Dennis at Book Cover By Design

The Wolfkin Saga emblem designed by Kellie Dennis, property of SJ Himes.

http://www.sjhimes.com

WARNING: Contains graphic sex, violence, dubious consent, mentions of child abuse and rape.
For mature readers only.

CONTENTS

DEDICATION

To my husband. Apologies for ignoring you the last few months while I wrote this book. You never doubted me, and for that, I will always be grateful.

To Amanda C., thank you for editing this jigsaw puzzle of a manuscript. You are a goddess of charity and helpful insights.

To Amanda B., thank you for the early help and encouragement. You have, better than most, an idea of just how hard this has been, and how much fighting it took to make this book happen.

To Stacie P., may you always be one of the first people I reach out to and say, "Hey, read this will you? Tell me if it's too weird? Or not weird enough? More sex, I can do that."

To all of my family members, friends and coworkers who dealt with my nonstop chattering about werewolves and men falling in love with men: THANK YOU!!!

To Matt T., Surprise! For being constantly annoying, and yet endearingly supportive by channeling our favorite psychotic baby and his talking dog.

Without everyone's patience, encouragement, and real interest and support, this would never have happened.

To the fans of shifter lore and m/m love: may you find the same enjoyment in this book as I did.

AUTHOR'S NOTE

This is a work of fiction, obviously. But—there are some very real, and very nasty, real-life situations in this book, and some content may be considered triggers. Sexual assault, violence, allusions of child abuse, blood, gore and the average depravity of mankind is in this book, along with love, lust, forgiveness and daily angst.

As with all things in this life of ours, use your best judgment about what YOU are capable of reading and handling.

Enjoy!

PART ONE

SHAMAN GRAY SHADOW

WHISPERS FLITTED about the hushed atmosphere of the clan council room, hard to pinpoint to any one particular were-child. The fire crackled softly, shooting out short-lived sparks high above the red hot coals. The great room was dark the only light, the fire centered deep in the sunken floor, casting its orange glow on the stone tiers that rose up along the walls of the council house. Scents of sage, smoke and pine, wet fur and warm blood mingled, an intoxicating blend that teased the senses of the many cubs huddled expectantly at the feet of the Shaman. He raised his gaze around the room, and the few fools brave enough to be whispering quickly quieted. He settled back on his seat, the great stone chair well-worn and adorned with thick bearskins. It was a place of honor reserved for Alphas and Shamans, and woe be to the foolish werewolf who was neither yet sat there uninvited.

His eyes flashed silver in the flames, and the air moved in an inexplicable breeze that smelled of cool winter nights hunting under a full moon. It was summer now, yet the shaman's power rose within the council house, changing the air's scent, the temperature, even the atmosphere.

The Great Shaman began his tale, and the shadows around the stone throne shimmered, gaining depth and movement.

He spoke, and as the tale began, his words and will spun out the images of ancient wolves running across snow swept tundra, great gray beasts with shaggy coats and jaws bred to bring down the greatest of prey and predator alike.

KANE, HEIR to Black Pine Clan, sat carefully in the back of the council house, unnoticed by the fidgeting cubs. He'd snuck away from the party in the square, the gathering's last night drawing a huge crowd. Beer and wolfkin usually led to fights, sex, and Challenges, and he wanted no part of any of the three. His place as Heir was secured, by his Alpha's decree and Kane's mastery of his own gifts as an alpha, so no challenger, even drunk, dared step forward. Beer didn't keep wolves drunk for long, their metabolism burning the alcohol off quickly, so there was enough on hand to drown a fraternity, and the stench was too much for him. And the sex held little appeal, as the majority of unmated wolves at the bonfire were females looking for an unattached alpha or high-ranking beta to seduce into a last minute mating pact before the gathering ended. Most of the females who hadn't found a mate this gathering were the ones worth avoiding, too cloying and clingy, more interested in a prospective mate's rank and influence than the poor male himself.

Kane wanted no part of that. He had his own lover, and Burke was exactly what he needed, what they both needed. Neither were interested in creating a bond outside of casual sex and friendship. Burke was more his friend than lover, anyway, and as the other alpha was his lieutenant as well, romance would just makes things messy. Running the Clan, hunting, and an occasional fuck kept them going.

The fire was reduced to embers, and Kane was glad for it, not wanting to disturb the Shaman or the cubs by bringing attention to himself, the darkness deep enough to hide his bulk as he hid in the back. An adult at what was ostensibly a history lesson but felt more like story time would just ruin the magic.

And magic was what this was. Shaman's magic, spirit magic. Kane never grew out of his childish fascination with it, and it still stung to some degree that when he hit puberty and his gifts emerged, he became an alpha instead of a shaman. He was happy now, but it would have been all kinds of fun as a young teen to experience even half of what the weakest of shamans could do.

Kane let himself slip away to his childhood, feeling like a cub again, watching as the Clans' greatest shaman spun history lessons and tales of legend out of shadows and smoke.

GRAY SHADOW sat above the children and youths of his clan, and he met as many of their wide-eyed stares as he could. The great gathering of the wereclans of the Northern Appalachians and the surrounding ranges brought many children this year, more than in gatherings past; their people were thriving, even with the advent of humanity and their aggravating technologies. The humans' last Great War was long over, and the clans had flourished in the wake of all the young human males dying so far from these shores. There was less competition for land, jobs, and food, and as long as they kept to the Laws of clan and man, and were vigilant, the clans were able to expand their territories. Once smaller packs were growing in numbers. That Great War was generations past now, and this new modern era was blessed with plenty enough young wolves to cause havoc and mayhem.

One of the worst offenders of past mayhem was hiding in the back of the council house even now, fully grown and pretending he wasn't there. The Shaman sent his eyes over where Kane was hiding, and pretended not to notice that the Clan Heir was avoiding matchmaking females and drunken upstart alphas looking for a beating. Kane was thankfully a wiser wolf now in his young adulthood than he had been as a whelp, and he was more likely to be stopping the trouble these days than starting it. The cub still had a temper, but age was easing its grip on him. He let Kane think himself invisible, and returned his attention to the collected youth of the clans at his feet.

He was the oldest of the shamans. Gray Shadow they called him, his birth name long forgotten by the clans in the many years since his youth. He alone held the greatest gifts of their people, in illusion, healing, spirit walking and mastery of the elements. Of the two hundred clans across the globe, Gray Shadow was known to all, and petitions for him to take apprentices came every year, clans seeking to have their young shamans taught under him unrelenting. Gray Shadow had only just released his last apprentice from his service this past spring, young Michael, a competent and trustworthy shaman after recently passing his trials. Even his Clan's Alpha expressing Gray Shadow's desire for a season of rest before taking on a new apprentice did little to stop the influx of requests for training, and Gray Shadow was thankful that Caius was the type of alpha willing to handle all the denials.

Gray Shadow held the illusion of an ancient dire wolf in perfect stillness, the great beast frozen in a leaping crouch, jaws open wide, fangs long and white, with claws spread. The assorted cubs oohed and aahed appreciatively when he'd spun it from the shadows, using the lazily drifting smoke as the base for the illusion. He could craft it wholly from the air and by bending the light, but the effect was far more dramatic when he gathered the smoke and made the ancient animal seem to flex and grow as he manipulated the illusion.

He cast the cubs all one last warning glare, ensuring their silence before he continued the rest of his story. This was the last tale he'd tell before releasing them to their minders. Their history was important, and every cub must be taught the story of their origins. Their Laws came from their history, and no one was exempt from the Law.

Gray Shadow drew the skins closer to his legs, the thick brown and black pelts obscuring his form in the flickering light from the fire. When he spoke, his voice was low and full, and a hint of his inner wolf crept into the words. His eyes flashed silver in the shadows and flame, and the cubs shivered in response, instinctively reacting to the old wolf's authority.

The illusion moved, falling from its aborted leap to walk calmly around the shaman, tiny cubs staring up in awe as it walked over them, gasping when they could make out the ceiling through the dire wolf's underbelly. Gray Shadow guided the illusion until it stood at his shoulder, where he had the great beast sit docilely, dark eyes glinting like black diamonds. Its coat moved in a breeze that wasn't there, frosted from a long ago winter's night.

"Long ago, in ages past, our Great Mother gave to her favored children a gift. She set us apart from the rest of humanity, and gave us the ability to become wolves. Great wolves of the far north, strong in limb and tooth. The dire wolves of the northern reaches claimed many a man's life for centuries untold, and after the sacrifices and prayers of our forefathers, our Goddess gave to our ancestors the shape of their greatest fear."

All the cubs leaned forward, transfixed, staring at the illusion, as he broke down the dire wolf, and spun out a tableau of a frozen tundra, men clad in leather and fur running for their lives from a great pack of dire wolves, the beasts far bigger than the men they hunted.

Gray Shadow bent his will, and the scene changed, and he siphoned more smoke from the embers, bending the light of the fire to craft a moon high in a clear winter sky, a white expanse of unending snow dotted by the huddled forms of men on their knees. They screamed, pleaded and prayed to the Great Mother on Her silvery throne high in the heavens, and She answered them.

The moon was all encompassing, glowing so brightly in the illusion that its light sparkled over the raised faces of the cubs, their eyes wide in wonder. Gray Shadow bent it again to his will, and the illusionary supplicants on the ground began to twist and shriek soundlessly, writhing as their bodies broke, erupting into gray and white mists that enveloped them entirely. Silver lightning arced within the clouds surrounding each man, showing brief black silhouettes of twisted limbs and melting bones, reforming muscles. The men and their crude leathers were gone, as the mists receded, and the moon shone down on a new breed of creature, born again as wolves, powerful and fearsome.

"The clan grew once they had nothing to fear from the hunters in the night, and as their numbers increased, the clan split. Red Fang Clan birthed Red Claw and Bright Moon Clans, and the first three became the genesis of the nearly two hundred clans that span the world today. We are great in numbers, and powerful."

Gray Shadow made sure to meet the eyes of the children of the Alphas in the room, for the next part of this tale was vitally important. The sons and daughters of the Alphas of the gathered clans must know this part of their history, so as to understand their ancestors' folly.

Again he changed the scene of light and smoke, to show the forefathers of their race. Giant men and wolves, hardened by the trials of their constant struggle to survive, ruthless and relentless. Grim warriors and powerful sorcerers snarled at each other and fought bloody battles, the cubs jumping and hiding in their seats as Challenge after Challenge and attack after attack on humans went unceasing, the horrid scenes playing out over their heads.

"The Alphas, our leaders, were granted the strength to lead, command, to wrest obedience from the wolves of their clans. The gift of command gave the strongest of alphas the ability to hear and speak to every wolfkin mind, joining wolves into clans and packs. They had total control over their people, from the smallest child to the strongest warrior. Alphas of old could force the Change upon any of their people, or prevent it entirely, by using a type of mental influence inherent in all alphas. Some Alphas could kill with the power of their spirits, commune with our ancestors, and control the wild creatures of the woods and plains. They could heal even the most grievous of wounds, including those caused by that baneful metal, silver. Some could walk the world as spirit wolves, leaving their bodies behind, to spy upon friend and foe alike, undetected. There are tales of myriad other abilities the Alphas had at their command in the old days, tales of gifts that nearly destroyed the world, and our people with it. The most dangerous and potent of an alpha's abilities was that of the Voice, the gift to wrest free will from any wolfkin, be he alpha or beta. Used with ill intent, the Voice had the power to utterly and completely destroy the mind and individual thoughts of any wolfkin it was borne against.

The Alphas of old, my little cubs, had power beyond measure."

The children of the clan leaders and lesser alphas scattered about the room either nodded gravely, or sneered as they elbowed their neighbors. He noted which cubs did what, and sighed softly, deploring the folly of raising children to be exactly like their parents.

The illusion changed again—to a horrific scene of a bloody battlefield, wolves adorned in armor and spiked collars charging ahead of wolfkin on horseback, swords in hand. Human armies fell one after the other, and Gray Shadow did not spare the cubs the most gruesome scenes. They were predators, and while most of them were too young to Change, they'd surely seen their parents and older siblings hunt and bring down game.

"We once stood to conquer the world, and many of our greatest alphas throughout our histories attempted to do so several times over the centuries. Once, my sons and daughters, the children of the first Clan, Red Fang, became so powerful that our ancestors nearly overwhelmed the humans, and turned this world into barren hunting grounds that ran with blood."

A scene of death and blood. Countless dead humans and wolves littered a far flung field of corpses, crows circling overhead, carrion animals scavenging on the flesh of the dead. It was harsh and jarring, and it was necessary. History was not all tales of love and romance and happy endings. It was death and pain and blood.

Gray Shadow heard the few whispers and growls, most from the militant and bloodthirsty clans of Red Wraith and Ashland, the direct descendants of the remnants Red Fang

Clan. Their pack members were of an aggressive and violent nature, and it was without fail that at nearly every gathering since the clans' inceptions that those particular packs instigated most of the fights.

"The Great Mother, from her silvery throne high in the sky, saw her favored children turn their backs on the humans, and begin to treat them not as cousins, but as prey. We wolves had not the compassion and mercy we once had as humans, and as generations passed, we lost more and more of what we treasured most about ourselves when we were human. Alphas of unspeakable power swept through lands unchecked, leading armies of werewolves, killing and enslaving countless peoples. Humans were being slaughtered, and the power of the clans grew to the point of all-out war with the surviving human nations. We were still outnumbered by humans, a hundred to one, and regardless of our longer lifespans and abilities, if they had all turned on us together, we would have died, down to the last greybeard and suckling cub. Our Great Mother saw our fate, and intervened to save her favored children one last time."

Gray Shadow looked around the room, seeking for a set of eyes that knew the answer. This tale was the oldest of them all, and not many of their youngsters knew it, even if their own home clan shamans taught it. Old tales, if told as a chore, were oft times ignored by the younger wolves.

He dismissed the battle scene, and put out his hands, collecting the smoke. He created a solid black wolf that rested easily on his palms, the tiny form visible despite its size. A small orb of light burned from within its chest, as bright as a star in the clear night sky.

"Who amongst you, my little cubs, knows what the Great Mother did to rein in her wayward children?" Gray Shadow asked quietly, peering intently at the tiny faces turned up at him, the shadow wolf shining like a rainfall of obsidian dust.

"The shamans!" a lilting young voice piped up from the rear of the council chamber, and Gray Shadow chuckled indulgently. It was the same little one he sought, knowing the answer as he was taught at Gray Shadow's knee.

Kane started where he sat, and Gray Shadow bit back a laugh as the Heir stared in consternation at the tiny cub not too far away from where he sat. Kane had spent the entire tale as fully absorbed as the cubs, and the cub's shout snapped him out of it. His face heated as he caught Gray Shadow looking at him, and the shaman let him off the hook by nodding in approval to the tiny cub who'd spoken.

"Yes, cub. The shamans." Gray Shadow leaned forward, and whispered through the taut silence that held them all together, every eye focused on him and the tale he told. "When the power of the Alphas grew too powerful, and war was inevitable, our Great Mother reached down from her silver throne, and tore in two the soul of command and spirit that resided in each Alpha."

Gasps and whispers reached his ears, and Gray Shadow leaned back. He raised his hands, releasing the shadow wolf, and the cubs all jumped as the tiny star burning in its core was suddenly torn in two. Another shadow wolf appeared next to the first, smaller and sleeker than the original. The sundered half of the orb hung in the air, waiting.

"The Great Mother, in her everlasting wisdom, removed the spiritual and mystical powers from the Alphas, and gave them to the gentlest and meekest wolves of each clan. The abilities that left the Alphas an absolute power were stricken from them, and given to those among the clans who did not seek violence or domination. Once the rift was final, she returned to the Alphas their powers of tooth and claw, strength and command. The wolves that were granted the gifts of the soul and spirit were the first Shamans among our kind."

The sundered half pulsed, so bright it was nearly too much in the shadows of the council house. It settled gently into the chest of the smaller shadow wolf, and flashed once more. Both wolves now had a star burning brightly where their hearts should be, pulsing together, one with a reddish and black hue, the other, gold and silver.

"So it was that all-out war with the humans was avoided. The Alphas, bereft of the gifts they had abused, turned then to the new Shamans for assistance in conquering the humans. To their vexation and shame, the Alphas learned their ability to order the total obedience of any werewolf of their clan was useless against the Shamans. No Shaman can be coerced by an Alpha, and so the Shamans were spared the horror of being forced to battle. The Shamans were gentle souls who sought only peace and love and the care of their people. They used their abilities to instead care for their clans, as was the intended purpose of the Great Mother. The Shamans are found now in all the major clans, and for those packs that are too small to warrant a shaman among them, we shamans travel from pack to pack, so all our people may be nurtured."

He paused, and breathed deeply. "So the threat of war faded, and we as clans blended into the world of humans, hidden yet separate. We now strive for peace and harmony, within ourselves and with the rest of the world."

Gray Shadow lifted his hands, and the shadow wolves with the starry hearts dissipated, the cubs moaning softly in complaint, shifting as the light show ended.

"Tell them about the girls!" A little voice shouted out again from the back, and Gray Shadow grinned. He knew that voice, for it belonged to a small cub dear to his heart. His grandson was one of the few cubs here in this room who knew their histories as well as Gray Shadow. "Tell them why we don't have female Shamans!"

Kane jumped again, and Gray Shadow found it harder this time not to break out laughing. The alpha glared at him, but soon gave him a wry smile of amusement as the tiny cub not far from him practically started jumping with excitement where he sat.

"Yes, I'll tell them about the girls," Gray Shadow said to the little cub, smiling, before addressing the room at large. The serious part of the history was over for now. "Our Great Mother, her wiles sharper than those of her bloodthirsty Alphas, put in place a measure to prevent any Alpha from abusing the power of a Shaman."

Gray Shadow waved a hand, and the cubs cheered as the shadow wolves returned. He made them slightly larger this time, one a male, the bigger muscles and frame proclaiming it an Alpha, complete with a red aura indicative of an alpha's power and gifts. The other was smaller again, but now female, a delicate yet still formidable example of a beta in her prime, mother and warrior in one.

"When we mate, my cubs, there are two types of bonds. One is the most common, referred to as a mating bond. This is akin to human marriage, vows and promises of fidelity and loyalty. This can be a love match or one of convenience. Historically, this is also the only mate bond that can be abused. If one of the pair was dominant or ruthless enough, then a mating could be forced upon the weaker of the wolves. This is very rare, and has never lasted long, as a shaman would never tolerate such an abomination in his clan, and has the power to dissolve an unwanted mating. The magic of a bonding ceremony can join the wolves involved at a very deep level, especially if one of the pairing has a strong spirit. For instance, a female beta, one mated to an alpha with the Voice, can manifest a lesser version of her mate's ability. The stronger the bond between the pair, the more likely gifts will bleed across, and more powerful the shared ability. This happens in most pairings, all that varies is the depth of the connection."

The female beta glowed red when a thin cord of red light wafted out from the male, weaving through the female beta, her new aura nearly the same shade as the male's, just not as vibrant.

“This can also work in reverse. If a female is born an alpha, a beta male can access alpha gifts through the mate bond. The birth of a female alpha is very, very rare, and has only ever happened five times in our history.”

Gray Shadow twisted his hands, and reversed the power flow, the male this time receiving it from the female wolf. Several cubs gasped in shock, scandalized, and Gray Shadow knew this was because not many shamans taught this part of their history, considering it legend. If he hadn’t seen a female alpha with his own eyes as a child, he would have thought it legend, too.

“This side effect of the mating is usually not under conscious control. The alpha cannot completely stop his powers from being accessible, at most he can inhibit the majority of it if he’s strong enough, if he has mastered his abilities. The beta female can also choose not to use the power available to her as a result of the bond. Because this is a phenomenon that can’t be totally controlled, it is why the Great Mother placed one condition on the new Shamans when she made them. If a male alpha mated to a female shaman, then the alpha could conceivably develop access to shamanic magic through the mating bond. Having access to that power in the first place is what drove the ancient alphas mad with bloodlust—and that, my cubs, is why there are no female shamans.”

Gray Shadow saw the nods of understanding from the cubs, and Kane was enraptured as well, even though he was an alpha, and the topic at hand wasn’t quite flattering to his class.

"Now, for the next type of bond. The soul bond." Gray Shadow erased the wolves, and re-crafted them, mere silhouettes this time and not as detailed. Each had a tiny star shining in its core, and they floated above the cubs, drawing every eye in the room. Even Kane was taken in, charmed by the magic show.

"A soul bond is a bond between a male and female wolfkin without the benefit of the mating ceremony and its magic forging a connection between the pair. A soul bond occurs when two wolves meet, usually when both are adults or near enough, and their souls join at a level past all manipulation by shaman, alpha, or ceremony. It is a natural and powerful event, unstoppable once the process begins, and the two separate souls of the wolves involved....become one." Gray Shadow focused his will, and the twin stars pulled the wolves together as if affected by gravity. Each star throbbed as one, their lights joining, until the flame of one was indistinguishable from the other.

"The more contact between the two wolves involved, the faster the process, and it can only be broken by death. When this type of bonding occurs, my dear cubs, it is a gift from the Great Mother, a blessing on the pair and their clan. Children of such a mating are considered blessed, and many of our heroes have been the children of soulbonds. It is magic so profound it can only come from our Goddess, and is sacred above all Her Gifts.

Because it is a gift from the Great Mother, we need never fear a soul bond between an alpha and a shaman, further guaranteed by the gender of all shamans since the First."

Gray Shadow stretched subtly, tired from augmenting his tales with shadow, smoke, and firelight. The illusions faded, and Gray Shadow dropped the shadow wolves. He sent a small smile to the tiny cub who was grinning and squirming in his seat, proud to share this one slip in his professional demeanor. The cub was the child of a soulbonded pair, and was very proud of the honor.

"Black Pine Clan is lucky to have a soulbonded pair—my son Josiah, to the daughter of our Alpha, Marla. If any of you can mind your manners, and you are curious enough, you may ask them about their soulbond. Just be polite—they may both be betas, but they have big teeth."

Gray Shadow grinned at his grandson, who giggled, a bright smile wide on his tiny face.

"So my little cubs, that is why all Shamans are born male—to prevent an exploitation of shamanic magic by an alpha through the matebond. And as there has only been a small handful of female Alphas in our long history, and none of them had the strength to force a bonding on a male Shaman—we need never fear again that our leaders will be driven mad by absolute power—that of Shaman and Alpha combined."

Kane was nodding, as if to himself, and Gray Shadow sent him a faint smile of approval. He was an alpha to respect, a wolf who was content and happy with who he was. He was like all alphas to some degree, but his temperament was gentler and less self-absorbed, a stark contrast to most of the younger alphas these days.

A swath of brilliant moonlight broke across the council room, and Gray Shadow laughed aloud as the assembled cubs jumped at the intrusion. Gray Shadow nodded to the female beta standing politely by the door, and she gave him a tremulous nod in return. She was a member of the host clan, Red Fern Clan, who tended to the structures and buildings of the state park where the gathering was being held. It was bedtime for the littlest cubs, and the older ones would wish to spend time around the bonfire in the main square with their families.

"Goodnight, my cubs. Return to your mothers and fathers, and dream sweetly under the watchful gaze of our Great Mother. Remember, my cubs, that she is wiser than us all, and knows what we need and what is best, in spite of our own selfish desires."

The cubs sprang to their feet, and Gray Shadow winced at their exuberance, the whole lot of them as energetic as if they just awoke instead of having spent the better part of the night sitting on a cold floor listening to old stories. He felt very old all of a sudden, and he sat until the last of them bolted from the room.

Kane stayed seated until most of the cubs were gone, then slowly unraveled his tall, lanky frame from its cramped position along the back wall. The tiny pup who knew all the answers was still in the back, playing with his shoelaces, but casting quick, shy glances at the alpha from under his thick lashes. Luca was a flirt, regardless of his target's gender, and saw it as a challenge to get as many wolves as he could wrapped around his little tail. The alpha's natural charisma was seemingly irresistible to Luca, and the alpha sent the cub a quick wink, which made the little wolf giggle. Kane responded with a gentle smile, and a soft pat on the cub's head as he walked to the door. Kane gave Gray Shadow an abbreviated bow, a mere dip of his shoulders, as if in thanks for letting him observe before he ducked out past the female beta at the door. Gray Shadow nodded back, and turned his gaze to the tiny cub still left in the council room.

His little grandson, a precious five years old to his several centuries, wandered up through the stone and dirt tiers to clamber into Gray Shadow's lap. He hugged his grandson tightly to his chest, and wrapped him in one of the many bearskins that draped the stone throne.

"Grandpa?" his grandson Luca said, burrowing into the furs and tucking his head under Gray Shadow's chin. "Am I gonna be a shaman one day, just like you?"

Gray Shadow hugged his grandson, and walked to the door, the young female beta still waiting for them, eyes down, and doing her best to pretend she was furniture.

"I do not know yet, my little cub. You are the youngest of my many grandchildren, and you have several summers to go before I know if you will be shaman, alpha, or a steadfast and wonderful beta. But of all my children and grandchildren, my little wolf, you are the most like me, so that may be your path."

"What if I'm just a beta, Grandpa?" Luca whispered, and Gray Shadow could hear the worry in his tiny voice. His older cousins must be teasing him again, all of them already confirmed in their powers and traits as shaman, alpha or beta. Gray Shadow had two grandchildren confirmed as alphas, and one was a budding shaman. The rest, bless their sweet natures, were betas, and happy to be so. Little Luca was only five summers, and Gray Shadow would not know of his true nature until he hit puberty, or perhaps sooner if his abilities were strong, and the Change came early.

"There is no shame in being a beta, Luca. Almost all of our brothers and sisters in the clans are betas. Only a few are alphas, even fewer are shamans. And not all alphas are clan leaders, as their fathers and grandfathers rule for many years. Some alphas will never see themselves become clan leaders, as they have brothers ahead of them in succession, or they haven't the strength to hold against a stronger alpha." Gray Shadow shifted the weight of the tiny boy in his arms, and left the council house, the young female beta at his heels. "And not all alphas and shamans have the same level of power, or the same abilities. Many alphas have the great strength and power of the warrior, yet lack the Voice, and many shamans can speak to the spirits, but cannot heal. Not all alphas and shamans are equal, Luca."

His grandson, while young, was incredibly intelligent, and Gray Shadow always took the time to explain things to him, no matter the topic. Deep in Gray Shadow's heart, he wished for Luca to be a shaman, for he saw in his grandson the compassionate and sweet, obstinate nature his clan would need when he was gone. His other grandson, Ezekiel, was only a few months into his apprenticeship in Russia, and was of a brasher, more abrupt nature than Luca. Zeke had the powers, but not the patience. Perhaps he would learn some before he returned home after his trials.

"I'm gonna be a shaman, Grandpa. Just like you." Luca fell asleep as Gray Shadow carried him out into the cool night air, the last summer moon high in the sky, a week away from full. Autumn was battling with the final days of summer, and the inevitable victory of the colder moons was fast approaching. He smiled, thinking his lectures passed in one ear and out the other of the little cub, soothed to sleep by his grandfather's long strides.

"And you may be one day soon, my little wolf," Gray Shadow whispered in Luca's tiny ear, and he walked to the Clan Leader's cabin where they were staying for the gathering, his son and Luca's father waiting on the porch of the large wooden structure.

"Hey Dad, you have fun telling campfire stories again?" Josiah teased him, reaching out to take his son from his father. Josiah was young for a wolf, only fifty summers old, and he had spent most of his early adult years begetting numerous children. Gray Shadow saw parts of himself and Josiah in Luca, and he had a special place in his heart for his youngest grandchild.

"Shush, whelp. Not long ago, you were one of those seated at my feet, begging me to tell another story before bedtime." Gray Shadow clasped a hand on his son's shoulder, smiling at the two of them. Luca cuddled up to his father, a tiny bundle of soft snores and awkward limbs.

"I know he loves the old tales. You had a big crowd tonight, which I was surprised to see. Most of the clans are leaving tomorrow for their home territories." Josiah rocked Luca gently when the pup stirred, soothing his son back to sleep.

"I believe my lessons have become a new method of babysitting. I think every mated pair with kids left their children at the council house tonight so they could attend the festivities at the square," Gray Shadow chuckled as he caught the scent of fire, beer and roasted meat on the night breeze, and his ears heard the faint far off sound of music and laughter. He thought briefly about joining his Clan Leader at the fire, but dismissed it just as quickly, not wanting to dampen anyone's spirits by having the scary Shaman Gray Shadow show up at a party.

"Not every mated pair. Marla and the kids are inside sleeping with Andromeda's brood, I just stayed up to wait on you and Luca." Josiah mentioned his soul bonded mate, Marla, the first born beta daughter of Caius McLennan, Alpha of Black Pine Clan, the home clan of Gray Shadow and his family. Andromeda was the Clan Leader of Red Fern, and their hostess while in Baxter.

Half of Josiah's children were grown and mated already, with a handful left under the age of ten. Female wolves were fertile for decades longer than humans, and males could father pups until the day they died. Wolves were allowed to mate once they hit seventeen years, which is exactly what Josiah and Marla did, having soul bonded in their early teens and anxious to have the ceremony, even though it was unnecessary, to celebrate their union.

Their kind would have overrun the humans in population if it didn't take so long for werewolves to conceive. The average length of time between pups was five or more years, with gestation around ten to eleven months. Multiple births from a single pregnancy was common, resulting in twins and triplets at about half the rate of single births. This encouraged many mated pairs to stop having children after one instance of a multiple birth, or stopping at one live birth so as not to risk a multiple the next time around. Female werewolves also had the option of controlling their fertility, and they could prevent pregnancy as easily as they could Change, and they did so with practical efficacy.

Another factor in controlling the populations of the clans was the regrettable nature of the wolfkin themselves—quick to anger and violence, clashes for dominance, mates and territory, all lending to countless early deaths of young wolves every year. If a Challenge was offered, and accepted, the loser could be healed by a shaman or their own wolfkin healing abilities, but as was usual in a Challenge, the victor rarely left the loser alive to have time to heal.

With centuries to reproduce, many mated pairs had no more than one or two children and the majority of beta pairings had only one. It was the families of alphas and shamans that strove for larger numbers of children, so as to increase the odds of having offspring born with the traits and abilities of the two classes. The power was hereditary, and the more children a shaman or alpha had, the more likely it was for that power to be passed on. Not to mention that in these days, as ones before, the families of alphas and shamans had better means—wealth, food, land, and territory, and were able to support larger litters.

Gray Shadow was wealthy, a long life spent frugally and wisely leaving him and his numerous descendants comfortable for many decades to come. Most wolves were the same as they grew older, with greed long considered a human failing.

Their own Alpha, Caius McLennan, was a wealthy man who did business in Augusta, with his clan seat not too far out from the capital. He had a large family of his own, with many of his own cousins, aunts and uncles, and their children part of his family pack. Caius' own heir, Kane, was young at thirty summers, but very powerful and highly gifted. He was the son of one of Caius' distant female cousins, born with the Voice in full measure and a powerful wolf-form to match. Young Kane was the most dominant and powerful alpha Gray Shadow had seen in their clan in several generations, and if it weren't for his own innate kind and respectful nature, Kane could have already wrested control of Black Pine Clan from Caius.

The gathering of the Northern Clans took place in Baxter State Park in Maine, away from the curious eyes of humans. Black Pine Clan held all of Maine north of Augusta, and over the border into Canada, thousands of square miles, and the lesser clans and packs under McLennan's rule resided throughout that area. Clans from the southern half of the state, from within New England, and regions of Canada came to the gather, which occurred every five years. This gathering was Luca's first of many to come, and he would forge friendships and bonds with the children of the allied clans of the north.

There were six major Clans here at this gather, and nearly three times that in lesser clans and small packs. Not every wolf came to a gather; wolves were left behind to guard territories, care for the old or very young, or those under punishment for crimes against their Laws.

"Tomorrow we leave for home, Josiah. Make sure our pack is ready to go at first light," Gray Shadow instructed his son, and Josiah nodded with a faint line of worry on his brow.

"We expecting trouble, Dad? I know you said something about humans in the area, questions asked about the 'massive family reunion' taking place up here the last couple of weeks."

"It is better to be cautious than dead, my son. Humans always get curious about the clan gatherings, seeing as how there's a few hundred of us coming to these things, with more every time. Gatherings were easier to hide before the human population got cars and phones. I'm not expecting trouble, just a desire to avoid the traffic jams and the snarling tempers. Most of the clans are leaving after lunch. I'd like to be gone before the mass exodus back to civilization occurs, and the roads out of here are deadlocked. The vans are ready to take us back to Augusta, and I'll be here for you and the children before dawn."

"Yes, sir," Josiah grinned at him, and his eyes drifted to the female beta who stood silently in the clearing, not yet released from attending to Gray Shadow as he executed his role as Shaman.

"Thank you, Claire. You may go."

Gray Shadow waved to the shy female beta who still hovered behind him, and she nodded back, no longer needed now that his duties as Shaman were over for the evening. She drifted off into the night, and Gray Shadow breathed in deep. The air was cooling further, and the pines rustled in the faint breeze. He tasted the tangy pine sap and a hint of dark earth, and his skin itched, the urge to Change and run through the trees strong and seductive.

"I'm going for a run, Josiah. Goodnight, son," Gray Shadow said, and clasped his shoulder one last time before heading for the woods. Luca slept on, undisturbed by the talking, content in his father's arms.

"Enjoy the night, Dad."

KANE MOVED through the shadows, avoiding the fire in the square, heading for the cabin he shared with Burke. His best friend-cum-sometimes-lover was most likely reading, not a fan of parties either. Kane looked forward to a quiet night before returning to Augusta in the morning, and he was glad he took the time to attend the history lessons. He smiled, thinking of the magic he'd seen, and the sweet, charming cub who'd known all the answers.

Luca was adorable, and smart, and his giggle was infectious. Kane sighed, catching a glimpse of his own cabin through the trees, glad to be going home in the morning. Maybe when he got back to Augusta he'd make a greater effort to know his clan mates better, and see if he couldn't get Luca to laugh again.

AMBUSH

THE DAWN brought a cool breeze as Gray Shadow's pack loaded into the two vans he'd rented for the round trip from their home territory to the gather. Cousins and some of Caius' own family members were opting for an early departure, and would be leaving with Gray Shadow and his family pack. Laughing cubs, grouchy and snarling teens, and resigned and annoyed parents all made as much noise as possible while Gray Shadow watched indulgently from the porch of the Red Fern clan leader's cabin, his great head resting on his paws. Gray Shadow was large for a shaman, nearly the size of the average alpha, as if his body reflected the level of spirit and earth magic that hummed under his skin. He was gray, the basis for his name, yet he was every shade of gray, from the dark dust of shaved metal to the vague wisps of fog that spun through the pines in the early dawn light. His age was merely hinted at in this form, a spattering of white furs lightly spread throughout the dark fur of his snout.

He'd spent the night as a wolf, running through the pine forests of the park, enjoying the peace and quiet to be found under the fragrant boughs. He seldom slept anymore, his mate long dead now this past half-century, dying not long after giving birth to Josiah. So he had no one to return home to when the moon set each morning, his hours his own. His children were grown, his shamanic duties over for now, and he found himself at loose ends more and more. Usually he would run with Caius, but the Clan Leader of Black Pine was busy with the other Greater Clan Alphas, and he didn't want to disturb his friend's political maneuvering.

His kind were not bound by the cycle of the moon as most legends spoke of by the humans, and could Change whether it be day or night. Some few legends spoke of monsters who could conquer the moon and walk as man or beasts regardless of the time of day or the moon's phase. Those legends were very close to the truth, and tended to pop up in human populations near clan homes and territories.

A tiny hand suddenly gripped one of his ears, and Grey Shadow held still as his grandson used it for balance as he climbed over his grandfather's lupine form. Luca sat on his grandfather's shoulders, and Gray Shadow hid his wince as Luca let go of his ear and grabbed the fur on the back of his head instead. Luca was small for a cub of five years, and his weight was slight, but like all young children, he tended to be unintentionally rough. He was taking after the stereotype that shamans were smaller, slighter than their beta or alpha counterparts, and Gray Shadow was glad for it as the little cub tugged on tufts of fur and heels energetically kicked at his ribs.

"C'mon Grandpa! One more ride?" Luca bent down and draped his slim arms over Gray Shadow's muzzle, whispering loudly in his sensitive ears. Gray Shadow let the wolf equivalent of a grin pull back his lips back from his fangs, and he sneezed, making Luca squeal with giggles and sit back.

Hold tight, little cub. Gray Shadow whispered softly in the mind of his grandson, the telepathy shared by all wolfkin strongest in their lupine forms. Luca giggled, and squirmed as he grabbed another handful of fur.

Gray Shadow carefully stood to all fours, and balanced the weight of his grandson on his shoulders. He waited to make sure Luca had a solid grip, then sauntered down the porch steps towards the vans. Everyone was seated, the side panel doors open as they waited for Josiah to double check everything before departure. Gray Shadow paced alongside the vans, and Luca blew a raspberry at his older siblings, who groaned in jealousy at the sight of their baby brother getting a ride wolf-back.

"Dad, you spoil him," Josiah said without heat, peering into the first van, securing a pup's seatbelt. He grinned down at his father and son, and went to take Luca from Gray Shadow's back.

As is my prerogative, whelp. Grandfathers are meant to spoil their grandchildren. Gray Shadow archly informed his son, a short wave of his tail taking any sting from his words. He pranced back from Josiah, and Luca squealed again at the movement, laughing. **I'll take him for one last run through the woods. I should be able to beat the vans to the park gates.**

"You sure, old man? That's a long run, and you were running all night."

Gray Shadow narrowed his eyes at his son at the old man

comment, and Josiah grinned, holding up his hands and tilting his head to the side, playfully exposing the arch of his neck in a show of submission. “No offense meant, Dad. Have fun.”

Josiah checked the remaining van, and Gray Shadow waited while his son got in the driver’s seat of the first one and the Alpha’s daughter the second, before both vans pulled away from the rented cabin.

“Let’s go, Grandpa! I wanna run!” Luca begged, and Gray Shadow obliged. He ran lightly across the clearing, reassuring himself Luca wasn’t going to fall, before diving in a headlong rush past the tree line.

The shadows were cool under the great pines, and the sound of his passage was nonexistent as Gray Shadow ran around the towering ancients. In this form, he could see the life force of everything in the woods, a slow trickle of liquid lights colored yellow and green, with vibrant hues of red and blue intermingled. The life force seeped from the cells of every living organism, and evaporated into a fine mist that was invisible to him, even with his shamanic Spiritsight in use. There were no shamans alive today who could see the life force once it joined the great rivers of energy that traversed the globe. Shamans could see the energies of the natural world, where the life force of all living things mixed with the radiant energy from the sun, moon and stars. The elements were tangible things, and the strongest of shamans could not only reach out and touch the variant energies of the world, but manipulate them as well.

Gray Shadow raced through the trees effortlessly, leaping

streams and small hallows, stricken trunks and tumbles of rocks. Luca was laughing and howling, his voice shrill in the old wolf's sensitive ears, but urging him on as he kicked up speed. Gray Shadow reached out with his mind, casting his awareness ahead. He saw as multi-hued sparks of light the life forms of deer and bear, and the deep red of a catamount at the farthest reach of his awareness. Tiny little flickers of light for the vermin in the ground and the flittering birds in the boughs, the green slinking glow of snakes in the bushes. Within his mind and the overlay of his Spiritsight, Gray Shadow could see and feel the vibrant miniature suns that burned within the beloved members of his family pack, not too far away as he followed the vague direction of the road out of the park. There were similar beacons of light miles out, other wolves enjoying the fine weather for one last run before returning to familiar territory. His family pack were to the east and south, and he adjusted his course through the trees to beat the vans to the park entrance.

Luca's heart was beating fast with excitement, a thrumming sound like that of a hummingbird's wings. Gray Shadow could see in his mind the powerful radiance that burned in his grandson's soul. Its light was so similar to Gray Shadow's own, a silvery, liquid-like tumble of life energy and a hint of something *more*—Gray Shadow laughed with pleasant surprise in his mind, now certain that Luca would grow to be a shaman once he hit puberty. He'd never thought to examine Luca with Spiritsight, and it was like looking in a mirror. The lights that burned in his spirit and soul were too familiar, too close to Gray Shadow's own power signature that he could see no other future for Luca. His grandson would be no beta, nor alpha; the shaman's path was waiting for him. He was already powerful, and his shamanic talents grew in his young heart, just waiting for his body to mature enough to be able to use them. Once Luca hit his majority, he just might outstrip Gray Shadow in ability and strength.

Gray Shadow exulted in his discovery, and his muscles burned with exertion and joy, the companionship and promise of the cub clinging to his back and the comforting love of his pack just ahead through the trees giving him an extra bounce in each leap. Luca wrapped his little arms as tightly as he could around Gray Shadow's neck, and the elder wolf spurred himself on, hearing the rumble of engines ahead through the trees, the scent of asphalt and humans at the park gates riding on the wind. His ears pricked forward, and he could hear voices, the off-tonal quality of humans glaring against the smooth timbre of his son's ever-steady timbre.

Gray Shadow mentally chided himself on being distracted by his Spiritsight, Josiah having used that time he spent admiring the world to beat his father to the park gates. Gray Shadow raced up a small incline, paws digging into the fragrant dark earth, when he heard the first sharp report of a gun firing. He instinctively ducked and held still, wondering where the hunter was and how close he was to being shot by some idiot human.

DAD! Josiah's mental scream raced out into the early morning air, and slammed into Gray Shadow's mind, full of pain and shock. Something was wrong. His cub was hurt, and

Gray Shadow got a hazy image from his son, of blood running from his shoulder, his arm useless as a human dressed all in black and armed with a large gun dragged him from the van. Not hunters then, but humans attacking in force.

I'm coming! Gray Shadow screamed back, mentally clutching at the tenuous connection to his son. He could hear more guns firing, and screams from the children. Men were shouting, and it sounded like a war was breaking out just over the rise. Shrieking howls and deep throated growls erupted from Changing bodies, and the scent of blood and angry werewolves filled the breeze.

NO! Josiah's mental scream was so sharp Gray Shadow halted at the edge of the rise, his muzzle seconds from breaking free from the cover of the tree line and entering the large clearing where the park gates were located. **Get help! Protect Luca!**

His son was right; he had a cub crying, clinging to his back, and he couldn't run headlong into danger with Luca depending on him.

CAIUS! Gray Shadow spun his mind out far to the north, seeking his clan Alpha. He quivered with the urge to run into the clearing, but his son's warning was prudent. He had a cub on his back, his soft whimpers of fear reminding Gray Shadow to stay still, and hidden. He pushed his mental call out to its limits, and tried again, screaming for his dearest friend and Clan Alpha. **CAIUS!**

Gray Shadow felt it, when the connection was made, locking in place with his Alpha's strength augmenting the link. *I hear you, mo ghra. What is it?** Caius' solid and fortifying presence filled the distance between them, and Grey Shadow sent his Alpha every rioting emotion he could through the link.

Ambush at the gates, humans with guns, attacking our cubs! HURRY! Gray Shadow called, and he felt Caius' answering mental roar of anger and fear. Caius' rage was a heady thing to experience, but Gray Shadow welcomed it, knowing Caius would come for him and his family.

Suddenly other minds entered the pack link, pulled in by the Alpha, and Gray Shadow felt the mind touch of Kane, Caius' heir, and other alphas he didn't know. They traced the link back to Gray Shadow, and he let them in, letting them see through his eyes and hear through his ears. Gray Shadow crept forward a step, and he could see the park gates.

The vans were stopped, the doors thrown wide, and his heart shattered under grief and rage as he saw the blood running from the limp forms littering the asphalt of the park entrance. Human men dressed in black combat gear and large guns dragged uninjured wolves still trapped in human form towards the park gates. One of his kin was in wolf form, collapsed unmoving on the pavement, as if caught mid-leap by a bullet. A large vehicle was parked on the other side of the gate, rear doors open wide, and human men were trying to force several of his family members into the vehicle.

Howls lifted from the trees in the far distance, Caius having alerted wolves in the area to what was happening at the gate. Through the link to Caius, he could feel the Change rolling over the alphas, and their headlong rush into the woods and down the roads to the gates. The wolves of the gathered clans would be here in mere minutes.

The humans all turned toward the howls from the north, and Gray Shadow's heart leapt in his chest as he saw Josiah start to Change, his body rippling as he fell to the ground. The human standing over him screamed as Josiah latched his warped, half-formed jaws around the man's calf, and the rest of the humans milled about in confused terror. Chaos erupted as more of his family began to Change, adrenaline forcing it on them faster than usual. Humans began to fire randomly, and Gray Shadow's restraint snapped.

Hurry, Caius. I must stop them. Gray Shadow stepped clear of the trees, and forced his will out into the clearing, tearing at the air between him and the humans attacking his family. Steam boiled into existence as the air heated, and the wind stopped, as a solid wall of energy ripped towards the humans standing over the wolves on the ground, weapons firing. A wall of super-heated air crashed into the humans near the large vehicle, and several screamed, skin blistering, clothing smoking, weapons suddenly too hot to handle. The energy required to do this was extraordinary, and Gray Shadow shuddered at the effort, pulling back his will for another strike. Spirit fire was dangerous, and the level of destruction it could reap was staggering. He could force all the air out of the clearing instead, but that would suffocate his kin as surely as the humans. As long as his family stayed down, any one of them still alive would be safe from the burning wall of air.

Stay down! Change if you can, and run! Gray Shadow flung out to his kin, and hoped some were still alive or awake enough to hear him. He sent a new wave of spirit fire towards the humans, forcing his body and mind to keep supplying the energy to sustain the new blast. If not for Luca being too near, Gray Shadow was desperate enough to draw more power from the life forms around him, but that would affect the cub as well.

Luca clung to his back, sobbing as more humans cleared the front of the strange vehicle and tried to assist the stricken men on the ground. One of them saw him where he stood, and yelled, pointing in his direction. Bullets whizzed past his head, and Gray Shadow ducked, pulling back among the heavy tree branches. Luca cried out, and Gray Shadow smelled the fresh scent of hot blood. He looked over his shoulder, to see a line of blood running from Luca's torso.

His grandson was hit, shot by one of the humans. He dropped the new attack, and pulled his will and power back, changing his intent. He assessed Luca in an instant, the bullet lodged in his small shoulder, his tiny form falling into shock. **Caius, Kane. Hurry, please.**

It was as if the forest was alive with howls and roars of challenge, wolves streaming through the trees from the north, the departing clans all alerted to the ambush at the gates. Gray Shadow turned to run north, to seek safety and help in the sheer numbers running his way, but a spat of bullets ripped past his muzzle, halting him. He heard the high-pitched whine of dirt bikes, and saw through the leaves several humans on bikes aiming in his direction. The humans on the bikes fired again, and he was forced to slide down the small hill, paws scrambling for purchase.

Shaman! We are close, we smell the humans. Almost there! It was Kane, his deep mindvoice usually comforting, calm even in his hard lope to push faster through the trees. Gray Shadow sensed how close the alpha was, but he had trouble on his heels now, and couldn't wait for help.

Not close enough! Luca's been hit, and I'm being chased by humans on dirt bikes. I'm heading west towards the river. Gray Shadow sprinted, and Luca nearly spilled from his back. Gray Shadow whipped out a tendril of power, and forced Luca's tiny body to his back, keeping his injured grandson from falling.

* *At the gates.** Caius called, and Gray Shadow heard the unspoken sob of grief and pain in the Alpha's voice, a fleeting image of his daughter Marla collapsed on the bloody road, frozen mid-Change. **Kane, Burke, help Gray Shadow.**

Gray Shadow let the voices fade out, maintaining only enough of the link to lead the alphas after him through the trees, the mind link a far surer method of tracking than scent or sound. His focus was bent on the forest floor before him, and the fading life on his back. He used his power to augment his faltering body, fueling his muscles, forcing himself to move faster than he was usually capable. The burning air attacks left him weakened, having had no time to prepare for the strenuous spells.

Luca was succumbing, bleeding fast and his light dimming. Gray Shadow raced as fast as he could through the trees, the horrible buzzing whine of the bikes and the sharp bursts of gunfire close behind him. He needed to lose the humans, or he was going to lose Luca. The cub was seriously injured, and Gray Shadow couldn't heal him and maintain this headlong pace at the same time.

The sweet scent of fresh water was ahead, the river rushing madly down from the hills, and hopefully he could get across before the bikes caught up to him. If he couldn't, then the boulders along the river would have to do as cover. Gray Shadow spared a fraction of speed to send Luca a rush of his own life energy, bolstering the cub's heartbeat, trying to slow the blood loss. He couldn't do much, and he was losing ground to the mechanical monsters chomping at his tail.

I'm almost there, Shaman. Keep running, I'm coming! Kane urged him, and Gray Shadow caught his scent on the wind, over the stench of exhaust and humans. He heard a flicker of grief from Caius, the Alpha now hard on his heir's heels, and Gray Shadow trembled with grief of his own, for it must mean more were dead than living at the gates for the Alpha to leave the site of the ambush.

At the river, just before the waterfall. Hiding in the rocks. There are three bikes, five humans on my trail. Armed with semiautomatics. I need to heal Luca. Gray Shadow darted among the large boulders that lined the bank of the river, where the bikes could not follow. Several towered high above him, and there were nooks and crannies where he may be able to hide. He raced over a flat stretch, claws marking the granite, the noise of the bikes dying out as the humans stumbled from their bikes, looking for him and Luca.

Gray Shadow ducked behind a large boulder, the river rushing wildly mere feet from him, and he hunkered down, letting Luca gently spill from his back. He could heal in either wolf or man shape, and if he stayed wolf, he'd have a better chance of attacking the humans if the alphas didn't make it in time. Luca was pale, and his heartbeat weak. Blood covered his torso, dark red and pungent in the damp air.

Luca? Hold on cub, I'll help you. Keep breathing. Gray Shadow rolled Luca to his back, hidden by the boulder, and put a paw over the wound, sending his awareness down into the tiny cub's body. He found the bullet, and the shattered shoulder blade where it was lodged. He focused, ignoring the approaching footsteps and the harsh breathing of the pursuing humans. It helped Luca was his kin; the connection between them was easy to forge. He urged Luca's body to obey him, and using the muscles that would one day warp and twist to initiate the Change, Gray Shadow forced them to slowly expel the bullet. This was similar to what Alphas could do when they forced a Change on a werewolf, whether it be to wolf or man. He couldn't force a full Change, he could merely lead the muscles to respond to the spiritual pull of the Change itself, and localized it to the wound. It was hard, harder than it should be, and the effort drained the shaman further. He caught the scent of something pernicious, and growled softly.

Caius...Kane. The humans are using silver laced bullets.

I can smell them, and you. Almost there. Stay hidden. Kane told him, the alpha near enough now that Gray Shadow smelled him in return, and heard the hard panting breaths of a predator fast approaching. He could smell Caius and another alpha, farther out from Kane but coming in fast, their scents strong on the milling winds. He continued to ignore the humans, his focus totally on the cub.

The bullet popped free from the flesh, and rolled to the rocks. Gray Shadow was able now to pour everything he had into the cub, the silver's influence over the injury gone, and the wound knit and the bones shifted. Gray Shadow merely helped along the cub's natural ability to heal, replenishing his blood supply, his young heart beating stronger, the tempo sure and certain.

Luca's eyes fluttered open, and Gray Shadow licked his little face in relief. He huddled over the cub, and just in time, as a human whirled around the edge of the boulder, aiming a shotgun at Gray Shadow's head. The shaman froze, lips pulling back in a soundless snarl,keeping himself between the gun and the cub now awake beneath him. The human tugged a radio free from his jacket, and clicked it on.

"Team Leader to Base, I've got the shaman. He's got the runt, too." The human gazed at them with steely, emotionless eyes, and his finger stroked the trigger of the shotgun as he held it aimed at the shaman's head. "Bring a tranq gun to the river, north of the falls."

Gray Shadow felt more than heard the silent approach of Kane. He knew the alpha was there when the sharp scent of fresh human blood was carried on the damp river breeze. The man holding the gun on him didn't react, unaware that his compatriots were being silently culled amidst the maze of boulders.

"Understood, sir. On my way with tranquilizers and restraints. Secondary exit plan in place, primary vehicle disabled," came the reply over the radio, and Gray Shadow's eyes narrowed. The ambush was starting to sound like a military or private mercenary job, and this explained why the humans would chase him and Luca through the woods with hundreds of wolfkind minutes away and closing in fast.

The humans were after shamans. And since shamans rarely left the clans, the humans came to the clans.

"Check with our contact, make sure the beasts aren't onto our escape route," the man with the gun ordered over the radio, and Gray Shadow grumbled at the implications.

Contact? A human spy in the park? Or a traitor in the clan?

"Play nice, dog, and I won't put you down. You so much as twitch, I'll blow your brains out across the rocks and drown the runt in the river," the human whispered, somehow sensing the rising wave of blood-red anger in Gray Shadow's heart. The shaman tensed, muscles coiling. Luca shivered with fear under his grandfather, tiny hands clutching at his forelegs. The cub was awake and listening, and Gray Shadow sensed the boy's fears as his grandson instinctively reached out with his mind, trying to initiate a link, searching for reassurance. He responded without thought himself, and bolstered the boy's connection to his mind, stilling the cub, so as not to draw attention to himself.

Keep the human focused on you, Shaman. If I take him now he may fire, and he's too close to you for him to miss. Kane's mental whisper sent relief rushing through Gray Shadow, and he saw the hint of a black wraith moving over the light grey stones behind the human. Kane was huge, larger than the black bears found in the northern reaches of the untouched forests, and he stalked the man who held the gun unwavering on the shaman and his grandson. *When I tell you to, pull a witchy trick and make him look away.*

Witch trick was an old term used to describe the conjuring of illusions, and Gray Shadow hoped he had the strength left to do so. He must; Luca needed him, and he refused to fail the cub. Gray Shadow kept still, eyes locked with the human, and sent his will and focus out to a spot near the trees. He gathered the light and forced the air particles to collect, shaping them to his will and guiding the shapes with a deft touch. It went slowly as his strength faded and waned. He must do this, and he tried again, wishing for the first time in his long years to be younger, his endurance not what it once was in the twilight of his life.

He knew the illusion was ready when the power drain was steady; all he needed now was Kane's word to unleash it. He didn't have long to wait, as Kane was a black blur of movement behind the human as he flowed the last distance between them. *Now, Shaman!*

Gray Shadow loosed the illusion, and two werewolves

tumbled from the trees onto the rocks, snarling and roaring at the armed human. He saw the fake wolves approaching, and jerked, the gun wavering between Gray Shadow and the rapidly approaching illusions, eyes wide in shock and indecision. Kane leapt as the human made up his mind, seeming to realize the wolves weren't real, and he brought the weapon to bear on Gray Shadow. The shaman was deafened by the shotgun's blast as the gun fired. The stench of gunpowder and blood flooded his sensitive nose, and he heard screaming and snarling.

"Grandpa!" Luca was screaming at him, and Gray Shadow tried to move, to comfort the cub. He staggered on his feet, and his vision blurred. Something was wrong.

Gray Shadow blinked, and his feet refused to move. He felt cold, and he couldn't hear the river anymore. Just his heartbeat, loud in his ears, an offbeat sound that grew weaker and weaker.

Gray Shadow collapsed to the rocks, Luca at his side, wailing. The shotgun fired again; once, twice, the discharge of each shot oddly enough something he could hear. He saw a blur of black as Kane and the human fought, blood running from Kane's shoulder and hip. The human stumbled backwards, and Kane lunged for him again.

Shaman! I'm here, hold on old friend, don't let go..... It was Caius, at last. Gray Shadow tried to respond to his Alpha, but his mind couldn't remember how to form the words. He was growing cold, the sun warmed rocks under him not enough to hold back the creeping chill. He realized in a corner of his mind that he was dying, and that there was a hole in his chest from the shotgun's blast.

He saw a blur of colors, and he watched, detached from his body, as Caius and another alpha breached the trees, leading more wolves. The human man was dying, bleeding out from his ravaged throat, the shotgun useless, clattering to the stones. The human fell backwards, his feet tangling with the shaman's body. The dying man fell towards the rushing white water below him, and Gray Shadow tried to howl in terror as the dying man's fingers caught Luca. The cub and the shaman's murderer toppled off the rocks, and the last thing Gray Shadow heard was Kane's cry of anguish as the alpha plunged into the river after the cub.

THE RIVER AND THE WOLF

KANE HELD his breath as water submerged his head, soaking his thick fur, clogging his ears. He snapped his muzzle shut, and kicked hard for the surface, powerful strokes of his hind legs propelling his head clear. Everything was muffled under the water, and he flinched at the cacophony of its rush over granite boulders once his ears were free.

**LUCA!* Kane called, hoping the cub could hear him, that he was old enough to respond. Most cubs could only hear and not reply to mind calls at his age, and he would have trouble finding the cub in the water without a link to his mind.

Kane swam, bracing himself with outstretched paws as he was hurtled towards partially submerged rocks and trees. He strained his neck high, and caught the barest glimpse of solid black a few yards downstream. The human. He was floating, going with the current, and Kane knew he was dead, the final slash across his throat insuring the human hadn't survived the plummet into the water. If the human was that close, then the cub may be as well.

He pushed himself harder, and rounded a sharp bend just as he heard the change in the river's roar. The water was rushing faster, its pull stronger, and there was a deafening rumble he could feel more than hear over the current around him. The waterfall.

Here the river narrowed, the rapids frothing white, and the strength of it was extreme. It was bitterly cold, even in summer, the runoff from mountain springs and year round snow melt, and he was thankful for his dense coat even as it sought to drag him under, soaked through to his skin.

Need to get out of the water, I can't do anything if I'm trying not to drown myself, he thought, and he lunged at the first opportunity, claws scrabbling for purchase on a water-worn tree. His legs churned and he stumbled momentarily, shaking the water from his long black fur. He was running before the droplets could land, streaming along the bank in a blur and eyeing the human's body as it bobbed in the current.

LUCA! Kane couldn't see the cub. He could only see the human, arms loose, legs floating heedlessly. There was no cub, and Kane's heart sank, the possibility of the youngster already having drowned a very likely occurrence. His last glimpse of the cub had been the human's fingers wrapped in the collar of his t-shirt when they fell, and Kane could only hope that death had maintained the grip on the cub.

The falls were yards away, a drop of 50 feet that descended into a deep pool before the mountains separated the river into tributaries before combining again miles downstream. If the cub was still in the water, he could be swept away in any direction. Kane put on more speed, and ran to the cusp of the falls, lunging out onto a boulder, his teeth sinking into the boot of the human corpse, and he yanked hard. His claws sank deep, flaking the rock under him, and he managed to keep the human from being dragged over the falls.

No! Kane's heart broke. The human had lost his grip on the cub. Luca was downstream... over the falls.

Kane dropped the body in disgust, and leapt from his perch over the falls, angled towards the bank. All four paws dug their claws deep into the nearly vertical shale cliff side, and he took the fastest route to the pool below without actually going over the falls in the water. He fell, claws ripping shale shards free from the earth, and he dug in just enough to narrowly avoid crashing into the rocks below. Kane let go a dozen feet above the boulders lining the deep basin at the foot of the falls, and twisted in the air like a cat, landing in a run on all fours. He raced to the water, eyes scanning, nose twitching, ears pricked, every sense on high alert, hoping to find some sign of the cub.

Caius. Haven't found the cub yet. I'm not giving up. He couldn't tell if he was still close enough for his Alpha to hear him, yet he felt a tiny mental nudge, with a hint of his packmate Burke sending an affirmation he'd heard. Burke would tell Caius.

The cub was wolfkin, for all that he was only a tiny thing, and he yet may live. Kane wouldn't stop searching until he found Gray Shadow's grandson, alive or dead. He couldn't bear to think that the sweet, charming cub from the history lessons the night before might be gone, his light extinguished.

LUCA CHOKED, air bubbling in his chest. It hurt, more than anything he'd ever felt before, and he coughed, only to have water rush back in his lungs. He was cold, and he couldn't feel his hands or feet. He was so cold that his terror was out of reach, as if he wasn't feeling it, his mind shrieking for his dad, his grandpa, all of his terror-filled cries an echo from outside his little body. The cold was creeping in, numbing his skin and muscles, and the water was a foul drink as it mixed with the contents of his stomach. He was flung hard against an object he never saw in the water, and sparks of white light exploded behind his eyes as pain bloomed on the back of his head.

The white sparks faded, and the water numbed the pain. It numbed everything. He was so cold. His fear left slowly, seeping away into the current, and he struggled to remember why he was fighting. He was tired, and he hurt, and he couldn't fight the wave of black nothingness that flooded over his thoughts.

"BREATHE! DAMMIT, breathe! Gray Shadow, *mo ghra,* don't stop breathing!" Caius knelt naked beside the great shaman's side, a large hand pressed hard over the gaping hole in the wolf's chest. The shotgun blast had ripped a hole the size of a closed fist deep into the shaman's body, and Caius could smell the rich blood that flowed in his heart, telling him without any healing gifts of his own that Gray Shadow was wounded, and mortally.

"Sir? Two shamans from Black Pine are coming, they'll be here soon." Burke, his heir's best friend and lieutenant, hovered at his shoulder, naked as well and streaked with blood over his face and shoulders. Caius barely spared him a glance, his mind focused on keeping Gray Shadow alive until his healers could get to the river.

Caius could feel, like the faintest of breezes, Gray Shadow's mind within the mental link Caius refused to relinquish. He was afraid if he let the link drop, the shaman would slip away. "Tell them to hurry," he growled under his breath, and he pushed harder on the wound, trying to keep his hand from slipping in the blood soaked fur.

Gray Shadow couldn't die. Not like this. Caius wished, not for the first time in all his long years as Clan Leader that his meager Voice worked on shamans. If he could, he would order the shaman to live until the healers could save him. His old friend and clan shaman was too dear to him, too important to his people and clan to let die. All the cold places of his heart warmed when he was with Gray Shadow, and a life that almost counted as eternal would be forever lonely without him. All he could do now was fight to keep the connection between his mind and Gray Shadow's open and strong, his thoughts feeding the shaman strength and a desire to live.

"Burke," Caius whispered harshly, teeth clenched. He refused to feel grief yet, but he must know.

"Sir?"

"Who's dead?" Caius had spent only a few heartbeats of time at the gates, all the humans either dead, injured or after Gray Shadow and Luca by the time he and the clan alphas got to the ambush. It had taken Gray Shadow's plight to pull him away, the humans hunting his wolves a target for his rage.

Burke knelt at his side, dark head lowered in grief. He was a big man, like most alphas, and he could barely achieve the submissive posture that etiquette required of a lesser alpha addressing Clan Leader. Caius snorted in exasperation, impatient to know. Burke exhaled roughly, and Caius could hear the sadness heavy in that sound.

"Three of Josiah's litter are dead. Marla, his mate and your daughter, is dead as well. Josiah is alive, though silver-shot in the shoulder, leg and hip. Shamans are attending to him now. Of the 20 wolves assaulted at the gates, only those four are dead. None were taken, though it was near thing. It seems Shaman Gray Shadow interrupted a mass abduction attempt by the humans. Numerous injuries among the wolves, sir. The humans are all dead, most succumbing to severe burn injuries and shock. It looks like the humans used some form of silver-laced aerosol on the vans, as the shamans are reporting gas burns. Most of your kin are having trouble Changing, or are stuck in partial forms." Burke shifted on his knees, his eyes locked on the barely breathing shaman laying on the rock between them. His head tilted as he listened to the multiple minds within the mental link. Caius had passed control of the link to Burke, to keep his focus solely on Gray Shadow, pouring his strength along the thin thread of thought to the mortally injured wolf.

Caius refused to give in to his grief. He swallowed back the howl of loss and despair that threatened to tear free from his throat, stamping down on it ruthlessly. His daughter was dead, some of her children dead as well. His grandchildren. Gray Shadow's grandchildren. He would not let Gray Shadow pass too. He didn't want to live without Gray Shadow. He would lead, but the hollow reaches that howled in his soul would never hear the echo of Gray Shadow's magic if he died. Caius would die on the inside, one lonely day at a time.

He would need all his wits to handle the ramifications of this morning, and to keep his people safe. He couldn't perform his duties as Alpha, Clan Leader of Black Pine, if he was overcome by grief. This act of aggression by the humans must be dealt with swiftly and wisely, to keep Black Pine from appearing weak and vulnerable in front of the other Clans.

"Kane?" His Heir had dived over the rocks into the river. He was alive, that much Caius could sense. He could not tell if his grandson Luca lived or not, and his heart hurt as if bruised at the thought the cub was already dead. He dared not devote any more of his attention on the younger alpha and his grandson, the energy required to seek Kane out over the distance between them all going to keeping Gray Shadow's mind engaged in the mental link.

"I can hear him, Sir, he's searching for your grandson Luca."

“Great Mother help him find the cub.” It was all Caius could do....pray.

Caius heard the patter of many feet racing across the boulders, and spared a quick glance over his shoulder. The wolves milling silently along the shore parted, letting two of Black Pine’s shamans through. A medium sized cream colored wolf and a larger deep brown skittered to a halt at his side, transforming swiftly into a platinum blonde haired older man and a younger brunette, both of them shamans who learned their calling under Gray Shadow’s tutelage. The blonde, River, reached past Caius, and he let the shaman’s smaller hands take over, holding pressure on the wound. Caius could feel the power of the blonde’s spirit magic rise as he used his gifts, ignoring him and the other alpha completely. The young man, Michael, placed his hands on Gray Shadow’s side, head bowed, with his shoulders curving in as he too poured his magic into the grievously injured shaman.

“Alpha Caius, can you hear him?” River asked softly, his eyes shut tightly, face a mask of concentration.

“I hear the faintest of echoes, and I’m refusing to let his mind go.”

“Good. Keep him here. Do not free his mind, or he will die.” He shifted on his knees, mindless of the sharp edges tearing at his skin. “Let me in the link with you.”

Caius reached out without hesitation, aligning River’s thoughts into the delicate connection. He shined to Caius’ mental eye as a small yellow sun, the palest of golden flames, a welcome addition to Caius' attempt at grounding Gray Shadow's spirit and mind. He was able to step back the slightest amount as River used his link to Gray Shadow, calling wordlessly to the other shaman. The link glowed brighter, filling in, becoming a more tangible thread.

"The human used silver shot," murmured Michael, head still bowed, his words laced with a faraway quality. "I cannot force out the silver."

"If I can make Gray Shadow strong enough, he can heal himself. He's the only one I know who can force silver out in such a large quantity," River whispered, his voice hissing both in Caius' head and in his ears.

"Do what you can." Caius stepped away, letting the shamans work in peace. He tugged Burke to his feet, and led him to the wolves gathered near the tree line. They all sat submissively or backed away, eyes averted to the ground, as he and Burke stopped beside the remains of the humans responsible for the attack on his people.

Caius kept the mental connection to Gray Shadow, holding the shaman's mind tightly, while letting that part of his mind settle to the background, freeing the majority of his focus for other matters. He would know instantly if Gray Shadow or the other two shamans did.

Two of the humans were torn to pieces, Burke having finished them off once Kane disabled them, his heir more intent on getting to Gray Shadow and Luca than in killing the humans. Caius wished for a moment that he had gotten there sooner, to tear the ambushers apart himself. The remaining two were relatively intact, just their throats ripped open. The four were wearing some sort of paramilitary gear, bullet proof vests and heavily woven fabrics designed to protect against knife blades. Caius yearned to know who sent them.

"Search the bodies. Here, and at the gates. Their vehicles, clothing, weapons—search it all," Caius growled the order at his wolves, and Burke relayed his words through the pack links to the wolves at the park gates. With a murmur of rippling fur and muscles, several of his beta wolves Changed, their naked human forms crawling to the dead humans, fingers far more useful than claws and fangs at searching pockets. He supervised as they searched the bodies, pulling off weapons, emptying pockets, tearing apart clothing.

"Rangers are in route to the park, Sir. Sentries are reporting three park authority vehicles approaching the gates," Burke whispered to him, his dark brown eyes vacant as he listened to the wolves placed along the roads to observe anyone leaving or coming to the park. They hadn't been in place this morning as the clans were supposed to be departing, and Caius mentally kicked himself for this mistake. If they'd been on sentry duty, he would have known humans were approaching the park this morning before Gray Shadow and their family left.

A shiver of something dark, a hint of doubt, slithered through his thoughts, and his brow furrowed as he pondered the implications. What were the odds the humans would choose this morning to attack, the only morning out of the last couple of weeks that sentries weren't on duty?

"Have an alpha from our clan, a shaman who can craft illusions, and a pack of betas hold the gates. Evacuate the injured and dead back to the cabins. Remove the ambushers' bodies and vehicles to the park center as well. All wolves not here with us or securing the gates, or on sentry, are to return to their family packs and their clan leaders. Inform the Greater Clan Alphas that I will be returning once I've determined the park and our people are secure." Caius relayed his orders to Burke, still glaring down at the dead humans, his people piling everything they found on the humans at his feet.

"Yes, Sir." A pause, and Burke nodded to himself, the orders sent. Burke was an accomplished Speaker, his thoughts dancing easily from one mind to another as he spoke to the necessary wolves to execute Caius' commands. When Kane's time to lead came, he would do no better than to have Burke as his second in command, as true Speakers were as rare as alphas with the Voice in full measure.

Caius knelt, and he ran a finger through the small pile of items. He scented human sweat and the acrid aroma of overly processed foods, and the oils used to clean their weapons. He found no identification cards or papers. One of his female betas shuffled over, and held out a Kevlar vest to him, her slim finger pointing to a small spot along an inside hem.

He took the vest, and peered at the spot. His blood ran cold for a heartbeat, before an enraged snarl crawled free from behind his teeth. A small imprint of a property logo peeked out near a slit in the fabric where the plates were inserted, and he read the words ‘Remus Acquisitions and Technologies’. The betas nearest Changed back to wolves, and they all drifted back from him, eyeing him warily. He was not unduly violent with his people, but an alpha’s temper was wise to avoid no matter the personality.

“Sir?”

“Wolf hunters. Government sponsored, paramilitary wolf hunters.” Caius snarled again, and claws erupted from his fingertips, several popping through the Kevlar plates with a sharp sound.

“No one enters the park. No one leaves. Not even the park rangers. Only wolves under my direct orders may cross the borders. I need all sentries doubled up, no wolf is to be alone in the woods.” Caius shot to his feet, the assembled betas shrinking back. Burke stood calmly at his side, the younger alpha unafraid of his Clan Leader’s temper.

“Done, Sir. Reinforcements are being sent to all sentry positions.”

“Good,” Caius snarled softly, lips curled back from the incisors that grew to small fangs from his upper jaw. “All strangers are to be stopped, by any means necessary.”

Caius didn’t wait for Burke’s reply, spinning on his heels and striding back to Gray Shadow and the two shamans.

GRAY SHADOW floated in a warm, unrelenting darkness. A space so vast, so empty, that he could see or hear nothing. He was alone, and content, his awareness narrowed down to his inner most thoughts. He was essence, pure spirit, the confines of body and earth discarded.

He swirled through the darkness, changing direction on a whim, or resting in the quiet nothingness. There was somewhere he must be, but he felt no rush to get there.

Gray Shadow.

He felt the touch like a brush of air, cool and soft, twisting in the nothingness before fading away. There was a hint of familiarity, and Gray Shadow pondered idly why that was. He'd always been here, in this warm place of darkness, hadn't he? So wouldn't he know why something was familiar?

Gray Shadow! Shaman!

Shaman.

Hear me, my teacher. Come back to us.

Someone was calling him. Gray Shadow. His name.

Shaman.

A crack formed in the dark, a narrow sliver of light, piercing in its intensity. He flowed in the darkness, and the light seeped into the shadows, gathering around the edges of his current reality. He wasn't afraid. The light pulled him together, compressing his spirit, and the light settled around him in an embrace full of confidence and control. It pulled him gently towards the crack in the warm nothingness, and through to the other side.

Gray Shadow snarled breathlessly in pain, eyes wide, the mid-morning sun rising overhead spearing straight through to his brain. His chest hurt, and the hands pressing hard on the wound didn't help the sensation of broiling agony. He tried to move, anything to alleviate the pain, but his legs didn't respond to his brain, and the hard rocks under his side were warmer than his whole body.

"He's awake!" A slim pale shadow leaned over him, blocking out the worst of the light, and he blinked, focusing past the sun spots in his eyes.

"Gray Shadow, keep breathing. You've been shot with silver, and we need you to help us get it out. You need to force out the silver." River. His River, an apprentice of his from many moons ago who was a shaman now, strong and calm, as immutable as the body of water he was named for.

Silver....shot? *Gray Shadow tried to speak, but found his tongue didn't work in his current shape.* Wolf-shape. I Changed. What happened? Why am I at the river, and how did I get shot with silver?

"Yes. I'm sorry, I don't have time to explain. We're barely holding you together, I'll explain after you get the silver out of your body. You need to hurry, we can't hold you here for much longer," River pleaded with him, his pale blue eyes and platinum blonde hair as brilliant as the sun above. Gray Shadow blinked, and saw the spirit of his former apprentice burning brightly to his Spiritsight, with a tenuous cord of light running from the center of River's chest to his own, little pulses of light in time to the other shaman's heart. River was literally sustaining him, restoring Gray Shadow's strength until he could heal himself.

"Thank the Great Mother, he's alive." He knew that voice. The deep rumble was akin to gravel grinding together, tempered by an Old World accent that gave his Clan Alpha a distinguished mien despite his rough warrior exterior. Caius stood naked behind River, holding something black in his hands, his face torn by grief and anger. *What happened?*

River was pouring energy into him, faster and faster, and Gray Shadow accepted it, spindling the golden light inside his own spirit, reinforcing his heart. Gray Shadow turned his mental eye to his own body, and shuddered in dismay and a sick sense of inevitability. He could see the shards of silver glowing with a baleful light amongst his ribs and muscles, several pieces lodged in the exterior walls of his heart muscles. He was dying, regardless of River's borrowed strength. He would be dead if he didn't force out the silver, the metal keeping his body from healing the wounds caused by the shotgun blast.

Shotgun blast? He was shot? He remembered....running. The woods. Guns firing. The river. Anger. Grief. Fear. Luca.

Luca.

LUCA! He cried, trying to move, his wounded heart pounding as adrenaline coursed through his damaged body. His grandson. Taken over the rocks into the river, Kane following. **Where is Luca?**

"Shit! Gray Shadow! Calm down!" River tried to hold him still, but couldn't remove his hands over the bullet wound. Another set of hands held him down, and a part of him dimly noticed the presence of another of his former students, the taciturn Michael. Both shamans tried to restrain him, but Gray Shadow had only the driving need to save his grandson, fear overriding his sense of self-preservation.

Be still, Shaman. Even with his natural immunity to the Voice, Gray Shadow still responded momentarily to the inherent authority in that mind voice. Caius. He stopped fighting, and his muscles complained bitterly at his attempt to get up. He didn't have the strength for this.

Luca went into the river.

Yes, I know. Kane is searching for him even now.

He hasn't been found?

He felt Caius' hesitation to answer, and realized as he did that his Alpha was in his head along with River, and had been since his first desperate call when the ambush began at the gates. He felt Caius' grief and anger, his pain. He got flashes of images, the most prevalent of them a young woman, blood pooled under her, dark red hair covering her face. Marla. Dead.

Who.... Who is...gone? He didn't want to know, but he must. His daughter-in-law, his son's soulmate, was dead. His heart ached more from the impending grief than the silver tearing at the struggling organ.

Shaman...heal yourself first, then I'll tell you.

TELL ME WHO DIED. Gray Shadow wasted precious energy demanding the truth, his mental strength faltering for a split second. Gray Shadow sent out a weak mind call along the blood connections he'd established in his family pack, and felt the voids of dead wolves just as Caius responded.

Three of our grandchildren and Marla. Caius whispered softly, his own grief an overtone that was inescapable. Caius stood with his head bowed, eyes closed. Gray Shadow was swamped by pain, purely of the heart and soul. His grandchildren. Marla.

He felt Josiah, his son lost to his own agony, both of the soul and body. He sent a wave of love and horrible relief that he was alive to his youngest child, but he was too weak to tell if Josiah felt him, his son's pain tremendous. Grief rode his son, and Gray Shadow knew that Josiah was fighting a battle with pain on his own, surrounded by the broken bodies of his cubs and mate. Marla was not just Josiah's mate.... She had been his soulmate, bonded at a level past the commonplace of vows and affection. For Josiah to even be alive after the death of his soulmate was a testament to his son's strength......and a hint of the hell he would be living in with his soulbonded mate dead.

River was glaring at Caius and himself, the pale shaman clearly fed up with the delay in healing, muscles in his arms straining from pushing on the gaping entry wound.

Gray Shadow caught a whisper of doubt from Caius, his thoughts briefly turning to the sound of the rushing waters mere feet away. He believed Luca to be dead as well. Kane hadn't found him before the waterfall. Their youngest grandson was dead too.

**No.* Gray Shadow growled, and it took every ounce of strength he had to turn his head at last, and look at the river. It was furious, white capped and rushing so fast a small cub would be battered against the rocks in seconds. *Oh, my tiny cub. Not my Luca.*

**He's gone, my brother. He's gone.* Caius tried to reach out to him, but Gray Shadow closed his eyes, and withdrew from Caius, and did his best to hide his thoughts from River.

**What are you doing?* River's alarmed voice whispered in his head, trying to see his thoughts, the cord of light connecting them flaring once before settling, the stream of life energy still flowing. River was powerful, he may be able to prevent Gray Shadow from doing what he must. He couldn't give up on Luca.

When he'd sent the echo along the family pack lines, he hadn't gotten a sense of emptiness from a void where Luca should have been if he was dead. His youngest grandson was alive. He was out there somewhere, unconscious and hurt. Kane wouldn't be able to find him, not being a part of the family pack, and not a shaman trained to identify pack and family members by life force signatures. The shamans within his family were still apprentices, and his own former apprentices were not part of his family pack, with no natural blood connection to Luca. For one of the other shamans to establish a link to Luca in time to find him before he died was impossible. No one could find Luca by life energy in time......except Gray Shadow.

*Luca lives, Caius. I can feel him. Our grandson lives.*

*Are you certain?*

*Yes.*

*What are you planning?!* Caius demanded, his mind voice growing even more worried, and angry. _*Heal yourself, dammit!*_

*There is a traitor, Caius. The human who shot me mentioned a contact, someone in the clans. The humans are after shamans. They knew me, and Luca, on sight. It's why they chased us. There are humans nearby, who were coming as reinforcements of the men who hunted us. Find the traitor, and the humans. Do your duty, and protect our people.*

*Gray Shadow, don't do it. Whatever you're thinking, don't do it!*

*There is no time, Luca is dying and Kane cannot find him. Josiah is my heir, he knows what to do. Goodbye, mo ghra.*

Gray Shadow withdrew as far as he could from the outside world, while still staying aware of his body. He needed an anchor, and his body would be it. Hopefully he could find Luca quickly, before his body succumbed to silver poisoning and blood loss.

Gray Shadow cast off the bonds from his Alpha, and deftly removed his thoughts from River, letting the other shaman maintain the cord to his body. They both tried to stop him, Caius trying in vain to make the Voice work on him, with River sending out nets of light, trying to hold his mind and spirit in his body. Gray Shadow took less than a second to send to Caius an emotional burst of exactly how much he'd enjoyed every second of the last several centuries at the alpha's side, and then he worked his spell.

The humans called it astral projection, the clans called it spirit walking. None of the currently living shamans could do this, but for Gray Shadow, and it took extreme stores of energy and strength. He was dying, and the silver was sapping his magic, each drop of blood seeping past River's hands a second off his life. His life in exchange for Luca's was an easy decision for him to make, and he made it without fear.

Gray Shadow slipped away, his spirit forming briefly on the rocks beside the wolves kneeling next to his body. He nodded once to the wolves who looked up in shock at the glowing form of his spirit-wolf, before Gray Shadow turned his muzzle downstream. The magic in the blood of his grandson was calling to him as surely as if it was dripped in a trail for his nose to scent. They had similar spirits, he and Luca, and he could sense, in the far distance, a faint glimmer on the horizon of his awareness that was the cub. Gray Shadow began to run, his spirit form moving as fast as thought, flowing over the river as if it were a solid earthly path, and not a wild ribbon of water carved through the mountains.

A thin cord of silver and gold light spun out from his spirit wolf, connecting him to his dying body. He prayed to the spirits of the living world and the Great Mother that the cord would hold, just long enough for him to save Luca.

KANE THUNDERED through the underbrush, twigs snapping under his paws, earth churning as he leapt and dodged the towering pines. The trees were thick here, and he was forced back from the river by the lack of shore, a steep drop taking place of the rocks. He would continue along this branch of the river for another half mile, then head back and take another branch. He wasn't giving up. If there was no sign of Luca along this part of the river, he would return to the basin at the foot of the falls, and start over down a new branch. He would search them all until he found the cub.

HE HURT. Badly. His chest was on fire, and he couldn't escape, whimpering, fingers digging into the wet dirt under him. Luca coughed, and water bubbled from his throat, but he couldn't draw in enough air. He was cold, his legs still in the water, and his head hurt just as badly as his chest. Luca tried to open his eyes, but his body was as confused as his thoughts, and he couldn't do more than cry feebly.

Daddy! Grandpa!

GRAY SHADOW paused above the falls, standing on the rushing water as it plummeted down to the basin below. He thought he'd heard something, and he tilted his spectral head, expecting it to be one of the shamans or his Alpha, trying to call his spirit back to his body. He would fight them on this, saving his grandson was more important than them needing him alive. He'd lived long enough. River and Michael were capable and well-trained; Black Pine would not suffer overmuch in his absence.

Grandpa. It was a plaintive whimper, so clear in his ear it was if the cub was curled in his arms, trying to nap and complaining about too much noise. He was close.

Gray Shadow threw himself from the falls, directing his path by thought and willpower. He soared through the pine groves, feet immaterial and striding far faster than any physical gait he could muster. He wove through the ancient giants, their life force shining in pools of green and yellow, the oldest with cores of vibrant deep blue that bleed out to green. He sifted the colors of life that blocked his view, and followed the river west and south, this smaller branch of the great river leveled out and gentle, unlike the others that traveled through the mountains in white capped fury.

He saw it, a small sun of silver white light. A tiny orb to his

Spiritsight, flickering beside the blue lights of the river. Luca.

Gray Shadow moved as fast as this form would allow, and re-materialized above the cub. Luca was laying on his stomach, tiny fingers curled into the damp earth, lower legs still in the water. He was soaked through, his t-shirt and shorts clinging to his thin arms and legs.

Luca? He could not speak aloud in this form, nor could he touch.

His magic was still strong, strong enough to help the cub until help came for him. No response from the cub, his thoughts faint, as faint as the lights of his spirit. The frigid water from mountain runoff was killing the cub, and blood ran in a thin trickle from the light corn silk hair on his head. Bruises littered his arms, and Gray Shadow was certain the boy had internal injuries from being buffeted about in the river.

Luca was breathing, albeit raggedly, his lungs partially filled with water, and his heart beat was slow and laborious. Gray Shadow lowered his spirit form next to the broken cub, and fought back the urge to howl in despair and frustration. He could not pick the cub up, nor use his magic to heal him. He was too weak to physically affect Luca in this form, his own body dying, the thin golden cord tying him to his corporeal form thinning with every minute that passed.

Kane? If the alpha was nearby, then he could at least help, keep the cub warm until shamans came. He heard nothing, his strength failing him, his usual reach with mind calls diminished.

The flickering orb of silver white light that glowed within Luca was still strong, and Gray Shadow wanted to weep seeing how alike his grandson's nascent magic was to his own. If only the cub were older, he could shift, and the Change would spur his natural healing. Luca was only five summers, and the youngest a wolf had ever been recorded making their first Change was nine summers.

Luca... not like this. I won't let you die like this. A thought came to him, wordless, more instinct than complete realization. It was a subtle epiphany, but it may work. Gray Shadow curled his spirit wolf around the cub, and reached out to the tiny orb of light within his grandson.

The initial touch of spirit to spirit was always a shock, like touching a moving wall of cool water with a warm hand. Their light flared, two fires burning brighter on first contact. Gray Shadow sent what strength he could to Luca's spirit, and sought out the pathways in his heart and mind that led to his slumbering wolf. He was no Alpha to order the Change to an already awakened wolf within a stubborn clan mate; his power lay in the less physical aspects of their kind. While the body was the vessel for the Change from man to wolf and back, it was the spirit of the ancient dire wolf within them all that let them become more than human. It was that spirit which Gray Shadow sought.

The Shaman went deep, guiding Luca's spirit to that place inside his soul where the tiny shadow of the wolf he would one day become slept. He was years away from being ready, his spirit and body not yet aligned nor mature enough for the

Change to happen on its own now. Yet Gray Shadow was old, his wolf and man fully joined to make one soul and spirit, both halves experienced in how to interact with each other. His duality was functional and seamless, and if he could show Luca at this primal level how to connect to his wolf, then the boy may be able to Change.

Grandpa? Luca's whisper was faint, full of exhaustion.

Sshhh, Luca. I'm here, just watch me. Reach out to your wolf. He's waiting for you. See? Gray Shadow led Luca's mind to that small, quiet place, where the vaguest hints of a curled up wolf cub slept in the shadows. Gray Shadow's old wolf was big, and fully melded to the human side of him, and Gray Shadow stepped to the sleeping wolf cub, letting Luca see as he walked what the man blended seamlessly to the wolf could look like. Two spirits become one during the first Change, never to be undone.

He's sleeping. I'm tired. Can I sleep now?

No Luca. Wake him up. Reach out and hug him. Then you'll both feel better.

Sleepy.

** I know, my little cub. Be strong. You can do this. Wake your wolf, and you can rest, I promise.**

Luca was stubborn, even dying and exhausted. His spirit trembled, edging towards throwing a fit and refusing to cooperate, and risking death as he wasted his few reserves of energy.

Gray Shadow gave him what energy he could, feeling himself falter, the connection to his own faraway body thinning rapidly. The cub must Change, and now.

Luca. You can do this, you're a shaman just like me. Wake your wolf, and show me how strong you are. Less cajoling and more of an order, and Luca responded. His orb of silver-white light zipped through the shadows of the darkest parts of his soul, akin to a wolf-den dug out of a stone cave, towards the young wolf that slumbered peacefully, tiny head tucked under a colorless plume of a bushy tail.

Yes! Wake him, Luca! Gray Shadow followed, watching, waiting, impatient and hoping.

Luca shivered, the light bouncing off walls of damp black earth and gray stone that didn't exist, and he hovered in front of the slumbering wolf pup. The light grew, and Gray Shadow sent him all the love and reassurance he could. To be brave. He could do the impossible.

The spirit cub glowed, unmoving, becoming more substantial the closer Luca's spirit got, the brighter he shined. Colorless fur darkened, each wave of color more defined. The bushy tail quivered, the tip thumping on the cave floor as if it were real. Luca laughed, and flew closer, so close, nearly touching now, and Gray Shadow could hear another heart beating. Luca's wolf.

He almost missed it. One moment Luca's spirit shined like a miniature sun, independent and contained. The next, Luca was within the wolf, lighting him....no...*them*....lighting them both up like a starry vista painted on an ink black horizon. The cub lifted his head, gray snout capped by a solid black nose, eyes as silver as the ones Gray Shadow saw in the mirror, ears pointy and big for his small head.

Yes! Run Luca! Run! Gray Shadow exalted, happiness overriding his own exhaustion. Luca the wolf rose to his feet, gangly and clumsy, yet beautiful. He took one hesitant step, then another, tail sweeping out in an excited arc. **Follow me, Luca. Come on, one last step.**

The cub wagged his tail, and tried to run, tripping over his feet but following Gray Shadow's spirit with the enthusiasm of youth. He led the way, pulling his consciousness from Luca's, returning to the real world beside the river just in time for the Change to embrace his grandson.

RIVER CRIED out in frustration, and Caius knelt at his side, one hand heavy on the Shaman's shoulder. Gray Shadow was still unconscious, his spirit walking far from them, searching for their grandson.

"What is it?" Caius asked, fearful of the shaman's answer.

"He's deliberately pulling his own life force out of himself. He's draining himself for some reason," River growled, sobbing past his anger. "Great Mother, no."

"River?" Michael moved closer, eyes worried, tears of his

own streaking down his cheeks.

"Gray Shadow is doing something, I can't tell what. It's drawing tremendous power from his body. I didn't know he was this strong.... He knows....he knows it will kill him. Whatever it is he's doing...... He's not planning on surviving this."

USUALLY WHEN a cub shifted, Changed, for the first time, it was an awkward, drawn out and painful affair that left cub and parents exhausted and hurting. It was very near to actual birthing, and just as messy. Many times an alpha would assist, to order the last few waves of the Change into completion, if the cub wasn't strong enough to do so on his or her own. Hands and feet first, torso last, or vice versa, always a mess.

This time..... Gray Shadow rejoiced as the Change came over Luca. It was like watching the spirit be reborn; there was no pain, no warped body parts or cries of fear. Luca rolled to his back, eyes open to the canopy above, human brown melting away to be replaced by mercurial silver, shining like shards of a mirror. A white and silver mist coalesced around the cub, his spirit manifested in the physical world. Tiny pinpoints of brilliant white light sparked in the mist, little bursts of lightning arcing as the cloud grew and solidified. Silver stars shimmered in the cloud, as if he were seeing the night sky through breaks in a storm. Gray Shadow pulled back, lest his spirit-wolf mingle with the Changing cub, and he watched the impossible, a transformation that his people had long attributed to myth and legend. Not since the days of the First Wolves had a Change happened like this.

Luca yipped, a writhing wiggle of half-seen limbs and gray fur that Gray Shadow could just make out through the sparkling cloud. As quickly as the mist formed, it was gone, sucked back into the cub, now a true wolf standing on four splayed paws. Luca shined for a second, miniscule spots, like distant stars, glimmered in his eyes and along his coat, before the magic faded, leaving a soaking wet cub shaking on a river bank.

I am so proud of you. Gray Shadow refused to let the cub hear anything from him but pride and love; his heart was breaking. By encouraging the melding of boy and cub so early, without Luca having any training, Gray Shadow had inadvertently torn down any walls that inhibited Luca's magic until he was mature enough to wield it effectively. His power was now his own, fully accessible. There would be no waiting for Luca to hit puberty to learn what he was—he was a shaman now. Untrained, and incredibly pure in power.

And Gray Shadow would not be there to teach him.

Gray Shadow heard an offbeat echo along the cord tying him to his body. Deep, yet erratic. His heart. His body was about to die. The weakest of cries shivered along the cord, as if River or Caius were calling him back. Caius' call made his heart ache sharply, but he refused would not regret his decision to save Luca. He ignored the pleas, refusing to leave Luca until the very last, when he had no choice. The child may be a wolf now, but he was still a tiny thing, helpless and alone in the woods.

Forgive me, Caius.

Luca tried to walk, the Change giving him strength, but not coordination. He tried to see every part of his newly transformed body, but didn't watch where he was stepping, four legs not any easier to handle than walking on two. More legs to trip over things. Luca fell on his haunches, yipping in surprise, tail wagging regardless.

I did it! I did it Grandpa! Luca crowed in happiness, his mind voice clear and true. Gray Shadow dropped his muzzle to the cub, and Luca tried to lick him, confused when his nose passed right through Gray Shadow's. He shook himself in surprise, head cocked to the side, one ear flopping. Gray Shadow laughed, and sent Luca a warm rush of love and pride through their blood link. Luca brightened, feeling it, and sent an answering burst of elation.

Yes, my little cub. You did it. I am so proud of you. Can you be strong for me now? There is one more thing you must do for me.

What? Luca asked, his youthful voice happy yet wary, as if he was about to be asked to clean his room or take a bath, interrupting play time.

I can't stay, my sweet cub. I must leave you. So you must hide.

Leave me? Hide? But...

I'm dying, little one. Luca quailed at his words, confused, hunkering down, with his ears flattening to his skull. **Don't be scared. You'll be alone for just a little while. Hide until Kane finds you.**

Kane? Gray Shadow didn't know it was possible to convey sniffling tears through a mindvoice, but Luca did it, tearing his heart into bleeding chunks. The poor cub didn't understand, and he wished he could spare him this experience, but there was no help for it. Luca was strong, and would survive.

The cord to his body was about to break, and he would die, fading away like the mist that still clung to the pines nearby. He didn't have the strength to return the distance to his body, let alone heal the damage to it. It was a blessing of the Great Mother that he had survived this long, and he would thank Her in person once he was on the other side. This had been a one way spirit trip into the woods, and it was worth it. Luca was alive.

Kane. The nice alpha who winked at you last night during story time, remember? He's searching for you. He will protect you, keep you safe. Hide until Kane finds you. Trust Kane. Gray Shadow felt it then; a tensing, a tightening in the cord, and a heartbeat of time passed—and a snap ricocheted down the cord. **Kane will help you.**

His end was there, death not a stalking predator but a cool breeze of rest on a sweet summer wind, and he could almost hear the whispers of his ancestors through the trees.

I love you, Luca, Shaman of Black Pine. Be strong.

Gray Shadow didn't fight the inevitable. This was an end to be proud of; there was no shame in letting go. His ancestors and Goddess were waiting for him. The golden cord broke, shards of light dissipating in the air, and Gray Shadow felt the subtle pull of something potent, overwhelming yet so welcome. He stepped back from Luca, the cub whimpering, yet with his head held high. Gray Shadow watched his grandson for as long as he could, his spirit waning, small pieces of him drifting away in the soft breeze from the river.

Love you, Luca whispered, and Gray Shadow let that love follow him into the unknown.

CAIUS MOURNED his friend and Clan Shaman, the ache of his loss a gaping wound to match the injury in the fallen wolf's chest. Caius ran his fingers through the dense fur, feeling the silky soft undercoat, the warmth that still clung to the shifting gray patterns. Gray Shadow's wolf-form was beautiful, even in death, and that beauty tore at Caius. He bit his lip until he tasted blood, and bowed his head.

"Mo ghra," Caius whispered, the Old World endearment slipping free before he could control himself. No one was close enough to hear him, hear the slip that once would have been fatal to them both. The shaman was gone, now, and Caius wished he could follow.

River and Michael held each other not too far away, the

pale shaman crying softly into the dark brown fur of the younger wolf. Michael had shifted the second Gray Shadow's heart beat that final time, as if he couldn't face his grief in human form. River didn't care who watched or heard; Caius recalled that River was one of Gray Shadow's first students, over two centuries old now, and the tie between former apprentice and master was strong, even centuries later.

"Alpha." Burke. Dependable and steady Burke. He stood a few steps away, head bowed, not wishing to intrude. Caius could smell the sadness that wracked his tall frame, the bitterness of pain and grief. The wolves along the river all smelled like pain, their bodies low to the ground, ears back, shoulders hunched. They were quiet, waiting. No howls of grief would come, not yet.

"Yes, Burke?" No tears choked his voice. He would not cry. Even this tiny amount of sentimentality was too close to being seen as a weakness. He was Clan Alpha, and must not show weakness, not now, not this morning. His family, his blood, had been attacked, never mind that the branch was under Gray Shadow as patriarch. Gray Shadow was the Clans' greatest shaman, unrivaled in talent, ability, skill and power. He was a remnant of the old days, when shamans guarded the clans alongside the alphas, fighting for survival against all enemies. Black Pine's supremacy in the north was due mostly to Gray Shadow; his death was going to upset the balance of power.

And Caius's heart would never recover.

"The park rangers are stopped at the gates. No other humans have been found within the park borders. Sentries are reporting fresh spoor from the last few hours of several wolves leaving the park through the woods. We have trackers following the scents back to see where they came from, and to identify the wolves who left. No signs the wolves ever returned." Burke paused, and Caius waited, not looking up from the body at his side. "Kane is out of my range, and the last I got from him was that he was still searching for Luca."

"Gray Shadow said that the human who shot him had reinforcements in the area. Send some packs out, no less than five wolves in each pack. Find where these humans are. They must be close. Restrain first, kill second."

Burke nodded, and started to get that vacant yet intense expression in his eyes that said he was speaking telepathically.

"Wait."

"Sir?"

"Have a pack go after Kane. He's been out there for hours now. Have the wolves you send help him search until sundown.... And if Luca hasn't been found, come back." He would need Kane now, more than ever. The young alpha's mastery of the Voice, in its formidable full measure, was Caius', and Black Pine's, best protection now against rivals.

"Until tomorrow, Sir?" Caius could hear the doubt, the sadness in his voice. He didn't believe Luca lived, either. Gray Shadow was dead. His closest friend and companion for centuries was gone. The greatest shaman the clans had ever known was dead, and Caius could only see Gray Shadow dying if he had nothing to live for... if he failed to save their grandson. He wouldn't die if Luca was still out there, still needing to be saved.

"Just do as I ask, Burke."

"Yes, Sir."

Caius ran his fingers over Gray Shadow's face, the great skull under his hand still strong and conveying an aura of power, even in death. His eyes were closed, the silver orbs hidden now forever. He could be sleeping, sunning on the rocks and dreaming, if not for the gaping hole in his chest and the blood pooled under his body.

Caius pushed his hands under the dead wolf's torso and hindquarters, lifting him gently, standing as he did. He cradled Gray Shadow to his chest, tail and head hanging limply over his arms, blood dripping from soaked fur.

He turned from the river, leaving the bloodstained rocks behind, and the place where he lost another of his precious grandchildren. The betas clustered at the shore scurried away as he strode for the trees, head up and his shoulders back.

Beta, alpha and shaman followed him as he walked into the trees with his sad burden, the wolves of Black Pine mourning silently. They would not cry out their sorrow until their Alpha freed his voice, and gave his grief to the moon.

KANE STUMBLED in the water, his front legs losing their grip on the rocks. Ice cold liquid filled his nose and made him sneeze, waking him up from his near catatonic daze. The sun was setting, the air cooling, and mist was racing in through the trees. He was exhausted, having ran more miles and swam longer today than any other day in his short 30 years. His paws were cut and bleeding from the rocks along the river, his chest burned from running, and his legs were going numb. He hadn't eaten that morning before the shaman's cry for help came through the clan bonds, and he was exhausting stores of energy he couldn't spare. It was nearly a full day since he last ate, and the pace of his searching was done at a near gallop. Changing required a huge amount of calories and protein, and he couldn't bring himself to stop his search and hunt, not while there was a cub still missing.

Kane pulled himself from the river, trying half-heartedly to shake the water from his coat, but giving up as he stumbled again. He struggled up the bank, and collapsed, leaves and pine needles sticking to his fur. He grumbled at the annoyance, and feared he would fall asleep the longer he lay here. He needed to find the cub, before night fell and chances of finding him alive grew slimmer. The temperature was dropping, and there were not just werewolves in these woods. Bears and mountains lions roamed the dense forests, and humans too. None of those predators would be kind to a lost cub, and the humans would make things difficult with their misplaced concern and penchant to overreact to wolves and children occupying the same space.

"Kane?"

He jumped, black head turning to the nearest tree. He must be tired, to not sense Burke's approach. His lover and lieutenant stood beside a large tree, not ten feet from him, naked and bloody. He carried a dead turkey in one hand, the other bracing against the tree as if he needed it for support. Burke didn't look as badly as Kane felt, though, just drained. Grief was a bitter tang in the air, and Kane huffed, annoyed at the reminder of the day's events. Not annoyed that the other wolf was grieving as he was, but that the grief was a reminder he had yet to find the cub. That he was failing a member of his clan, one so helpless that he needed Kane, someone—anyone to save him.

Caius send you? He refused to Change, to speak as a man. To do so would be to give up. He knew it was foolish, but the man was weaker, an unconscious concession to something stronger. It's why Burke stood out of reach of claw and fang, bringing an offering to appease his wolf. Kane sniffed loudly, a grumble and an excuse to scent for more wolves. They were out there, several of them hiding.

"I came for you, instead of someone else as I'm sure he meant; but yes, he sent me." Burke took this as permission, and came closer, sitting naked in the pine needles beside his alpha, his long body occupying far less space than his size would lead one to expect.

And the others, the ones hiding beyond the trees?

Burke snorted, and tossed him the dead bird, the scent of blood and meat pricking Kane's interest. He caught it in his great jaws and dropped it over his front legs, licking at the few drops of blood coating the feathers. Burke glowered over his shoulder, and the sound of faint growls came through the branches. Kane sent out a low rumble of his own, and the growls in the trees cut off, the sound of paws finding pounding on the needles as the hidden wolves ran off. Kane was Heir for a reason—he was no lesser alpha to poke at.

"They were convinced you wouldn't notice them." Burke tried for levity, but it fell flat. He gave Kane a small smile, a mere lifting of his lips and lacking any emotion. "Shaman Gray Shadow is dead."

Kane lowered his head, and breathed through the pain. In and out, and did his best not to howl his rage and frustration at the moon, still hidden under the horizon as the sun set.

"Caius sent us to help you search for the cub...then bring you back at sunset." Burke's voice was soft, a bare whisper of breath. Kane heard what Burke wasn't saying. Caius believed his grandson to be dead, and was calling Kane home.

It's sunset.

"Yes, it is. But I'm in no rush." Burke reached out, and poked at the turkey. Kane put a large black paw on it, and raised a lip at the other alpha. Burke poked the bird again, goading him, and Kane snapped at his hand, the Speaker laughing as he pulled his fingers back in time to avoid losing one. Kane gave in, and tore into the bird, spitting out feathers until he got to the meat.

Caius will be displeased.

Burke just shrugged, fingers playing in the pine needles, trailing through the soft blanket the needles made that they sat upon. If Burke wasn't worried about their Alpha, then Kane wouldn't worry either. Burke was always telling him that he wasn't choosing his battles wisely, backing down when he should fight, and fighting when he should talk instead. Burke was usually right, too.

"The pyres are set to burn at midnight. We have time to rest. Then we can search some more, and return to the park. Hopefully with a cub in tow, too." Kane knew Burke didn't believe Luca was alive, but his lieutenant-lover-best friend was a kinder soul than Kane, and didn't say so out loud. He would help Kane search, and when they could search no more Burke would patiently run beside him on the way back to the park, and the funeral pyres waiting to be lit.

Kane didn't react outwardly to the hand that ran over his head, and down his neck. Kane ate, his hunger an aching emptiness in his gut, and Burke pet him, an action allowable now that the others were gone. Such a caress was more for Burke than for him, the other alpha fighting back tears, and if pretending to comfort Kane instead comforted Burke, it was the least Kane could do for the poor wolf. He would never tell Burke that the gesture soothed his hurts as well.

LUCA SHIVERED, drawing himself farther under the fallen

log, his fur still damp. He was scared, and the sounds his now supersensitive ears kept picking up weren't helping any as the sun set. The forest came alive with sound, and the murmur of the nearby river did nothing to quell the noises coming at Luca from all directions. He heard birds settling down to sleep in the branches, little animals burrowing in the earth under his paws, and the clicking of insects so close to him he could reach out with his snout and touch them.

He was very hungry, his stomach gnawing at his backbone, a phrase he'd heard his daddy say all the time but never understood, not until now. He wanted his mom, and nothing more than to climb into bed after supper and sleep under the covers in his own room.

Luca tried to curl up smaller, another wave of shivers racking his small frame. He was happy to be a wolf, even if he was hungry and cold and wanted to go home, and he couldn't wait to show his dad or Grandpa Caius. They were going to be so proud of him. Grandpa Shadow had taught him to find his wolf before he left, and Luca flinched away from the thought he would never see the great shaman again. Grandpa Shadow said he was dying, and that he had to leave, but he was a powerful shaman, and he couldn't die. This must be a test, a trial like his cousins bragged about when they were going through their shaman training. That's what this was, a test. To see if he was strong enough to be a shaman.

Grandpa said that Kane was looking for him. Told him to hide until Kane found him. So he'd pass the test if he waited for Kane. Grandpa said to trust Kane, that Kane would find him and keep him safe. So he would wait and hide, because he trusted his grandpa, and he wanted to go home. The alpha was nice, and Luca liked him, feeling safe when the big male was nearby. Making Kane smile made Luca happy, and he hoped Kane would smile if he did as he was told and waited for the Heir. Most alphas made Luca nervous, especially his uncle Roman. Uncle Gerald was a big softie, but he had a temper sometimes, and his uncles were lesser alphas. Except for Kane, Luca didn't like alphas much. Even Grandpa Caius made Luca nervous sometimes.

Luca fought to stay awake, jerking every time he heard something in the trees. If Kane was going to find him, he didn't want to be found sleeping. He was so tired, and the earth was warming under his body at last, all working to make his head droop and eyes shut.

WAYWARD

CATHERINE MEDEIROS, Ph.D. in Biology, and Director of Luna Wolf Rescue and Research Sanctuary in New Brunswick, swore viciously as another mosquito snuck a snack from her neck. She slapped her hand over the offender, managing to knock her hat off in the process.

"Easy, Cat, or you're gonna scare off the wildlife."

Cat sent a glare to her research partner, Glen's easy going smirk solidly in place as he casually navigated the underbrush in the near dark. She was having trouble seeing where to put her feet, never mind the super-megawatt torch she was using to light her way. She had trouble seeing where she was going even in her labs at the research center, and trekking through the woods in Maine being eaten alive by bugs was not her idea of fun. Her glasses were fogging up as the temperature changed, and she kept having to wipe off the moisture.

Glen Mitchell was a big man, older than she by at least ten years, placing him in his late thirties, and he never put a foot wrong. He spent most of his time in the woods, photographing wolves in their natural habitat. He was a big supporter of the wolf restoration projects, chronicling the species' return to eastern Canada and the northern United States. She was here in Baxter State Park with him to substantiate or disprove rumors that wolves were back in Maine, actual functioning packs and not loners just passing through.

Cat waved the torch at him, gesturing angrily. "I think the wildlife is hiding from the monster bloodsuckers. I haven't seen any sign of wolves here in Baxter since we arrived three days ago. Ouch!" She smacked another flying leech, this time on the back of her hand, and ended up dropping the torch. Glen laughed, and set down his pack on a large flat rock. He carried most of the camping gear as well as his camera equipment, since she had trouble just carrying herself through the trees without tripping. Glen was used to being the pack mule, as he refused to replace any more gear broken by an uncoordinated scientist.

"We'll be camping here, since the river is about ten yards to your right. Don't fall in."

"Ha-ha, you're so funny. You better hope I don't push you in, buster." Glen snorted at her, since she was about half his size and stick thin. She glared at his back, trying not to laugh, and went to pick up her torch, dropping her own, much lighter pack on the ground.

Cat leaned over, eyes following the intense beam of light to where it illuminated a cluster of old windfall, logs covered in moss and greenery. She was thinking it would be a good place to sit if there wasn't a bee's nest in it or something else equally unpleasant when she saw the fuzzy ear tips.

Heart pumping loudly in her chest, hands shaking with excitement, Cat knelt down on the damp earth, eyes straining. She hoped she wasn't dreaming, her desire to see wolves here in the park giving her hallucinations. She got a better angle, and sucked in a deep breath, bugs and discomfort forgotten.

"Glen," she whispered, and the big man stopped unpacking, freezing at the urgency of her words. "Come over here. Carefully."

She never took her eyes off the gray wolf cub, the tiny bundle of fur and big ears curled up under a log, tail covering its nose. Glen knelt down next to her, silent despite his size, and followed the line of her pointing finger. The cub was small, and she felt her heart contract as a shiver ran through his whole body. He was cold, and she wondered where his mother was. He looked to be a few months old, and wolves this young were never left alone for long.

"We need to leave. Quietly, too. His momma has to be around here somewhere, and she won't be happy that we're this close." Glen put a hand on her shoulder, and went to stand. They both froze, as Glen's movement finally woke the cub, his eyes opening and ears turning in their direction.

Cat felt her heart jump again, this time in awe. The pup's eyes were an unbelievable shade of gray, almost silver, and they flashed like mirrors as he blinked in the torch's beam. The poor thing tried to draw back, but the space under the log was too small for him, and he couldn't go anywhere. Glen froze, then slowly lowered back to his knees, one hand reaching out towards his camera. The cub was beautiful, extraordinarily so. He was gray, like most wolves in North America, yet it was his coat pattern and eye color that set him apart. Dark gray, almost gunmetal in depth dusted his muzzle, before brightening to a misty gray that swept over his shoulders and down his back, with actual bands of different gray tones wrapping around his torso and legs. She couldn't see his whole body, but what she saw was enough for her to know he was the most striking wolf she'd ever seen.

Glen lifted his camera, and she heard the whirring of the lenses as he zoomed in on the cub. Glen sucked in a breath, and clicked away, taking several pictures before lowering the camera. "Here, take a look. You need to see this." He sounded off, as if he couldn't believe what he was seeing through the lens.

Cat gingerly took the camera, not wanting to pull her eyes away from the cub hiding in the logs, afraid he'd disappear. She took the camera, eyes flickering over the zoomed in pictures before taking a longer look. She brought the camera close to her face, unsure of what she was seeing.

"Glen, how old would you say he is?" Cat whispered, hoping her partner would say what her brain was thinking, but what her gut was saying was wrong.

"His size puts him around ten to twelve weeks....but his teeth and musculature, limb development looks younger than that. Scroll over to where he lifts up his lip..." Cat flipped pictures, and she saw the frame he was referring to, "-and his teeth, eyes and ears are saying he's around five to seven weeks. God, he's beautiful, too."

"Shit. That's what my gut says, too." They'd both spent years of their lives looking at wolves, and what she was seeing didn't make sense. "Is he just really big for his age?"

"Must be. Probably the only surviving pup in a litter, so he got all the food. That would make sense."

"Yeah, that does make sense. Oh, wow. Umm...." She trailed off, as the cub moved. She was disappointed, thinking he was about to run away, never to be seen again. She had her proof that wolves were back in Baxter, the pup's presence evidence of breeding pairs at the minimum. Instead of running to the bushes, the cub stood on shaky legs, and tumbled from the pile of logs. He moved as if he didn't know his nose from his tail, clumsy like most pups, but a cub of ten weeks or so should be more coordinated, substantiating their opinion he was actually much younger.

They both froze, and Cat found one of her hands had grabbed Glen's wrist in a death grip as the cub got to his feet, and oh-dear-Lord, slowly walked over to them. He was lovely, and his tail was out straight, head level to his shoulders, his posture curious and not aggressive. The cub would be glorious when he lost his puppy coat and got the spectacular adult coat of the gray wolf. He seemed to remember how to walk the more steps he took, and Cat and Glen held absolutely still as the cub came right up to them, black nose stretched out as far as he could reach, sniffing loudly. The cub wasn't afraid, just nervous.

As he got closer, Cat could see that he was damp, and his legs were muddy, tail too. He smelled like river water, and she had a sneaking suspicion he must have been in the current. It would explain his shivers, and damp fur. The cub snuck in cautiously, and his nose was inches from her free hand. Her fingers twitched, the desire to touch him nearly overpowering, yet she held back. He was a wild creature, and she couldn't treat him like a pet.

She held firm right up until his tiny little pink tongue came out and licked the back of her hand, whimpering pitifully as he scooted closer. He put his head under her hand, making her pet him, and she fell in love instantly.

"Cat...." Glen warned, but the cub's tail was wagging, and he was suddenly in her lap, whining and licking at her face, her arms coming up instinctively, hugging the cub. She laughed, the licks tickling her, and she tried to keep him from falling as he all about climbed her torso to give her kisses.

"Dammit, Cat..." Glen suddenly found himself with an armful of wiggling cub, the little wolf jumping from Cat's lap to the flustered photographer's. Glen tried to abstain, but the cub's enthusiasm soon put a reluctant smile on the older man's face. "He's charming, isn't he?"

He wasn't acting like a wild animal. He wasn't afraid, not anymore, yipping happily as Glen scratched behind his ears, practically throwing himself in joy on the man. Glen smiled, and Cat laughed as the cub rooted in Glen's coat pockets, his nose working loudly.

"Think he found your jerky stash, Glen."

"Yeah he did." Glen managed to get the plastic pouch away

from the cub, who promptly sat on his haunches and perked up his ears, tail wagging. He looked so much like a Labrador she had as a kid she felt a niggling suspicion firm into conviction.

"Glen, I don't think he's wild." Cat pointed at the way he was sitting, and the pup yipped, raising one foot and pawing at the air, eyes fixed on the jerky in Glen's hand. "Look at how he's acting. He's used to people."

"Yeah, I can tell. I've never seen a wild wolf pup act like this. He's acting more like a dog than a wolf." The pup seemed to understand, and he almost glared at the photographer before his attention returned to the jerky. Glen laughed softly, and rubbed his head. "Sorry, pal. You're nice for a mean, evil varmint."

That got Glen another look, but Cat just smiled, thinking she was seeing things after hiking around in the woods all day getting drained of her blood supply by the local pests.

"Where do you think he came from?" Cat asked, as both she and Glen relaxed on the ground, the pup between them with a chunk of jerky, making happy growls as he chewed on the dry meat. "He obviously isn't wild."

"Nope. Someone's pet, probably got dumped out here when he got too big. Happens a lot, unfortunately." Glen was right; people thought it would be cool to have a wolf as a pet, and as the cubs got older and much, much bigger, (and inevitably more aggressive) they were often dumped in parks and reserves, lacking in the skills necessary to survive in the wild, and the required caution of humans to keep them safe. They often became nuisance animals, hunting around human populations and eventually becoming too bold. Most 'tamed' wolves either died from starvation or disease, ended up in sanctuaries, or sadly were shot by local wildlife agencies. "Whoever had the cub most likely heard the same rumors we did about wolves out here, and thought it would be a good place to dump him.... I hate people sometimes."

"Yeah, me too. He isn't going to make it on his own. And we don't even know for certain that there are wolves in Baxter. We can't leave him here." Cat waited for Glen's denial, but to her amazement, the photographer didn't immediately say anything, eyes on the cub. The cub was watching them as they spoke, quicksilver eyes darting from her to Glen and back again. He had this air about him as if he understood what they were saying, and he politely took another piece of jerky as Glen held it out to him.

"Damn, he's cute." Glen couldn't stop staring at the cub. Cat watched as the cub charmed the socks off her partner, and she smiled, thinking that she wouldn't have to say a word about bringing him back to the sanctuary—the cub was convincing her partner all on his own. "He's used to human food, too."

"He sure is cute, for an animal that'll grow to be nearly two hundred pounds and can take down a full grown elk. Look at the size of his paws—he's gonna be a monster." Cat smiled as the cub perked up, staring at her as he swallowed the last piece of jerky, tail thumping the ground. It was if he liked her prediction, though she knew that was silly. He was just reacting to the appreciation in her voice, her body language conveying affection.

Glen sighed as the cub got up, and crawled sneakily onto his lap, snuggling in like he'd sat in someone's lap a million times before. The cub rested his head on Glen's knee, and the big man petted his fuzzy head, rubbing his ears. Both cub and man sighed in unison, sounding so alike Cat couldn't keep from chuckling.

"Looks like Luna Wolf Rescue and Research Sanctuary just got another guest." Cat nudged Glen's shoulder as the big man stroked the cub, not denying her claim. She'd make the appropriate calls tomorrow to get him over the border, and their charter was equipped to handle wolves. It wouldn't be the first time they rescued a wolf from a bad situation, and she sadly thought this wouldn't be the last time, either.

KANE HOWLED, his fury and frustration shaking the trees nearby. His throat was raw from their mourning cries to the Great Mother in the sky above, and his howl was ragged from every harsh emotion tearing apart his equilibrium. Only Caius and Burke remained unaffected, every other wolf within striking distance running away. The moon was high in the night sky, dawn not far off. He was exhausted, and the funeral pyres were burning down to embers, visible through the trees and reminding Kane that he failed to save Gray Shadow and Luca.

"He could still be out there! I don't understand how you can just abandon your own grandson to certain death!" Kane roared, lashing out, his fist snapping a sapling in two, wood splintering with a loud crack. Caius remained unmoved, and Burke wisely stayed quiet, standing behind Kane and not drawing his attention.

"Gray Shadow went to save him at the cost of his own life. He died, which a shaman of his strength and ability would not have done if Luca was still alive to be saved. I believe Gray Shadow would have been able to tell us if Luca was alive, or that he managed to find him before they both died. I know this is hard, but I cannot sense Luca through the bloodline links, and neither can Burke find his mind. Josiah cannot find the cub's mind, either, and if anyone other than Burke or Gray Shadow could do it, surely it would be his own father," Caius told him, impassive, his stern face revealing nothing. Kane doubted Josiah was capable of finding anyone, or anything, past his grief—his soulmate was dead, and it would be a miracle if the beta lived past dawn. Caius' own daughter and three of his youngest grandchildren were reduced to ash on the pyres dying in the field, and Kane couldn't understand how he could just give up on the possibility that Luca could still be alive. "We need to focus on the traitors, and the humans responsible for this attack on our people."

Kane growled, and began pacing, fists clenching as he fought to restrain his temper. He didn't see the harm in sending scouting packs to search the rivers in the morning, and going farther out. The answer to why no one could reach the cub was easy, at least to Kane. They just hadn't gone far enough.

"And no sneaking out at first light to search, Kane. I need my Heir here. We have too much to do, and too little time. The human authorities are sniffing around, and I wouldn't put it past Remus Acquisitions to send another group of hunters. Someone out there wants shamans, and a group of wolves—our own kin—helped them. This is too crucial a time for my Heir to be out wandering the woods when we're under attack." Caius pointed at Kane, accentuating each point with a jab in his direction, making the younger alpha want to snap at his hand. "The other Clan Leaders are waiting on us at the council house, and my Heir will be there at my side in a solid show of our strength. We will not show vulnerability, no matter that we lost the greatest shaman the clans have ever seen."

"Then maybe I shouldn't be your Heir, if this is how you treat your people. Apparently you feel justified to sacrifice one cub for the sake of appearances, even your own flesh and blood," Kane told his Alpha, refusing to cower as Burke stiffened in fear and Caius went glacial in fury. He was aware he'd crossed a line, and he was willing to accept the consequences.

"You are my distant cousin's son. You have the strongest Voice in generations and Black Pine needs you. I admit to needing you. My own sons are only half the alpha you are, which is why I accepted you into Black Pine and named you my heir," Caius strode forward, crowding in his personal space, the same height as Kane and nearly as strong. Kane didn't yield ground, annoying Caius further. Kane was centuries younger, and had the benefit of youth, yet Caius had decade after decade of fighting experience, and Kane doubted for a brief second that he would come out the victor if he and Caius ever came to blows. "But I will not tolerate insubordination, not even from my Heir, and I will remove you from that position if you test me on this. And I won't send you back to your mother, either."

A fight to the death, then. Kane was too strong to leave unaligned. He could Challenge Caius for the position of Clan Alpha, and Caius was afraid of him.... afraid he might succeed. So Caius was safe as long as Kane was his Heir and happy to be so; but if Kane was unhappy with his Alpha and his place as Heir, then Kane was a threat. And Caius hadn't become Clan Alpha by leaving threats unchallenged—he would kill Kane, even if he needed him.

Caius said nothing, both alphas refusing to look away. Kane could smell Burke's stress levels rising, the longer both alphas held each other's gaze. Kane refused to look away. He was right, and Caius was blinded by grief and anger, and was feeling vulnerable by this morning's attack and what it implied. Just because his word was law didn't mean he was in the right.

Kane could almost feel Luca out there, alive and waiting to be found. Kane didn't know why he wasn't doubting the cub's survival, when everyone, even his own family, believed him dead. He knew Luca was alive, felt the cub's continued existence as surely as he felt the magic in the moonlight that showered over them. Kane wanted to search until he had a body to prove him wrong.

Tension grew, and neither alpha blinked. Burke faded into the background, forgotten. Kane could feel the Clan Leader's anger rise the longer Kane refused to cave; he was expecting a blow to fall any second. So it was with an absolute shock to his system when the Alpha broke first. It was a tiny shift in his eyes, but enough. Caius growled, and spun on his heels, turning his back on Kane, his long legs eating up the distance to the trees. Kane was shocked, too stunned to do anything but stand still and watch as the Alpha of Black Pine backed down and left, heading in the direction of the council house.

"Strike one, Kane. I won't tolerate many more before I remove you," Caius' voice carried out from the trees, and Kane didn't doubt the threat in his words. If he ever went up against Caius' will again, he'd better be prepared to kill him. "And stay out of the woods."

"Fuck," Burke breathed out in disbelief. Kane couldn't move as Burke came to his side, a big hand resting on his shoulder. He was shocked that he 'won'. A small victory, but enough of one that Caius saw him now as a threat to his reign instead of a willing supporter.

"Fuck," Kane agreed. Both men waited in the trees, staring at the darkness where Caius disappeared, the funeral pyres nothing but piles of ash and embers, with trails of smoke heading up to the moon.

LUCA WAS confused. He'd found people, and they were nice. The female human petted him and cooed at him like he was a baby, and kept talking to him about how pretty he was, and how big he was going to get when he grew up. This made him happy, and every time he tried to tell her thank you like his momma taught him, she acted like she didn't hear him. The human male was no different, except he liked to play rough and fed Luca tons of yummy food that his mom never gave him.

He slept that night on the big human's lap, warm and feeling safe for the first time since his grandpa disappeared into the mist. He wasn't used to the dry meat the male fed him, and his tummy filled fast, and rumbled in complaint. He was petted and scratched, and he finally fell asleep until morning.

When he got up to go relieve himself, he remembered his manners and found a tree away from the others, just like he recalled his daddy saying to his older brothers and sisters after they first Changed. The human female watched him, and she seemed afraid he was going to run away, as she followed him everywhere. It got annoying, so he stayed nearby, watching as the big male packed up their gear and they got ready to leave. He was excited, and he kept trying to make them hear him, but the humans acted like he wasn't speaking at all.

Luca tried to tell them his name, and that he was lost, and that he wanted to go home, but neither one of them heard him. It was like their heads were broken. Didn't humans speak to each other in their heads like the wolves? They made words with their mouths, and yet they didn't talk to him like he was used to his family talking to him, both words and mind. They didn't respond when he said that Kane was supposed to find him and take him home, and they didn't hear him when he asked them if they had shamans, too.

Luca got even more confused when he tried to become a human cub again. He thought about being a boy, and using his mouth to speak to the humans so they could take him home, or help him find Kane, but he couldn't figure it out. He spent a few minutes trying to Change, but just ended up falling over and growling at himself, and the human female laughed, telling him he was cute again.

The big male smelled good and had more food on him. Luca was distracted by the scent of the dried meat when the female slipped a thin rope over his head and around his neck. He stood still, bewildered, trying to see what was around his neck and why it was there.

When it tightened as she stepped away he got scared. It was tugging and pulling and his feet didn't move with the rope. He fell over, and tried twisting away, whining and nipping at the rope. He fussed, crying, and he wanted his mom and his dad and wished his grandpa would come back.

The female was making distressed noises, trying to calm him down, and Luca was having none of it. He snapped at her when she reached out, and Luca yelped when the big male loomed over him and picked him up by the back of his neck.

"Don't think the leash is a good idea, Cat." Luca cowered, ears back, and the big male pulled him to his massive chest and pulled off the rope, handing it to the female who frowned down at it. “I’ll carry him.”

“You’re carrying most of our gear too, Glen.” Luca was confused, wondering why the big man was named after a small place in the woods when he was big enough to be named after a mountain.

“Then it’s a good thing the car isn’t that far away. God knows you can’t carry him, and you’re not dropping my camera equipment again. Come on, I want to go home and he’s gonna get heavy real quick.”

Luca submitted, the big male holding him with authority, just like Grandpa Caius. Luca felt confused again, wondering how Kane was going to find him if the humans were going to carry him away. Maybe he’d hid too well and Kane couldn’t find him? He whined, resting his head on the big male’s shoulder, and was restless until a warm hand stroked his back a few times.

“Easy, little wolf. We’ll take care of you.”

SINS OF THE BROTHER

EACH STEP the wolf's paws made on the flagstones left white slashes across the expensive polish. Long gouges marred the priceless floor, but Sebastien Remus wasn't going to tell his guest to calm down and cease his pacing. He enjoyed having all his limbs intact.

"Are you certain you got away without a trace?" Sebastien asked, sipping on his scotch on the back porch of his mansion, the rich liquor burning a trail as it flowed over his tongue and down his throat. His stomach was churning, and if it wasn't for the previous glass he'd gulped down before his guest arrived, he wouldn't be half as restrained as he was right now.

The wolf, a large beast that was a brown and black brindle with dark eyes, stopped its pacing and turned a menacing head in Sebastien's direction. Eyes devoid of any humanity stared back at him, and he had to fight down the mouthful of scotch to avoid choking as every instinct in him told him to run. He sucked in a breath, trying to be subtle, but the beast seemed to know he was fighting off the urge to flee, and he let his lip curl back at it, refusing to show fear. He may be nothing to this beast, but he was a wealthy man, with hundreds of people on his payroll, and no one, no *animal*, was going to intimidate him.

The monster on his porch silently shifted on its big paws, the snap of bones bending and warping, and grunts of vague distress filling the warm evening air as his guest took on human form. He looked away, out towards the skyline of Augusta, and deliberately, for the sake of his stomach, avoided watching as the monster finished its transformation, and knelt panting on the flagstones.

"They got away clean. I used the masking agent to clean my tracks and stayed behind for the blood sample. The others barely made it out in time before they closed the borders," snarled the naked man, lifting his head and chewing at the words. Sebastien rolled his eyes, and waved a hand at the small table beside his chair, where the bottle of scotch and another glass sat waiting. Beside it was a tube of red liquid, priceless and the beginning of a new world order. "They would have torn us apart, and then come hunting you."

"Don't be so dramatic."

"Dramatic? Dramatic?! Do you comprehend what will happen if Caius, or any of the other Greater Clan Leaders, discover who was behind the attack this morning?" His guest stood, and instead of filling the other glass, grabbed the eighteen year old bottle of scotch and drank straight from it in several long draws. Sebastien made certain the glass tube was secure before casting a glare at the beast who drank his best scotch.

"That's a thousand dollar bottle, you animal."

He got a snarl in response, as his guest flung himself naked on to the other patio chair.

"It was supposed to be a simple job, Remus. Care to explain what happened? We'd have the shaman and his heirs, along with millions of dollars, if you'd only done your fucking job like you were hired. That blood sample I got may not be enough to rectify this disaster."

"Information was inadequate," he retorted, thinking about the men he'd lost in that very expensive waste of an operation earlier that day. Highly trained mercenaries were hard to come by, and even harder to keep employed if their coworkers died in large numbers on 'training ops.' "I was told the shaman was old, and that there were no alphas in his family pack, nothing but betas and brats. My men were burnt alive by that *old dog,*" he sat up, and moved his feet off the patio recliner and faced the monster in human form beside him. "It was your job to supply me with adequate information, and I lost almost two dozen men because of your incompetence!"

"He was old, dammit! Oldest fucking shaman in the Clans, and there were no alphas in his family pack that were there! You just didn't listen to me when I said a shaman was dangerous."

"Magic," he scoffed, putting his crystal glass down on the wooden table with a harsh clink. "Party tricks and sleight of hand are nothing against bullets."

The monster threw back his head and laughed harshly, lank brown hair moving in the faint wind. His blood chilled at the human sound coming from the creature's throat, and he stiffened his spine, refusing to show his discomfort.

"Sleight of hand that can burn men alive, manipulate the elements, travel across vast distances in seconds, use telekinesis and pyro-kinesis, telepathy, accelerated healing, and countless other abilities that can fucking rule the world, and you discounted them all because you *don't believe in magic!* Fucking moron." The monster shook its head, and took another drag on the bottle. "We had a deal, Remus. You failed to hold up your part of it. I got Gray Shadow's blood, so my end wasn't a total loss."

"I won't fail the next time. I can have a new op planned and ready to move in the next twelve hours. There are more shamans out there, from what my intelligence tells me. We can get fresh samples, and a living specimen." Sebastien stood, and gazed out over the landscape as the sun finished setting. "Now I need you to leave, my brother will be here any minute, I'm not explaining why I have a naked man on my porch."

His guest smirked up at him, a nasty excuse of a smile that twisted his seemingly human features into something.... *wrong*. He stood, a hulking man covered in dirt and smelling like wet dog, the odor enough for Sebastien to take a step back in disgust.

"Oh, you don't need to worry about explaining about the werewolf, Sebastien," came a voice from the back door. Sebastien whirled, and his little brother Simon stepped casually over the threshold. The monster slowly moved closer, and Sebastien struggled to understand what was happening. His little brother was supposed to be coming over for dinner in an hour, not talking about werewolves he wasn't supposed to know existed.

“You know?” Sebastian spun to glare at the monster, and sneered at the chuckle rising from the naked creature on his porch. “Did you tell him? I wanted him kept out of this!”

“I’ve known the whole time, brother dear. Just as I know you fucked up a job that was going to make us all obscenely rich.” Simon shook his head and chided him with a thin, wagging finger as he pulled out a cell from his jacket with the other. He hit a button, and held the ringing phone aloft as it connected on Speakerphone.

“Nine-one-one, please state your emergency.”

“Please help! I think my brother’s been kidnapped! There’s blood everywhere and I can’t find him!” Simon suddenly screamed into the cell, making Sebastien jump, startled and confused. His brother glared at him with flat, dark eyes, and Sebastien felt a cold, sinking sensation coil in his gut.

He was about to shout, to do something, but he never finished the thought as a burst of pain and white lights exploded in his temple. He heard the faked terror in his little brother’s voice as he fell, and then his thoughts faded away.

SIMON REMUS played the concerned little brother to the cool-voiced dispatcher on the other end of the line as the alpha werewolf lifted his unconscious brother over his shoulder, and strode off the porch and down into the back yard. Blood dripped from Sebastien's head and down the finely muscled bare ass of his assailant, and Simon leered at the sight until he caught a glimpse of the scotch bottle in the monster's free hand. He snorted, turned it into a sob, not wanting to clue in the dispatcher to his perfectly calm state.

He answered questions with an appropriate degree of hysteria as the werewolf carried away his brother, the tall creature quickly swallowed up by the darkness under the trees. Sebastien would be dead by morning, his body found in a bad part of town, the slain victim of a kidnapping gone wrong, dumped by his kidnappers as they fled the city.

In reality he was being taken to the Clan Leader of Black Pine, a sudden dead end on the trail leading to Remus Acquisitions. Caius McLennan would not spare Sebastien Remus, not with his precious daughter and grandchildren dead, and there was no proof leading to Simon's involvement. The beast who just left with his brother would see to that. With the CEO and owner dead and unable to tell anyone who had hired him or who he was working with, Simon was safe to continue on and improve upon their plans. No one would look to the grieving young man who would bravely take over his brother's company in the wake of his death. His brother's mistakes would not come back to haunt him.

Sebastien had screwed up a mission that was posed to make them millions, hell—billions of dollars, and he'd even had the audacity to try and keep him out of it, too. Simon reached out with his free hand and picked up the shaman's blood. Despite being taken from a corpse and hours past adequate preservation, the blood was still worth millions. His brother's death wouldn't affect the bottom line for long.

He looked down at the marble, its smooth finish marred by blood and claws. He pretended to cry as he wondered how easy it was to get blood out of stone.

PART TWO

GHOST

FOURTEEN AND A HALF YEARS LATER...

"STOP! OH MY GAWD! Glen, he killed it!" He ducked his head as Cat's scream of frustration soared through the laboratory, his claws skidding in haste over the white and black tiles, dodging the torn towel flung his way. It fell short, and he huffed softly in amusement as it flopped limply, like a dead bird.

The wolf flashed her a toothy grin, red tongue lolling from the side of his muzzle, tail flagging high. Cat tossed her hands up in the air, hair fuzzy, glasses askew, as she gaped at the wreckage of the once lone couch situated along the one clear wall of the lab, a horrendous monstrosity of puke green, and a yellow reminiscent of urine stains.

Glen strode from his office, still powerful and strong after all these years, just a few more lines around his eyes and mouth. He was still an alpha to the young wolf, and moved with a calm authority that resonated with him, even when his human alpha was angry. He wasn't, not this time, just resigned.

"Ghost...," Glen sighed to the wolf, wiping a hand over his

mouth as he struggled not to laugh, eyes lighting on the destroyed couch. “I told you he wasn’t a fan of that couch, Cat. It looks better torn up.” Glen sent the wolf they named Ghost a quick wink, and he wagged his tail once in reply.

“Glen, he ate the couch. Ate it! There’s stuffing everywhere! I was planning on having our guests up here, where would you like me to have the meeting with the conservation officers now?” Cat grumbled, kicking at the white stuffing littering the floor, damp from saliva and coated in gray hairs. Her shoulders slumped, and the wolf dropped his tail, cocking his head to the side, watching as the human beta sat disconsolately on one of the numerous steel stools beside the table in the middle of the room.

He hadn’t meant to make her sad. It was funny when she got frustrated, but it never lasted long, her mood lightening quickly. She always made the funniest sounds when he did something outrageous, squawking like one of the water birds he hunted in the autumn, hands flapping like wings, hair going every which way.

Ghost stepped lightly across the floors his feet soundless, great black claws making no noise as he wound his way through the mess, before approaching the female, the one named Cat. He still found that name confusing after all these years since she never changed into a cat, and she smelled totally human. A human woman who smelled faintly of the gray wolves kept in the enclosure outside the building, but still a human. Yet they called him Ghost, and he was not one of those faint lost souls that haunted the old pioneer cabins out in the wild woods, past the sanctuary boundaries.

He dropped his giant head in her lap, mindful of how small she was compared to him. Ghost had vague memories of giant wolves, much larger than he currently was, great beasts that ruled the dark pine forests in his dreams, and spoke in his mind. Ghost did not feel small, yet a part of him knew somehow that he really was, his memories of giants on four paws faraway, yet painful.

He whined, slowly blinking his liquid silver eyes up at her, nudging her hands with his nose. She tried to glare at him, but he widened his eyes, tail wagging, and she groaned, dropping a hand behind his ear and scratching.

It was his turn to groan, a rear paw spasming with the urge to scratch as her thin fingers wove through his thick fur, finding the same spots that always itched. He wasn't carrying the tiny parasites that sometimes bothered the smaller wolves of the sanctuary, but his skin still dried out from the central air that cycled through the large building that contained the laboratory, Glen's photo studio, and the rooms the humans used as their den. It was winter, the cold season of death and slumber laying heavily on the wilds of New Brunswick. He had learned about maps over the years by sneaking out of the wolf enclosure and finding his humans in their den. He learned about a lot of things that humans liked, and the things they liked to do, and it wasn't all that different than what he was accustomed to as a child. He knew more than the gray wolves that were content in their run outside the building, simply because he knew there was more out there past the fence, and he could get out any time he wanted. Glen and Cat eventually stopped locking him up, letting him come and go as he pleased, patrolling his territory and sticking his nose wherever he wanted. They were his pack, Glen and Cat, more so than the simple creatures that ran behind their fence, convinced they were free.

"We've got an hour until they're supposed to be here, babe. I'll clean this up, go take a shower and relax. Everything's ready for the meeting. I'll put Ghost out with the puppies. He never gets into trouble when he's in there."

Ghost sent the human alpha a glare, annoyed at the insinuation he was still a cub. He was nearly twenty years old, ancient for a wolf....and very young for his kind. He fought back the dim memories that threatened to confuse him, and remembered that he was here and now. There was a small fenced in area right outside the building, where the youngest of the sanctuary's 'guests' were kept, all of them wolf cubs under six months, too young to be released with the grown wolves in the main enclosure. They were close enough that scents and sounds traveled the short distance between the two pens, so that the cubs would be at least known to the grown wolves if they survived long enough to be added to the sanctuary's pack. Ghost had spent a few weeks in there himself, until the disparity in his growth cycle became overwhelmingly obvious, and Cat brought him into the lab to study him and his unusual physiology.

Ghost pulled back from the female, and shook his great head, hackles rising and falling, before darting away from the humans. He far outweighed the female, and the male was not as strong as he. If he didn't want to be locked up with the puppies, he wouldn't be. Ghost ran to one of the windows, skidding through the guts of the couch, and nosed the latch. The lab was on the second floor, overlooking the rear yard and the high fence that enclosed the wolf run.

"I swear he understands us," Glen grumbled as Ghost opened the window, the lever swinging the pane out and away from the frame, then sent Glen and Cat a haughty look before jumping out the window, hurtling to the snow covered ground below.

He landed in the thick wet stuff, sneezing away the flakes that coated his nose on impact. He could hear them as easily as if he were still up there in the lab, as Glen moved to the window, reaching out to shut it.

"He's an odd one, that's for sure. What other wolf knows how to open windows, and jumps two stories into a snow bank? And I know Ghost can open doors too, I've seen him. I stopped trying to keep him out of the kitchen years ago. I'm hoping the reps from the other research center the conservation officers are bringing will have some answers. I gave up thinking he was a gray wolf about twelve years ago, once he outgrew even our largest resident wolf." Ghost shook out his fur, and sighed, hearing Cat's suspicions aloud for the millionth time in the last few years. "He doesn't act like a wolf, either. Doesn't age like one, either. If he wasn't so obviously a wolf of some kind I'd say he wasn't an animal at all."

Ghost lifted his head, and sniffed loudly, sucking in the swirling scents on the cold breeze that whipped over the sanctuary. He shook once more, not smelling anything of concern on the wind, and trotted to the wall of the building, snuggling under the window high overhead. It was free of snow under the second floor overhang, and the dried leaves blown there made for a comfortable bed. He could hear them above him moving around, probably cleaning.

The sanctuary slumbered under a thick blanket of white, the trees heavy with the wet snow, the wind a steady source of sensory input as it weaved through the buildings and the forest. He smelled the puppies in the small pen to his left, snuggled together in a pile inside their wooden den, sleeping until it was time for supper. He looked north, and caught the smallest hint of dark orange eyes that blinked once before retreating back into the thick foliage of a giant pine. The wolves were hungry, winter urging them to eat more to replace the energy spent to stay warm. Cat would be out soon, feeding the pups first, then the adults. Ghost had no taste for butchered meat, preferring to catch his own supper. He'd already eaten, and he was more interested in what Glen and Cat were discussing than tracking winter rabbits.

In the weeks and months after Glen and Cat found him by the river, the two humans treated him as any other wolf pup. Fed him, gave him a warm place to sleep, and tried to comfort him as he howled his loneliness every night, missing his family, his home. As time passed, and they continued to ignore his mental attempts to communicate, he stopped trying. He couldn't recall when it was he gave up trying to get them to understand him, and turned his attention to the wolves at the sanctuary. That turned out to be slightly more successful than talking to the humans. The wolves knew him by scent and instinct as a stronger predator, and if he tried really hard, he could sense the half-formed thoughts of the wolves murmuring inside their minds. They were smart, just not as smart as Ghost, and they knew it. While he couldn't talk to them as he had to his grandfather, they heard him, and obeyed.

When he failed to change back into a boy, Ghost's wolf grew swiftly. He learned to run, leap, hunt, and communicate as a wolf. The memories of his grandfather faded as he grew further away from his past, the wild northern woods seducing him, comforting him. Pack life as a wolf was easy. Straightforward. His loneliness came on him at odd times, like when he snuck into the labs and snuggled with Glen as he watched football on the television, or when he went on car rides with Cat as she traveled to the nearest town. Those trips stopped, though, once he got too large, and people started to notice how different he was. Humans got nervous easily, and around here most humans had guns.

The first time the peaceful ease of his life at the sanctuary changed happened when his wolf-form grew to adulthood. It happened quickly, and he wasn't normal, if the confused and impressed exclamations from Cat and Glen were anything to go by—he was too large. Too big, too muscular. His body was shaped differently, nothing like the smaller gray wolves here.

Too smart.

No pen could remained locked, no door shut, no snack was safe from him. If he didn't want to stay in the enclosure with the other wolves, then he didn't. If he wanted to go for a run, he went. And minding the manners he learned by watching Cat tutor her summer interns, Ghost remembered every time to shut doors and latches behind him, so the real wolves never got out, too.

He knew he was worrying them when they started to install something he called 'thumb-locks', devices that wouldn't open unless a hand with an opposable thumb attempted it. Combinations, buttons, and more. He remembered the first time he opened a combination lock, not with teeth and tongue, or claw and awkward digit—he used his mind.

It was so easy he startled himself. He'd run up to the gates of the wolf pen, smelling some deer a few hundred yards away, and he wanted to eat something other than butchered beef. Expecting to meet a latch that just needed a nose to open, he'd been stymied by the combination lock. There were numbers inked on it, the scent of the marker fresh, and it made his nose itch. The three digits brought to mind fuzzy recollections of lessons at a large table, a sweet smelling older woman with reddish brown hair reading to him from a book, counting. He couldn't recall what they were exactly, but he recognized them anyway.

Sitting on his haunches, Ghost tilted his head, and glared at the offending chunk of metal. He wanted out. He wasn't a sheltered wolf battered by tragedy, incapable of fending for himself. Not like the others there. He could take care of himself. Seconds after sitting down, the tumblers spun, untouched, the wind warm as it moved around his head and to the lock. With a satisfied snick, each one fell into place, matching the numbers inked on the lock. With a grunt, he'd nosed at the lock once it fell open, and tipped the latch. The gate swung open, and he bounced through, ecstatic to be out, eager to hunt. He turned, pushed the gate shut with his head, and nuzzled the latch until it fell into place, ensuring the wolves couldn't follow him out.

Ghost turned towards the woods, his nose twitching with the scent of deer, and then he tumbled to a stop once the reality of what he'd done hit him. He opened that lock. Without touching it.

His cry of delight morphed into one of despair, as he fought back the encroaching memories of a large gray wolf, a starry sky and miniature suns, and a dark room filled with kin and magic. He didn't hunt after opening the lock. He ran instead, fleeing from the certainty that he was living a life that wasn't his. He wasn't meant for this. Ghost spent hours shaking in a damp cave, his whole body shivering from a cold that seeped through his bones. He was missing something, incomplete..... He was in a dream, long overdue to wake up. Hours in the darkness, eyes shut, afraid to remember, but wanting it all the same. The morning after, Ghost limped back to the sanctuary, since he had nowhere else to go, no one other than Cat and Glen to wonder where he was and miss him. It was all he knew for certain.

Shaman... It was a whisper from the depths of his soul. A memory.

Voices above him called him back from the past, and Ghost heard the rumble of an engine coming up the drive. He'd lost track of time, and realized that Cat and Glen were talking about their visitors. He stood, and shook himself out, before padding silently around the building, stopping at the corner where the drive came right up to the front of the laboratory. It was a large vehicle, one that Glen called an SUV, and he smelled of want when he spoke of them. It was a weird thing to want, when wanting food and snuggles was something far more important. At least to Ghost.

He kept out of sight, only peeking around the corner enough so he could see, as four humans exited the black SUV. The wind blew their scents to him, and he breathed deep, eyes narrowing as his mind processed the separate smells. Two were dressed as officers of some kind, matching clothing and the scent of trees and snow marking them as the conservation men. The other two men were different, and he couldn't discern some of what he was smelling. Stale sweat, nerves. Fear. And pain.

He watched, but saw no signs of injury on either stranger. One was tall and thick, and moved like a predator, eyes watchful, each stride efficient and calculated. Yet there was something off about him, as if he was pretending to be prey instead of predator. False smiles, handshake too quick and hard. The other was shorter, and older, and was nervous, though he was doing his best to act calm. Maybe the predator man was the alpha, and he was displeased, making the small beta human nervous, though Ghost only saw calm confidence and a subtle edge of danger as he moved. That one was dangerous.

Glen greeted the four men at the front door, inviting them

in, voicing the silly pleasantries that Ghost tried to understand. Humans were weird. Who wants to talk about the weather, when all you have to do is look outside? Or asking about their drive, when one sniff will tell you that they stopped twice on the way here, and ate nasty snacks that stank of something Cat called preservatives?

They were in the building, and Ghost hesitated. They were here to discuss him, and part of him wanted to know what they were going to say. Something was bothering him, the two foreign men with the conservation officers making his skin shiver with suspicion. They didn't smell right. Yet if they were going to talk about him, and poke and prod at him like Cat used to, then he didn't want any part of that. Humans liked using needles and machines when they should just use their noses.

It was the thought of the fragile Cat with those strange males that made up Ghost's mind. Glen was a strong alpha, but he was human. He was also outnumbered, and if they got rude, then Ghost didn't want his pack undefended.

He bolted around the corner, and raced to the front door, taking the handle in his teeth and tugging down. The door popped open, and he slipped inside, the door shutting automatically behind him as he ran down the hall and up the stairs, heading back to the lab. He stopped outside the shut door, and stretched out on the tiled floor, able to hear every word and movement. If something went wrong, he could be through that door and on the interlopers before Glen and Cat got hurt.

“Dr. Medeiros, it’s a pleasure to meet you in person. Our correspondence remains the highlight of my week. Hopefully I can help you with your problem.” That must be the older man, as he sounded shaky, yet pretending to be sure and certain. Ghost smelled the two officers closer to the door, off to the side, the beeps and chirps telling him at least one of them was playing with one of those human toys, a ‘smartphone’. They were crunchy, and boring, and Cat yelled at him something fierce when he tried to play with hers.

“I’m so glad you could come, Dr. Harmon. I’m hoping you can help us out as well. Ghost is a mystery, and I’d dearly love to figure him out.” So they were there about him. Not good. His sense of unease grew, and he resisted the urge to growl, not wanting to let on that he was there.

“I’ve got the pictures you sent, along with the blood tests. I ran the DNA several times, but it came back inconclusive.” Ghost had no idea what that meant, and he waited, hoping the strange human would say something understandable. “The pictures look to be very similar to the gray wolf, yet I took into consideration the scale once I saw his measurements. I’ve never seen a gray wolf that large before, not outside of a specimen from two hundred years ago stuffed in a museum, at least. Does he really weigh in at over ninety kilos?”

The male doctor sounded excited, and the sour scent of his sweat wafted out of the room, under the door. The other men in the room stopped fidgeting by the lack of sound from them, and he could practically sense their riveted attention.

“That he does. I’ve never seen a wolf so large before. Portions of his anatomy are slightly different, too. His shoulders, neck, and head are proportionally larger, along with his legs being far more muscular than the average gray wolf. I've timed him from one end of the wolf run to the other, and his speed is faster than any other gray wolf recorded over a similar distance. He shouldn't be that fast for an animal his size, but Ghost is." Cat sounded so proud of him, and she was happy. Confused, but happy. "I have a theory, but it's so off the charts I really need another opinion on this."

Please don't say werewolf. I like it here. I may not know where my real home is, but this place is the only home I've known since I fell in the river and you found me. Don't say werewolf. I don't know where to go if I leave here.

"Do share, I'm excited to hear it."

"Glen agrees with me. The similarities are common enough that I can reasonably assert that Ghost isn't a gray wolf at all, but a dire wolf."

Silence greeted her statement. Ghost shuddered, the true name of his wolf-form whispering to him, taking him back to his past, the night before the river tore him away from his family, his pack. Dire wolves. Great predators that roamed the ancient world, and hunted man.

"Canis dirus? My dear Dr. Medeiros, they went extinct thousands of years ago." Dr. Harmon was lying. He was saying one thing, but the rapid thump of his heart and the rank sweat Ghost could smell through the door belied his words. He knew something.

"I would agree sir, if not for the fact that everything about Ghost says otherwise. Size, speed, body shape, even his coat and coloration. If I were equipped to perform DNA tests I'd be able to confirm it, which is part of the reason why I reached out to you. I'm certain, beyond all doubt, that Ghost is a dire wolf."

"Well.... I admit the evidence is compelling." The male doctor tried to sound doubtful, but Ghost could hear the agreement in him. He wanted Cat to think he didn't believe her, but he did. It was more than that; his excitement told Ghost that he *knew*.

"I think that at some point, someone found a remote wolf population in either Russia or Siberia, and took the cubs. We found Ghost as a puppy in Baxter State Park, and he was used to human interaction. I theorize that since the wolf populations here in southern Canada and the northern States are so closely monitored that someone wanted a wolf as a pet, but couldn't get one from here. So I think some lucky smuggler happened to find a surviving pocket of dire wolves, took the cubs, not knowing what they'd really found, and sold them to unsuspecting buyers in the States. Then, once it became difficult for his owners to keep him, they dumped him in the state park, in an area where wolves were rumored to be." Cat was so certain she was right. Ghost shivered, thinking about how close she actually was to the truth, yet at the same time how very far away from it she really was. If only she knew the truth.

"A very enjoyable theory, Doctor. Full of intrigue and thrills." Ghost quietly growled at the subtle snark in the foreign doctor's words, aimed at his packmate. Cat was a smart woman, for a human. She was wonderful, if annoying. No one talked to her like she was a foolish cub. "May we see the animal in question? Perhaps an examination in person would help me come to a conclusion about his origins."

"Oh. Um... he's outside. He usually runs free." Cat sounded embarrassed, a den mother unable to restrain her wayward cubs. Ghost panted in amusement. "He'll come back to the lab soon, it's getting on to suppertime."

"He doesn't run away? Surely such a degree of freedom is dangerous, for him and humans?" That must be the strange alpha human. He was moving, feet making a bare whisper of noise as he went towards the part of the lab where Cat was standing. Ghost twitched. The thought of that dangerous male near his alpha's mate made him nervous.

"Ghost has never caused any trouble. Well, aside from getting through locked doors and the refrigerator. And he hates my taste in furniture." Cat laughed, and the men in the room chuckled.

"So, this wondrous wolf isn't in here? He's outside?" the strange alpha asked, and there was something in his words that made Ghost tense.

"Like Cat said, he'll be back soon. He never misses a meal." Glen was speaking now, and Ghost reacted to the tension in his voice. Something was bothering his alpha.

"He'd better. At least I don't have to worry about his interference when I kill you." Ghost shot up from the floor as Cat screamed, two rapid popping noises coming from the room. Glen shouted, and the scent of sulfur and blood came to Ghost as he slammed into the door. He hit it so hard the door flung off its hinges, sailing over two men collapsed on the floor, crashing into a table covered in equipment.

The strange alpha had Cat cornered on her stool, a gun pointed at her head, the barrel oddly long, not looking like the smaller weapon that Glen sometimes carried when he left the sanctuary. Ghost crouched low to the floor, ears back, lips pulled back from his fangs, a roar of white-hot anger building in his chest as he took one slow, slinking step after another over the threshold, towards the aggressor who threatened his packmate.

"Fuck! Remus, that's him!" the foreign doctor stammered, rapidly stumbling back as Ghost crept closer to the man threatening Cat. He cleared the edge of the table, able to see Glen kneeling on the floor, blood running from a deep gash over his left eye, wavering as he attempted to stand. Glen fell back to his knees, and the strange alpha tightened his grip on his human weapon, shoving the end of it closer to Cat's head.

"Stop right there, abomination." The interloper spoke to him directly, his eyes locking with Ghost's. He stopped, the growl of rage spilling over his bared teeth, rumbling up from his chest. "I will kill her if you take one more step. And don't act like you don't understand me. I know full fucking well you're not a dumb house pet."

Ghost paused, his growl dying off, yet he didn't relax, ready to pounce at his first chance. This human knew. He knew that

Ghost wasn't just an over-large, too intelligent animal. He knew. *Werewolf. Wolfkin.*

"Change, now. I prefer you without fangs and claws," the interloper ordered, and Ghost crouched lower, claws digging tracks in the tiles under his paws. He shook his head once, an abrupt negative that made the man with the gun narrow his cold, dead eyes at him.

Ghost bit back the urge to snarl a challenge, and feared that this human would see that he was broken—he was wolfkin, a werewolf, who was stuck in one form, untrained and lacking the knowledge to return to his human body. He'd spent the last fourteen years as a wolf, and he couldn't recall what it was like to walk on two legs instead of four. The boy Luca was gone, as surely as if he had drowned in the river that warm summer morning.

Ghost fought back the familiar fear of being trapped in a similar situation. He saw an overlap of an image, of cowering under his grandfather's great wolf-form, another man with cold eyes holding a weapon on them both, threatening to end their lives. It was the agony of that memory that pushed him, made his heart beat harder—he would not let history repeat itself. No one he loved was dying again. He wasn't a cub anymore. Form-locked he may be, but he was his grandfather's blood—he was not helpless.

"Harmon! Get the tranquilizer ready," the aggressor snapped, and the human doctor jumped, digging at his pockets, pulling out a couple of black boxes. He was fumbling, awkward, and Ghost could taste his anxiety as it flooded the room. He pulled a syringe and a vial from one of the boxes, dropping the other on the floor where it made a soft beeping noise and lit up a small screen.

"Now, you're gonna hold still, and Harmon is gonna knock you out. If you turn on him, or make one move I don't like, you can say goodbye to your pet humans." The strange alpha waved his free hand at his doctor, the smaller man swallowing nervously, hands shaking as he fought to draw a clear liquid from the glass vial in his hand.

"What are you doing? What's going on?" Cat stammered, finally finding her voice, tears running down her cheeks. Glen groaned weakly as he finally collapsed all the way to the floor. The man with the gun shoved the barrel in her face, making her cry out. Ghost growled, muscles readying for his leap.

"I'll do it! Harmon, hurry the fuck up and stick him!"

"Okay, okay!" Harmon paled to bone white, but crept forward with the syringe filled and ready.

Ghost quivered with the desire to kill, saliva dripping from his fangs, eyes locked on the man hurting Cat. The scent of blood was overpowering, filling the room, clashing with the fear and adrenaline scents that rose from the doctor now standing at his side. He didn't move, afraid that one twitch on his part would result in a bullet tearing into Cat's skull.

A slight pain bloomed in his shoulder, and he turned his head with a snarl, the human doctor backpedaling away, the syringe held in his hand uncapped and empty. Ghost wondered what happened until he felt a dragging sense of fatigue roll over his mind. Cat watched in confused horror as he shook his head, fighting the urge to lay down, to rest. His anger drifted out of reach, and his claws withdrew from the tiles.

"How long until that kicks in?" the interloper growled at the male doctor, grabbing Cat by her arm and yanking her to her feet. Ghost tried to leap at him, but his brain couldn't seem to tell his feet what to do. His chest heaved, lungs and heart slowing, as if he were about to fall asleep.

"He should be out any minute now." The male doctor nervously threw the syringe in the trash, wiping his sweaty hands on his jacket. Ghost fell, breathing heavily, trying to fight off the drug coursing through his body. "I used a silver nitrate derivative as the base for the sedative, it'll keep him under for a while. I'd say he's a beta from the size of him, so he'll be out any second. It works on the betas and lesser alphas that we have at the labs."

"What did you do to him? What the hell is going on?" Cat cried, her toes barely touching the floor as the large male held her by her arm, easily controlling her as he lowered his gun. He sneered at Ghost, who could do nothing but blink slowly, mouth open, paws twitching.

"Keep an eye on him, Harmon." The human alpha ordered the smaller male doctor, who nodded, eyes still tracking Ghost while he struggled to stay awake. "I'll need some time to take care of our hosts."

Betas. Lesser alphas.

Betas... Alphas. How does the human know... what is he

doing to Cat and Glen?

The interloper pulled two pieces of metal from his pocket, and he threw Cat against the table, wrenching her arms behind her back and tying her wrists together. *Handcuffs,* his mind supplied idly, the words coming to him from the memory of watching cop shows with Glen on TV.

Darkness was coming. His eyes stopped blinking, the edges of his awareness dulling, his chest rising and falling so slowly he couldn't even tell if he were breathing. Ghost watched through the blur in his eyes as the strange man stepped over him, after throwing Cat to the floor next to where Glen was still passed out. He smelled blood even as his brain began to shut down, the drug working fast, his shoulder burning as the poison spread through his veins.

Silver. Beta, alpha... beta and alpha. Silver kills us unless a shaman...

Shaman. Grandfather. Gray Shadow. Shaman.

He called me a shaman as he died, disappearing on the wind. Luca, Shaman of Black Pine.

I REMEMBER.

I am a shaman.

It was if the thought, the remembrance, was a catalyst, and a bolt of white-hot energy raced through his mind and muscles. A glow settled over his dimming eyes, and lights grew within the two humans laying on the floor. Cat was crying, sobbing, but all Ghost could see was a tiny star that shivered in the shadow of her body, deep in her chest, a pale blue light that fluttered, as if shy. Beside her, barely conscious, Glen remained where he'd fallen, and his body faded out as Cat's did, a small dot of light twinkling within his chest, the pure yellow of dandelions that sent out tendrils, racing from the center of his body, to his skin, focusing on where his shoulder was touching Cat's hip.

The lights were so entrancing that Ghost almost succumbed to the drug, so distracted by what he was seeing. He jerked, a small spasm, but enough to drag his gaze from his packmates to the human male grumbling to himself as he watched his cohort mess with the dead conservation officers behind Ghost. There was light in his chest too, and Ghost stared, mind and thoughts clearing as he watched the baleful pale green star pulse in time with his nervous heat beat.

Ghost closed his eyes, finally able to blink, and he found himself looking at a starry expanse, a deep lake of black that shined with dozens of lights, the brightest of which was so near to him that it *was him.* A silver white star burned with a fury he could not bear to watch, but he could not look away. Dark pewter lines of liquid flowed through the lake of darkness, winding towards his light, coming from where he somehow knew his shoulder was, where the syringe punctured his flesh. He was seeing the drug, as it attacked him from the inside, rendering him helpless. He snarled, soundless to the outside world, yet it echoed here in the calm black lake of his spirit, and the star that was him shined brighter at the sound. His anger rose, frustration and an instinctual desire to be free making the silver-white star grow, burning brighter, hotter, more violently, a writhing mass of light and soundless challenge. The snaking tendrils of poison withdrew from the growing light, and Ghost, *Luca,* poured more power into his body, his spirit, calling to the other faraway stars across the horizon when he began to falter.

Light came, in thin rivulets, winding through the heavens that existed behind his eyes, answering his call. As he chased the poison through his body, the light from the other stars poured in, buffering him, fueling him. He heard with his earthly ears a startled gasp, a sharp beeping coming from nearby, and the rumble of a beast enraged. As the poison fled from his internal light, retreating back to the point it entered his body, he heard a startled exclamation from the outside, so loud it made him snap back, and his eyes open.

Cat was staring at him, eyes wide with concern and fear. The male doctor was staring down at his feet, where the other black box he'd dropped was beeping erratically, going crazy. Ghost blinked, and breathed deep, rolling up from his side, pulling his feet under him.

"Not a beta. Not a lesser alpha. Shaman. He's a shaman," the male doctor breathed in astonishment, unable to tear his eyes away from the box squawking at his feet.

"What are you rambling on about?" the aggressor demanded as he climbed the stairs, entering the lab, his dark shirt soaked with the blood of one of the slain officers. He stopped in the doorway, startled, and Ghost snarled, moving swiftly, placing his large body between the predator and his packmates.

"Remus! It isn't a beta! It's a shaman!" screamed the male doctor, throwing himself backwards, falling to his rear in his haste, fear snatching at the air in his lungs. "Shoot it, shoot it!"

Ghost roared as the man drew his gun. Lifting to point at his face, finger settling on the trigger. Time slowed, and Ghost let his fury loose, a red-hot wave that came from all around, collecting in front of him, making the air warp and burn, ozone crackling as a wall of burning hot gas rolled across the space between the man who hurt his pack and Ghost. He acted without thought, distant memory of another doing the same anchored deep in his subconscious, barely guiding him when the spirit-fire hit the gun.

A scream was the interloper's answer to Ghost's attack, the gun exploding in his hand, glowing shards of metal fragmenting across the lab. Nothing came at Ghost or his packmates; the wall of air still rolled forward, trapping the man on the floor and the now wounded gunman. Blood ran from an injured hand, and clothes smoked as Ghost's rage pushed the wall of air. He stepped forward, one paw at a time, charged with anger, his will driving the wall, forcing the two human men to scramble to the door.

The doctor wasn't fast enough, his entire right side exposed to the burning air, clothes blackening in seconds, the smell of burning flesh erupting as he screamed, ineffectively batting at his clothing, eventually falling through the open door into the hall. The human alpha grabbed at his shirt collar with his uninjured hand, and dragged the male doctor down the hall to the stairs. Ghost followed, the human alpha staring back at him with hate-filled eyes the whole way as Ghost herded them with the wall of burning air, down the stairs, and back down the hall to the front of the building. The paint peeled and the carpet smoked; the wooden stair rail blackened and smelled horribly; Ghost pushed on, an eerie sense of calm settled over him, the ease at which he bent the air to his will a vague worry in the back of his mind.

The two men spilled out the front door, past the body of one of the dead officers, into the vehicle. The male doctor was still screaming, and the aggressor's eyes silently promised retribution to Ghost as he stood in the doorway, gathering his will for one last push. The hot gas slammed into the driver's side of the SUV, singeing the paint, causing the tires to smoke as it was thrown into gear. The SUV sped away, and Ghost dropped the spirit fire, chasing after the vehicle as it took the gravel drive away from the sanctuary, the accelerator bottoming out.

Ghost nearly overtook it as the SUV cleared the front gates, and he skidded to an abrupt stop, watching as it disappeared amongst the trees. He listened as the engine eventually faded, miles between the attackers and his territory. Ghost threw back his head and howled, victorious, anger and rage and power shaking the snow from the nearby trees.

Answering howls from the wolves behind the building pulled Ghost free from his fury. He dropped his head, his claws digging into the gravel as he padded soundlessly back to his packmates.

He ran through the front door and up the stairs, and back

into the lab. He stepped around the tiny puddle of poison that glittered evilly on the tiles where the shot was expelled from his body, and he stopped once he reached Cat's side. She'd managed to work her cuffed hands to her front, and Glen's head was in her lap, his eyes fluttering drowsily up at Ghost, the blood flow stopped under the towel Cat had pressed to his forehead.

He met her eyes. Human to wolfkin, they watched each other, unblinking. He lifted a paw, and batted gently at the cuffs, focusing briefly. Two soft snicks, and the cuffs fell away, clattering to the tile floor.

"Ghost?" she said, softly, a quaver in her voice. He sighed, and sat, his head above hers even sitting. He watched, nearly able to discern every thought racing across her expressive face as she processed what she had seen. "Ghost?"

He shook his head, not as a wolf would, but as a human would, once from side to side. Her eyes widened, and she froze. It was Glen who reacted, but not in anger or fear. His human alpha lifted a shaking hand, and ran his fingers through the thick fur that covered his chest, scratching as he had a million times before over the years.

Their questions would come. If only he could answer them.

WHAT WAS ONCE LOST

"FATHER?" TIMIDITY should never be heard in an alpha.

Caius eased back in his chair, carefully closing the manila folder in front of him before lifting his eyes to his sons. Roman and Gerald stood side-by-side across his desk, both wolves tall, fit, and mean. Both were handsome, in a common sort of way, brown-haired and tanned skin. They both took after him to some degree, yet Caius always saw their mothers when he looked at them. One the result of a failed mating, the other a cub born from a liaison that should have been brief and unremarkable. His sons matched the stereotype of what alphas were supposed to look like and how to act, yet they lacked one important trait between them.

Power.

They were both lesser alphas, and Caius was reminded daily of his failure to produce a suitable Heir of his bloodline every time he saw them, or his actual Heir, Kane.

Roman, the eldest, born over two and a half centuries earlier to one of Caius' former mates, was staring down at him, face bruised and cut. His dark suit was strained across his shoulders and chest, an ill-guided move to make his burly physique blaringly obvious. His muscles had done him no good last night against Caius' Heir. He was looking far better than he did hours before, the rapid healing of their kind quickly repairing the bite and claw marks Kane left on Roman during his failed Challenge. Roman was trying not to glare, discomfited, blatantly upset at having been summoned from his bed this early in the morning where he'd no doubt been wallowing in self-pity. The scent of sex and blood wafted off of the lesser alpha, and Caius spent a second wondering how many betas his son had gone through the night before trying to assuage his manhood after his bruising loss.

Gerald, his other son, was a generation younger than his brother, born of a brief affair and just as lacking in greater alpha qualities as his elder brother. He wore a dark tee and even darker jeans, black boots and leather jacket all trying to make himself seem tougher than he actually was. All the youngest son was good for was chasing betas, most of whom trounced him soundly for attempting to take liberties. Gerald was spoiled, mean, and petulant, an eternal cub who refused to grow up. Caius had been too occupied with Clan duties when Gerald was an actual cub, and he'd spared little time in the rearing of his own child. Here was the result, a bully and a brute who spent too much time following Roman around and harassing betas than either wolf did in trying to better their stations.

Caius sighed, and let his eyes flick over the framed picture sitting on the corner of his desk. His daughter Marla had been a tiny cub of ten years old when that picture was taken, the black and white photo not showing her dark red hair or rich brown eyes. When she'd found her wolf at the tender age of eleven, a scant year after that picture was taken, he'd never been prouder of any one of his children. He was cursed with a multitude of sons, all of them lesser alphas of varying degree, and it had taken the birth of a beta daughter for him to feel something other than obligation and grudging affection for his offspring. He'd loved his daughter, and the day her soul-bond to Josiah was made , his heart broke. His little girl, brave and stubborn and beautiful, had given her love to her soul-mate, who thankfully was a wolf of their Clan, the youngest son of his dearest friend, the shaman Gray Shadow. He hadn't needed to say goodbye to her as she followed her mate, and instead was gifted with seeing each and every one of her own cubs born over the years.

He pulled his mind away from the memory of the last birthing he'd attended, the one of his littlest grandchild, Luca. That memory was both dear and despised, and recent events, like the ones depicted in the folder on his desk, were sorely testing his ability to control his emotions.

It took their union, and the plethora of cubs they would have, to thaw the final remaining pieces of Caius' heart. The litter of grandchildren had been another curse though, in the end, for there was no surer way to break a man than to have him see his grandbabies die. He'd lost four of the youngest, and even though he'd killed the man responsible for their deaths and his daughter's, it had done nothing to heal his heart.

He was left, in the end, with his dearest friend, his daughter, and four of the youngest grandchildren dead. No others had been born yet after the tragedy fifteen years prior, and he was glad of that fact. He could not abide learning to love another cub, only to have fate cruelly take them away. His eldest grandchildren were all grown now, and spread throughout the Clans of the North and across the country. Ezekiel, Gray Shadow's only descendent to become a shaman, had missed the catastrophic events at Baxter by virtue of being on the other side of the planet, deep in the wilds of northern Russia, and his other grandchildren followed their cousin's example by spreading out to the four corners of the country. They'd all left as soon as they could, their hearts weighed down by grief and tragedy, though none mourned as deeply as Caius.....or Josiah.

"Father, you summoned us?" Roman asked, doing his best to sound diffident. Gerald just appeared to be bored, picking at a hangnail and letting his brother do the talking.

"I did, yes," Caius replied, and went back to observing his sons. Rumors were floating about, and Roman's recent attempt to usurp Kane was merely cementing some of his own suspicions.

The sons of kings always succeeded their father through one of two ways: by being named heir and taking the throne after a natural death of the king, or through regicide. He had no intention of dying any time soon, and his sons' behavior in the last few years was making it hard for him to believe they wouldn't eventually be tempted to remove him forcibly. Killing one's own sons was never lauded, no matter the circumstances, so to keep his power and place secure, they must leave. Roman was more of a threat than Gerald, being marginally smarter, and impetuous. Gerald merely followed his nose and his brother's lead, so once Roman was gone, Gerald would find himself killed off through his own careless actions.

Being his offspring was not a bonus. Not in Black Pine. Their Clan was the strongest, and again the most revered, despite Gray Shadow's loss almost fifteen years earlier, and it was all due to his Heir's doing. Kane's power was known far and wide, and the Voice he carried nearly made up for Gray Shadow's loss. His Heir's skill with human technology, weaponry, and his ease at navigating through the complex and contradictory human legal system made him an asset to Black Pine. All of this benefited the Clan, and Caius was thankful for it, yet all of that glory garnered left him bitter.

If only his sons were stronger, more powerful, with even half the potential of Kane, then he would have been able to name one of them Heir, and kept the Clan's succession in his direct bloodline.

Kane was powerful. Where his sons would only be able to take leadership of Black Pine from him by treachery, Kane could do it with the tiniest of inclinations. His sons would soon be dethroned, the Clans taken over by another, stronger alpha, unless they preemptively and simultaneously murdered every able bodied alpha in New England. Kane could not only take Black Pine and all its sworn lesser clans and packs, but also keep it safe from all challengers. The young alpha was that strong, and it infuriated Caius to no end that Kane didn't even act like he ***wanted*** to be Clan Alpha. He appeared content to be the dutiful Heir, respectful, followed orders, and offered wiser insights than he should have been able to at the tender age of forty-four. Every year that passed left Caius with the undefinable and horrid sensation that the world saw him for what he really was, a broken and bitter wolf belittled by the far-reaching glory of his mighty Heir.

He missed in that moment Gray Shadow's ever-steady presence with a vicious ache that stole his breath and made his heart stumble. The shaman's face floated in his thoughts, his lightning quick grin and sharp eyes glowing. Caius banished his friend's visage, and found his center, prepared to do what he must.

"Has it to do with Kane's mission to Worcester?" Roman asked eagerly, eyes glinting.

"It does." Caius looked past Roman's shoulder, and spoke to his younger son. "Gerald, go pack. Kane will be leaving soon, and you're going with him. You have thirty minutes."

Gerald gaped at him, shock plain on his features, clearly not expecting to even be included in the conversation, let alone on a cross-Clan mission. Something other than shock ran through his eyes, and Caius couldn't get a grasp on whatever emotion it was before it was gone. If he didn't know better, he might have called it relief.

"Don't just stand there, whelp. Move it!" Caius snapped, and the lesser alpha jumped, and all but ran from the room in his haste.

Roman watched his brother leave, and he turned back to Caius, jaw tight, eyes narrowed. Caius smirked, and returned his attention to the manila folder in front of him, not opening it. He didn't want to see the dead wolves in the photos, not yet.

"Father?"

"You, Roman, you will stay here until you've recovered sufficiently from your injuries. Then you will leave as well."

"And where will I be going?" Roman demanded, growling.

"I don't care."

Roman took a step back, as if struck, and Caius remained impassive to the shock on his son's face. Rumors of his desire to take over Black Pine through any means necessary would one day lead his son to making a foolish mistake, and it was better for him to leave. Leave before Caius was forced to kill him. If only Kane hadn't spared him the night before, this situation would be resolved already. With Roman gone, and Gerald in a position to make an unforgivable transgression, the trouble his sons brought to the clan would be taken care of, and Caius could then focus on more important matters.

"Once you are healed, I suggest you go on a trip, perhaps to the Old World. We have distant kin remaining in the Greater Clans over there, and they may be swayed to sponsor your admittance to a new Clan."

"What?" It was clear Roman wasn't taking this seriously.

Caius stood, and Roman took another step back, an instinctive move on his part.

"You are no longer welcome here, in my territory. Your

constant planning, your fruitless Challenges against Kane and his position as my Heir are an embarrassment to this Clan. Take the time while you recover to think about where you want to go. If not the Old World, then perhaps somewhere here in the States. Your other brothers may even petition to their own Alpha's for you to find a place with them. Or maybe your nieces and nephews, Marla's children, would welcome their uncle with open arms. Perhaps go and search out Ezekiel in Russia, I really don't care."

"You're banishing me?" Roman snarled, fists clenched.

"Yes, I am. Don't waste your time arguing me, either. You need this time to consider where you're going to go."

Roman wore a look of total befuddlement, and past that, anger. Caius would have felt sympathy, even compassion, if he had seen anything in his son's eyes besides rage under the confusion. There, that glow in his dark eyes, was evidence of guilt at thwarted plans to try and usurp his own father for his place as Clan Leader. He didn't need actual proof, for as Clan Leader, he was judge, jury, and executioner all in one. His word was law, and final.

Caius bemoaned the lack of integrity and intelligence in his sons, and dismissed Roman with an idle wave of his hand. Roman looked like he was going to argue, but he snapped his mouth shut when Caius leveled a stony glare at him. Roman stormed from the room, and Caius could hear his snarls as he climbed the stairs to his room.

Wishing again for Gray Shadow, Caius put his hand on the

folder containing the photos of slain wolfkin. He was so weary of seeing his people die and being unable to stop it.

"KANE!" CAIUS' roar reached through the mansion, echoing off the walls, finding the ears of the two alphas who were loading the weapons and supplies into the back of Burke's SUV. The garage doors were open, the February air biting and harsh, and the scent of fresh snow filling the concrete space. The lights were off overhead, the gray midday sun casting faint shadows, their breath frosting as they worked.

"Fuck, Kane. What the hell did you do now?" Burke asked, chuckling as Kane rolled his eyes, safely out of sight of the Clan Leader.

"I beat Alpha Caius' son last night in a personal Challenge, remember? I don't think he'll be happy with me for a while." Kane snorted, meeting Burke's eyes over the rear seat of the SUV, where the other alpha was stacking duffel bags. Burke shook his head ruefully, smiling at Kane. "I don't think Roman will be happy with me, either." Roman was one of Caius' sons, and not the first one Kane defeated in personal Challenge, just the most recent.

"Oh yeah. You'd think our fearless Clan Leader would be happy that you spared his worthless son instead of snapping his neck. He hasn't that many sons left to be wasting them one by one, in Challenge after Challenge like this." Burke shut his door, and Kane shut his, the booming echoes bouncing through the five car garage. The two alphas joined up at the rear hatch, moving in tandem to shut the door together. Burke flicked a finger over Kane's cheek, the single faint line of a rapidly fading scar the only remainder of the fight with Roman the night before. Kane pushed him away, chuckling.

"I think he's embarrassed that his sons keep losing, really. If he'd just step up and tell them to stop, I wouldn't have to keep beating them down," Kane shrugged, zipping his leather jacket up to his chin, and pulling on his driving gloves. It might be Burke's SUV, but Kane drove. "Lemme see what he wants, I'll be back. Warm it up." He gave Burke a smile and a slap on the shoulder before he left the garage, his best friend shaking his head.

Kane's long legs ate up the distance between the garage and the Clan Leader's study on the first floor of the mansion. It was a great sprawling room that doubled as library and office, two massive fireplaces on either side of the room, with a wall of windows floor to ceiling behind Caius' desk, overlooking Augusta, the city covered in the snow that fell gently from the gray skies.

Caius was seated at his desk, the Alpha's brow furrowed as he barely acknowledged Kane's entrance to the room, despite having hollered for him across the grand house. Kane walked down the length of the room, over rugs as expensive as the house they sat in, past furniture as old as the city that the mansion sat above on the hill. Black Pine Clan's seat was here, in Caius McLennan's home, their territory vast and far-reaching.

Kane stopped in front of his Alpha's desk, waiting patiently. The scent of bourbon, smoke from the merrily burning fires, and Caius' own musk rose to meet Kane's nose. There was a hint of sharp pain, but not the physical kind. It was a scent Kane was accustomed to sensing near his Clan Leader, ever present since the morning Gray Shadow died, and he knew better than to mention anything. One thing Caius would not tolerate was mentioning the late shaman.

Kane smelled the fading scents of both Gerald and Roman, and was glad they were gone. He had no desire to see either of his Alpha's sons. He breathed deeply again, the combination of smells as delightful and comforting as they were when he was a young cub, fresh from his mother's small home in Hartford, barely sixteen and yet fully in possession of his alpha abilities, and the coveted Voice. That was nearly thirty years ago now, and yet the memory was as immediate as if it happened that morning.

"Are you ready to leave?" Caius' words snapped him out of his reverie, returning him to the present. Kane quirked a brow at his Alpha, but Caius had yet to lift his head from the file he was reading, one large hand smoothing over a picture with which Kane was all too familiar.

"We were just about to depart. We'll be in Worcester by this evening. I'll be meeting up with our team there, and the Ashland Alpha and his people as well." Kane told Caius calmly, refusing to fidget, or show any impatience with his Alpha. Caius knew all this already. There was something else going on. “We plan on breaching the apartments tomorrow morning, just after dawn.”

“Good. I expect a report every afternoon until this....situation is handled. I want everything you can find on who is responsible, if not the traitors themselves. Do not fail me.” Caius ordered, at last lifting his steely gaze to Kane’s. He refused to show anything but calm indifference, his temper having not cooled over the years, just becoming easier to control. His casual, unruffled attitude continued to annoy his Alpha, and Kane suspected it was because Caius could no longer contain his own emotions. He acted in control, the archetypal leader, yet Kane saw the cracks in his armor. That bitter summer morning almost fifteen years before haunted Caius still. It haunted Kane too, yet he carried his pain quietly now, deep inside, where it was safe, a failed promise goading every action he took from that day forward. He would never fail a clan mate again.

“Understood. With your permission, Alpha, I’ll be on my way.” Kane waited to be dismissed, a small smile on his lips, voice sure and even.

“Not just yet. You’ll be taking Gerald with you.”

Shit. What the hell is he doing?

Gerald was one of the Alpha’s oldest surviving sons, a lesser alpha of unremarkable qualities, just barely counted as an alpha by virtue of his bulk and his meager ability to influence other, weaker-willed wolves. He was a bully and didn’t give two shits about how badly his behavior made Black Pine look.

If not for Caius being his father, Kane would have been comfortable regulating Gerald to the lowest ranks of the betas, and away from any authority. He was two hundred years old, and no smarter than he was the day he sailed across the Atlantic to join his father in the New World. Mean, spoiled, and he carried a chip on his shoulder that Kane could drive through with Burke's oversized gas guzzler.

"Sir?" Kane sincerely hoped Caius wasn't serious. Gerald was not someone he wanted on this mission. He was quick to anger, didn't take orders well, and violence was his answer to everything. Not to mention he was still carrying a grudge at being defeated by Kane in a Challenge the autumn after the tragedy at the summer gathering.

Not long after Kane made Caius blink the night of the funerals at the gathering, Gerald decided to Challenge him for his place as Heir. He lost. Kane spared him, not wishing to antagonize his Clan Leader further, yet Caius seemed to see Kane's mercy as a weakness and an insult.

None of this history explained why Caius wanted Gerald to accompany Kane on a cross-Clan mission of this magnitude.

"No argument. Take him, use him. He's yours. Just be gone." Caius slapped the file shut, and leaned back in his leather chair. Kane bit back a retort, and nodded once, before turning and walking for the doors. He felt Caius' hard gaze following him from the room, and Kane stood taller, shoulders back, confidence in every step. Technically he shouldn't have given Caius his back as he left, but he wasn't backing out of the huge room like some peon from medieval times.

Kane exited the study, and made his way back to the garage, mindful of the other clan members he met in the halls, some of them his distant cousins. He nodded, meeting their eyes briefly as he walked, not stopping to chat. The betas stepped aside and waited politely for him to go by; the lesser alphas merely nodded and kept on their way, moving over as a concession to his rank. There were no other greater alphas in the clan house other than himself, Caius and Burke. The remaining greater alphas of Black Pine lived nearby, since having them in the Clan house was an invitation for disaster. Too many greater alphas in one place led to fights and spilled blood. The clan house was busy today; his mission was on everyone's lips and minds, no matter it was supposed to be a secret. The members of his team must have told their mates, and then once they knew, everyone knew. His team had departed the night before to set up surveillance and a perimeter, and Sophia, Kane's First Beta and team leader in his absence, was waiting on Kane and Burke to finalize details before they breached the building in the morning. It was at Caius' insistence that they wait, the Alpha believing they stood a better chance at catching the traitors responsible if they left things alone at the target site, hoping one or more of the ringleaders would show.

"Ready, then?" Burke's falsely cheerful voice broke him out of his thoughts, and Kane looked up to see his Speaker standing at the closed driver's side door, leaning against it, as if guarding the vehicle. He saw why when he glimpsed Gerald prowling near the hood, a dark look marring his Neanderthal-heavy features as he growled to himself, a bag flung over his shoulders. He reasoned that a spoiled whelp like Gerald wanted to drive, and was trying his best to intimidate Burke into moving before Kane returned.

Not gonna happen, buddy. It may be my best friend's car, but I drive.

"Ready. Gerald, you'll be in the back, there's a file on the mission I want you to read before we get to Worcester," Kane stated, falsely cheerful, heading straight for the driver's side door. Burke gave way with a snicker, opening it swiftly. The doors must all be locked but this one, as Burke darted inside, over the center console, and into the front passenger seat before Kane even finished closing the door. He hit the locks for the back, and the Alpha's son glared at him as he rounded the hood and got in the back, slamming the door. He very annoyingly sat in the center, obscuring Kane's view in the rearview mirror, and he even kicked the back of their seats a few times just to make his point.

"Comfortable?" Burke sniped, sounding way too cheerful, hiding his aggravation at the other alpha's childish behavior. Burke was withholding his opinion on Gerald's presence; not wanting to antagonize the Clan Leader's son. Burke didn't fear a fight, he just didn't want one. Burke rarely did anything he didn't want to do, which made him perfect as Kane's lieutenant, who didn't want a second in command who was nothing but a mindless grunt, blithely following orders. And having his second-in-command be a Speaker was just a bonus.

"Shut it, pansy," Gerald growled, lips pulled back from his teeth, clearly put out with Kane's lieutenant. Kane wondered what he missed while he was talking to Caius and these two were alone in the garage. Kane caught Gerald's eyes in the rearview; he made sure that the lesser alpha got a glimpse of how little patience Kane really had with him, his black eyes burning brighter for a second. Gerald grumbled something unintelligible and sat back with a sigh. It was better that way; Kane had no desire to use the Voice on so trifling a matter as bad manners, especially on a wolf who was centuries old and in need of a time out instead of exposure to a juggernaut mental coercion he could not withstand.

"The file is in the duffel bag to your right, on top. Please read it thoroughly; we have a few hours until we get to Worcester, so you'll have time to be on par with the rest of the team," Kane smiled cheerfully, and threw the SUV in gear, Burke smiling at him gleefully as the big vehicle roared out of the garage, eating up the snow on the mansion's long driveway.

Burke sat back, clicking his seatbelt on as a concession to the Maine patrols looking for violators. He ignored the surly wolf in the backseat yanking at zippers and shoving at bags as Gerald grudgingly sought out the file Kane mentioned, making a great show out of being told what to do. Kane bit back his smirk, catching Burke's eye briefly as he navigated the vehicle through the snow, heading south.

WORCESTER, MA, was the quintessential small New England

city, full of historical landmarks, snarky East Coast accents, a coffee shop on each corner, book stores everywhere, and a crumbling warehouse district that hovered like an expanding blight on the landscape, courtesy of the recent economic downturn. Winter hugged the streets as Kane navigated the SUV through the businesses and warehouses closed down for the evening, eventually parking on a side street several blocks from their target. They were at the edge of the warehouse district where it abutted failed housing complexes, and their target building was in the nearby block of abandoned buildings. He double-checked the GPS, confirming the coordinates his team sent for the meeting with the Ashland Alpha, Heromindes, and Kane's team.

The night was darker, far darker than it should be with streetlights on the corners, and the snow seemed to fall thickest here as the three wolves exited the SUV . Kane tasted the air, the sweet scent of fresh snow, and the tangy mingling of multiple wolves came and went as the wind constantly changed directions. He joined Burke and the dour Gerald on the curb, eyeing the lonely street one last time before heading for the unmarked door halfway down the block.

Kane knocked, a staccato beat to alert his team locked inside, not wanting to risk a mind call, wary of alerting the wrong wolves to their presence. Heromindes was an Alpha, and would be able to sense any private mental conversations going on in his vicinity, if not being able to discern the words, and he didn't want to be rude to the resident Clan Leader. Not to mention the possibility of the traitors being nearby. While it took an alpha of incredible power to 'listen in' on a private mind to mind connection between two wolves, there were the rare lesser alphas out there, plus unaligned alphas of the greater variety who had the affinity to hear any wolf, over great distances. Burke was one of those greater alphas, making him Black Pine's only Speaker.

For the last twenty years, across the country, wolves were disappearing. That wasn't unusual, considering their species' inherently violent nature and the fights that broke out amongst the lower ranks of each clan and pack. Wolves got killed by accident, murder, silver-based drugs and misfortune all the time. Sometimes they would even be kidnapped by enterprising government entities or private corporations that resulted in Kane and his people getting them back with fang and claw, or Caius and his veiled threats to get the missing wolves returned. What was different in the present situation wasn't that wolves were missing—it was the number of wolves missing from the same area, during the same narrow time frame, and the occurrences were greatly increased in the last ten years. Whole family packs were vanishing; minor clans and roaming packs were disappearing in large chunks, with no viable reasons or suspects.

The missing wolves would be found, eventually. Dead. Dumped in mass graves along lonely back country roads, in landfills, quarries, any place with minimal human traffic and exposure to wildlife, insuring the speedy decomposition of the remains. The wolfkin were being kidnapped and killed in larger and larger numbers, and the allied Clan leaders of the Northeastern clans struggled to stop the disappearances, and find the people responsible. No one knew why, but the prevailing theories were experimentation, and hunting for sport.

The only thing the disappearances had in common was the appearance of strange wolves in the area of the missing wolves in the days preceding each mass abduction. It was considered polite for wolves to visit the established pack if they were traveling or moving into a claimed territory, to get permission to stay or to just be courteous, so as to avoid fighting. Most clans and packs were laid back about territorial disputes, allowing a few strangers to pass through unmolested, as long as their business was quick, and nothing untoward happened to draw the attention of the humans in the area. Having strange wolves in a claimed territory who did not approach the established clans or packs were noted, and the alpha or highest ranking beta in charge would report the behavior to the Greater Clans.

That happened this time, in Worcester, last week. Ashland, the Greater Clan of Massachusetts, received complaints from the local family pack, the Suarez family, who held the southern edge of the city, reporting that half a dozen strange wolves were in their territory and weren't following established protocols for visiting wolves. Any time contact was attempted by the Suarez pack with the interlopers, they disappeared. This was reported to Clan Ashland, who sent a pack of lesser alphas and high ranking betas to deal with the trespassers. Yet once that pack arrived, and went to the territory belonging to the Suarez family pack, they were gone. Twenty wolfkin were missing. Fifteen adults and five children were gone, their homes broken into, signs of a struggle everywhere, and the scent of unknown wolves laden over every surface.

Kane knocked again and backed off from the door as he heard footsteps approaching. Burke relaxed beside him a second before Kane felt the mental touch of one of his betas, Sophia, who was the ranking member of his team.

She opened the door, weapon up, the barrel pointed right at his head. A grin lit up her pretty features, her dark hair pulled back in a long tail high on her head. She was shorter than him by over a head, and weighed a hundred pounds less, but she was an exceptional fighter, and far older than her twenty-something-looking age suggested. She led when he and Burke were called away by other duties, and she did it well, often teasing Kane and Burke that if she were a male, she'd be their alpha, instead of the other way around. Kane was of a mind to agree.

"Alpha Kane, Alpha Burke, welcome to Worcester. What the hell took you so long?" Sophia dropped the gun, flicking on the safety and holstering it on her thigh. She stood back from the door and waved them in, and Kane heard the low grumble from Gerald as the lesser alpha passed Sophia where she held the door.

"Alpha Gerald, I was not informed you were coming," Sophia said, features tight in displeasure. She was polite, and very reserved. Gerald was not popular with the females of Black Pine, especially the high-ranking ones, the females with the strength and willpower to resist his meager allure and poorly disguised noxious attitude. Gerald had the unfortunate habit of seeing them as a challenge, and hounded them at every turn.

"None of your business, beta. Father sent me along, so watch your mouth," Gerald snapped, and Kane turned in time to see him leaning down in Sophia's face, inches from her, the posturing of a wolf threatened by a stronger opponent written clear in the tense lines of his body. Kane shook his head, wondering if he'd have to explain to Caius why his son was broken before the mission got underway. He and Burke watched the interaction between the beta and the lesser alpha with interest.

They dropped their bags, just in case Sophia needed help moving the body, and leaned against the entranceway wall, just as Gerald made the colossal mistake of poking Sophia hard in the shoulder with a large, meaty finger. He must have been expecting her to drop her eyes and tilt her head, or even fall to her knees—he really wasn't expecting the reaction that he got to his unwanted touch instead.

Gerald groaned in pain and shock as he face-planted the wall, one arm twisted high behind his back, the joint straining. She lifted him by it, until he was standing on the tips of his toes, his free hand clawing at the wall. He howled as she twisted higher, and Burke bit back a snort of laughter. Kane elbowed him, thinking laughter wasn't the best thing as Sophia sent them a wicked glare. Sophia leaned in to the hold she had on the larger wolf, her tiny frame belying the immense strength at her command. She was older than all three of them, a wolf long versed in combat. Once upon a time, she wielded a sword instead of a gun, in ages past.

"Touch me again, Gerald, unranked son of Caius, and I will

rip you apart. I answer to Alphas Kane and Burke—and they know better than to touch a woman without her permission. Stay out of my way, and I won't Challenge your piece of shit ass." She twisted one more time, and Gerald slapped his hand on the wall three times, like a MMA fighter in the ring. He caught himself surrendering and growled in frustration.

"Bitches don't Challenge," Gerald snarled, and both Kane and Burke winced as Sophia punched the pinned wolf in the kidney with her free hand, making him yelp. "Okay! Dammit, let me go!" Gerald yelled, and Sophia dropped him, backing away as the lesser alpha dropped to his knees, cradling his abused arm and whimpering. Sophia reached out, and calmly shut the door, locking it before stepping around Gerald.

"Alphas? This way please, the Clan Leader of Ashland is expecting us." Sophia gestured down the hall, and she led the way, all three of them ignoring the moaning fool left in the entrance of the closed business. They grabbed their bags, and left Gerald to sort himself.

"Any problems?" Kane asked, shifting his duffel over his shoulder. Burke paced behind him, long strides slowed as he kept an eye on the hall behind them. Gerald was just the type to come up from behind and attack, especially after being beaten.

"None, sir. All team members are accounted for, and we have surveillance in place. Alpha Heromindes has supplied us with three additional teams, all lesser alphas." Sophia turned at a junction in the hall, leading them deeper into the building. The lights were off, the faint glow from the emergency lights providing more than enough visibility to navigate. They wanted this building to look empty, and having unnecessary lights on would merely attract attention. Their night vision was superb, though in human form not as powerful as it was in their wolf bodies.

"No shamans?" Burke asked, as they entered a large storage room in the rear of the building, the ceiling twenty feet overhead, a long table set up with small lamps along the far wall, surrounded by wolves. Some were in wolf-form, great hulking beasts that tracked their entrance, eyes reflecting the low lights from the lamps.

"Actually, there is a shaman..." Sophia trailed off as a man stood from the table, and approached them. He was pale, and slim, his body more delicate than the average wolf. He was no alpha, and there was the faintest hint of a yellow-gold aura that sparked with every step. Kane saw his features as he cleared a deep shadow, and felt his heart twist in pain and welcome, a memory of a warm summer night and the scent of funeral pyres rising briefly as the shaman came within arm's reach.

"Shaman River," Kane murmured in greeting, holding out his hand, pain and bitter disappointment briefly choking his words. Shaman River gripped his hand, and said nothing, the delicate bones of his hand full of a strength of a different kind than Kane's. He hadn't seen Shaman River since that ill-fated day almost fifteen years ago, at the gathering where Gray Shadow and his family fell.

Kane beat back the memory of rushing waters, and a broken promise, the biting hint of burning pine as the murdered wolves who were sent back to the Great Mother. Kane gripped River's hand tightly, and ducked his head, not wanting anyone to see the pain he was experiencing. It was foolish to feel this way, after nearly fifteen years. He'd done his best, and it still felt like he hadn't done enough that day. He had made a vow as he raced the river, a vow to himself and the Universe to keep searching until he found Luca. Yet that promise came to naught, the cub lost to the river and time. His strength and abilities were nothing against death, no matter that his heart said Luca lived. His mind knew better.

Kane.

A touch of warm golden light swept a balm of peace over his thoughts, his name a mere whisper in his mind. Kane bit his lip, glad for the deep shadows, and the shaman's body obscuring the other wolves' line of sight. He couldn't afford to appear weak, not now.

Kane. You did not fail Gray Shadow. Or Luca. You did more that day than anyone, myself included. Don't carry guilt along with grief. The golden light traveled from River's hand to Kane's, rising up his arm, relaxing him as it spun out questing tendrils towards his chest. Kane let the light in, and River took full advantage, the shaman's own sense of peace and contentment easing the ache in Kane's heart. It felt like forever, as the shaman banished the guilt and grief. He didn't remove it, he merely let Kane regain his equilibrium, his confidence, until he could control his own emotions.

There you are. Feeling better?

Yes. Thank you, Shaman.

Kane sighed, and opened his eyes, not realizing he'd shut them. Burke and Sophia were waiting patiently, and Kane discerned that while it may have felt like minutes had passed, in reality it was merely seconds, and neither Burke nor Sophia had seen the shaman soothe Kane's emotional injuries. Not many wolves were attuned to seeing the mystical side of a shaman's workings, and Kane was more sensitive than most. Kane nodded in thanks to the shaman, and River dipped his head, features calm, unruffled, as if nothing had happened.

"Come. Heromindes is waiting," River told him, squeezing his hand once before dropping his grip, gesturing to them as he walked back to the table and waiting wolves. Kane followed, head high, heart rate back to normal. There were nearly eighty wolves in this room, only a third of them his own, and the scent of something other than total confidence would upset the precarious balance between the separate packs. Kane must be so strong that Black Pine's fewer numbers would not be seen as a weakness. Ashland was an ally, yet they did not hesitate to Challenge other packs if they wanted something, and Sophia with her prowess, and Burke with his mental abilities, were appealing to other packs.

Kane saw Heromindes once they got closer. The Alpha of Clan Ashland was a giant of a wolfkin, topping out at over six and a half feet, and nearly three hundred pounds. There was not an ounce of fat or wasted flesh on his body; he was intimidating in the truest sense of the word. Dark hair pulled back in a braid that fell to the middle of his back, whispering over his shoulders as he moved, tied with a black leather string. His heavily muscled arms were bare, as if it were summer, and not the depths of February in the Northeast. A black tank covered his torso, so tight it looked painted on, revealing a tightly sculpted chest and stomach, and his long, thick legs were wrapped in skin tight black combat pants, his large feet in equally black boots. The only part of him not black was his skin, a rich golden hue, and his eyes, a brilliant green that flashed as he watched them approach.

Kane felt the instinctive urge to curl his lips and snarl a challenge at the other alpha, his urges as an alpha telling him he must be the biggest bad-ass, nastiest predator in the room, and that Heromindes was a serious threat to his supremacy. Kane stamped down hard on those urges; he was not a young, unruly alpha jockeying for position, and nothing like the foolish Gerald and his ilk. Kane was Heir to Black Pine, and while he may be slightly smaller than Heromindes, he was not weaker. Kane smiled instead at the Clan Leader, unable to hide the glitter of his wilder spirit as his baser nature scoffed at the other alpha, frustrated he could not throw aside rational thought and fight this wolfkin to the death.

Heromindes' eyes glittered back, and Kane caught a hint of the Clan Leader's own desire to fight in the vibrant green fire of his gaze. Everyone held still, as Kane walked alone to Heromindes, the rising tension in the room freezing the occupants. Instinct held the lower ranked wolves in place as their alphas decided who was to lead, and who was to follow.

"Greetings, Heromindes, Alpha of Clan Ashland. I am

Kane, Heir of Black Pine. I come as requested, by permission of Caius, Clan Leader of Black Pine, to lend assistance in the recovery of your clan members," Kane relaxed every tensely corded muscle, and gave Heromindes a dip of his head, never once taking his eyes from the larger alpha. He was an Heir, not a Clan Leader, and it was Heromindes' territory in which he stood. He could afford to be polite, and not step on the other alpha's toes. "I bring my lieutenant, Alpha Burke, who serves as Black Pine's Speaker, and lesser alpha Gerald, son of Caius. I hope my team has been helpful while you awaited for us."

"Greetings, Kane, Heir of Black Pine," Heromindes nodded in return, a vague movement, and he waved to the table, where the remainder of Kane's team sat on one side, and presumably the higher ranking wolves of Ashland on the other. His voice was a deep rumble of sound, oddly accented, like most of the old wolves Kane had ever met, their speech patterns and inflections forged in times long past. "Have a seat. Your people have been most helpful, and I appreciate Black Pine's assistance in this matter." Heromindes relaxed as well, and it was if the lessening tension between the two alphas gave everyone permission to breathe again. Wolves began to talk softly, and Burke took their bags, piling them off to the side by some crates.

Burke sat next to Kane as they took the empty seats beside the Clan Leader, with River next to Burke, and Sophia standing at attention behind the two Black Pine alphas. Kane saw Gerald shuffle in, every inch of his profile shouting anger and embarrassment, and he found a place to sit off to the side, snapping at two Ashland members in wolf-form, who made the barest effort to move over so he could sit on a crate. Kane looked to Heromindes, who was watching Gerald as well. He saw the Clan Leader quickly assess and just as swiftly dismiss the son of Caius, and their eyes met for the barest moment as they shared derision for the lesser alpha and his rude behavior. Kane would watch Gerald, and so would the Clan Leader. He would be trouble, and soon.

"Your Sophia has been a dream to work with, Kane. A capable and talented beta. She and your team have narrowed down the location of my missing wolves, here, about two blocks away from where we are currently." Heromindes pointed a sturdy finger to a spot on a large tablet that was laid out on the table, double tapping the screen, a map of south Worchester enlarging. Two dots blinked red on the map, one for the building in which they sat, the other a multiple story building nearby. Heromindes tapped the red dot for their target, and a picture from a satellite website popped up, showing a five story apartment complex, shut down and vacant, a large For Sale sign out front, ten foot high chain link fences wrapping around the front and sides visible in the picture.

"Good. I was informed that my wolves have successfully scented out the Suarez wolves are inside. No sign of the traitors?" Kane asked, leaning over the tablet, as Heromindes tapped it again, playing what looked to be live action video feeds of the building, snow falling past the lens on multiple angles.

"Nothing on camera, but we have fresh scent, and movement inside. There are humans in the building." Kane looked up at Heromindes, one brow raised in question at that piece of news. The Clan Leader nodded, confirming his statement. "We can't hear the Suarez wolves through the pack links, and I cannot reach them, either. It may be drugs or injury interfering with our abilities. The most I'm able to discern is that they are alive. We can't narrow down the scents well enough to parse out the traitors, but the scent of humans inside the building is strong. Your scouts report there is no scent of sickness or drugs on the humans, as there is on the majority of wolves inside. I'm of the opinion that the humans are not captives, but working with the traitors."

"I would agree. This is shaping up to be exactly like the previous incidents that have been occurring in Black Pine territory. We need to move fast, before they kill the Suarez wolves. We can't wait for the traitors to show up and reveal themselves, not if you want your people alive," Kane spoke, adrenaline revving up his heart rate. They needed to move, and fast. It was already too long since the Suarez wolves were taken; if the traitors didn't get whatever it was they wanted from the Ashland wolves soon, then they would be killed, exactly like the wolves abducted in similar situations in Black Pine territory. "Most packs were killed in the first week after they went missing; your people have no time."

"Agreed. We move now." Heromindes nodded to his people, who all stood and backed clear of the table, heading for stacks of black combat gear littering the far wall of the room, or stripping down, preparing to Change. "I will ask that your people take the lead. Mine will secure the perimeter, and provide backup."

Kane stood as well, and his people with him. Sophia came immediately to his side, her short body a bundle of raw energy, the scent of her blood rushing through her veins filling the air around her. Kane grinned at his top beta, who grinned back. Burke stripped his gear, dropping his clothing on top of their bags, and Kane's lieutenant knelt on the cold floor as the Change took him over. They all politely looked away, as no matter how experienced or old a wolf was, Changing was an awkward and painful endeavor, and no one liked an audience.

"Burke is my Speaker, Alpha. He will coordinate the incursion, if you would be so kind as to allow him into your pack links." Kane gestured to the large chocolate-brown dire wolf that appeared at his side, head level with the top of his waist. Burke was impressive in his wolf-form, large and sleek, not overly muscled, but still considerably strong. Even more impressive were his mental abilities; his telepathy so far beyond any other wolf in the combined Northeastern clans he had no equal. Burke's deep snort of amusement reminded Kane that they weren't alone, and he shouldn't be running his fingers through the brown wolf's hackles. Kane pulled his hand back, and saw the glimmer of amusement in the Clan Leader's eyes as he kindly pretended not to see anything.

"Very well. I've heard of Speaker Burke's abilities, and I am thankful he's lending them to us." Heromindes faced the large wolf squarely, and Kane felt the cool rush of power from the Clan Leader using his pack connections, sending out active lines to wolves present. Kane caught the mental line tossed his way, drawing in the wolves sworn to him, before mentally 'handing' the entire web of connected minds to Burke. His lieutenant took them all easily, and Kane was able to see in his mind the effortless way Burke wove the Black Pine wolves and the Ashland pack together, with his mind acting as the bridge. Kane could sense the Ashland wolves, and from the startled looks they were getting, the Ashland wolves could sense them in return through the new links. Speakers were as rare as alphas gifted with the fully developed Voice. This wasn't easy—only the most powerful of alphas could handle this many minds, and overcome the natural walls built between different packs. Burke could have done this without Heromindes, his mind strong enough to breach the inherent defenses of the Ashland pack links, but it was far, far easier to do this with cooperation.

Kane felt Heromindes' awe at Burke's extraordinary ability, before the Clan Leader got himself under control.

Count yourself lucky that I can sense his unwavering devotion to you, Kane. If he was not so content to be yours, I would Challenge you for him. He is an asset I would dearly love to have in my own Clan. Kane heard the private thought Heromindes sent him, and the truth under the slightly wry tone. **If not for his love for you, and your Voice, I would not hesitate to take him from you.**

Thank you for the compliment, Alpha. Burke is indeed exceptional. And he is mine. Kane replied, meeting the Clan Leader's gaze dead on. **Shall we begin?**

Under your lead.

Thank you.

“I need everyone’s attention,” Kane spoke, keeping his voice level. Every set of eyes turned to him, and Kane made certain his face was blank, no emotion evident. “Black Pine will lead the initial incursion on the complex. Ashland wolves will secure the perimeter. No one escapes, friend or foe. Kill only if necessary, last resort. We need the humans alive, but priority is the safety and recovery of the Suarez wolves. Sophia and I will lead the strike team once the perimeter is locked down. Clan Leader Herominds and Speaker Burke will be handling communications, and Shaman River will enter once the building is ours, to attend to the Suarez wolves. I believe you all have your assigned teams and positions already.” Kane saw Sophia nod in confirmation, and he turned back to the wolves watching him, mindful of the Clan Leader watching and listening.

“That’s it. Move out. Speaker Burke will alert you all when we start,” Kane ordered, and the assembled wolves arranged themselves in preordained teams, the rear door of the building opening silently to the back alley, as they poured out, two and four-footed death and retribution racing towards the apartment complex.

“What about me?” Gerald snarked from his spot on the crates, arms crossed, a petulant frown on his two hundred year old face. Kane and Heromindes both sent him a look, no patience with the lesser alpha and his attitude.

“Stay here and guard the gear.” Kane grinned at the growl and pout from the unranked alpha, and he followed Heromindes out the door, the winter air clearing his senses and focusing his mind. He had traitors to hunt.

A BULLET ZIPPED past Kane's face, inches from killing him. He plastered himself to the wall, too big to be anything other than a prime target in the narrow hallway. Sophia dropped to her knees at his feet, firing twice, killing the human who was shooting at them in the hall outside the last apartment they had to clear. Four more dead humans littered the length of the dingy hall, the overhead lights flickering, the walls streaked with blood and claw marks, some fresh, and some old.

Kane helped Sophia to her feet, both wolves stepping over the dead humans bleeding out all over the torn, ragged carpeting. Kane dropped his weapon, the harness for the now empty shotgun pulling the weapon around to his back, out of the way. He flexed his hands, and his fingers sprouted inch long claws, black against his blood-streaked lightly tanned skin. Sophia brought her shotgun up, the short barreled weapon ideal for close combat. Blood covered them both, the breaching of the abandoned apartment complex taking far too long.

They paused outside the door, Sophia dragging the limp corpse away from the threshold, blood soaking the thin gray carpet underneath. She dropped the body with a soft thud, and knelt on the floor, shotgun aimed at the door. Kane stood to the side, ready to kick in the door once she was ready.

Burke, breaching last door. Humans dead in hall, fifth floor, northwest corner of building, I can smell multiple wolves inside. Have Shaman River ready. Kane alerted his lieutenant, and he got a wordless reply, a sensation akin to a brush of cool fingers on the back of his neck. He heard a whispering in his mind, a constant hum of words, and it told him that Burke was speaking to multiple wolves at once, conveying status updates and orders.

Sophia? Ready? Kane asked the beta at his feet, and she smiled, white teeth flashing in a feral grin, her sweet face a macabre mask of bloodlust. The blood sprayed on her face made her appear uncivilized, the shade of a warrior long dead and turned to ash. He grinned in return, a growl rising from his chest.

Kane spun on his heel, one large booted foot lifting, kicking forward fast and hard. The cheap door splintered in a cloud of shards, raining across the room. He kept his momentum going, spinning out of Sophia's way as she entered the room in a blur of black combat gear, looking for threats. Kane followed on her heels, body partially Changed, fangs splitting his jaws, nails turned to razor sharp claws.

It was a small apartment, and they were in the living room, thin pallets arranged sloppily on the floor, huddled bodies on each. Sophia cleared the corners, and sprinted down the hall, clearing what must be the kitchen and bathroom as she went. Kane sent a quick look to the wolves on the floor, noting chests rising, and the scent of sickness and blood. They were alive.

He followed Sophia, his beta stopped outside a closed door

that must lead to the apartment's bedroom. It wasn't locked, the doorknob missing and the hole for it empty. Sophia knelt quickly, took one look, and promptly stood at his side, radiating fury. Her whole body was humming with it, every muscle tense.

Kane was too large to kneel and look, and he quirked a brow at her, questioning silently what she saw. She held up four fingers, two alone, then two more, a pause in between. Two friendlies, two bad guys. She pointed to where the corners of the room would be, and grinned, her teeth sharper now than they were minutes ago, her eyes glowing. Kane felt a rush of air come through the hole in the door, and the scents coming from inside the room made his blood boil and his body wrack with shivers, the urge to Change and kill nearly overwhelming.

Kane tapped a clawed fingertip to the barrel of her gun, and Sophia frowned, not wanting to put away the weapon. **Sophia. We need them alive. As much as it pains me, we need the humans alive. They know who the traitors are.**

Fine. Alive doesn't mean whole, her words were growly and dark, and Kane nodded once in agreement. Alive did not mean whole indeed.

Sophia put the gun away, her harness maneuvering the weapon just as his did, to her back and away from her arms. She stripped her combat gloves, and her nails grew to claws, her deep brown eyes burning black and green as her wolf-form crept over her in small increments. She knelt on the floor in a crouch, her body twisting enough to accommodate a leap from the floor. She nodded, and Kane smashed the door open, the cheap wood panel swinging on its hinges, crashing into the wall.

Sophia leapt, halfway across the room before the door even hit the wall. Kane was a blink of time behind her, leaping for the opposite corner. There was a large bed in the room, two thin and bloody bodies on it, and two humans were on either side, huddled in the corners, guns in hand. Kane saw the humans fire, time slowed, the bright flash of a shotgun aimed in his direction. He felt the silver shot graze his ribs, the pain negligible, and he forgot about his injury as his clawed hands sank knuckle deep in the human's torso and arms. His weight crushed the human male under him, squishing him in the corner, the gun dropped to the floor as the human's arms broke.

Kane lifted the human and rotated on his heels, throwing the semi-naked man towards the door, the space there clear of furniture. The human hit hard, and lay limply, alive but broken. Kane sniffed scornfully, and turned his head in time to see Sophia pinning her target to the wall, zip strips binding his hands, blood dripping from over a dozen long slashes over his face, neck, and shoulders. Alive did not mean whole. Kane huffed, satisfied, as she dropped her prisoner on top of Kane's, both wolves indifferent to the whimpers of pain from the humans.

"Sir, you were hit." Sophia pointed a clawed finger at his side, where the shotgun blast had grazed his ribs under his left arm. He felt the burning sting of silver, but it was minor. His body would force the silver shards out, and if they didn't come out on their own, a shaman could cut him open and excise the remaining pieces.

"I'll be fine, minimal silver exposure," Kane told her, his attention on the wolfkin in human form on the bed. His breath caught in his throat, and even the lack of air couldn't dispel the scents of blood, pain, fear and sex. Silver and some kind of drug permeated the sick smell that came off their bodies, and Kane reached down a clawed hand, gripping the shoulder of the nearest wolf on the bed. He gently applied pressure, and flipped the small body over.

It was a young male wolf, his dark golden skin and black hair matching him to one of the Suarez youths, one of the five missing children. He looked to be about thirteen, all gangly limbs and awkward joints, and Kane could not sense the boy's wolf spirit on him. He was pre-Change then, puberty not yet far enough along for his wolf to emerge. Blood covered his naked frame, dirt and semen on his thighs and hips.

Sophia was attending to the other wolf on her side of the bed, a female, just as young, and Kane could only assume she was the youth's sister. She was naked, in the same state as the boy. Both were unconscious, eyes cracked open enough to show the whites, mouths open, slow, strenuous breaths barely moving their chests. The smell of silver and some kind of drug oozed from their pores, and Kane felt his stomach roll as he fought back the urge to vomit.

Burke. I need Shaman River, now. Kane looked to his beta, the hard-nosed warrior woman crying sob-less tears as she stroked the brow of the abused cub, pushing back lank black hair from a face that was beautiful, even under layers of dirt and bruises.

“Sophia.” Kane tried again, voice cracking on her name. She looked at him through watery eyes, and the wolf receded from her face, leaving a woman behind, a beta with the instincts of a mother with cubs to protect. “I’m going to check on the wolves in the front room, stay with the cubs.” He was going to ask her to go check herself, but Kane saw on her face the need to stay with the cubs. He agreed; if they woke, they may not want a male near them, since the odors on the cubs and in the room made it clear the human males were their abusers.

She nodded, sitting on the bed, and she pulled off her jacket, wrapping it around the girl. Kane found a blanket on the floor beside the bed, and covered the boy. He felt like crying himself, his anger draining away, swamped by a sickening dread and pain. Kane left the bedroom, stepping over the injured humans, ignoring them completely. They would tell Kane everything he wanted to know, then they would die. Horribly.

Kane, complex is secure. How many wolves? Burke asked him, his mental voice giving Kane an anchor. He latched on, sending Burke a wordless image of the two cubs on the bed, and he walked back into the living room, letting his lieutenant see through his eyes. There were five wolves drugged senseless in the living room, all naked, beaten and dirty. Most were young, late teens and early twenties. Only seven wolves recovered; seven out of twenty.

Kane felt Burke’s rage, and the echo of Heromindes’ anger

as Burke shared the images with the Clan Leader. **I have seven of the Suarez wolves. Two cubs. Five adults. Alive. They need immediate healing. Two human hostages, alive. Where is Shaman River?**

"I'm here, Kane." The shaman ran through the door of the apartment, eyes burning gold and sky blue, as he took in the wolves on the floor in a quick glance before sprinting past Kane, down the hall to the bedroom. Heromindes was seconds behind River, and Kane met the Clan Leader's eyes as he ducked his head, clearing the threshold of the apartment.

Heromindes' eyes were green fire, his teeth sharpened to points, his hands clawed. Anger rolled off the Clan Leader as he took in the state of his wolves on the floor. He was panting, and Kane watched as the Alpha fought back the urge to Change.

"Where are they?" Heromindes growled, the words almost indistinguishable in the rumble of deep sound.

"The humans are alive, in the back room." Kane darted forward, blocking the Clan Leader as he made to head that way. Heromindes growled at him, a fearsome sound of challenge as Kane stopped him from presumably tearing the human abusers apart. "No, Alpha. We need them alive. *We need them alive.*"

"Move!" Heromindes ordered, the Change coming on fast. If the Clan Leader killed the humans, they may lose this chance to find out who the traitors were. The Suarez wolves may know, but they were days away from being coherent enough to tell them anything useful.

"No." Kane stood his ground, and braced himself for a fight. He didn't want to fight Heromindes, even if it was like this, outside of a Challenge. If Heromindes attacked, Kane would stop him, short of killing him. And even outside an official Challenge, Heromindes would be seen as weak when Kane won, and the power structure of Ashland would suffer, leading to an imbalance of authority as challengers made constant plays for the position of Clan Leader. It was a position Kane did not want, and when he stopped Heromindes, the Ashland Clan Leader would suffer a major loss of pride, and Black Pine could lose an ally.

"No, Alpha. Control. You need control." Kane had no doubt he could defeat the other alpha, no matter the size difference or experience. No doubt at all, and he let that conviction come across as he spoke to Heromindes. Let the Clan Leader see it in his eyes, smell it in his scent. If Heromindes tried to get through Kane to kill the humans, he would lose. "Hear me, Alpha. Regain your senses and think."

Kane would swear to his dying day that he did not mean it. That the dread of fighting and defeating the Clan Leader of Ashland pushed him past his own control, and let a tiny shred of the Voice out. It was small, a mere slip, yet the barest brush of the Voice that Kane commanded was enough to knock Heromindes back several feet, shaking his head, hands coming to his face.

Kane swore softly, and stamped down hard on his wayward talent, repressing the Voice, the ability to command instant and total obedience from any wolf, be he alpha or beta. His talent was so strong Kane feared that even a shaman may not be immune, and he refused to use it unless a situation was urgent, as even the tiniest exposure was enough to leave a wolf rendered mindless and wholly obedient.

Kane waited, breathless, afraid of the damage he may have done to the Clan Leader, hoping that he hadn't done anything irreversible. It was rare, but the Voice unleashed in its full glory could forever destroy the free will of a wolf, leaving them a mindless slave to an alpha. It was that version of the Voice in eons past that resulted in the ancient alphas going mad with absolute power, coupled with the spirit gifts that were once theirs, before the Great Mother stripped them, creating the shamans.

Kane froze as Burke bounded into the room, the great chocolate brown wolf coming to his side immediately. Burke took one look at Kane's face, and stilled, and his lieutenant then turned to the Clan Leader. Heromindes was shaking, fully human hands covering his face, shoulders slumped, covered in sweat brought on by stress. Kane could hear other wolves approaching, and he prayed to the Great Mother that Heromindes was all right, not wanting anyone to see the Clan Leader in his current condition. Regret rose like bile in his throat, and Burke huddled against his hip, Kane's fingers digging deep into his thick fur.

Heromindes was shaking, so hard as to fly apart, and Kane swallowed nervously. He may have broken the Clan Leader of Ashland. He wanted to vomit, feeling as vile and dirty as the humans responsible for tormenting the stricken wolves lying unconscious on the floor.

Hear me, Heromindes, Alpha, and Clan Leader of Ashland. Hear me, and obey. Kane risked this, risked destroying the Clan Leader in order to save him. He released the Voice, keeping its power restrained to thoughts along the link between himself and the other alpha, not wanting Burke or the other wolves approaching to be exposed. **You have your free will, your thoughts and actions are yours alone. Your strength is intact, your command and authority unchallenged. Hear me, and believe.**

It seemed eternity before Heromindes responded, Kane's words echoing in his head, as Kane carefully released the Clan Leader from his influence. It may have worked, using the Voice to repair any damage it caused. Kane waited, hoping, afraid he may have ruined a fine leader and a good wolf through carelessness.

Heromindes dropped his hands and stood taller, as Ashland and Black Pine wolves poured into the apartment, stopped by the sight of the two alphas squared off, and the Suarez pack members drugged on the floor.

"Attend to their injuries, and summon another shaman. Get vehicles here, one for the prisoners," Heromindes ordered, his scent quickly clearing of stress and fear. His eyes were a calm, gentle green, and Kane let go of his worry, relief coursing through his veins as the Clan Leader issued orders. Wolves sprinted to obey, some kneeling by the Suarez wolves, others turning and running back down the hall, jumping over dead humans still on the floor.

Kane breathed, relaxing, Burke at his side doing the same. He would apologize later, alone, and he hoped Heromindes would be able to forgive him.

Kane moved aside as Heromindes made for the bedroom, where Sophia and River tended to the two cubs. He needn't fear that Heromindes would kill the prisoners, not now. Whether Heromindes would try and kill him for his transgression was another matter.

ESCAPING THE PAST

"GLEN? CAN you stand?" Cat asked as Ghost paced the floor, ears pointed towards the front of the lab and the drive. He didn't trust the trespassers not to return. They wanted him for some reason, and he didn't doubt that they would be back.

"Yeah, I can stand. Give me a hand." Cat put every muscle she had in it, and Glen still did most of the work getting to his feet. Ghost watched, worried, the blood seeping now instead of flowing freely from his human alpha's head wound.

Glen watched him in return, thoughts clear on his expressive face. He was wondering about Ghost, but not afraid. There was no fear on his features, in his movements, no trace of it in his scent. Ghost huffed, and pointed his nose back to the door, scenting, ears straining.

"They still out there, boy?" Ghost turned his head back to Glen, surprised. His human was watching him, a new understanding in the way he looked at the wolf. Ghost gave up trying to scent the trespassers, and padded back over to his humans.

"They gone?" Glen asked again, and Ghost braved meeting his eyes. He dipped his snout, a wolf version of a nod, twice. Cat gurgled in shock, eyes round, but Glen just smiled, a small lift of his lips. "Good."

"Go back to guarding the front, there's a good boy." Ghost glared at Glen, but he went, sitting in the doorway of the upstairs lab, muzzle pointed down the hall, ears and nose on high alert for a scent or sound that didn't belong. He kept one eye on his humans, the other on the hall.

"Cat, grab our camping gear, our survival packs, all the emergency supplies. Sat phones, passports, everything. We're buggin' out." Glen pressed the heel of his hand to his forehead, the other bracing himself up on the table. "I'll get the truck ready."

"We're what? Glen, we need to call the police!" Cat exclaimed, red hair frizzy, her hands making knots as she ran her fingers through her hair over and over. "You need an ambulance!"

"And tell them what, babe? That we had two scientists kill two conservation officers, assault us, drug and try to steal our wolf, who turns out is something called a shaman and isn't really a wolf at all, who can apparently do magic and communicate like a person?" Glen asked, exasperated, clearly in pain. He wasn't yelling though, and Cat stood still for a long moment, mouth hanging open, staring at her mate. Ghost huffed loudly in amusement, tail thumping on the doorframe as he contemplated Glen's easy acceptance of the situation. He was a fine alpha, for a human.

Cat snapped out of her daze, and blinked a few times. She closed her mouth, and nodded, running from the lab towards the rear door, where their den was and their camping gear.

"C'mon boy, let's go get the truck started," Glen walked up to him, and Ghost stood, bracing the big human with his shoulder. Glen dug his fingers deep in the fur on Ghost's shoulders, and the wolf walked Glen down the hall, to the stairs. They went slowly, and Ghost stopped at the front door once they hit the bottom, scenting for danger before guiding Glen out. They both avoided the body left beside the drive, freezing in the harsh winter wind, blood no longer flowing from the bullet wound in the center of his forehead.

Glen appeared to be regaining strength with each step, the frozen gravel crunching under his boots as they made for the garage. Ghost bolted ahead, nose to the ground, sniffing for trespassers, but there was nothing, just the days old scent of Cat and Glen, and the crunchy sweet smell of squirrels. Cat had a feeder that she stored in the garage during the winter months, and it drew in the giant rodents even when it was empty. He shook off the desire to follow the tempting scent, and met Glen at the door to the garage, keys jingling in his hands. The large steel and concrete barn that acted as the sanctuary's garage was as chilly on the inside as it was outside, and the smooth concrete made his paws ache from the cold.

"Ghost, go check on Cat, get her moving," Glen ordered him as he turned on the sanctuary's truck, a silver and black vehicle nearly as old as Ghost, which Glen lovingly referred to as 'his baby'. Ghost cocked his head at the human, still wondering at the ease Glen had in addressing him not as an animal, but a thinking person. Ghost didn't argue this new change in their dynamic, woofing softly, and he sprinted from the garage as the big truck roared to life.

Ghost paused at the top of the drive, scenting the wind, looking for hints of the trespassers. He couldn't smell anything, but the wind was blowing in the wrong direction and they could be coming back and he wouldn't know until they were close, with more members of their pack. He dashed through the burnt and broken front door, and ran up the stairs back to the lab. Cat was running around, dropping gear bags and backpacks in a pile near the door, before running back through the rear door of the lab, to where the humans had their den.

"Can't carry all of this... Oh! Ghost, you startled me, bad boy." Cat scolded him absently, running her hands through her red hair for what must have been the hundredth time, ticking on her fingers a list of everything she thought they might need. Ghost wasn't sure what buggin' out meant, but it seemed to involve a camping trip of some kind. It wouldn't be the first one he'd been on with his human packmates. Ghost eyed the pile, many of the bags as big as Cat, and heavier.

Ghost grabbed the nearest bag by its straps, and pulled it from the pile, carrying it in his jaws. He dropped it in the gravel of the drive just as Glen parked the truck, engine running. He and Glen ran back inside, the human slightly unsteady, but moving fast enough. Together they carried the packs downstairs, Glen even dropping a strap around his neck before handing him another to hold in his jaws. Ghost grumbled around the fabric but followed his human alpha, the bags bumping on his chest and forelegs.

"Glen..... What about the body?" Cat asked as they rejoined

her upstairs, holding an armful of coats, staring down at the other dead conservation officer, where he was slumped partially propped up on the wall, eyes staring, dulled by death. Blood was pooled under him, and Ghost grumbled, annoyed at the blood he just noticed on his paws, prints on the white and black tiles from where he walked through the puddle several times. The trespassing alpha named Remus had dropped the other body beside the front door, and Ghost had regained consciousness and chased them off before the other body could be moved.

"Leave him. Nothing we can do for him, or his partner downstairs. We need to go, and now." Glen put a hand on her elbow, and guided her from the lab, helping her step over the blood. Ghost crowded behind her legs, keeping her moving forward.

"What about the wolves? The puppies?" Cat asked, tears in her voice, and Ghost sensed she was at the end of her resolve.

"We can call one of the summer interns to come up here and take care of them, or we can contact the police after we've gotten some distance between us and the sanctuary. We gotta go babe, we can't take them with us." Glen and Ghost between them managed to get a very flustered Cat into the truck, and Ghost ran in front of Glen before he got behind the wheel.

He sat, and put a paw on Glen's thigh, and he stared up at his human alpha, silently asking him to wait. Glen met his eyes, and while Ghost could not actually speak to the human as he would to a wolfkin alpha, his human seemed to understand. Other humans would not care for Ghost's cousins, not as his human packmates did. The sanctuary wolves would not be safe.

"You have five minutes buddy, make 'em count," Glen told him softly, and he hopped up into the truck, shutting the door.

Ghost ran around the building, and went straight to the wolf run, the high chain link fence gate locked securely, the snow deep and untouched. He pounded through the snow, and sent his will out ahead of him, listening to the tumblers in the lock spinning as he approached. The lock fell away as he reached the gates, and he reared up, slamming both front paws on the fencing. The gate groaned as it opened wide, the bottom bar scraping through the heavy wet snow as he pushed it.

Ghost howled, calling. He could sense them near, the wolves of the sanctuary pack. A heartbeat of silence, then they answered, the deep call of the female alpha of the pack closest to him. She flowed over the snow, soundless, smelling of pine sap and blood from yesterday's butchered meal. She was a large black and brown wolf, her thoughts a warm swirl of gold and green, none of them word based like his, but a mix of emotion and desires, and an entrenched wariness that he understood well. He was bigger, faster, more powerful, yet not alpha, and it left her confused.

A shadow of a star burned in her heart, and Ghost called to it with the vibrant star that shone inside of his own, pulling her forward. The pack came at her heels, a half dozen elusive wraiths that kept their heads low, tails tucked. They were shy with him, wary, not as brave as their matriarch.

Her eyes were a deep orange, startling and pure. She kept her head up and tail out, supreme in her domain. Instinct and a half-practiced technique formed over the course of the last fourteen years sent the pack matriarch a series of images, a deep-seated need, of towering pines and mountains, far from humans and their roads. She blinked, slowly, as he repeated the urge on her to run, to lead her wolves far away, away from humanity and their traps and guns. He gave her what he could, the knowledge of what to avoid, what to hunt, tugging at the edges of her mind, filling it with what he knew of surviving in the wild, calling to her own instincts. She had been born behind this fence, years after he was found and brought here as a cub, and she knew nothing of the wild. So he dug deep, looking for the memories that weren't, the instincts that could never be tamed, and pulled them to the light.

Ghost withdrew, and he heard in his head the lonesome cry of an ancient wolf, and felt the thunder of paws on rich black earth. The female wolf shook her head, as if she heard the same call. Ghost backed away, and ran to where the puppies were kept, the female on his heels. Again he sent out his will, so easy now, and the locks popped open. They heard them coming, little yips and cries greeting Ghost and the female. Three cubs poured out from the warm wooden den, awkward little bodies almost six months of age, from the same litter of a slain pack. Cat had saved them before local cattle farmers put them down, flying all the way out to a place called Montana and back.

Ghost opened the door of the puppy pen, and they tumbled out into the snow, their coats thick despite their age, and the cubs mobbed the female. She gave him a look that transcended species, exasperation and a grudging affection. Ghost sent her a wordless entreaty, and she answered him by nosing the pups, guiding them towards her pack.

A horn blared, and Ghost jumped, startled. He sent the wolves of the sanctuary one last look, as they slowly made their way out of the wolf run, north towards the tree line. The cubs bounced through the snow, the other females of the pack taking cues from the matriarch, surrounding the little ones. They left, not once looking back, and he felt a faint echo of longing, a part of him wanting to follow.

He ran, satisfied, mind now dedicated to his own pack. His humans. They were all he knew, all he loved, and he belonged with them. Ghost cleared the side of the building, and he ran to the truck, the side rear door of the extended cab open. He flew into the back, claws scrambling on the cloth seat. Cat reached back, yanking the door shut as Glen hit the gas. The cab was warm, and he immediately felt overheated, his dense coat adequate outside but stifling in the truck. He panted, eyeing his humans as they left behind the sanctuary. Ghost dropped his head on the shoulder of the driver's seat, snuffling at Glen.

"Cat, turn on the radio, listen in on official channels, see if anyone called in a disturbance at the sanctuary. Our guests might be coming back," Glen murmured, driving fast on the icy gravel road, handling the large vehicle well despite the conditions. Glen pushed Ghost's nose away from his face, and he snuck a quick lick in before he sat back.

"Where are we going?" Cat asked, clicking on the radio

over her head, scanning the channels.

"They were after Ghost. Willing to kill us, and anyone else in their way to get him. He's obviously not a regular wolf. I'm thinking they knew that, from the moment you sent in the DNA samples." Glen continued to drive, barely slowing the truck once they hit the paved highway, heading south. "He was young when we found him. Every young thing has parents, family. I'm thinking we messed up big time all those years ago when we found him by the river."

"He was just a cub, a baby. Of course we took him," Cat complained, glaring at Glen. "We thought his owners dumped him."

"I'm thinking he was lost, Cat. Like any other kid, lost in the woods, happy to see grown-ups, even if they weren't *his grown-ups*." Glen stressed the last words, looking briefly at Ghost in the rearview mirror. Ghost sat back up, and nudged Glen's head behind his ear, licking him happily. Finally, his humans understood. Glen gave him a smile, tinged with a strange joy, and sadness. Sorrow, even.

"You're talking like we *kidnapped him,*" Cat said harshly, eyes wide, staring hard at her mate.

"Cat—we did." A long, heavy moment of silence settled in the air between them all, and then Cat slumped back in her seat, rubbing her face.

"So how are we supposed to find his family? I'm guessing that's the point you're getting at? How are we supposed to find them? We can't go around asking people if they know of any sentient wolf packs that may or may not have lost a cub fourteen years ago." Cat demanded, sounding stressed.

"We'd heard rumors of wolves in the area for months, Cat. Months. That means there were wolves there at the same time we found him. His species was there, I know it. We're going back to where we found him, Cat. We're going back to Baxter State Park."

Ghost whined loudly at Glen's declaration, heart pounding so hard surely his humans could hear it. He did not know the name of the place where the gathering happened, but he remembered that it was a special place, one the packs.....no, the *Clans* traveled to every few years. If it was a wolfkin place, then there must be wolves there sometimes, if not all the time. He remembered a dark haired woman telling him that he was a newborn the last time the gathering happened, and was too young to go. He knew he was five summers old when he fell in the river, and if the gathering happened once when he was born, and again when he was five summers old.....

He may not be able to remember numbers all that well, or do something Cat called math, but he had toes, and could count as high as the ones he had. A gathering was coming. When the spring rains dried and the earth was warm through the night, the gathering would happen. The Clans would return. His mind was awash in memories, half-formed and chaotic, his heart pounding, and his nerves tingling. Words barely remembered tumbled in his head, and he lay down on the seat, whining softly.

Family. Pack. His Clan.

Black Pine.

Home.

A LONG WAY BACK

"SIR, WE have seven of the Suarez wolves. Thirteen are still missing. No sign of the traitors." Kane spoke to his Clan Leader, the webcam's image indistinct enough to grant him some buffer between himself and what he was certain was a look of extreme displeasure on Caius' face. The ultra-powerful netbook was braced precariously on the center console of the SUV, and he held it in place with one hand, the other on the wheel, watching over the screen as the Ashland pack handled the scene.

"I ordered you to hold off until we identified the traitors, Kane." Caius was displeased, no getting around it. Kane tried to look contrite, and hoped the fuzzy signal was enough to mask his grimace. He would never admit that he'd had no intention of waiting once he got here and the Suarez wolves were located—rescue first, plan retribution later.

"Caius, we have two human prisoners. We'll get something out of them," he said, exasperated. He flinched, hoping Caius didn't catch the lapse in decorum. It was time to get this conversation away from Caius' favorite pastime of digging at Kane and on to taking care of the survivors. "Shaman River has a request he wants me to pass on to you."

Caius growled, but sat back in his leather chair. A shaman usually didn't request permission to do anything, unless it had to do with territory lines. And an alpha was wise to listen, no matter the status of the shaman, or their home clan.

"What is Shaman River doing in Ashland territory?" Caius asked brusquely.

"I'm not one to question the wisdom of a shaman, Sir, or his actions," Kane answered slowly, "but having River here made the difference in saving the Suarez wolves."

Shamans had the autonomy to go where they pleased, and answered only to Clan Leaders in everyday, non-magical and non-spiritual matters. When it came to their craft and their duties as Shamans, they answered only to the Great Mother, and the Goddess brokered no interference to her will. Kane was agnostic, as were most wolves, but tradition held that no one, not even Clan Leaders, forbade a shaman from executing his duties, no matter where they took him.

Caius glared, his jaw set. A deep breath, audible over the tiny speakers, came to Kane, and he held still, waiting. Caius waved a hand, signaling Kane to speak.

"The survivors need specialized care, Sir. More care than Ashland's shamans are trained to handle, or have the skill to heal. Shaman River is requesting that he be allowed to bring the Suarez wolves into our territory, and taken to his home clan, Red Fern. He'll be staying with them as their primary healer." Kane spoke clearly, enunciating each word so he didn't have to repeat any. This was tricky, the potential for politicking getting in the way of helping the Suarez wolves.

"They cannot be treated there, under his care?" Caius demanded, sounding impatient.

"Heromindes doesn't want the family pack left here in Worcester, Sir. He's afraid a Challenge will be made to the youngest adult, one of the survivors, an untested alpha. The Suarez wolves hold southern Worcester for Heromindes, and it's a lot of territory, a temptation to any alpha in the area not already established. One of the wolves we rescued is an untried alpha, barely out of adulthood. He is certain to be killed in a Challenge if he isn't removed from the area, and Heromindes wants the remaining family members to stay together. Heromindes doesn't want to see the family suffer any more losses."

"He has you calling him by name now, does he?" Caius growled, leaning forward, his lips pulled back in a snarl. "Remember not to get to friendly with him, Kane. He has an Heir of his own, Heromindes has no need for mine."

"Yes, Sir." He felt it prudent not to say anything else. Every word out of his mouth lately just served to piss off his Clan Leader. In fact, Heromindes hadn't given Kane permission to call him by name—that was just Kane forgetting, too stressed out from his earlier slipup with the Voice to mind his tongue. Heromindes was doing all his talking through Shaman River or Burke, giving Kane a wide berth. He may not be able to apologize to Heromindes if he couldn't get near the other alpha.

They sat in silence for a short time, Caius not speaking to Kane, though thankfully not ending the video call. He needed an answer to the Suarez wolves' problem, and soon. He wouldn't put it past Shaman River to just head north, Suarez wolves in tow, and then explain the situation to their Clan Leader after the fact, if at all. River was much like his mentor, Shaman Gray Shadow, stubborn and devoted to a fault, agreeing to an alpha's whims only when it suited him.

"What of my son?" Caius asked suddenly, out of the blue, making Kane come back abruptly from his musing. He'd completely forgotten about the Alpha's aimless and surly son in the mayhem after the raid. He raised his eyes from the screen, quickly looking over the small crowd in front of the building. He spotted Gerald hounding Sophia as she waited for him to finish the video call at the curb, breath puffing out in white plumes in the cold night air. She was very admirably disregarding the lout.

"He did very well guarding the gear back at the base during the raid, Sir. No complaints from the Ashland pack, at the moment," Kane offered, trying to sound as if he wasn't pissed off that Caius decided to send Gerald along on a mission of such importance, no experience whatsoever and not a fan of any of Kane's wolves, or of Kane himself.

"You had him babysitting the gear?" Caius snorted, and Kane breathed easier, hearing the mirth in his Alpha's voice. "He didn't wander off, poke his nose where it shouldn't be?"

"Not that I am aware, Sir. Other than a mild dustup with my beta, Sophia, Gerald has kept to himself."

"Still bothering that same beta? He'll learn when she breaks a few bones." Thankfully Caius didn't sound upset. That was one thing unchanged about Caius—he did not tolerate his wolves harassing the females of the Clans. "If he knows what's good for him he'll behave."

Kane didn't respond, knowing that last bit was rhetorical enough he didn't need to. In his opinion Gerald had plenty of time to learn the hands-off rule in the last two hundred years. He just didn't care. Caius sighed, and Kane waited, trying to be patient.

"Very well. Shaman River may take the Suarez wolves into my territory. Red Fern still holds the gathering lands, under the rule of the White Wolf. He may take them there."

"Thank you, Sir..." Kane snapped his mouth shut when Caius spoke again.

"I'm not done." Caius waited a second, then continued. "None of us are sure why the Suarez wolves were taken, and these seven left behind. It's possible their captors were in the process of moving them, and were intending to come back for them. They may know who their abductors were as well. That means they are still in danger."

"I agree, Sir."

"Good. You'll be handling their protection."

Wait. What?

"Sir?"

"The gathering is in six months, Kane. It'll be held in Baxter State Park again this year. With the recent abductions and killings, we need advanced security. I will not have a repeat of the gathering fifteen years ago, do you hear me? This gathering needs to happen flawlessly, no incidents. I was planning on sending you ahead anyway to secure the park, I'm just moving up my timetable."

"Sir..." The gathering was in six months. He wanted Kane out of the way in the deep woods for six months while unknown enemies were hunting their people and abusing cubs?

"No arguments, Kane. Protect the Suarez wolves, and secure the state park for this summer's gathering." Caius was unmoving, and Kane bit back his retort, angry at being regulated to park ranger and nursemaid. He had traitors and killers to hunt. "Have Heromindes contact me in regards to the prisoners. I want them here in Augusta. I will learn what there is to know of the traitors myself."

"Yes, Sir." He refused to acknowledge that he growled, would in fact deny it if asked.

"You should have adequate bodies for the job, with your 'strike team' with you. Take them north as well. I'll have whatever supplies Red Fern requires sent north once you get there. Send my betas the information tomorrow, they'll sort you out." Caius leaned forward, one hand out, as if to end the call. He paused, and Kane groaned at the malicious grin lighting up his Clan Leader's face. "Oh, and take Gerald with you."

"Yes, Sir." *Fuck.*

The video feed dropped, the call ended. Kane slapped the laptop shut, growling under his breath. He eyed Sophia through the window, wondering where Burke was and what he'd have to say. He wanted to call his lieutenant, but figured he was with Ashland's alpha, and restrained himself.

He opened the door, and got out, the February air dry and biting. The snow had stopped falling, and it crunched under his feet as he jumped to the curb.

"Sir?" Sophia looked calm, but the dull wind was sure to be hiding the smell of her annoyance, Gerald standing far too close to her back for Kane's liking. She was his beta. Not Gerald's. *His*.

Kane growled, letting out his frustration into the night air, and Gerald jumped, glowering, but backing away from Sophia. She grinned, biting her lip to keep from laughing.

"Beta Sophia, please alert my team that we will be leaving as soon as Shaman River has situated the Suarez wolves for transport. Make sure we have everything, and everyone." She nodded, and at his signal took off down the sidewalk, surefooted on the snow and ice. Kane turned to Gerald, stopping the lesser alpha as he made to follow. Kane couldn't tell if he was stubborn or stupid.

"Your father has assigned you to my team, Gerald." Not precisely true, but close enough. Kane was Heir, and Gerald was a lesser alpha. Dominance and rank won out against birth status every time. Gerald would obey, or pay for his disobedience. "I expect we'll be getting along perfectly, won't we, Gerald?"

The lesser alpha's face went from horny, to smug, to mildly fearful in a handful of seconds. Kane let him worry, and took off after his beta at a sedate walk, offering his back to Gerald. He heard Gerald snarl quietly at the implied insult, but he followed quietly enough at Kane's heels.

SHAMAN RIVER wasn't sleeping, but he appeared to be, eyes closed, arms relaxed, with the young female Suarez wolf huddled in his lap in the rear of the SUV. The boy was sleeping as well, tucked to River's side, occasionally tensing and shaking as he dreamt. Just the three of them crowded on the bench seat at the very back of the vehicle, and Burke couldn't resist turning around in his seat every few minutes, eyes running over them, reassuring himself that they were still sleeping undisturbed.

You'll give yourself a crick in the neck if you keep looking over your shoulder like that. They're fine Burke, stop it! Sophia was laying on the center seat, stretched out, boots off, jacket bundled under her head as a pillow. She was short enough that her toes only just reached the edge of the seat, and her black clothes blended in with the shadows as Kane drove them north. New Hampshire was about to give way to Maine, and the gathering grounds at Baxter State Park should be reached a few hours after dawn.

I can't help it. I... Burke struggled to find the words, his heart sore, thoughts fragmented. Who could hurt children like that? How could any wolf, no matter their allegiance, hurt cubs to such a degree, or let humans use them so? It went against every instinct their kind had, their species fanatically devoted to the wellbeing of their young, no matter their parentage. Very young cubs were immune to feuds and Challenges, and were never held responsible for the transgressions of their parents. In ancient times, battles used to be halted by the arrival of children on the fields, as mothers and wives brought their young, hoping to stop the bloodshed long enough for the wounded and dying to be removed and tended to. Cubs had even served as guarantees of peace at treaty signings and diplomatic meetings, as no wolf with honor would risk a cub's safety by resorting to violence.

It was Law—cubs were off limits. All cubs were untouchable and protected by the Law until they reached adulthood at seventeen years, and even then they were so very young that wolfkin were often coddled and protected until their late twenties and early thirties. Their species was very long lived, and the older wolves never considered a younger truly grown until about fifty or so summers.

Burke was forty-nine, five years older than Kane, who was very young to be a Clan Heir. There were many elder wolves who saw Kane and Burke as cubs yet, and if not for their rank and unique strengths as alphas, they would be hard-pressed to receive any respect.

He realized he was still staring at Sophia, her brown eyes

flashing obsidian and green as they reflected the light from oncoming traffic on the other side of the highway divide. Burke huffed a soft apology for staring, and turned around, pulling his mind back, so that the shining lights he saw only in his head, the lights that were the minds of the other wolves in the SUV, dimmed and subtle.

Kane was quiet, both big hands at ten and two on the steering wheel, fingers loose, shoulders relaxed. Burke ran his eyes over his alpha, and leaned back into the corner made by his seat and the door. He tried to relax, to forget the horrors he'd witnessed in Worcester. Watching Kane was peaceful, relaxing, the connection between them intimate and true, even though they stopped being lovers not long after that disastrous gathering almost fifteen years before.

Sometimes he missed the nights they'd spent tangled in the bed sheets, hot and sweaty and exhausted, both freshly fucked and aching from marathon sex sessions. Burke grinned, remembering, and he bit his lip to keep from chuckling at one particular image that crowded his thoughts, of Kane getting caught in the sheets, tripping and hitting the floor one morning after they'd been rudely awakened. His lover had smacked the floor so hard he'd thrown himself into the Change. Burke had crowed with laughter, tears running down his cheeks, at the sight of the intimidating Clan Heir in his great black wolf-form, thoroughly entangled in white cotton sheets, completely confused and embarrassed.

What has put that smile on your face? Kane's thoughts whispered through the empty space between them, slipping past Burke's mental walls. Kane was the one wolf Burke's mind let in automatically, a habit that was the result of so many years living and working side by side.

Thinking of that morning you fell out of bed and ended up on all fours instead of two. Burke sent Kane a mental image of that morning, and he felt his friend's fresh exasperation and grudging mental laughter.

As your Alpha, I order you to forget that morning and erase those images from your mind, Kane told him, and Burke sent him a mental snort, refusing to countenance the very thought of forgetting that morning. He felt Kane's answering laugh, a warm echo down the line between their minds.

Kane? Burke asked quietly, eyes shut, moments from sleep as the smooth motion of the SUV lulled him into a relaxed state. The memory of them together was sweet, and it coaxed out a question from the recesses of his mind. A thought he'd never meant to ask, as the consequences of getting an answer could be raw and painful, for the both of them.

Yes, Burke?

** Why did we stop sleeping together? I wasn't that upset, it just ended so abruptly.**

He waited for several minutes, sleep held off, afraid he'd asked the wrong thing at an even more horrible time. When Kane spoke to him, Burke relaxed, thankful his best friend didn't sound too upset.

** I... I don't know. I felt... different, after that day. As if... as if I wasn't myself anymore. Like I was waiting, on the edge of a cliff. Knowing I was about to fall, but not knowing when. I still feel like that, actually. I haven't felt the urge for another wolf's touch since that horrible day.**

** Was it so very bad? Losing Gray Shadow and Luca, and the others? Do you think...** Burke had a suspicion of what changed in his friend, his former lover, an instinct so faint and unclear that he struggled to make it coherent enough to say to Kane. Old legends crowded his mind, and he was too tired to speculate.

Do I think what?

Never mind. I'm tired. His courage was about to desert him, as his body started to go limp, his mind languid and slow.

Not getting out of it. Finish that thought Burke. Kane told him, his thoughts full of curiosity.

He was about to, but sleep came up on him fast, and Burke succumbed, snoring softly.

Burke slipped away, and he dreamed of two wolves running in the snow, under a full and bright moon. One was black as the deepest shadows of the night, and the other, every variation of gray in spectacular patterns. The black shadow and the gray wraith raced together over the frozen reaches of his dream, and Burke wondered in a foggy haze who the gray wolf was, having never dreamed of him before. He was a stranger to Burke, but he was also heartbreakingly familiar.

The gray wolf looked like someone long-dead and dearly missed.

NIGHT CAME on quick as they drove. The window was cracked an inch or so and let in the cold air as the truck headed south, the border to the States just ahead. Ghost dozed, head on his paws, listening to the sounds outside the vehicle, and to the soft thump of Cat's heart as she slept, her head resting on Glen's shoulder.

The sweet, cool air rushing in through the window filled his nose, and he breathed deep, lungs full of clean air and rapidly changing scents. Exhaust, leather, the humans in the front seat, it all mixed with the smells coming in the window, the harsh odor of cold metal, the chemicals used on the roads that melted the ice and snow, and the vague hints of many humans, the merest hints of warm bodies traveling fast.

The truck was moving at a good clip, its suspension rocking softly, and Ghost let it relax him. They were being hunted for certain, by predators he couldn't understand, and Ghost let the worry go. No human could attack at these speeds, not like Ghost could, racing alongside a deer before he leapt for its throat or hamstrings. Humans were soft, and hated discomfort, even the toughest of them, and Ghost felt safe resting. He slept on and off until the truck began to slow, and he yawned, flashing his white fangs as he stretched out, claws scratching the seat.

"Border's just up ahead. Wake up, Cat," Glen nudged his mate, and Ghost peered over the seat, looking out the windshield. Cat grumbled but sat up, slowly dragging her mind awake as she rubbed her eyes.

The border checkpoint was a row of booths in a long line across the road, many smaller buildings on either side. Ghost understood borders, as they were a concept akin to a wolf's territory. Though where wolves would know the place their territory ended and another pack's began by scent and landmark, humans had invisible lines drawn on paper, and buildings sitting in the woods, guarded by men and women in uniforms and metal weapons.

There was a line of vehicles queued up at the border, only a few lanes open at this time of night. Glen slowed the truck as they approached the end of the line. He took a quick look over his shoulder behind them, then back to the line of cars ahead. Ghost smelled the rising tension in his human alpha, and whined.

"Ghost, I'm going to open that rear window all the way, and I want you to jump out. We can't call you a dog, not here, not this far north. Every border agent here knows what a wolf looks like, and we can't explain why we have you," Glen slowed the truck even more, and the window next to Ghost opened all the way. Cold air whipped freely about the cab, and Ghost looked out. "The area here is fenced for a few miles in each direction, so you can't take to the woods. Head there to the left, where the other lanes are closed. You can get through. Do it fast, they shouldn't care about an animal crossing the border, not if they think you're wild instead of someone's escaped pet. Thank God you don't look like a dog."

Ghost huffed in agreement, and licked Glen's ear. Cat reached out, and ran her small fingers through the fur behind his ears, scratching him. She was worried—he could smell it in her scent, see it on her face. Ghost thought for a moment that maybe he should look like a dog, since humans hated shooting pets, but loved to shoot wolves. He dismissed the thought, and looked out the window.

"Okay buddy, meet us on the other side of the border, there's a curve in the road about a mile south of here. It shouldn't take us long to get across, Cat and I have done this a few times, we know the agents here. We'll pull over and wait for you once we get through. Don't get shot." Glen sent him a look in the mirror, and Ghost saw worry in his eyes as well. He licked Glen's ear again, and growled gently, trying to reassure his humans. He would be fine. Human bullets couldn't hurt him badly while he was a wolf, not unless they got a lucky head shot or were at close range, and his bones were dense enough he may survive even that. Ghost wondered where his surety came from, since he'd never been shot before, but he was remembering things now, things he hadn't thought of in a long time, and he would worry about it later.

Glen slowed the truck almost to a crawl, about a dozen meters from the rear of the nearest vehicle, and Ghost didn't hesitate, squeezing his large body through the window. Paws hit ice-cold pavement, and he shifted his weight when the momentum of the truck and his abrupt landing on the ground made his pace falter. He ran, ahead and to the left. He heard the truck behind him as Glen put it in line, and he headed south, straight for the border. It felt strange running on the smooth, well-maintained road, clear of ice and snow. He felt the sting of the road salt on his paw pads, but ignored the discomfort, aiming his nose for the closed lane farthest to the left.

The booths were all well-lit, the arms across their single lanes down, and with jagged steel teeth rising from the pavement under the long, steel bar. He would be able to duck and leap through it no problem, and put on more speed, claws grabbing at the pavement under him. He ran hard, nearing the border, and as the lights of the crossing began to grow brighter, he knew he was visible. He heard off to his right a startled shout, a human catching sight of him as he finally entered the bright fall of lights that shone down from high overhead. He stretched out, at a pace that devoured the ground, going faster than he ever had before, the flat road and rough surface letting him call up his full measure of speed.

Humans were crying out, alarmed by his presence. Men in matching clothing came out of the buildings to the left, above the booths, stopping in their tracks just as he made the lane he wanted. He ducked under the steel bar, then leapt in a high, graceful arc over the jagged steel teeth that rose from the ground. Voices cried out in shock and some few sounded pleased.

He smelled the burning scent of guns, undrawn, the powder within them little blinks of red on his mental horizon. Ghost saw the warm pulsing stars of the humans, his weird double sight settling over his mind as he ran even harder, buzzing past the startled men lining the road on the other side of the border. He wasn't through yet; he'd only managed to clear the northern side, and the southern side, the part that belonged to the States, was less than a hundred meters away. People were shouting, and he heard the crackle of radios, the words indistinguishable in the excited chattering of the people behind him, and now, ahead. He stayed in a straight line, and breathed deeply, swiftly, filling lungs with fresh air, his muscles burning in a pleasant fashion.

He was feeling confident of his ability to get through unmolested when the first pop of a gun rang out, followed by another. Shards of road exploded inches from his nose, and he dodged a step to the side, feeling the bite of multiple stings as his muzzle was littered with miniscule fragments. Someone was firing at him. Ghost dropped his head, and ran on, lowering his body, stretching out more as he ran, trying to make himself smaller. But ahead of him, in front of the lane where he needed to go stood man, gun drawn.

BURKE YAWNED, and Kane did his best to relax. His friend was driving now, rested after taking a short nap, and the others were sleeping still. He always drove, but he was tired, and didn't feel like causing an accident as they traveled north.

They'd stopped earlier for gas and restrooms, and were still a couple hours away from the park. Kane wished they could have stopped at the clan home in Augusta before coming north, but River had shaken his head, eyes lingering on the cubs piled together on the rear seat as they fueled up. The team's other SUVs were occupying the other pumps as they fueled, and Kane was thankful it was so late at night, since they must have looked like some kind of crazy military convoy from an action movie.

While they'd taken the time to get the cubs cleaned up and immediate needs like clothes and shoes seen to in Worcester, the cubs still smelled like pain and violence, and Kane agreed with the unspoken thought that bringing the young ones near many strange wolves would provoke violence. It was their instinct to protect their young, no matter who they were or what clan they called home, and the wolves at the mansion would get overstressed by the condition of the cubs. Overstressed wolves always got violent. Kane didn't feel like putting the cubs or his clan through that, so on they went to Baxter. Red Fern Clan was small, and well used to Shaman River bringing home wolves needing long-term care. The condition of the younglings would be stressful, but tolerable on the clan's collective nerves. River had called his family, and the one known as the White Wolf was expecting them a couple of hours after dawn.

Kane sat in the passenger seat in the front, and peered over his shoulder, meeting River's eyes. The shaman was wide awake, a cub on either side of him, their tiny heads burrowed in his shoulders, hiding. They were sleeping still, and Kane had a suspicion that River was keeping them under somehow. He looked at the cubs again, and then back to River, and he got a small dip of the shaman's head. So River was keeping the cubs under until they got to Baxter and Red Fern. That was a good idea, considering what they'd been through. A shaman meant safety and comfort, yet not even River would be enough to manage two severely abused cubs surrounded by strange wolves, two of them alphas. While neither Burke nor Kane would harm a cub, they were accustomed to other wolves being wary of them, and only a few wolfkin found the natural draw and appeal of an alpha easy to enjoy once they got past their nerves.

He found himself experiencing a quick flash of déjà vu, remembering the long ago night of the gathering, a shaman telling stories and a sweet cub showing off for him, trying his best to get Kane's approval and attention. He shrugged off the memory of the lost cub, and sent a brief prayer to the Great Mother that Luca was at peace, wherever he was.

Kane looked back to the front, and put a hand on Burke's shoulder, squeezing hard once. He needed the contact, the touch. Seeing the cubs like that, knowing what had happened to them, made his heart sick, and a bitter anger boiled under his self-control. He felt impotent, and he cursed the time it had taken for Caius and Heromindes to agree to send Kane and his team after the Suarez wolves. They may not have been able to prevent the abuse, but they sure as hell could've ended it sooner.

Burke smiled at him, one hand coming off the wheel and

up to his, squeezing back. Kane let his hand sit for a moment, then gently pulled away. He didn't want Burke to get the wrong idea, especially after the question he'd raised earlier in the evening. Kane didn't really know why he stopped turning to Burke for sex. It had been great, and uncomplicated.

He let Burke think it was the tragedy that long ago morning nearly fifteen years ago that made him pull away, made him change their relationship. He hadn't lied to Burke about how he felt; there was something different, something inside of his heart that felt off center. He felt like he was waiting, that light and eager, yet oddly tense sensation of impatience that usually heralded good news or a favored event. It came and went, vague and indistinct at first, then as the years went by it deepened, coming on suddenly when he was relaxed, or tired, and leaving him feeling expectant, eyes raised, searching, senses alert. Yet even after all these years, nothing happened, and he learned to adapt, to live around that odd sensation when it came over him. If it had been unpleasant or trying, he would have asked a shaman about it, but it never left him feeling badly, so he kept it to himself. It felt almost intimate, personal, and he feared losing it all together if he shared it with anyone. Part of him was convinced he was picking up the mental thoughts and emotions of his clan members, but he wasn't Clan Alpha yet, and so he shouldn't be picking up on the wolves of Black Pine like that, not unless he deliberately opened a direct line to another wolf's mind. It may well be him sensing Burke or Sophia, the two wolves he personally called his own, but they were rarely around when it happened, so he had to discount that theory fairly early.

What truly left him confused was that the sensation started the night before the tragedy at the gathering, when he sat and listened to Gray Shadow tell stories of the past, crafting illusions from smoke and light. He bit back a sad smile as he recalled that night, how peaceful he felt, even with the soon to be lost Luca sitting not too far away, answering every one of the shaman's questions. He sighed, remembering how silly the little cub had been, sneaking looks at him under his lashes, a flirt at five years of age. He felt ill, thinking about how less than twelve hours later, Luca would be lost forever, along with the Alpha's daughter, Gray Shadow, and three more of his grandchildren dead.

He thought of it now, and he wished for something to ease the hurt in his heart, the nasty, sick ache compounded in his chest after rescuing the Suarez wolves and finding the cubs. He'd gladly take phantom emotions with no discernible cause than feel as wretched as he did now. It was late, he was tired, and he needed to be at his best when they got to Baxter. Red Fern was led by River's sister Andromeda, the White Wolf, a beta centuries old, one of the oldest wolves Black Pine and the surrounding clans could claim in their territory. Andromeda was a wise and wicked creature, the mother of many cubs, and she had the distinct honor of birthing some of the most promising betas and shamans seen in generations. She was a contemporary of Gray Shadow and Caius, the three of them friends from the Old World, and they'd come over to the New World around the same time. He enjoyed her wit and dry humor, and he needed his mind sharp to deal with her. She wouldn't be too much trouble, but he always ended up walking away from their conversations feeling like a freshly scolded whelp.

Kane leaned the seat back, and stretched out as far as he could, lacing his fingers together in his lap, and shut his eyes. He yawned again, and let himself slip away, muscles relaxing. He felt it then, the eager and breathless joy, and wondered if wishing for it summoned the sensation. It was as if he was getting close to something, that he was about to experience joy, on the limit of sleep and wonder. He fell, just the littlest bit, and slipped into the waiting dream.

It happened fast, and was jarring, even in sleep. He knew he was dreaming, yet he had no control over what he was seeing and feeling. The joy turned to nervousness, stress. His heart was racing, and he saw in his mind a row of buildings, lights blazing, and smelled bitter anxiety and cloying fear.

He was running, on paws instead of feet, claws digging hard into what felt like pavement, lungs burning, limbs snapping forward in a blur of speed, tail outstretched behind him. Cold air seared his lungs, and he smelled car exhaust and metal. Humans were around him, too close, and he wanted to keep running, to escape. The way ahead was blocked, and fear lanced through his heart as he faced the man in front of him, gun raised, aimed right at his head. To stop was to die for certain, and he had nowhere else to go but forward. The shot was loud and shocking, and he felt the burn of the bullet.

Kane shot upright, a shout on his lips, breathing hard, both hands slapping onto the dashboard of the SUV. He panted fast, air rapidly filling his lungs, and he would swear for a second that he could still feel the bullet shot by the man in his dream, tracing a path from his shoulder, down his side, to his hip. He looked down, expecting to see blood, but there was nothing.

"Goddess! Kane, are you alright?" Burke swore as he jerked the wheel in surprise, looking over at him in concern. Sophia cursed loudly as she almost toppled off the seat to the floor. He sat still, eyes scanning the road ahead of them, part of him expecting to see the border crossing from his dream. He didn't know how long he was asleep, but whatever that was, it had come on fast and strong, and he still felt the cold burn of the night air, and the sensation of pavement under his paws as he ran.

"I'm... I'm fine. Just a bad dream." Kane sat back, and tried to relax. His heart was racing, and he felt sweat cooling on his forehead. By the Great Mother, that was the oddest dream he'd ever had.

"Some dream. You've never done that before, you sure you're okay?" Burke got the SUV back under control, and slowed down, as if he was about to pull over. Kane heard the shaman in the back, whispering to the cubs, and he smelled their fear. They must have woken up when he startled Burke into swerving.

"I'm okay, I swear. Bad dreams, nothing more. Everyone okay back there?" Kane didn't turn around, not wanting to stress the cubs.

"All is well, Alpha. Just startled. We're fine." River said

that to him as much as to the cubs he comforted, and Kane kept his attention to the front. They settled down, and Kane heard Sophia grumbling as she sat up, pulling her boots back on, and clicking the seatbelt back into place. She was up for now, it seemed, and he felt bad. It was close to dawn by the moon's position low on the horizon, and he didn't think he'd be able to fall back asleep either.

"Once we get to Baxter, I vote for sleeping the rest of the day," Burke said softly, and Kane exhaled roughly, nodding in agreement. It had been a hard twenty four hours.

He watched the moon, still bright and amazingly clear, and felt his heart settle. He thought of the dream, and wondered how he came to be visualizing about crossing the border in wolf-form. He recognized it as one of the border crossings between Canada and Maine, having crossed it several times before, and he was at a loss as to why he'd dream about it now, and in that context.

He played it over in his head again, and drew in a soft, startled gasp, freezing on a sharp mental image. He caught a glimpse of one of his legs outstretched in front of him as he galloped towards the human male holding the gun, and the fur covering the limb wasn't midnight black. It was stormy gray, with a band of dark pewter in a line across his toes.

Kane stared up at the moon, and wondered if it was possible for a wolfkin to go mad at just forty-four summers. Madness for their kind usually only afflicted the extremely old, and he wasn't even fifty yet. Still very young by their measure of time.

The pain lingered, and he ran a hand down his left side under his jacket, wondering.

GHOST LIMPED into the woods, whimpering as each step of his left legs brought on a piercing wave of pain. The bullet had missed his head, instead running along his side, from his upper left shoulder, along his ribs, and digging a deep furrow in his skin all the way to his hip. He could run just as fast, and managed to bowl over the human standing in his way as he breached the last hurdle of the border crossing.

Once he gained the other side, he'd ducked and weaved through northbound traffic, and made it to the woods. He didn't know why the human fired at him, since he wasn't attacking anyone, but humans did stupid things. He was very clearly trying to avoid people, yet the human shot him anyway. He snorted in derision, and loped along the road, just inside the tree line. He was at the first bend in the wide road south of the crossing, and found a small incline to sit on, so he could keep an eye out for his humans. Glen said he would meet him here, and so he would wait. Glen always did as he said he would, and Ghost licked his side with one eye on the road.

The pain was lessening swiftly, the skin closing around the injury so fast he barely got a taste of blood through his thick coat before it was gone. He huffed, satisfied, and resumed watching the road. He had a feeling it would be a while before Glen and Cat joined him, watching as vehicles that didn't belong to his humans drove past.

The moon was bright, and its light broke through the bare branches above him, and he saw the flow of light rising from the sleeping trees nearby blend with the liquid silver light of the moon. He watched the ebb and flow of light for a while, sniffing at it, walking through it, and he managed to make it move around him, as if he stepped into a stream of water instead of light. He blinked, and it faded just a little, and it wasn't so distracting.

He lowered himself down, head on his paws, tail tucked around him, and waited. The woods were quiet, and the soft lights he could see with that his vision were dim and barely noticeable. The trees slept, and there was nothing larger than an owl within striking distance. It was strange; with this new sight, he could see behind himself as well as to either side, all without turning his head in that direction. He mentally explored the sleeping woods in his immediate area, still staring at the road, and he could see the tiny dulls stars that belonged to humans inside each vehicle as they passed his hiding place.

Ghost began to count the humans, slowly, trying to remember what the woman with the long, dark red hair had taught him all those years ago as they sat at the kitchen table, his siblings playing loudly in the living room. He was thinking about whether or not fourteen came before or after thirteen when he saw Glen's truck coasting along the curve of the road, Cat's window open, her anxious face peering out into the darkness.

He sat up fast, and darted down to meet them, stepping out in front of the truck. Glen slammed on the brakes, and Ghost wagged his tail as his human alpha shook his head, Cat letting out a squeal as they stopped a few feet away.

Cat opened the rear cab door, and Ghost wasted no time getting in the truck. Glen pulled them back into traffic, and Ghost rested his muzzle on the human's shoulder. His head was bigger than Glen's, and his human's shoulders, while broad, were barely big enough to support him.

"Don't try and snuggle with me, buddy. I said run across the border, not scare the crap out of half of US Border Patrol and Customs. They shut the whole border down when the shots started. It took them over an hour to figure out what happened and start letting people through again." Glen sounded mad, but Ghost could smell his human's concern and fear. He licked Glen's cheek, and snuggled in closer, as well as he could while sitting on the backseat. Glen sighed, and reached up a hand, scratching the little divot between his eyes, a place he could never reach on his own. "I really wish you could talk, this would be so much easier."

Ghost gave his human a soft growl in agreement, and sighed as well. He really did wish he could talk. If only he could remember how to find his human form again. He didn't even remember what having fingers felt like, much less how to speak like a person. He had trouble remembering his birth name, let alone how to form sentences and what words to use. He'd been Ghost, the wolf, for so very long that Luca the wolfkin boy was a distant dream, indistinct and far away.

Cat snuggled back up to the both of them, and Ghost let himself drift, sandwiched between the two people in the world who he knew loved him, even if he was broken.

He rarely dreamed. Life as wolf was simple, uncomplicated, and he had little to sort out in his head as he slept. Yet when he did dream, the dream was always the same. It was a torture he could have done without, but he yearned for the pain of it all the same. He dreamt of a wide field covered in snow, nothing but a brilliant canvas of stars above and the company of the wind as he ran. He would stop, in this lonely dream of his, and lift his jaws to the heavens and call. Again and again his cry would go unanswered, for what seemed like lifetimes. He would fall to the snow, hopeless in his loneliness and grief, willing the cold to take him...until a howl reached him, and echoing answer winging over the snow fields. He would leap to his feet in his dream, and race up a small hill, to see a dark silhouette of a wolf standing at the crest. Yet no matter how hard he tried, he could never get to the top, the black shadow of the mystery wolf forever out of his reach.

It was a dream he hated having, and he thankfully only experienced it a few times a year since he reached what he assumed was his majority, his time as a pup over.

When he was still little he crept into bed with Glen and Cat, sleeping at the bottom of their bed, their feet tucked under his ribs for warmth. When he got too big for that, Cat got him a thick, comfy rug that she put near the door of their inner den, what she called their bedroom, and he slept across the door, guarding his humans. Some nights, especially during the summer, he spent the nights out in the woods, hunting and running, and calling to the moon. He always got an answer from the sanctuary wolves, but he never once heard the cries of his own kind. He was far away from them, and couldn't remember how to find his way back. Loneliness followed him through the forest, and he eventually stopped going out alone at night, staying with his humans, unable to bear the ache in his heart. He had people who loved him, but they weren't ***his*** people. Yet what they gave him was all he had, and he loved them back. Even if they spent years thinking him a tame, overly large animal. He spent most of his years with them thinking the same, since he couldn't make himself be a person again. He'd stopped trying, the pain of failure too much to bear again and again.

The truck's motion on the road rocked him gently, and he pulled away from his humans, stretching out as best he could on the backseat. Sleep found him slowly, peacefully, and he went willingly into the rare dream he sensed waiting for him. He expected to see the snow fields, and braced himself for the loneliness to crawl out from his spirit.

This was a new dream.

He was at the river, soaking wet, and it was dark. He wasn't a cub anymore, and he felt new, different, his heart full of pain and a weird eagerness that left him off balance. The logs around him were damp, and the air was cool. Insects sang and buzzed, and he kept his head low as bats flew above him, snagging tiny biting bugs from the air. His new ears twitched and pointed at each noise he heard in the dark, and he waited.

He was scared, but he would wait, just as Grandpa Shadow told him to. Kane was coming, he had to wait for Kane. Grandpa Shadow told him Kane would keep him safe. He heard a whisper of a thought, in a beloved voice that made his heart hurt with a sharp sting of grief.

He's searching for you. Hide until Kane finds you. Kane will keep you safe.

He was aware he was dreaming, the world around him immaterial no matter how real it felt. So when the night brightened, and the humans never found him hiding in the logs, he looked up in the gray light of predawn and saw a great black wolf standing over him, he knew at some level that this never happened. Yet it felt like it was supposed to.... That this is what his morning after a night of horrible heart break was meant to be.

The scent of warm fur, sweet breath, and the dark eyes above him were so familiar, as if he'd run beside this wolf every night for eons. There was a heaviness to his body, a heat that ran through his blood and made his limbs shake. His heart thrummed madly, and every sense exploded. The ground under his paws was richer, steadier, the strength of it more tangible. The wind was cool and gentle, and smelled of living things and clean water. It carried the black wolf's intoxicating aroma to him, swirling around his head, over his muzzle, across his tongue. His ears heard the deep bass of a powerful heart, beating slowly, each thump comforting and alluring.

He didn't feel the same anymore, yet he never felt more

real, more like himself, in years. This was a dream, he was never more certain, and yet he ached for this reality, and he wanted to stay here, content and whole.

The black wolf stepped closer, and looked down at him where he hid in the broken pile of logs and bushes. No aggression, no threat was in the lines of that powerful body. Only a sense of waiting, of patience. As if he was asking something, and Ghost... Luca... had the answer.

He wasn't afraid. Kane had found him.

Ghost stood from his hiding place beside the river, and stepped free, standing tall, fully grown and strong of body, mind and heart. He felt a sensation of rightness, of equilibrium, and reached out his head, and the great black wolf met him halfway.

A FLARE OF light across his eyes woke him, yanking him rudely from the riverside dream. Ghost sat up, as a large semi roared past the truck, horn blaring. Dawn sent an overcast and seedy glow over the road, and Ghost curled his lip at the noisy vehicle as it pulled away. They were still driving, Cat passed out, Glen with one hand on the wheel, the other buried in her red hair, as she slept with her head on his leg.

Ghost growled softly so his human would not hear, upset to be woken from the rare peace he'd felt. He missed the dream with an ache that threatened to steal the breath from his chest, and he wished desperately for the sense of comfort and subtle joy that it had brought him. He recalled parts of it, and he felt a pang of loss to be taken out of that peaceful place. The image of the great black wolf sent a lance of sharp yearning through his heart, and he lay back down, whining.

He wanted to go home. Trouble was, he didn't remember where it was, or who was waiting for him. He struggled to remember Luca, the boy he had been, yet even those days of walking upright and having hands were dim and ethereal, vanishing if he got too close. He had a horrible, sinking feeling that he'd been too long the wolf, and the hope to one day be a man was out of his reach. He sensed he no longer thought as a man; that his mind was too much like an animal's, regardless of the realization of his calling. Shaman he may be, but untrained, and foreign to the ways of the magic that pooled and flowed around him, visible to him even as they traveled over the human's roads in a machine of steel and fuel.

What good was being a shaman and having magic if he couldn't fix himself?

THINNER THAN WATER

"GIVE ME a guarantee I'll have more concrete results in hand by this time next week," he said softly, hissing in Dr. Harmon's ear, "or you'll wish that magical dog had burned you to a crisp."

Simon Remus dropped the sniveling doctor back on his feet, and his legs promptly gave out on him, spilling him to the floor on his plump ass. Dr. Harmon scrambled to his feet, one arm bandaged in thick white gauze, most of his exposed skin red and blistered, but for where it was a pallid, leeched shade due to sick dread. Simon smiled, a wolfish expression, and that one look sent the fat little doctor running from the room, mumbling assurances before his off-kilter footsteps sprinted down the hall to the laboratory.

"Fucking humans, none of you are worth more than the stink of your fear."

Simon straightened his suit jacket, brushing invisible lint from the immaculate gray wool, tugging on his cuffs. The stitches on his right hand itched, but he resisted the urge to scratch at them. He took his time, calming his heartbeat, before spinning to his guest.

The man, or beast, really, was unchanged by the years.

Simon, now in his mid-thirties, was still in the prime of his life and fit; whereas this thing, this wolf, masquerading in the form of a human man, appeared to be in his early twenties, ridiculously youthful and in pristine condition for a being that claimed to be centuries old. It was his desire for that near immortality that made Simon mind his tongue and hold back his real thoughts.

"What we lack in bravado, I assure you, we make up in intellect, and where brains fail us, treachery compensates," Simon said as he walked to his desk, glaring at the irritating folder that bore the lackluster results from his scientists' failed experiments. Their attempt to genetically graft shaman DNA to a human was a non-starter—the dissimilarities between the two species was too vast. It was that distance in their species that drove Simon to maintain the uneasy truce he had with the werewolf—if he could meld a shaman's DNA to that of an alpha's, then he was one step closer to completing his goal. The lone sample they had was almost gone, degraded by time and diluted.

"Treachery," scoffed the werewolf, "is hardly worth mentioning as a virtue. Didn't you arrange the dethroning of your own brother?" The hulking brute threw himself down on the coach in Simon's office, disregarding his glare when a pair of leather boots unceremoniously dropped themselves down on his mahogany coffee table.

Simon dropped his glower when it became obvious the werewolf was unaffected, and he picked up the manila folder and threw it at the werewolf, the stack of papers inside giving it enough heft to make the distance. He snorted when the animal in man's clothing caught the folder without a single paper being lost, and without once taking his eyes off the ceiling. He was gifted with a return toss, and the papers scattered across the office when he failed to catch the folder as elegantly as his guest had.

"You're hardly one to talk of treachery, aren't you? How many of your own people have you killed in the last twenty years?"

"All lesser wolves, beta and alpha alike," the monster growled, and he finally chose that moment to look at Simon directly, eyes flat and cold. "And I'll kill whoever I need to, to get what I want."

"Your loyalty to your species is laudable," Simon muttered, and picked up a stray piece of paper from the mess that littered his desk and ran a finger over the DNA sequencing codes. Simon lifted his eyes, frustration at the lack of progress in their experiments and his minor burns and cuts on his hands and forearms digging at him. "Why are you here?"

"None of your business," Roman McLennan snarled, dropping his feet to the floor with a thud and standing to his full height. Simon eyed him warily, and made a conscious effort to restrain his own anger. "I'm on a sabbatical, that's all you need to know."

Simon snorted in disbelief, rolling his eyes, not buying it. Looked like Caius finally kicked his son to the curb.

Simon reached down for another piece of paper, this time

a color photo, one of a large gray wolf with odd patterns in his coat, with bright silver eyes. The same wolf that nearly burnt him and Harmon alive in Canada days earlier, and was the one who made the gun explode in his hand, earning him the stitches. It was his first encounter with a shaman directly, and he wasn't looking forward to a repeat of the experience. He suppressed his rage, and held out the photo.

"Since you're here, make yourself useful—do you know this wolf?" Simon asked, holding out the picture, and Roman took it after a short pause.

He was watching carefully, as the Clan Leader's son had a habit of not sharing everything he knew, choosing to parse out information in increments. So he saw the tightening of his grip on the paper, the way his eyes flew open wide, and the stuttered breathing as he took in the gray wolf's visage.

"Where did you get this?" Roman asked harshly, hands shaking.

"That's the shaman who nearly burned me and Harmon alive a few days ago in Canada," Simon said casually, leaning back on the edge of his desk, crossing his arms, mindful of his injuries. "We thought he was a beta due to his size. I wasn't expecting to see a shaman outside of clan lands."

"Canada? A few days ago? But... this wolf is dead," Roman breathed, and Simon got a good look at his face as the werewolf lifted his head, staring at the far wall, face leached of color.

"He certainly is not dead, whoever that mutt is," Simon

replied, still watching. This was interesting. "You told me shamans never leave the clans, their duties. So do you care to tell me what a shaman was doing at a wolf sanctuary in New Brunswick, masquerading as a pet?"

"What?" Roman snapped, looking back at the picture, fingers running over the gray wolf. "What the fuck are you going on about?"

"Harmon, through his contacts with the conservation departments in New Brunswick, was contacted by a woman who runs a wolf sanctuary in Canada. She claimed she had a new subspecies of gray wolf she needed help identifying. Harmon asked for blood samples and more information. The woman sent the samples, which we coded, and it came back as werewolf. He was the only one, and the sample was unique. We wanted more, since what she sent didn't survive the coding process. It was unique enough to warrant a trip over the border to collect him."

"This is the wolf?" Roman asked, waving the picture at Simon.

"Yes! Who the hell is that?"

Roman pulled in a deep breath, and for the first time in nearly fifteen years, Simon saw what looked like fear on the creature's face.

"This wolf... this shaman... should be dead." Roman held the picture facing Simon, and he looked at it, not knowing where Roman was going with this. He sucked in a noticeable breath again, and exhaled roughly. "If I hadn't seen his fucking corpse with my own eyes the day he was killed, I would swear to the Goddess that this was Shaman Gray Shadow."

"He's....that Shaman is dead," Simon said, hope stirring. Gray Shadow's bloodline was severed, the world's most powerful shaman dead these last several years, slain in an attempt to kidnap him and his descendants. If Gray Shadow was alive, then their work may actually come to fruition.

"I know he's dead, so this picture makes no sense. I took the blood sample for you from his corpse before they burned him, I know he's dead for certain. That wolf, whoever the hell he is, is identical to the wolf I knew as Gray Shadow. He must be related somehow...." Roman asserted firmly, then his voice trailed off, and his tanned face grew even paler. "Not possible," he whispered. "He died. He fell in the river, and drowned."

"Make sense, you fool," Simon snapped. "Who the hell are you talking about? Is this the other shaman, the grandson who was already apprenticed when Gray Shadow died?"

"No. No...this is not Ezekiel. He's still in Russia, his apprenticeship is over this summer. And his wolf-form is a deep auburn and black, subtle coloration, with green and brown eyes. Not this wolf."

"You told me, when we first began this venture together, that Gray Shadow only had one grandson who was a shaman. None of his sons became shamans, and only this grandson became a shaman. He's out of reach in another country on the other side of the world in the wilderness somewhere, so deep my agents never found him. If this demon-wolf—," Simon stabbed at the picture with a stiff finger, "—looks exactly like Gray Shadow, and you're certain the old shaman is really dead, *then who the fuck is this?*"

"All of Gray Shadow's line is accounted for. All of them, even the ones who died at the gathering, were accounted for, with the dead burned on the funeral pyres that night....all but one," Roman growled, and his eyes glowed for a second, a wild thing coming to life in their dark depths. "My nephew, Luca, went into the river that day, and his body was never found. He is the only wolfkin unaccounted for after the kidnapping attempt."

"Is this him?" Simon snarled, a bad habit he'd picked up from consorting with monsters for nearly fifteen years. He grabbed the picture, and waved it under Roman's nose.

"Is he an heir to Gray Shadow's bloodline!?" Simon shouted, heart racing.

Roman went still, his body subtly shifting from tense uncertainty to lethal and vicious predator. Simon gulped, and took a small step back, reminded yet again that while Roman McLennan was a lesser alpha and no power figure in the clans, here, in the human world, he was a monster with very big teeth who had no compunction slaughtering anyone who annoyed him.

"If it is Luca, I will find him," Roman growled past teeth suddenly longer and sharper, eyes glowing. "If Luca lives, and he is the shaman, then his power will be mine."

REIGN OF THE WHITE WOLF

THE CABIN was small, with a tiny bathroom off the wall it shared with the kitchen, one full bed, a table, two chairs and a rug in front of the stone hearth, cool now and unlit. Wood was stacked beside it, and more was out on the porch, under the overhang, dry and waiting to be burned. He breathed in deeply, and scented nothing beyond small furry vermin and the smell of humans, weeks old. This cabin was off the beaten path, out near the boundaries of the park, miles from the center where Ghost recalled the gathering took place.

"Does it even have power?" Cat asked, coming in behind him as she dropped her bag beside the door. He looked up at his human packmate, and huffed in amusement. He saw nothing wrong with the cabin, but perhaps it was a bit on the ....wild side for his humans. Cat looked exhausted and stressed; her red hair lightly streaked with gray was a mess, and her clothes were wrinkled and she smelled like she hadn't bathed in two days. Which she hadn't, actually.

Ghost moved out of the way, convinced the cabin was secure enough, and went back outside, dodging around Glen as he brought in more of their gear. He didn't care if there was power in the cabin or not, he had his fur to keep him warm, but his humans needed the artificial warmth. He heard Glen reassuring Cat, but he lost interest in their conversation when he got the view of the park from the porch.

The cabin sat in a small clearing, the towering pines hovering high overhead, the downy verdant wings of their boughs waving in the soft breeze that came in fits and spurts. Behind and to the left side of the clearing rose the mountain, and the narrow drive wound its way up the hillside, the only tracks left by Glen's truck. He smelled nothing on the wind but pine sap and wet things, but it was so weak that he would need to rely on his eyes and ears to sense his kindred if they were here. He was relatively nose-blind unless the wind moved with more strength through the trees.

Were there still wolves here? Were his kindred here, even after all these years? A part of him, the part of his mind that still thought like a human was afraid—afraid that after the violence of the gathering all those years ago, his people decided to leave, to hide. He remembered that keeping the secret was important, that only special humans knew. It was why he was taught at home by a woman he thought was his mother, instead of going to a human school like the older cubs did. The older cubs could keep secrets better than the littler ones.

He remembered being that small, wearing clothes... talking. Being able to say his own name. His name, the name his parents gave him.... he fought to recall their faces, but there was nothing but blurry, out of focus recollections and indistinct sounds.

He shook nose to tail, a tremendous shiver that wracked his whole body, and the planks of the porch under him moved as if they were alive. For a moment, the snow was gone, and the clearing before him was covered in tall sweet grass and wildflowers, the pine boughs waving in a high summer breeze. He shook himself, and the snow returned, the vision fading away. The sounds of summer were replaced by the oppressive weight of winter, and he wanted nothing more than to feel the heat of the sun on his back, smell the earthy breeze, and chase after the distant sound of running wolves.

Glen brought them into the park through an old access road, explaining to Cat that they didn't want to bring attention to themselves by trying to get into the park in the off-season by the main gates. Ghost was glad—what he remembered of the main gates left him feeling sick, as if he'd eaten spoilt meat. He heard again the echo of gunfire, felt the ravaging pain of the silver bullet in his shoulder, and he heard the sharp fear and frustration in his grandfather's mindvoice as he called for help.

Ghost ran out into the snow of the cabin's front yard, paws spread, head hanging low, shaking. He was swamped by memories, chaotic, none of them staying long enough to become clear before losing its place to a new one, all of them harsh and jagged and painful. He saw blood, and a human man in black, standing over them, a gun laden with silver-shot aimed for his grandfather's head. He saw a great black shadow running over the rocks, big paws not making a sound, hunting the man who would take his grandfather's life, the man who would pull him into the river and tear him from his family.

Ghost shook hard, so hard he fell, his heart pounding, mind

besieged. He heard someone calling to him, a loved voice crying out in alarm, and soft hands running over his face. His eyes were blind as the memories began again, from waking long ago early that morning before dawn, to climbing atop a gigantic gray wolf, to running through the wild pine groves, laughing and yelling in happiness. He saw his father! His father, Josiah! He remembered.... He was Luca, son of Josiah and Marla, grandson of Clan Alpha Caius and the powerful Shaman Gray Shadow.

He cried out, thrashing in the snow, his howl full of aching, hollow loneliness. It poured out from his heart, past his fangs, and it was forceful enough that it was sufficient to break him free from the cycle of images. There was a susurration in his ears, familiar sounds that his mind tried to piece together into a whole he could understand. He caught a chorus of howls, the voices of many wolves blending and twining as their song rose to the moon. A single howl returned in the echoes, high and thin, fading away as the memories loosened their grip on his thoughts.

He opened his eyes and blinked the snowflakes away, panting hard, to find Cat and Glen kneeling beside him in the front yard. He whined, and Cat petted his face, brushing off the snow, crying. Glen held him, head and shoulders only as he was too large for the human to hold in his lap anymore. His human alpha's heart was racing, smelling of nerves and worry.

"Hey buddy, you okay? C'mon Ghost, wake up." Glen was speaking in his ear, leaning over him, and Ghost rolled his eyes up, meeting the human's. He saw concern and affection, and Ghost again marveled at the man who helped raise him, wondering how a human could be so accepting, so unafraid. Would he be so brave if he knew Ghost was wolfkin, a werewolf, and a boy long trapped by a magic he claimed too early? How could this mortal man be so accepting, so at peace with the unknown, when he and his mate spent all their lives living in a world run by the barren philosophy they called science?

Ghost moaned, and rolled to his stomach, Glen leaving a hand on his shoulder. He waited, and when the world didn't spin, he slowly stood. His legs held him, and he lifted his head, ears up, listening. His howl had been loud, and he knew full well that it could travel for miles before fading out. If there were wolves in Baxter, they may have heard him, and be on their way. He waited, but there was nothing but the sound of his humans and the snow falling.

"Back in the cabin, let's go. We're all feeling the stress of the last day. Food and sleep first, then we'll think about what's going on." Glen patted him on his back, and Ghost nodded, waiting for his humans to go first before following. He sent a quick look around the clearing in which the tiny cabin sat, a part of him expecting to see the glow of eyes in the shadows. He was haunted by memories, and he feared what would happen if he ever came across one of his own kind. Whether he would be welcomed, or hunted.

"DO YOU hear that?" Andromeda paused in pouring the tea, the kettle suspended over a fine porcelain cup. She faced the window, open despite the cold, and Kane and Burke turned to look as well. The cabin was huge, and the kitchen windows had a view to envy, the mountains covered in dark green pines and thick layers of snow. It was snowing now, and Kane heard the soft hissing noise that it made as it landed on the ground.

"What?" Kane listened, head tilted, but heard nothing but the snow and the gentle breeze. The cubs and their family were upstairs, where River, Sophia and Red Fern's resident betas were tending to them. He heard voices, but not the words, not wanting to intrude on the family's privacy. He looked to Burke, who shrugged, obviously not hearing anything.

Andromeda stared out the window, her eyes focusing in the far distance, her head moving slowly side to side as if trying to get an angle on a sound only she could hear. Kane listened again, and caught a sound so soft he thought he imagined it. It might have been a howl, either wolf or wind, but it was gone before he could be sure. It was lonely, that faint echo, and he rubbed a hand over his sternum as his heart ached. The wilder part of him wanted to go outside, and answer that lonely call. He shook his head, and dismissed it as wind through the mountains.

"Never mind, it was probably nothing." Andromeda went back to pouring the tea, and returned the kettle to the stovetop. She sat back down, and sipped, her pale eyes closing in appreciation.

She was much like her brother in appearance, for all that

they had different mothers. They shared a father, a shaman who was two centuries dead and gone, one of their races' longest lived wolves in history, who sired River the same year he died of extreme old age. Elder Stormcloud was his name, in a time when wolfkin had use names, and not the traditional names of the modern era. Legend had it he had been born in a storm, and hence his name. It apparently suited his temperament too, which he then gave to his daughter.

Andromeda was old, yet her age lay on her lithe form delicately, only evident in the serenity in her eyes and the way she moved. Young wolves moved like humans—the older the wolf, the more time spent in their wolf-forms, and the more they moved like the spirit side of their natures. Her hair was nearly white, with a golden sheen over it that flashed in the light, and she was fair, her eyes a light blue. She was grace personified, with a dangerous undertone to her movements that left Kane with the impression she should be armed with a spear or sword, and not a teacup. Her wit was as sharp as her fangs, and she routinely left lesser wolves feeling the sting of her words.

Humans would call her beautiful, by their measure of beauty, and she was stunning to wolfkin eyes, even his. He may prefer his own sex, but even he was swayed by her appeal, so magnetic was her presence. He didn't doubt she could have him if she ever made the effort, and he would let her, if she didn't leave him so terrified. She would not though, as he couldn't see her ever having to seduce another wolf. She had plenty of cubs, birthed over her long lifetime, so she lacked not for suitors. She was mate-less, but that hadn't stopped her from having children. She was a rarity among their kind, a female beta, unmated yet a mother, and a fully recognized Clan Leader. He would be willing to call her a female alpha, one of the mythical creatures from their histories, yet she ruled not out of possession of the gift of command or the Voice—she ruled by skill, love, and a ruthless personality that spared nothing when it came to the protection of her people. The gift of command was an old way of describing the mental dexterity of alphas that let them handle the multiple minds of a pack and their influence over those minds, and the charm they exuded to other wolves. Burke was a Speaker because of the exceptional depth and range of his gift of command. There was no sign of the Voice in her either, so she was pure beta, pure woman, and she was beloved of her people. Her wolves followed her out of respect and love.

And when she was in her wolf-form, there was no creature more beautiful, or deadly. She was the White Wolf, a living legend, a creature as sharp as arctic ice and just as pale, teeth as white as her fur, her eyes the eerie glow of glacial blue. Andromeda was fearsome as a woman, and terrifying as a wolf.

“Keep staring, pup, and I’ll send you out in the snow to fetch more firewood.”

Kane jumped, and gave her an apologetic smile. Burke snickered, but he shut up when she looked at him, one pale brow raised. It was rude to stare at another wolf; such a behavior often preceded a Challenge. He had no intention of Challenging Andromeda (he’d probably lose, she was scary, his possession of the Voice or not), and he sent his eyes back out the window.

“So Caius thinks they may be in danger, even after their removal from that hell house.” Not a question. Andromeda flicked a finger up to the second level, her eyes cool, her features impassive. There was no reading her. Kane withheld his smile at her audacity to call his Clan Alpha by name and not title. But then she was probably the only one left who could. According to legend, she grew up with him back in the Old World. Gray Shadow was another, but he was gone these fourteen and a half years.

“Yes, ma’am. That’s why he sent us along with them and River, to keep you all safe,” he said, drinking some of his tea when she leveled a glare at his untouched cup. It tasted like wintergreen candy and cinnamon, and he drank some more, letting it warm his bones. “Their captors may make a move on them, since they might be able to identify them.”

He may be a greater alpha, and Heir, but he had no power in this room. She may be a female and a beta, but Andromeda was pure authority. Red Fern had no alpha, lesser or greater, and she ruled it with complete and total dominance. Her wolves followed her without question, and while their numbers may be small compared to other clans, Red Fern had the longest ruling leader of any Clan in the North America, even beating out Caius for that honor. She had a generation on Caius, taking over after the death of Red Fern’s last alpha, centuries earlier. Red Fern was an anomalous Clan; they produced only betas and shamans. No alpha had been born in the Clan in over two hundred years.

She even had the distinction of defeating several alphas who had, over the years, foolishly attempted to usurp her place in the Clan and take over. After the last Challenge and the headless alpha she left on the killing grounds about fifty years earlier, Red Fern and its leader were left in peace. He would not antagonize their hosts and her wrath by acting the Heir. Red Fern may bow before Black Pine, but they were a power to be reckoned with, especially Andromeda. He knew who he was, and so did she, and Kane was content to follow her lead.

"There's been no activity here in Baxter. Some humans on cross country skiing trips, some hunters we reported to the human authorities, and a couple of wandering idiots. No camping is allowed here in the winter months, not that many humans think to do so, but we send out routine sweeps to make sure. As of yesterday, all outlying cabins were clear. I have a continuous watch on the entrances, and sentries are posted a mile outside all the gates so we have advance warning of approaching humans. The human authorities are aware we hold the park, so as to avoid any chaos akin to what happened here fifteen years ago." Andromeda paused, and sent him a quick look, one he thought might be tinged with something soft, caring. He blinked, and it was gone. "I thought it prudent to inform the park service here of our existence after the tragedy years ago. They know enough to stay away unless it's an incident involving only humans, then we bring them in."

She meant the attempted kidnapping and killing of the wolves here at the gathering, where Gray Shadow and his three grandchildren, along with his son's mate, all died. Kane still refused to count Luca among the dead, his heart refusing to believe it, even after all these years.

It was an attempt by a private corporation to kidnap shamans, and it took Caius making a few calls and killing Sebastien Remus, the human leader of the company, to avenge the loss. The human had been taken from his home in the night, and deposited at Caius' feet, and Kane remembered with a heavy heart full of fruitless rage and satisfaction as the man bled to death after his throat was torn out by the grieving Clan Leader.

The human governments of the world were aware that werewolves, the wolfkin, existed and guarded the information from the wider populations of humans just as the wolves did. It was a secret impossible to keep, considering modern day technology and the sheer number of wolves and humans. There was an uneasy stalemate across species' lines—the wolves left humans alone as much as possible, and the same for the humans. The few organizations that did know about the wolves were restricted to the upper reaches of power, and while the secret did get out occasionally, it was dealt with ruthlessly. As long as the governments of the world kept their hands off wolfkin, the wolves never turned on the humans in wholesale slaughter. The human numbers were great, and while they could do serious damage with their modern weapons and tactics, they lacked the power of the alphas, and the clans' greatest defense—the magic of shamans. Humans had no magic, and nothing in their sciences could counter the spirit-magic of the shamans.

Kane long theorized that it was the lure of the shamans' magic that led to the abduction attempts at the gathering, and they never learned who hired Remus Acquisitions to try it. Gray Shadow's parting words to Caius confirmed his suspicions. The trail died with Sebastien Remus, and the traitors in the wolves were unknown. In a gathering it wasn't unusual to have wolves present who weren't known to all, and there were hundreds of wolves at the gathering almost fifteen years before. The wolves they theorized were involved in the attempt were long gone, and were never tracked down. The scents were similar to the wolves involved with the new abductions taking place in the Northeastern States, and Kane wanted to know who was responsible for betraying their own kind, and to sink his teeth in their necks. His instincts were telling him the same traitors were responsible for all of it.

"Your measures are impressive. I'm going to focus on the lesser known ways to enter Baxter, and patrols. My team works well with strange wolves, but I think we know each other well enough to get along without issue." Kane nodded to her respectfully, and then he remembered the less pleasurable reason for his visit this afternoon.

"I sense a 'but' hovering on your tongue, youngling." She sat back in her seat, pale eyes locked on his, and Kane flushed. She unnerved him.

"My Clan Leader, in his infinite wisdom, seems to be under the assumption that I am a suitable role model for his son, Gerald," he said sarcastically, and he drained his cup. He avoided the glee shimmering in Burke's eyes. His lieutenant had yet to speak. Wise wolf indeed. "He is the newest member of my team. I am now babysitter to a bad-mannered wolf old enough to be my grandsire."

Andromeda didn't respond. Her eyes gave nothing away, her thoughts hidden, and he couldn't even get a measure of her emotions through scent, so controlled was she. He looked forlornly at his now empty cup, and he barely restrained himself from jumping when she stood, and returned with the kettle. She was barefoot on the cold hardwood floors, wrapped in a seamless dress that covered her head to toe in soft cotton, dove gray and thin. It moved about her like a cloud, responding to her movements as if caught in an unfelt wind, independent of her actions. It was strange, and distracting. She poured him a new cup, and sat back down.

"Gerald's mother died birthing him, did you know that?" she asked, out of nowhere. Kane lifted a brow in surprise, and he looked at Burke, who shook his head. She spoke on, as if she weren't expecting an answer. "It is not often a wolf dies during the birthing. Lillian, his mother, was not Caius' mate. They were a brief affair, and she decided to keep the cub when she discovered she was pregnant. She sent word to Caius, but he was involved in preparing the Clans' migration to the New World, and he never made it in time for the birth. She was wounded by a human, who had learned her secret, and she lasted long enough to birth her son. Caius tracked her blood trail for days, and when he found her, she was gone. Gerald was barely alive. If Gray Shadow hadn't been with Caius at the time, Gerald would have died as well."

Kane sat back in surprise. He never knew this. It wasn't unusual for wolves to be conceived outside of a mate bond, but for a single wolf mother to decide to have the resultant offspring was. Females had complete control over their reproductive cycles, so the decision on Gerald's mother's part to have him spoke of a stubborn will and a potentially lonely wolf. If she were bonded, the affair never would have happened, and most females waited until they were mated to have cubs. Gerald's mother must have dearly wanted him to let the pregnancy proceed. Andromeda had succeeded in raising her cubs independently of a mate by sheer force of will and her position as Clan Leader. The pressures of single motherhood were nothing compared to running a Clan, and she had numerous wolves supporting her.

"So there was Caius, unmated, his other children long grown, with a newborn whelp. He was neck deep in organizing the removal of the Clans under his control to the New World, a task that took all of his time and concentration. I saw little of him in the early days of his reign, though in hindsight, I wish I'd seen more. I was already leading Red Fern when Caius assumed control of Black Pine, and the early days were full of chaos and strife. If he had only come to me... perhaps things might be different. I would have helped him, but pride before the fall and all that. Hindsight, again." She paused, and ran a finger over the rim of her empty cup. "But he is not one to shirk a duty, and he named his new son, and took him home. There he gave Gerald over to a succession of beta nursemaids, who, because of the era he was born in, raised the cub as a little lordling. No humility or modesty or discipline was given to his upbringing, and Caius, while not a cold man, never invested more than a token affection or attention to his then youngest son. His other children at home at the time were the offspring of his first mate, and she had been much loved, and missed, and her children received the wolf's share of their father's time."

Kane said nothing. What could he say? He felt a shred of sympathy for the young Gerald, raised by an absentee father and nursemaids, and he must have been lonely. Andromeda gave him a faint smile, as if she knew where his thoughts were going.

"So Gerald grew to adulthood, spoiled rotten, utterly ignored by his father, and with underdeveloped alpha abilities that were as much a disappointment to him as to Caius. When it came time for the exodus, Gerald followed his father, ever hoping to prove his worth, and always falling short." Andromeda gave him a cool glance, and then looked out the window. "You, Kane, are much as I imagine what Caius hoped Gerald would become. If only Caius had taken the time to raise his own child... So perhaps, if you were to think past your own discomfort and wounded pride in being saddled with a malcontent wolf, you may see that you are exactly what Gerald needs? You joked about being a role model for him—perhaps that is exactly what you are meant to be."

She paused, and took a slow breath. "Babysitter? No. You are an alpha. Act like one."

Kane sat silent, stunned, head down, eyes locked on the table and his cup, the tea cold. Burke shifted in his seat, the wooden chair creaking, and he sensed the other alpha was just as uncomfortable as he. Andromeda always did this to him, left him feeling like a cub reprimanded for bad behavior. He wasn't mad, though. While he may not understand Caius' motivations to leave Gerald in his care, he would not shirk his duty. He would take it seriously, as he should have from the beginning. Bad attitude and poor manners aside, Gerald was a wolf of Black Pine, and Kane's responsibility. If the taming of Gerald was Caius' intent in sending him with Kane, then he would honor the task and do his best. If it wasn't Caius' intent—then Gerald was now his, and Kane would treat him as he deserved, as all of his wolves deserved. With respect and care.

"You are wiser than I, Andromeda." He meant it to be light, but he couldn't manage it. He never knew his own father, the alpha who sired him dying in a Challenge before he was born, and he couldn't imagine being raised by a man who never spared him a thought, duty always in the way.

"And don't you forget it." She stood, taking their cups, and put them in the sink. "Go—do what you must to secure the park and the wolves now in my care. You will find little to do, as I learned my lesson dearly when it comes to securing my territory." He knew she meant the day Gray Shadow died. "Rest, run, hunt. Relax." She waved an elegant hand at the door, and Kane understood they were being dismissed. "Keep an eye on your wayward charge, or he will suffer my teeth. It won't be the first time that I've had to put Gerald, son of Caius, in his place, and it would be better if I didn't have to do it again. He may not live to benefit from your influence if that happens."

They stood, and left quietly as she made her way to the stairs, where above them her brother tended to the Suarez wolves. His last glimpse of Andromeda, First Beta and Clan Leader of Red Fern, was the swift motion of her ageless body as she took the stairs, so fast his eyes saw naught but a gray and white blur.

"WHAT WE know is simple, I'm thinking. One—Ghost is not a regular wolf. Sentient and fully aware." Cat was in front of the table, where Glen was sitting, Ghost underneath. She paced back and forth, hands flying as she spoke. "Two—Apparently me sending the DNA samples to the other lab sent those men after Ghost, so that means other people out there know about his species, and are willing to kill to get ahold of them. Three—Ghost can do.... well... okay, he can do magic."

She said that last part as if she were expecting to be laughed at, and Ghost thumped his tail on the floor, agreeing with every point she made. She was smart, and while she wasn't handling things as easily as Glen seemed to be, she was brave and resilient. Cat sent him a smile as she grabbed a large roll of paper from the table, and some empty mugs from the cabinets.

"Because we don't really know what is going on, I thought of a way to talk. Crude, but hopefully effective." Cat kneeled on the floor, unraveling a large sheet of white paper. She braced the corners with mugs, got up, waving at him to come out from under the table. He left the shadows and joined her.

There were three words on the paper in large letters, and he could read well enough to recognize them as 'yes, no and maybe'. He grinned, a predatory smile full of teeth and appreciation. She was very smart, his human.

"Okay, Ghost. We're gonna ask you some very simple questions, and you put a paw on your answer. You know what those words are?" She asked him, and he nodded, getting excited, tail wagging like a dog's.

"Do you know who is hunting you?" Cat asked first, looking as excited as he was.

He wasted no time in putting his paw on the 'no.' She had a notepad in her hand, and he never wanted to laugh as much as he did in that moment as she dutifully recorded his answer.

"Are you a species unknown to science?"

He had no idea what that meant, so he put a paw on 'maybe'. Again, she marked his reply.

"Are there more of you?"

A paw on 'yes'.

"Do you have a family?"

He didn't know if they survived the ambush at the gates, but he hoped they did, so he put a paw on 'yes' again.

"Can you do magic?"

A very happy and firm paw to 'yes'. She bit her lip, and marked his reply carefully, as if his answer was more unsettling than the fact she was having an intelligent conversation with a giant wolf that three days before she thought was just an animal.

"Are they after you because you can do magic?" That was Glen, finally asking a question. Cat glared at him for interrupting, but she wrote down the question and looked at him for his reply. He wasn't sure; how could he be? So a paw went to 'maybe', as close to saying 'I don't know' as he could get.

"They called you a 'shaman'. Is that what you are?"

Paw, with pride, to 'yes'.

"That morning we found you by the river, were you lost?" Cat asked him, pencil raised over the paper. She wasn't looking at him, but the paper on the floor, and he smelled a faint hint of sadness coming from her. It intensified when he put his paw on 'yes'.

"Do you.... Do you think your family was looking for you?"

It wasn't in him to lie, to tell an untruth, yet part of him wished he could. The sadness that came to her eyes was painful when he put his paw on 'yes'.

He knew Kane was searching for him that morning, his grandfather told him so before he died. If they hadn't taken him, he did not doubt that Kane would have found him. And if he hadn't, Ghost would have followed the river home, no matter his grandfather's orders to stay hidden. It was more of a hope, really, thinking of Kane finding him; he remembered the alpha with the kind eyes and the shy smile, and the monstrous wolf-form that fought to save him and his grandfather beside the river.

Tears gathered in her eyes, but didn't fall. She sniffled, and went to the next question. Or she tried, but she choked up, and put a hand over her mouth. She turned her back, shoulders hunching, and she sniffled again. He whined, distressed that she was sad. He couldn't do anything to take her pain, he couldn't hug her as Glen often did. His human alpha got up, and moved around Ghost and the talking paper on the floor, and hugged his mate.

Glen looked down at him, eyes just as sad, but glinting with a strength Ghost responded to, easing his guilt at his mate's tears. Cat cried on his chest, and Glen took over asking questions. "Are there wolves like you here in Baxter?"

He wasn't sure, but he thought there might be. Wolfkin never abandoned territory once claimed, he recalled that much. A hopeful paw to 'yes.'

"Are they friendly?"

Humans and wolfkin did not mix well. He had a feeling their situation was not normal. A paw to 'maybe'. He stared at Glen, willing the human to be cautious, to understand. He didn't want his humans hurt by his kin, but they might be if he wasn't around and they came across the humans. Glen nodded, as if he understood the danger, and Ghost hoped he did.

"Do you want to find them? Your people?"

He slapped his paw over 'yes' so many times his claws slashed the paper.

TO BE AN ALPHA

"BURKE, TAKE Sophia and some betas out, patrol the outlying borders and along the river," Kane told his lieutenant, as he zipped up his leather jacket, standing at the door of their shared cabin. It was actually the same one they'd shared fifteen years earlier, and Kane was trying not to let the memories get to him. He was thankful that the Suarez wolves were awake, and he planned on speaking to the adults as soon as he could. He should be out there patrolling as well, but he couldn't bear the thought of going near the river.

Burke gave him a nod, and a small smile. Kane tried to hide how he was feeling, but the night before had been long and lonely, and he fought tooth and nail with the urge to Change and run along the river, looking even after all these years for a long lost cub. It was a foolish desire, and he ruthlessly battered it down, refusing to give in to the guilt and weight of failure.

Luca was gone, no matter what his heart said. No matter how strongly his whole body yearned to run out there, every instinct screaming at him that Luca lived and was waiting for him...he restrained himself. He struggled to fight back the pain, the hole in his heart a screaming void of guilt and grief, and he feared it would never go away.

Suddenly, he was engulfed in a hug, Burke pressing his face in his neck, long arms holding him tightly. There was nothing sexual in the embrace, and he stood frozen for a second before he let himself hug Burke back. Best friend he was, before any other role. Alpha, lieutenant, Speaker—Burke was his best friend, and he loved him. And he knew that Burke loved him back. Burke had been by his side since the day Kane arrived in Augusta, the slightly older youth looking out for the lonely Heir, and forging a friendship that neither man could do without.

“Never doubt yourself. Please. I feel your guilt, your pain. You did not fail them. You did not fail Luca,” Burke whispered in his ear, and Kane buried his head in Burke’s shoulder, tears welling up unbidden. “His death is not your fault.”

“Why does it hurt so much? I barely knew the cub. He’s dead, he must be, but it hurts, as if he’s waiting for me to save him, and I just gave up on him,” Kane bit back a sob, clutching Burke as tightly as he could, the other wolf’s warmth suddenly essential to his survival. He missed touch, he missed the connection of flesh to flesh, and it bothered him again that he couldn’t think of another wolf sexually at all. He hadn’t even hugged anyone in years. The most contact he’d had was the occasional brush of his hand on Burke’s shoulder or arm, or a few handshakes or nose touches with clan mates. Impersonal touches, or slightly friendly. Burke was the only one who he felt comfortable touching, but even then those were fleeting moments.

Was he broken? Did his guilt cripple him, leave him impotent?

"It hurts because you are a good man, and good men never forget," Burke said softly, nudging his nose into the hair behind Kane's ear, a move so similar to what they'd do in wolf-form that Kane felt the pain all the sharper. Burke's big hands rubbed over his shoulders, soothing. He dragged in a deep breath, and held it, eyes tightly shut, and he let his last tears fall. No more tears. Coming back here to Baxter was almost more than he could handle, and he couldn't do his job and protect the wolves in his charge if he was constantly swamped by memories of his failure.

They stood like that for a while, and Kane absorbed the comfort his friend gave him. Burke's mind was a glittering presence that hovered at the edge of his perception, the other alpha remaining distant mentally to give him some semblance of privacy, even as they held each other.

"Better now?" Burke asked, as his tears dried, his breathing evened out.

"Yes. Thank you, brother." Kane lifted his head, and clasped Burke's face in gratitude, kissing his forehead before pulling away. "Sometimes you leave me wondering why I'm Heir, and you are not. You're far wiser than I, Burke."

Burke's arms fell away, and he gave Kane a smile that was both sweet and cocky.

"I wonder that all the time, whelp," Burke teased, gently shoving him with one arm.

"Whelp? You're like five minutes older than me, don't even start."

"Five years, not five minutes. Still too young to tell time correctly, I see."

"Be gone with you, insubordinate mongrel!" Kane laughed, and pushed Burke ahead of him out the door, where his friend promptly began to strip. Sophia was waiting out front in her wolf-form, a dark brown and black shadow that somehow blended in with the snow, despite the contrast. She was small, but compactly built with powerful muscles, and she very politely turned her head as Burke knelt in the snow outside the cabin to Change.

Kane walked on, averting his eyes as well, as Burke transformed from a tall, lean man with dark hair and light golden-brown eyes to a large chocolate-brown wolf with a deep, thick coat and brilliantly white teeth. Burke brushed past him as he sprinted to join Sophia where she waited patiently, pausing for half a second to let Kane run his fingers through the guard hairs along his back.

"Please keep me in the loop while you're out there," Kane told them, tapping his temple, meaning the mental pack lines, "I don't want to lose any more wolves to our mystery enemies."

Burke yipped in agreement, and he and Sophia took off down the path, towards the other cabins where the rest of the Black Pine wolves were bunking. Kane watched them go, and then turned his feet towards the big cabin at the top of the path. His boots slid in the melting snow and ice on the pathway, and he wondered if he shouldn't Change as well, four paws having better traction in the current conditions than booted human feet. He dismissed the inclination, as his wolf-form was very large, and he didn't want to intimidate the Suarez wolves. They were in a delicate place mentally and emotionally, and Andromeda's mental call to him this morning was laden with an unspoken warning to be careful with their guests.

He passed the council house, the large stone and wood building locked up until this summer's gathering. A memory came upon him, fast. Kane sat again in that building, surrounded by cubs, as one in particular flirted with him, all sweet giggles and smart answers. He paused briefly, eyeing the structure, memories threatening to again overwhelm. He was prepared for it this time, and pushed the grief away. He took to the path again, resisting the urge to look back.

Kane knocked on the front door of Andromeda's cabin, and it was opened by a young female, her light blue eyes and blonde hair proclaiming her to be one of the Clan Leader's descendants. She was clad in a dress identical to the one Andromeda had worn the day before, only lighter in color. She looked too young to be a daughter, so she must be a grandchild, or even a great-granddaughter.

"Greetings, child. I am Kane of Black Pine. May I come in?" he asked politely, smiling. He didn't want to intimidate her, and she blushed prettily at him in return. His smile grew, as she plainly was not afraid of him, her blue eyes twinkling.

"Let him in, Helen," Andromeda called down from where she was standing on the landing between the first and second floors. The young beta ducked her head, and opened the door wider, gesturing for him to enter with a slim hand. She was small, and so similar to her ancestress that Kane couldn't help but nod back, enchanted. Again with the blush, and a giggle.

Young Helen shut the door, and he took off his jacket, which she took without a word. Andromeda watched, her keen eyes tracking him as he smiled at the little one in thanks before heading for the stairs. He heard another giggle, and caught a glimpse of the young one darting off towards the kitchen. He looked back up at Andromeda as he climbed the stairs, and swallowed nervously at her stern expression.

"Don't make her fall in love with you, youngling. Your smiles are potent. If I didn't already know you preferred males, I'd box your ears." He stopped a couple of steps away, and found he was at a loss for words. He couldn't help it; wolves either gravitated to him, or stayed away. There was no in between, the power and allure of an alpha both blessing and curse. He probably shouldn't have smiled at her so much, though, feeling a little bit guilty.

"My apologies, Andromeda. She is beautiful, like her ancestress." Charm never hurt, and he had plenty when he wanted to use it. He meant his apology, since first loves were always painful, and he didn't want to make anyone's life harder. He had no inclination to be someone's unrequited love interest.

She snorted lightly, but her cheeks tinged with pink at the compliment. "Obvious that she's one of mine, isn't it? Father's blood breeds true, even generations later."

She gestured for Kane to follow, and she led him up the stairs to the second floor. She was wearing a dress again, the same type as the day before, barefoot and elegant. She turned down one of the halls that branched off the top landing, heading towards the back of the large cabin.

"Daughter?" Kane asked politely, hoping flattery would further soften the older wolf. She gave him a small smile, seeing right through him, but she answered anyway.

"Helen is the youngest of my great-great-grandchildren. She is fifteen years old, a newborn the last time you were here in Baxter. She found her wolf-form about a month ago, and did it seamlessly." He followed quietly behind her, hands clasped behind his back, head down, doing to his best to keep her talking, sharing. Wolves loved to talk of their children, and Andromeda was no exception. To mention that her descendent found her wolf-form with ease was a major point of pride in her lineage; most cubs found their wolf-forms through a painful, messy ordeal that lasted for hours, even days if an alpha couldn't be found with the Voice to force the process along. "Her mother let me name her, and she was the most beautiful baby I had ever seen when she was born, so Helen was appropriate."

He raised a brow at her in question, and she smiled ruefully, shaking her head as they neared the end of the hall and the last door. "I named her for Helen of Troy, youngling. Caius has much to answer for at the apparent holes in your education."

He grinned at her, thinking she might be right, and she opened the door. If it wasn't wolfkin history, he had little experience with it. The scent of fear swamped him, and he stepped back, instinctively looking for the threat that warranted such alarm from the wolves in the room. His eyes took in the two wolves present, neither of them the cubs. A young male, about twenty years of age, and grown female, who could be an older sister or his mother. They were both dark-haired, with golden skin and bright green eyes. They looked like Heromindes, and the Alpha's quick agreement with the plan to get the Suarez wolves out of Worcester to a safer location made a lot more sense. They must be blood-kin.

He saw nothing in the room to warrant their fear, which held a few couches and chairs, a sitting room of some kind that opened up to a balcony that overlooked the same view the kitchen had downstairs, just better. The smell of fear was coming from the Suarez wolves, and the young male stood in front of the female, hands clenched at his sides, eyes glowing as his wilder nature neared the surface. It was the reaction of a wounded beast, and Kane held still, not entering the room.

This was the young alpha, the only alpha of the Suarez wolves to be recovered from the apartment complex. The other alphas, his father and uncles, were missing still. He was covered with bruises and healing cuts, evidence of a severe beating on his lanky body, still thin and with the angles of youth. This young one was too young for Kane to sense if he were a lesser or greater alpha, his abilities not yet fully matured. He was brave, to face down an older, bigger alpha, and Kane met his eyes, unblinking. He would not harm this young one, but he would not tolerate defiance, either. The young alpha must accept that Kane meant them no harm, and then they could begin. He stepped over the threshold, Andromeda moving away, standing against the back wall, waiting. She would not interfere, understanding what Kane must do.

The young alpha growled softly, nervous, fists growing claws, and the female he blocked from Kane's view put a hand on his arm, as if trying to soothe or restrain. Kane took another step, and again, calm, relaxed, showing he was not affected by the aggression from the smaller male. He was over a foot taller, and looked down at the glowing green eyes that held more fear than fight. This wolf was wounded, hurt in ways that Kane saw as shadows hidden deep in the green orbs. He saw a shattered innocence that made him angry, angrier than he'd been in a long time, but he held it back, not letting on he was anything but in control. He could sense the pain and misery under the bravado, and he remained impassive, waiting, his heart breaking. He would not show it, not yet. This wolf needed strength from another alpha, from a power outside of himself. He was lost in his fear and agony, without anchor.

Kane knew he won the brief battle of wills when the young alpha's eyes filled with tears, the glow fading. His chin ducked down, his bangs hiding his face, and his shoulders drooped in defeat. Kane sighed, and slowly lifted his right hand, moving carefully, so as not to startle the other wolfkin. He brushed away a stray tear that glistened on a bruised cheekbone, being careful not to hurt. He ran his fingers through the youngling's long black hair, firmly gripping, and tugged him forward. There was no fight in him, and the younger alpha launched himself at Kane's chest, sobbing. Kane wrapped both arms around the shaking boy, and let him cry. This was a morning for tears, it seemed, and Kane fought back his own. This was release for the boy, one Kane suspected would be the first of many tearful episodes to come.

BURKE TRAILED after Sophia, her paws splayed wide as she ran over the snow, kicking it up behind her as she followed a thin game trail through the trees. Her size let her move faster over the recent accumulation, and she had several strides on him. Burke was bigger, and heavier, and he had to work harder to keep up in the wet, dense snow cover. She wasn't that far ahead of him, and the others were farther behind Burke. They didn't let the distance get too great, mindful of the safety in numbers, and Kane's edict.

He felt Kane in the back of his mind, not deep enough to speak, but there in case of need. Kane was always there, and Burke was glad for it. The other alpha was the only one Burke was comfortable letting in on such an intimate level, and Kane was the wolf to have on standby if something happened. Burke wasn't expecting this patrol to turn up anything, as the lady Andromeda and her Red Fern wolves were serious about protecting their territory. Several of her wolves were patrolling the other borders of the park, and he had very politely initiated a discreet mental link to the betas in charge, keeping tabs on their progress so he would know if they came across anything worth noting.

I'm not a fan of snow, but it is gorgeous here, don't you think? Sophia whispered to him, sending him a sly look over her shoulder before she took a hairpin turn around a fallen tree, heading downhill towards the river.

They were heading for the place where the river entered the park, a span of narrow valleys and hidden clearings, and several older cabins used by hunters during the appropriate season. No hunting was allowed in the interior of the park, attributed to the cabins and the humans' laws pertaining to firing a weapon near places other humans dwelled, but it happened on occasion that hunters broke that rule, and wandered deeper into the park. Andromeda had said the outlying cabins were clear, but that was two days ago, and humans were known to break their laws often, and without remorse, so the empty cabins could become occupied anytime.

Snow doesn't bother me. We live in Maine after all, it would be horrible if I did. Burke replied, and he put on a burst of speed, the cold air making his teeth ache as he breathed fast, coming abreast of her hindquarters as she slowed her pace. They were near the river. Burke heard the rushing waters that even February temperatures couldn't freeze, and the smell of small creatures taking advantage of the free-flowing water. Squirrels, rabbits, and somewhere nearby, some muskrats. They were chewy and smelled like wet grass, and Burke's stomach rumbled as he and Sophia cleared the trees, coming out onto the bank of the river where it flattened out into a snow covered rocky beach.

Think we can take the time to get a snack? Sophia must

have heard his stomach complain, and he gave her a toothy grin as she sent him an image of a large muskrat with hunger undertones. The other wolves soon joined them, a handful of mixed company, two Red Fern and two Black Pine betas. Burke sent them a wordless message to rest but stay alert, and sniff out some river rats if they were hungry.

Tiny prints in the snow revealed the constant traffic of other animals, and Burke trailed with his nose to the ground, following the nutty and warm scent of a very large squirrel back towards the trees. Sophia was doing the same a few feet away, heading further upstream. He heard a squeak and the snap of powerful jaws a second later, and he looked up to see Sophia settle down to eat a brown rodent. She sent him a wink, a hilarious and difficult action in wolf-form, and he grumbled back, nose to the ground as he sought out his own snack.

GHOST WATCHED as Glen cleaned his gun, the weapon broken down on the kitchen table. He sneezed as the scent of the chemical cleaner crept into his nose again.

Cat was sitting beside the hearth, a fire burning in the grate, her laptop on her knees. She had something she called a satellite link, and was doing research. Glen wanted her to check police reports for any news about the sanctuary, and both humans got extremely worried when she hadn't found anything. That sounded weird even to Ghost, since humans made a big deal about other humans killing each other, and two men were dead. All Glen said was for Cat to keep checking, and Ghost paced.

He sighed, bored, and nervous, wondering why he was in the cabin when his people could be just outside of reach, and all he needed was to run out there and look. He glanced again to the door, latched and locked, the snow falling in sporadic bursts visible through the windows. He was terrified, and he didn't know why. The night before he thought he heard howling, a distant chorus of many voices that rose toward the cloud cover. He hadn't left the cabin, shaking on the floor beside the bed where his humans slept. The cries never sounded again, and he went back to sleep, ears pointing towards the door, almost willing to hear them call out again.

Finally the odor got to be too much, and Ghost sneezed again, shaking out his coat. Glen sent him a sympathetic smile, which quickly turned to alarm as Ghost padded over to the door.

"Whoa buddy, where do you think you're going?" Glen called out, standing up, pieces of his weapon in hand.

Ghost snorted at the implication he couldn't take care of himself, and looked at the door. The lock clicked open and the handle turned, and Cat gave a little gasp as the door swung in, snowflakes finding entrance on the breeze. Ghost hadn't touched a thing to open it, and he walked out on the porch.

"Guess we know how he opened doors the last few years...." he heard Glen murmur before his attention was captured by the view outside the cabin.

The snow wasn't really falling so much as misting about; buffeted by the wind running through the trees. He snorted, clearing his nose of the harsh chemical, and breathed deep. Clean air, snow, and pine sap invigorated him. His humans came to the doorway behind him, and he looked at them over his shoulder. He whined, and shifted on his feet. He wanted to go, but he wanted to stay. He was torn, and he didn't know what to do.

He yelped when a boot landed on his rear, pushing him off the porch and out into the snow. He spun, growling, and sniffed in disdain when he saw the grin lighting up Glen's face. He wasn't hurt, and Cat was laughing quietly.

"Go on. I'm surprised you lasted this long without traipsing out there looking for your family." Glen waved out towards the mountains, making shooing motions with his hands. "Go on! We'll be fine here, we're not going anywhere. I've got my gun, and we won't leave the cabin. Go see if your people are here, and if they're friendly, bring them back for a visit."

Ghost wagged his tail once, surprised. Cat was nodding, albeit nervously, but his human alpha didn't look concerned at all. And he didn't know what his reception would be, much less how his people might react to him claiming the humans as his packmates.

"Go on, Ghost," Cat sniffled, but she held back her tears. "Just come back."

He whined gently, agreeing. He would come back for his

humans. They were the only family he had, regardless of who may be out there among the trees.

Ghost went, choosing a direction randomly. He didn't hear the door shut as he went, and he could feel his humans watching him as he entered the forest.

"I WAS AT school, Sir. I don't remember seeing them, the strange wolves, before they came for us that night," the young alpha, who went by Gabe, told him as they sat around the coffee table in Andromeda's sitting room. Coffee and tea and platters of what remained of their brunch covered the low oak table, and Andromeda had left them a while ago, after making certain Kane and the Suarez wolves would be all right alone.

Kane was sitting in an armchair, across from Gabe and the female who had indeed turned out to be his mother. She held her son's hand, not speaking, seeming to receive just as much comfort from his hand as he did hers. Kane hadn't pressed her for her name, as she was obviously frightened of him, not attempting eye contact or even looking at him, which was worrisome after he let her son cry on his chest for nearly an hour. He didn't push though, knowing she was wounded by her ordeal as well, and he let her be. It turned out that the other youngsters they'd rescued in Worcester were still too traumatized to talk to Kane, and River was adamant they experience zero stress, so that just left Gabe and his mother.

The young alpha had pulled himself together fairly quickly after his tears dried, and was willing to talk to Kane, sharing what he remembered of their abduction.

"You never saw the wolves who took you? Who reported them to the Ashland Alpha?" Kane leaned forward, hands on his knees. The female shrunk back, but the young male was no longer afraid of him, and remained still. Gabe shook his head regretfully, and sighed.

"Sir that would be my father and my uncles. I was at school in Boston, and I came home the night before we were all taken because my dad asked me to come back," Gabe explained, biting his lower lip, eyes haunted. "He was certain we were about to be Challenged for our territory, and he wanted everyone home in case the strangers made a move on us."

"They did, in a way. They just wanted your family, not the territory. Tell me about the night they took you."

Gabe drew in a deep breath, both his hands now holding his mother's, and he looked down at his lap. His mother gripped their fingers tighter, and he set his shoulders, sitting up straight. Kane gave him a nod of approval, and the younger alpha spoke.

"My dad, my two uncles and most of my cousins were all at our place, discussing what we were going to do about the strange wolves. We'd reported the interlopers to our distant cousin, the Clan Leader of Ashland, and he was sending wolves to help us deal with them." Kane nodded, his guess that Heromindes was related to the Suarez wolves confirmed.

Gabe drew another breath, and continued. “It was after supper, and we were in the TV room. It’s the largest room in the house, with big windows facing the street. We had just finished talking, and getting ready to watch a movie.... when....” Another breath, and he went on... “When the windows shattered, and these big metal objects landed in the room. We all jumped up, thinking it was humans vandalizing, but then the metal things exploded.”

Gabe visibly had to collect himself, tears pooling in his expressive eyes, mouth tightened by fear and remembered pain. His mother was completely withdrawn, almost hiding behind her son, her face buried in the back of his shoulder. She was young to be a mother, and she looked no older than her son. It was becoming very apparent that she was with her son not for his sake, but hers, and he was meeting with Kane with his mother present only because she couldn’t function without him with her. His heart broke for her, and he prayed that her mate, the boy’s father, was still alive. He and his two brothers, the older alphas of the Suarez family, were not among those recovered by Kane and his team.

“Take your time. You’re safe here, I promise.”

“It must have been silver in the canisters, Sir. My eyes and nose burned, and when I breathed it in, I thought I was breathing in fire, or acid, it hurt so badly. I tried to Change, but got caught partway, and I couldn’t walk. It was like learning to find my wolf for the first time, everything happening out of order, and it hurt.” Kane nodded, easily seeing the scene the younger man described. They had found traces of a silver-based aerosol chemical in the houses belonging to the Suarez wolves, and it would inhibit the Change if applied in large enough doses. “Everyone was screaming, I could hear my father howling, and sounds of a fight. I think my dad managed to Change all the way, and he was fighting whoever was attacking us.”

“What happened after that?” Kane was trying not to rush him. The boy was the most stable of the wolves recovered, and even then he had to be careful, as his ordeal had been horrific, and he didn’t want Gabe withdrawing like his mother.

“I passed out, Sir. I don’t know. I woke up...I woke up in that dingy apartment, naked and tied up with metal wires that burned my skin.” Gabe looked like he was about to vomit, swallowing fast and literally paling to corpse-white in front on Kane’s eyes. “Then....there were humans....”

Whatever he was thinking was enough to make him panic, and Kane leaned forward, across the table. He put a large hand on the youth’s shoulder, reached out with his mind, using the gift of command to pull the youngling out of his fear. He caught Gabe’s mind and pulled it to his own, pushing back the distress, and instantly stopping the panic attack the youth was about to have. Here he left the gift of command behind, and summoned the Voice, carefully unfolding the slumbering power from the depths of his own mind. He must tread lightly, and with extreme care.

Usually he would not be so callous with the mind of such a battered wolf, but Gabe’s reaction to his mind was instantaneous, his gratitude swamping Kane for a second before he put up a wall between their emotions. Kane raised the wall, a mental buffer between the boy's memories and his emotional and physical reaction to them, and Gabe's mind clung to his. Kane's mind was ordered, and calm, his emotions separate from his thoughts, and Gabe surrendered his mind, letting Kane handle the hard part of thinking and feeling at the same time.

You need not speak of what happened. I was there when we found you, I saw what they did to you. With your permission, I can see all that you remember, so you do not have to relive it by telling me.

Gabe's reply was swift and relieved, wordlessly pleading for Kane to spare him the task of recalling his abuse. Kane held his eyes, and the boy let go. Kane caught his mind, holding him, submerging his conscious mind, placing him in a state humans would call catatonic. Kane was able to physically let go of the boy at this point, and sat back in his chair. Gabe was staring, eyes blind, not even blinking, chest rising and falling evenly, slowly. His mother was staring at Kane in shock, and some rising alarm, but there was motion off to the side, a pale blur that materialized into a slim hand that landed gently on her shoulder.

"Your son is fine, Alpha Kane is helping him." Shaman River stood behind his sister Andromeda, as she comforted the female beta. "Come, leave them alone for a bit. Shaman River will stay here with them."

Andromeda patiently pried the female from her unresponsive son, and Kane gave her a nod of thanks as River walked around the chairs, standing at Kane's shoulder. The two females left the room, and the door shut behind them.

"You have taken over his mind." A statement, not a question. "You've extended the Voice past the influential stage to that part of it that lets you manipulate another wolf's thought patterns."

"Yes, I have." Kane was thankful there was no judgment in River's voice, only a calm professional curiosity and interest. "I'm not hurting him."

"I would not let you continue if I thought you were." Kane believed River could stop him, if he suspected Kane was hurting the boy, and he was very glad that it was River here, and not some stranger. It may have been fifteen years since Kane saw River last, but they all lived very long lives, and fifteen years was nothing between wolfkin. River was no stranger to object to Kane using his ability, the coveted Voice, in such a way. He appreciated the trust, and turned his mind back to the boy.

Kane sorted through the boy's memories, cringing mentally as he saw the rape of the boy, and his family, over the course of several days. Beatings and drugging and assault after assault, and he felt the boy's misery, his despair, and the wish for him to die, as a means to escape. Kane paused, seeing the buried desire the boy hid, even from himself, along with the shame of having been used so brutally. It was not his fault, but even the strongest of wolves could break under such conditions. Kane paused in his perusal of the boy's memories, and extended a mental line to River, inviting him in to see.

River hesitated, as this skated the edge of moral behavior. River was a shaman though, and the boy's injuries weren't just to his body, but to his heart, his mind, his soul. Kane was no shaman to help heal such wounds, and the hint he gave River of the boy's mental state would help the shaman heal the boy in the months to come. River took a lightning fast look at the glimpse Kane gave him, before withdrawing. He heard River sigh softly where he stood at his shoulder, full of sadness and compassion. River would have a surer idea of what he was dealing with now.

Kane finished examining the boy's memories, feeling sick to his core at what he'd experienced there. He batted away the feeling, not wanting to leave a hint of his own emotions behind for the boy to deal with on top of his own. Kane focused, narrowing down his view, and put an inaudible directive deep in the boy's psyche. Every time he started to become overwhelmed by his memories, Gabe would find the strength Kane left him. Faith in himself and his ability to heal, and belief that he could lead a life free of pain and fear.

Kane would not take his memories, as it was not his place to alter the boy to such a degree. Leaving the mental reinforcement behind was as much as he was willing to change without affecting free will.

Kane withdrew, sending the boy to sleep before leaving completely, and he slumped back on the couch, going limp. He would sleep for a short while and wake, fully aware of Kane's actions. If he had complaint, then Kane would remove the directive, even though it was more emotional bulwark than a controlling influence. He doubted the cub would ask that of him. River went to his side and put a hand on his forehead, eyes shutting as he used his healing ability to see to the boy's state. He dropped his hand away after a moment, and looked at Kane.

"Well done, youngling. I have not seen such a use of the Voice before. Usually alphas use it for less delicate things, for far more selfish reasons." Kane flushed at River's praise, and slowly stood. He hadn't seen any wolves in the boy's memories, only the humans that Kane and Sophia killed as they took the complex. The two surviving humans were soon to be delivered to Alpha Caius, and he would have to trust that his Clan Leader would learn who the traitors were through the prisoners. "If the Mother of us all had made you a shaman, you would have handled that life well."

"I need to check in with my wolves," Kane said, uncomfortable with the praise. It was his duty to help the wolves under his care, and what good was the Voice if he couldn't use it to take care of them? He wanted no part in spreading his dominion or wresting control from perfectly capable clan leaders, and this was a far better way to use the coveted Voice than taking lives and ruining other wolves.

River waved a hand at him, dismissing him from the room. It was so like Andromeda doing the same that Kane cracked a smile. He walked out of the room, closing the door on the sight of the shaman covering the young alpha with a blanket.

LEARNING A NEW PATH

GHOST STOPPED on a small rise, lifting his head to the breeze, and tasted the scents it brought him. He smelled the ever-present pine trees, and a small herd of deer to the north. Somewhere to the south and east was the smell of silt and mud, and damp earth, which must be the river. His heart stuttered at the thought of coming across the river that changed his life, and he pushed aside that worry. It was just water, nothing else.

His stomach rumbled, and he thought briefly about hunting for his midday meal, but he was in unknown territory and the scent of blood would be a strong signal to any and all predators that he was there. Thinking of scent made him nervous, and he looked back the way he had come, his tracks the only blemish in the otherwise pristine snow.

If anyone crosses my trail, they can follow my scent and tracks back to the cabin, he thought, glaring at his tracks in frustration. Most predators tracked by scent, but wolves went by sight, then scent and sound. Add in the sentient thought process of the wolfkin, and he was leading any potential wolfkin in the area straight back to his humans.

Ghost sat down, and stared back at his tracks in consternation. He wanted to go deeper into the park, but the farther he went, the likelier the chance of someone coming across his tracks. Any wolfkin here would know their territory, and could probably guess the location of the cabin based on the direction of the tracks. Ghost was risking his humans with every step. He thought about going back, but the tracks would remain, and he glared at them, highly frustrated.

The wind moved, subtle, across his muzzle. He was too busy thinking about what to do, whether to go back or onwards, that it took a strange hissing for him to notice what was happening. His tracks came up the small hill in a straight line, showing that a large animal at a fast trot had come through, but he blinked as he had trouble seeing them. When his eyes opened, shorter than a second closed, his double-vison was back. The snow glowed, shining like silver dust, and his tracks were a dull blight on the frozen expanse. Or they were, as the breeze he finally noticed blowing past his nose was rushing over the snow, lifting the fine top layer, and imprints made by his paws. He blinked, and shifted nervously on his haunches, the breeze started to die out, pausing with the tracks partially filled. He stumbled mentally, and finally grasped what part of his brain was sending out the instructions to the wind. It was like telling his tail to stop wagging when he hadn't told it to start, his body reacting instinctively to his moods and subconscious thoughts.

It took him a moment, but he resumed the wind's work, and the tracks filled, for as far as he could see. He was out of sight of the cabin, so he didn't know if this was erasing all his tracks, but he was erasing a large swath of them, so he'd have to trust that this would be enough. He let the wind die out, and shook his head, feeling tired suddenly. His stomach complained again, cramping slightly, and he whined even as he dropped his nose to the ground. He scented deeply, and could only smell the snow and the frozen ground underneath.

I erased my tracks and scent. I wasn't even trying!

He stood, tail wagging, excited. He could now search the park, and not risk his humans. It didn't make them totally safe, as wolves patrolled their territory regularly, but this was something he could do to keep them as safe as possible. He didn't want to put Glen or Cat in a dangerous situation, and he didn't want Glen shooting one of his kin. It might not do major damage, but Glen would shoot to kill if it meant protecting his mate.

He turned back to the park, the double-vision still in place, yet not as strong as a few moments prior. He saw dull glows in the trees, and from under the snow, but with the sun shining through the branches to the ground, the lights weren't as bright as they could be, not as distracting. A tiny glittering dart crossed the periphery of his vision, and he turned his head to see what it was. At first he saw nothing, but the sing-song call of *chicka-dee-dee-dee* settled his nerves. The tiny black and white bird trilled its call again, and he could see the infinitesimal spark of light from its tiny internal star shining through its feathers as it sang above him in the trees. It was a familiar song, and he wished again he could regain his human form, mentally feeling the desire to smile. The tiny life above him was enough to banish some of his loneliness, and he listened until the singer flew away.

Pleased, Ghost dipped his head, finding comfort in the sounds of the forest around him. He pulled at the double-vision, increasing the glows, backing off when it got to be too much. He found a comfortable balance, and realized just as it showed him what he assumed were living creatures, he could also see past the trees and brush. If he came across his kind, he might have warning, giving him far more options than relying on just his normal senses. Considering the constant swirling of the wind, that was a big advantage.

Now where to go? Deeper towards the center, where Glen said the main camping grounds were, or... He was torn, again, but decided to just point his nose and follow it. He was afraid of what he would find here, but he was no puppy to cower in a den and hide. He took off, nose and ears and double-vision scouring the woods in all directions, wondering if he would have the courage to approach his people if he found them, or run from them.

"ARE YOU going to confine me to the cabin like a puppy?" Gerald stormed around the main room of the cabin he was sharing with some of the Black Pine betas, and Kane stifled a sigh of exasperation as he waited for Gerald to stop ranting.

He'd come from Andromeda's cabin, intent on returning to his own before reaching out to Burke and Sophia to check on their progress, only to be stopped by one of the Red Fern wolves, informing him that lesser alpha Gerald was making a nuisance of himself. Apparently Gerald was throwing his weight around, sniffing after some of the younger, unmated females of their hosts' clan, and the Red Fern mothers were about to go to Andromeda with their complaints.

Mindful of the Clan Leader's warning concerning Gerald's behavior, Kane interceded and went to handle the lesser alpha himself. He didn't feel like sending Gerald home to his father in a body bag if Andromeda handled the situation, and he was reminded again that Gerald was one of his wolves, and his responsibility, no matter how onerous. The lesser alpha was in the communal mess hall, where the pack members gathered for large meals, and Kane had gone straight there, ordering him out of the cafeteria and back to his cabin.

"Tell me why I was informed you were bothering the females of our host clan," Kane demanded sharply. Gerald wasn't expecting that, and the lesser alpha stopped mid-stride and flushed. "Tell me the truth of your actions, and I may not have to treat you like an ill-mannered whelp and confine you to the cabin."

"I wasn't 'bothering' them." Petulance and anger, and some embarrassment were in his voice, and Kane waited, unsatisfied.

Gerald snarled, and spun to the nearest wall, punching the wood logs, the sound loud in the small living room. Kane was unimpressed, and didn't move a muscle. Gerald was no threat, and something was obviously wrong, the other wolf emotionally off-balance and lashing out. He was rude, and spoiled, but even he knew better than to harass unmated females in territory that wasn't theirs. Red Fern may answer to Black Pine, but this was Andromeda's land, not Caius', and Gerald was well aware of that.

"I was just talking to them," Gerald muttered, fists clenching at his sides, speaking to the wall.

"'Talking?' You were bothering underage females, and you ignored their mothers when they asked you to leave." Kane held back his incredulity, and he wasn't going to let Gerald out of this, no matter how uncomfortable the topic.

"I was just talking to them! I didn't touch a single hair on their heads! I was just asking them about...." Gerald spun back to him, glaring, but he stopped speaking mid-sentence.

"Asking them about what?" Kane demanded, meeting Gerald's eyes, holding until the lesser alpha dropped his gaze.

"If it was true their clan only produced shamans and betas," Gerald mumbled to the floor, and Kane bit his lip, trying not to laugh. He thought he knew what this was about. Younglings rarely minded their tongues, and were a good source of information, as adults spoke freely around cubs and tended to forget that their young had ears.

"It is true, Gerald. Red Fern has not produced an alpha in over two hundred years. Thinking of Challenging Andromeda for the honor of being Red Fern's first alpha in two centuries?" Kane asked dryly, watching the other alpha carefully. He blinked in surprise as Gerald blanched, shaking his head.

"Oh no, I'm not stupid. Andromeda would kill me."

"Yes, she would. In fact, she warned me she would take care of you if you didn't mind your manners while you were here," Kane informed him, and he watched as Gerald paled, obviously nervous at the prospect of having to face the wrath of the White Wolf. "So perhaps you should spend your time doing something else instead gathering information from cubs."

Kane waited, but got no response. Gerald was staring at the floor, and he seemed withdrawn. Something was wrong with Gerald, something other than being a first-class jerk with boundary issues. Kane stepped away from the door, and noted that Gerald flinched, as if expecting a blow. Kane made no move towards him, just sat in the nearest chair. Kane hadn't come here to beat on him, and a part of him saw a lot in that habitual reaction. How many times had Caius dealt with Gerald with his fists instead of words? Not once had Caius raised his hand to Kane, but then he long suspected that Caius was afraid of him, which left his Clan Leader steadily and increasingly resentful towards him.

Just because he never struck Kane, didn't mean he never struck his sons. He remembered Caius' lone daughter, Marla, and she had been treasured by her father, treated like she was made of glass and liable to break with one harsh word or glance. His sons were another matter, though. They were all lesser alphas or betas, none of them even coming close to Burke's level of power, let alone Kane's. That would be enough to make any father bitter, and look for an outlet for that bitterness.

“Sit down, Gerald.”

He waited, and Gerald hesitantly sat, a glower etched on his dark features. His mother must have been of a mixed heritage, as Gerald was darker than his sire, in skin and hair, and the only thing reminiscent of his father was the shape of his eyes and mouth. He wasn’t unattractive, not by any means, in fact was quite good looking, but the aura of discontent and anger he carried around with him left other wolves with the impression of ugliness. He wasn’t ugly—just his behavior and attitude were.

“Talk,” Kane told the other alpha, and Gerald raised his head, confused.

“What about?”

“Why you wanted to know the truth about Red Fern producing only betas and shamans.” Kane dropped his hands on the armrests of his chair, idly looking around the room, staying relaxed. If he kept this casual, Gerald might share.

It took several silent minutes, Gerald glowering all the while, but eventually the lesser alpha relaxed, drooping on the couch and staring at his hands. Kane was amazed by what a small amount of patience did to the older wolf, and he felt a stirring of anger in his heart towards his Clan Leader. Did Caius even take the time to be patient with his sons? Did he care? Why send Gerald away, essentially giving him to Kane, as if he were a lone wolf looking for a new home, and finding nothing but rebuttal everywhere he turned?

It was that thought, that hint of callousness on Caius' part that gave Kane an inkling of what might be running through Gerald's head. He breathed in deep breath, and let it out, easing the sudden ache his epiphany gave him.

"You weren't asking the cubs about Red Fern's lack of alphas to Challenge Andromeda, were you? You were asking because you wanted to know if you'd be welcome here." Kane knew he was right when Gerald's head snapped up, face blank, his dark eyes full of misery and despair.

This is a day for tears indeed. Everywhere I look, a broken wolf waits. If it's not violence or brutality, it's casual negligence and indifference.

"How.... How did you know? Did you read my mind?" Gerald snapped, but there was no anger behind his words, just tears he was fighting, and rejection. As if he were waiting for Kane to tell him he had no place asking for permission to join Red Fern. That he had no place anywhere.

"No, Gerald. I did not. You're an alpha, you would notice if I went prying about in your thoughts." Kane saw the surprise behind the pain that he would recognize the older wolf was an alpha, even if he was of the lesser type, so far down the power scale it could be argued he was a beta instead. *How long has Caius made his son feel worthless, for not being born stronger? A lesser alpha has value, just as our betas do. There is no wolf born among us that has no place in the pack.*

Gerald just stared at him, and Kane let the infraction go. Being stared at was rude, but Kane saw no challenge in the other wolf.

"Gerald, do you wish to leave Black Pine? Would you be content to serve Andromeda, a female, and a beta? She would not tolerate any incursion to her authority, so you would be seen as naught but a beta here, unranked and alone."

"I'm alone anyway," Gerald spat, clenching his hands on his knees. Not fully broken in spirit then, just battered. "My other brothers are content to ignore me just as Father does, or they have left for other clans. Only Roman remains, and he talks of nothing but dethroning you, and taking over Black Pine, but he is only stronger than me by a slim margin, and he couldn't even best your Speaker. Your easy defeat of him last week hasn't done a thing to convince him otherwise. I learned my lesson years ago, but Roman will keep after you until he has taken your place. I can't stay there anymore, Father will see to that if Roman doesn't beat him to it. He'll make me fight you again, and you wouldn't let me live a second time."

Kane sat back, thinking over Gerald's revelation. Roman was Gerald's brother, and the only other son of their Clan Leader still a member of Black Pine. The others were either dead, or had petitioned to other clans for admittance, most leaving after failing to defeat Kane in personal Challenges in the last twenty plus years. Kane had killed two of them in Challenges, after they refused to yield, leaving him no option but to take their lives. He'd defeated Gerald in Challenge years ago, and spared him once he yielded without hesitation. It had been a fight so swift that it was anticlimactic, as if Gerald had only challenged him because his brothers had, and lost.

"What do you want?" Kane asked, softly, the words hanging between them. Gerald looked at him, thoroughly confused. "It's not a trap, Gerald. Tell me what you want. Do you wish to leave Black Pine as your brothers have done, seek out a new place in another clan? I think you know how hard that would be, considering your current reputation and behavior. A Clan Leader would have serious reservations about letting you into their clans, even if your father asked it of them."

"Then it doesn't matter what I want, I won't get it. Better to be a lone wolf, than be where I'm not wanted, or seen as a burden." *The amount of hopelessness in his voice! Why did I never see past his bad attitude to the pain?*

"There is another option." Kane prayed this wasn't a mistake, but if this day was to end in something other than more tears and sorrow, he needed to change this wolf's future. At this moment, Gerald was still a Black Pine wolf, and Kane would never let one of his wolves suffer. "Your father gave you to me, whether that was his true intention or not, by sending you with me. I gather it's his way of getting rid of you, maybe even expecting me to kill you or chase you off. Callous, but then Caius has been a different man since the day Gray Shadow died, and I see no signs of him improving."

Gerald was staring, hanging on every word.

"So, Gerald, son of Caius. You are *my* lesser alpha. *My wolf.* You are one of my wolves now, no arguments, no question. You have a place with my people, my pack, my team, until you ask me to release you, or one of us dies. And I will only release you if you have shown yourself to be an ill fit, but only after an honest effort to try to fit in. If you wish to leave my pack, I will do my best to find you a home where you will be welcome. I expect total loyalty and obedience, and in return, I will protect you, care for you, and do my best to make you welcome. To make sure you are happy, and well-treated." Kane stood, and Gerald gaped at him, his dark skin leeched of color, shock obvious. Kane strode to the couch, and pulled the unresisting wolf to his feet. Gerald let him, limp and pliant, and Kane gave him a gentle shake. The other alpha blinked at him, and breathed in a ragged gasping lungful. It was obvious he was not expecting anything like he was hearing from Kane, and he took that as a good sign.

"Do you agree? Will you be one of mine, and follow me as your alpha? Answerable to me, and my lieutenant? Burke will outrank you, as will Sophia, but neither will treat you badly, nor will I. Let me show you how a true alpha cares for his wolves."

Gerald didn't answer, but Kane saw the reply he wanted in the other wolf's eyes. Gerald capitulated, and nodded, wiping at his eyes. Kane squeezed his shoulder, and dropped his hand. Gerald regained control, and Kane gave him a smile.

"My first task for you, my wolf, is to return to the communal hall and apologize to the mothers you made nervous earlier." Gerald flushed, but he nodded. Kane smiled at him again, and tilted his head to the door. "Come on then. An unpleasant task is better completed quickly, so as not to drag out the torture. And I need lunch, I heard they're serving corned beef sandwiches."

"Yes, Alpha."

Kane led the way to the door, Gerald on his heels, and Kane took encouragement from the fact that he could sense nothing from Gerald but a faint pain, and a nascent emotion that was too small to be anything but the beginnings of hope.

WHEN STARS COLLIDE

GHOST HUNKERED down, the group of swift moving stars on the other side of the hill making him nervous. He was at the bottom of a hill, hidden in a windfall of old trees and overgrow raspberry brambles. The night had come sneaking in as Ghost wandered through the park, the recent snowfall making it hard for him to catch the fresh scent of wolfkin. Twilight was taking forever, the shadows long and black, and he was thankful he was hidden at the base of the hill.

He wasn't too far from the cabin where Glen and Cat waited, south and east of it, and he had been about to return to his humans for the night when he saw the moving pack of stars running through the trees, and he'd made the bottom of the hill in time to hide.

He'd caught the scent of wolves a while ago, days old and covered in snow, and he'd followed it, thinking it might be a regular patrolling path, and the time between when it was laid originally and now making it likely they would be back. So he'd followed the trace, ramping up his double-sight, until he saw every flicker of life in a near-blinding rush of light, even as the sunlight died and night crept over the forest.

He could see the stars of the half dozen creatures on the

other side of the hill, as they climbed to the crest, the vibrancy of the lights and the similarity to his own internal star convincing him they were his kind. Wolves, wolfkin. His heart was racing, and his legs were shaking, and he could do nothing but stare as they stopped once they gained the top of the hill.

What do I do now? Hide, wait, or call out? Will they be friendly? Do I know them, are they my relatives? My family? Or strangers who won't tolerate a trespasser?

Ghost saw his first wolfkin in nearly fifteen years as a shadow of brown and black against the snow. His mind instantly told him that the wolf was a female, though her winter coat hid any distinguishing features of her sex. He didn't know how he knew, but he did, just as he knew that the large dark-brown wolf that appeared beside the female was a male. His instincts screamed that this one was an alpha, his size, the way he moved, the way the other wolves moved around him proclaiming that he was in charge. Ghost thought he was large, and he was, compared to real wolves, the ones back at the sanctuary, and large compared to his humans, but he was small compared to the brute standing on top of the hill.

The big brown wolf sniffed at the breeze, as the others milled about, some laying down in the snow, others rooting about the base of the trees, sniffing, probably looking for a squirrel or mouse to snack on. The wind was blowing from behind the hill and down it, which meant Ghost was getting a noseful of scents, while the wolves on the hill would not know he was there in the windfall. If he stayed quiet, then they could conceivably pass him by.

Ghost stayed hidden, fascinated by the other wolves, content for the moment to watch. They acted not as wild wolves would, not really. It was in the way they made eye contact, like people did when they were talking to each other. The big brown was sitting now beside the small female, side by side, both of them looking out over the windfall where he was hiding. He thought he heard a buzz, as if he were hearing humans talking over a great distance, too far to catch words. He narrowed his eyes at the wolves, and his double-vison showed him a thin collection of lines, little tendrils of light that all spun out from the big dark brown wolf, a thread to each of the other wolves. They were talking! He was hearing the dull echo of their conversation as they spoke mind to mind, and he got excited. He might be able to speak again! To talk, mind to mind, as he hadn't since the day he fell in the river!

He was about to gather his courage and reach out to the wolves on the hill, but they all moved, as if to an unspoken command. The big brown flowed down the left side of the hill, the others on his heels, heading north. They passed within meters of his hiding place, but didn't pause, and disappeared into the trees.

Where are they going? North, heading north..... The cabin! Glen and Cat!

Ghost shot out from the windfall, and took off at an angle to the other wolves, running as fast as he could through the trees for the cabin. This was an established patrolling pattern, and the cabin must be checked every few days. He had to get back before the wolfkin did, or Glen might be forced to use to his weapon, and he was no match against six wolves.

SPEAKER BURKE, the last cabin is a few hundred yards north. It was empty the last time we patrolled this part of the border, one of the Red Fern betas told him as they ran, her mental voice restrained and polite.

Doesn't hurt to check, Burke replied, and he took the mental cue on which way to go. They breached a dark grove of pines, and flowed down a small hill, covering the small open expanse in seconds.

Sophia was just behind him, letting him go first. If there was a threat present in the cabin he would determine what to do about it. She suddenly stopped, and he skidded to a halt, looking back at her in some alarm, thinking she might have landed a paw wrong and hurt herself. She had her nose buried to her eyes in the snow, and her tail was high, hackles raised.

Here! Burke, come smell this! Sophia was excited, and he loped back to her side, the others following. He dug under the snow where she was, and breathed deeply, the others spreading out. At first it was nothing, just snow and dirt, but he moved forward a few feet, breathing in deeply every step, when he caught it.

Do you smell him? Sophia asked, prancing at his side, her green and black eyes glittering in the shadows. He closed his eyes and concentrated, and he did indeed smell the foreign wolf.

Young male. Strong, moving fast. Smallish prints, probably a beta by the size. This smells fresh, but the trail dies just a pace or two to the south. Wonder how he did that? Do any of you recognize his scent? Burke directed that last part to the other wolves, and they all sent back wordless negatives. The Red Fern wolves did not recognize his scent either, so whoever this young male was, he was trespassing on Red Fern territory. Their enemy may have followed them to the park after all. Alone like he was he may be a scout, looking for weaknesses.

Kane! Burke called to the presence buried in the back of his mind, the place where Kane left the connection between them open at all times. He was glad for it, as he stared to the north, seeing now the tracks cutting through the snow. There was a wolfkin here, and he'd come from the direction of the cabin, which was supposed to be empty.

Burke? Kane's answer was immediate, his alpha's presence filling his mind. He sent Kane the scent impressions and the images of the tracks, and felt Kane's anger and satisfaction rise up in the other wolf. **I'm on my way. Surround the cabin, if he's inside take no action. Stop him if he tries to leave. We may have found one of our traitors.**

Understood. Burke took off for the cabin, passing along Kane's instructions to the others as they ran.

The scent was stronger now, clearer, as were the tracks

still visible in the waning twilight. They were only a few hours old, and Burke wondered how the trespasser had managed to conceal his scent and tracks. They should have come across signs of him earlier.

Burke saw a flash of light ahead through the pines, the glow of lamps through cabin windows. He also smelled humans, and the trail they were following came directly from the cabin. No humans were allowed in the park in the off-season, and the park rangers would not come onto the park lands without invitation from Andromeda. It looked like this may be their traitors, working in concert with humans in the slaying and kidnapping of their people. Anger rose in him, and he snarled, hoping he may have a chance to sink his teeth into the wolves who dared betray their own people.

Burke howled, the others crying out with him, and he broke into a small clearing in which a small cabin sat in the center. The lights were on, and there was a large civilian truck parked off to the side. He slowed to a halt a few yards from the front porch, and howled again.

KANE CHANGED swiftly, throwing his clothes to the ground, making the transition from man to wolf in seconds. He heard Gerald swear behind him, and drop to the ground, not as fast as Kane in changing forms.

He took to the woods, the connection between Burke and

his mind strong and clear. He knew exactly where to go, and he summoned his speed, his powerful black wolf-form devouring the miles. Kane was very large, even for a greater alpha, his legs long, his stamina unmatched, and he soon left Gerald far behind, his impatience to reach the cabin overwhelming. He would have his chance at last, Burke's anger at finding the cabin occupied by both wolfkin and human a sure sign that the trespasser was one of the traitors. If there was one, there may be others nearby.

**He's here, Kane!* Burke called, and sent him a blurry image of a gray wolf, head down, teeth bared in rage.

He ran faster, convinced he would arrive in time to see Burke and the trespasser tearing each other apart.

GHOST ENTERED the clearing just seconds after the other wolfkin did, the big brown wolf howling in rage. He saw Glen at one of the windows, gun in hand, and Ghost thundered through the snow, whipping his body around to an abrupt stop in front of the porch, sending snow in a shower over the other wolves.

He roared, the thought of Glen and Cat confronting the large wolves alone and armed with one small gun enough to terrify him. His roar shook the windows, and made the ground vibrate under his feet, the snow shivering with a hiss. He sucked in air, parsing their scents, his brain automatically identifying which wolves were the alpha, and betas, the female closest to him just off to his left side. These wolves were not friendly, their anger palpable to Ghost, rolling off them in waves. They growled back, surrounding him in a semi-circle, and he realized he was backing up when one of his rear paws touched the bottom step of the stairs. He lowered his head, lips pulled back from his own fangs, and he growled, refusing to give any more ground.

The big brown wolf snarled back at him, head down, eyes narrowed, saliva dripping from his fangs. He was larger than Ghost by almost half, and he was certain this alpha could rip him apart. He refused to back down, hearing Cat's fearful cries of alarm from the cabin, Glen trying to calm her down. Glen had his gun, and if Ghost could smell the weapon, then so could these wolves. They inched in closer, the female snapping at him from the side, and that was enough for Ghost.

He was no match for six wolves, not in a fair fight—but he was more than just a wolfkin, more than the simple betas and the lone alpha who bore down on him. The will of an alpha only had sway over him if he let it, and he had no intention of submitting.

He willed his rage, his fear, his uncertainty all into the wall of fire that erupted at the feet of the other wolves. They yelped, scrambling back, as the snow melted in a burst of steam, scorching hot. The ground in a semi-circle in front of him burned, the swiftly revealed wet grass flaring to black ash in the extreme temperatures. Through the steam and fire and the building smoke, he saw fear and surprise on their lupine faces, and he pushed out, widening the arc of the spirit-fire. He forced them back, and he stepped with the wall of expanding heat, flaring it again, making them run backwards and trip over each other in fear.

He stopped the wall's advance, and held it, now several wolf-lengths between him and the big male. They were no longer growling, their heads up, looking at each other in shock, and he caught the subtle buzz of their thoughts as they spoke to each other. The female sniffed the air, and took a step closer, and he sent a thin whip of fire at her nose, keeping her back. She dodged the flame with a shocked yip, and went to the alpha, hiding behind him, where she glared back at Ghost.

They watched him, now sitting or standing, no longer growling. If anything, they looked confused, and very upset, but there was no anger. The big brown wolf stared at him, his golden eyes thoughtful, and Ghost thought he felt something as he met the alpha's eyes through the wavering wall of intense heat. There was a brush of cool air over the surface of his mind, and he dropped his head again, growling, wondering what the alpha was doing.

Peace, Shaman. Forgive us, we thought you someone else. Peace. Ghost jumped at the first touch of another's mind to his in years, but he crouched down again with a snarl. He knew it was the alpha speaking to him, those golden eyes glowing as he spoke. There was another brush of that cool sensation, and Ghost snarled again, pushing back at it, not trusting this strange wolf. They recognized him as a shaman, but that meant nothing to Ghost, since they'd come into this clearing intent on violence, and his humans were still in danger.

We won't hurt you, or the humans you guard. Please, shaman, drop the sprit-fire, the alpha said as he lowered himself to the ground, and the others followed suit, every action they were taking non-threatening and calm. It was a rapid and extreme change from their behavior just moments earlier, and Ghost did not trust it, or them.

You came here with violence in your hearts, threatening my packmates. I don't believe you. Leave, now, or I'll scorch you all to ash. His first attempt at speaking mind to mind was stilted, and left him feeling raw, exposed. They all jerked as one, and he realized that instead of just responding to the alpha, he'd broadcast his thoughts to them all. He sensed more surprise, and he thought it was because he called the humans his packmates. The alpha confirmed this when he looked past Ghost to the cabin, where he figured Glen was watching through the window.

Packmates? the alpha was confused, and it came across in his thoughts.

Yes, my family! Now leave! I won't let you hurt them! Ghost cried, and he pushed more power into the spirit-fire, though he didn't advance it.

He sensed the alpha was about to answer, but he stood instead, and turned his great head towards the forest. A shadow ran from the trees, larger than anything Ghost had ever seen, a beast twice the size of the brown alpha. He trembled with fear and awe as a midnight black wolf flowed across the clearing, charging through the deep drifts with perfect ease. He was a relic of ages past, when teeth and jaws were meant to tear into wooly hides and bring down towering prey, in the dark days of humanity's birth...

He was so beautiful he made Ghost quake with alarm. Something so wondrous couldn't possibly be real, and each movement of his large paws, every glitter of white teeth against the unbroken black of his muzzle, all of it made Ghost stare, cold air rushing through his throat, feet tingling, muscles quivering.

The great beast was bigger than even the brown alpha, towering over the other wolves. He did not doubt that this was the greater alpha these six answered to, and he poured power into the wall of spirit-fire, though he feared that even his magic could not stop this beautiful monster if he wanted to kill them all.

KANE, WE WERE wrong, hurry!

What do you mean?

He's a shaman! A shaman? The trespasser was a shaman?

If the young wolf was a shaman, then he was not one of the traitors, as a shaman would never abuse his power by killing and abducting their people. This was not a foolish belief—the shamans answered to the Great Mother, and She would not tolerate such an abuse of power, nor could any shaman be coerced into betraying the wolves in their care. Whatever this shaman was doing here, he was not a threat.

He was seconds from the cabin, the glow from lamps and the scent of fire filling his nose. There was a strange aroma on the wind, and it drew him in, pulling him through the trees in an unerring path. He felt that breathless anticipation again, the one that came and went, so strong now it had his heart racing faster than his headlong gallop through the trees warranted. Something was about to happen, and he spurred himself to greater speeds.

He entered the clearing, and saw the reason for Burke's cry for him to hurry. The shaman stood in front of the cabin, head down, teeth bared, and there was a towering wall of spirit-fire between him and Burke's team. The young shaman was obscured from view by the wavering wall of heat, the warping of the air keeping him from getting a proper look.

He ran to Burke's side as the other wolves scrambled away, and Kane got his first clear view of the magic holding them away from the cabin. A wall of spirit-fire as tall as the cabin, in a wide half-circle curved in front of the shaman, making the air snap and burn, ozone wafting on the breeze. It was impressive, that one who was clearly in the first blush of adulthood would have the mastery, the power, to summon and maintain such a feat of magic. Spirit-fire was not a skill for a novice, and whoever this young wolf was, he was clearly a master.

Kane peered through the waves of heat, and sent a thought through the spirit-fire, hoping to calm the young shaman.

Forgive my wolves, Shaman. I am Kane, Heir of Black Pine, and these are my wolves. I promise I will not hurt you, nor will they.

For a second he thought he said something wrong, as the young wolf looked back at him in astonishment. He was about to speak again, when he heard a voice he thought he knew, as if reuniting with a long-parted friend after decades, and the sound of his voice was different than he recalled.

...Kane?

The wall of fire dropped abruptly, and Kane felt like he was struck by lightning, every strand of fur on his body rising, the vision of absolute perfection in front of him extraordinary and sublime. A supernova of white and silver light consumed his thoughts, and he was drowning in liquid silver eyes as they eclipsed his whole world.

KANE? GHOST replied, and he looked up, into the dark eyes of the alpha. What he saw there was an answering shock to his own, and he had no idea what to do.

He felt something in his chest, his heart, a wrench and twist, and he dropped the spirit-fire, head coming up, with his ears pricking forward. He wanted to whine and cry and howl, but he could do nothing but breathe, and barely that, his heart pounding as if it would burst. His legs felt like he'd run for days, yet he was alive with energy, and his thoughts swirled and his double-vision flared, almost blinding him.

The red star of the black alpha, of Kane, burned like the sun in the sky, and tendrils of light reached out from him, scarlet and crimson, and his own silver-white star sent out questing lines of light in return. The tendrils flared as they touched, and suddenly he was not alone in his head anymore.

He saw into the mind of the other wolf, and knew the alpha peered into his in return, and he felt Kane's astonishment, his confusion, and there...... under the shock, Ghost sensed an incredulous joy. He saw Kane drift through his memories, his thoughts, and he felt it when Kane made the connection to who he was, under the years of playing at being a wild animal. Kane reeled, and Ghost pushed at his thoughts, pulling the light that was Kane's mind back to his, wrapping every ray and beam of his own starlight around the alpha's mind, so he had no room to doubt that he was once Luca.

His whole being sang with a tremendous joy, a wellspring of happiness that would have made him dance over the snow if he could only find his paws to tell them to move.

He was home.

You died! The river took you! Kane whispered in his head, disbelief and a profound shock filling each word.

I'm alive, I'm here. Ghost trembled again, whining deep in his throat.

Kane! he let his joy go, flooding every part of his body and heart and mind—and the alpha responded. Suddenly his nose was buried in silky black fur, the big alpha rubbing and nudging at him, and he licked back at Kane, kissing his muzzle, and his paws were finally dancing.

Kane circled him, sniffing and rubbing that great big head of his over Ghost's head and shoulders, making rumbling noises in his throat, almost like a cat would purr, but deeper. Ghost whimpered as he danced, and he wove his body under Kane's front legs, tripping the bigger wolf, and they fell in a pile of limbs and fur in the snow. Kane put a big paw on his neck, holding him still, and licked his face, thoughts sweet and happy.

Luca, my Luca, Ghost heard his old name, whispered gently, and he was never happier. He burrowed into the warmth of the alpha's big body, his soul humming with joy, and a sense of utter rightness and completion filled him up.

BURKE WAS AT a loss for what was happening. One second his alpha was attempting to calm the strange shaman so he didn't burn them all to death, and the next, Kane and the stranger were all over each other, tangled together in the snow, kissing each other as if they were long lost lovers. Burke sat down, totally confused, and looked at Sophia, who had much the same expression on her face as he must have.

He'd never, ever, seen Kane act like this, and he cocked his head to the side, watching as his alpha licked the face of the gorgeous gray wolf, who squirmed his way into Kane's side like he wanted the alpha to swallow him up. Kane threw his big body over the young shaman, and pressed their heads together, rumbling in happiness.

So I think Kane knows the shaman, wouldn't you say? Sophia whispered to him, amusement lacing her words. He flicked an ear at her, and snorted.

It would seem so, but I don't know him. I've never met him before. Though he looks familiar, like someone we all once knew, Burke sighed and shifted on the cold snow, and he flicked an ear towards the cabin, hearing the humans inside whispering to each other.

What do you mean? Sophia asked, tilting her black head at him curiously.

He looks like Gray Shadow, Burke replied, softly, hesitant in his recollection. Sophia froze beside him, her attention returning to the young shaman who was damn near surrounded by the Heir's bigger body, both wolves whining with happiness.

Whoever he is, there's going to be trouble, Sophia said to him alone, and she leaned into his shoulder, and he looked down at her, confused. **A lot of trouble.**

What do you mean? he asked, but before she could answer, the cabin door creaked open.

A human male, robust and tall, in his early fifties, took a step over the threshold onto the porch. He stared down at the shaman and alpha, who were both still enamored with each other, not paying attention. Burke was about to alert Kane, when the odor of gunpowder and stress crept down the stairs, and that's when Kane finally looked up, and saw the gun.

Kane stood and put himself over the gray wolf, growling at the human on the stairs, fangs flashing white in the light from the rising moon.

HOMECOMING

GHOST TRIED to shove Kane off him, but the alpha put a paw on his back, pushing him under his big body, blocking his view of Glen standing hesitantly on the porch.

"Ghost? Care to introduce us to your friends? I'm assuming they're your friends, you seem to be getting along okay now," Glen asked nervously, but his scent held no fear.

Ghost wiggled, and finally got free of Kane and looked up at his human alpha. He yipped, tail wagging, and he pushed his shoulder on Kane's leg, trying to get the wolfkin alpha's attention. Kane was growling softly at Glen, and Ghost figured out why when he saw the gun held casually in his human's hand at his side.

He's not a threat, I promise. We had some trouble a couple of days ago, he's just being cautious, Ghost whispered hurriedly, trying to protect them both.

He called you Ghost, Luca. Both statement and confused question in one, it took Ghost a moment to figure out how to explain. He leaned on the black alpha, and sighed.

He calls me Ghost because he doesn't know my real name. He and his mate raised me, please be nice. Kane startled, and looked down at him, and he felt the alpha's confusion. He nodded, like a human would, and wordlessly pleaded with him to not hurt his humans.

Be careful, my little wolf, those puppy eyes of yours are dangerous. Kane said, and then he relaxed, the tension flowing out of his huge body. Ghost sighed, relieved, and stayed leaning on the black wolf, no urge to move. He was home. **What do you mean he doesn't know your real name? Did you not want to tell him?**

I.... I cannot. He lowered his head, ashamed, and tried to find the words to tell Kane he was broken. These wolves were raised normally, and must transform with ease between their two forms, while he had never done so, not even once, falling into his wolf-form as a cub and never finding his was back.

Luca? What is wrong....? Kane shifted, sensing his distress, and suddenly the alpha was back in his mind, and saw what Ghost could not share. That he hadn't been able to return to his human form, that he could not remember how, and Kane shifted through his thoughts, seeing the distance Ghost felt to his humanity, his thoughts long-set in the ways of a wolf. Every thought he exchanged with first the brown alpha, and now Kane, made his thoughts flow easier, and he was thinking again in a greater variety of words, but it was hard, as if he were constantly being pulled back and forth, between wolf and man.

**Little wolf, you are not broken. You are not the first wolf to lose himself in the Change. We can call you back, help you. I will help you, I promise. You are not broken, you are glori-*

_ous._*

You can? I'm not? He looked back up, not daring to hope, and Kane seemed to sense the difficulty he was experiencing, and the red glow of the alpha's starlight came to rest in the back of his mind, giving him strength. He felt like he was waking up, and suddenly his mind was clearer, freer, and he was filled by an intense wave of energy.

Glorious, my little wolf. Just glorious, Kane whispered to him, and tipped down his great head, giving him a quick lick across the nose. He squirmed, embarrassed and cheerful, and he looked back up to the porch when Glen coughed into his hand. *_I shall introduce myself to your humans, and then we shall see about fixing your little problem. What are their names?_*

The human alpha is Glen, and Cat is his mate. She is shy, don't scare her.

I'll behave as long as he does. And the gun needs to go.

Kane stepped away from him, and began to walk up the stairs. There were only four steps, and Ghost felt the Change roll over Kane before he saw it. When Kane gained the porch, he was a man, the wolf gone. Ghost exalted in seeing the Change and wanted to ask Kane to do it again so he could see how he did it, the alpha making it seem effortless, even as the wolf melted away in a jumble of fur and skin, so fast he almost couldn't see the moment Kane became a man.

A naked, tall, and very muscular man, who was luckily close enough to catch the very startled human alpha as he gaped. Glen's eyes rolled back in his head and he fell over.

The gun clattered to the porch, and Kane propped Glen up, looking back over at the wolfkin gathered in the front yard.

"I guess he wasn't expecting that to happen, huh?"

KANE PICKED up the human male and carried him effortlessly over the threshold, dropping him carefully in a chair at the lone table in the cabin. He heard a startled squeak, and looked up to see a redheaded human female staring at him in shock from the bathroom, a kitchen knife in one of her hands. He rolled his eyes, and stepped back from the unconscious human, looking around for something to put on. It was very apparent that while they may have raised Luca, they weren't fully aware of *what,* exactly, they had raised.

"Luca? Come on in here, calm her down so I don't have to disarm her please," Kane called out as he pulled on a pair of the human male's sweatpants, which thankfully fit him well enough. The little gray wolf pranced inside, tail high, and he sniffed curiously at the male he called Glen before sweeping gracefully into the bathroom.

Kane bit back an appreciative grin, realizing the little shaman would not thank him for thinking him pretty. He'd never seen a wolf more spectacular than Luca—than Ghost, as he apparently went by now. A coat in every shade of gray, in unbelievable patterns, and Kane realized with a jolt that he looked just like his grandfather Gray Shadow, just smaller. His heart hurt a little at that reminder, but he couldn't be sad, it was impossible. Luca was home. He was alive, and home. And he was glorious.

"You called him Luca," a female voice stated, full of curiosity, with a nervous edge.

He saw the human female come out of the bathroom, the knife left behind, and she stood with one hand buried in Luca's hackles, gripping tightly. Luca looked up at him, that pleading expression back in place, asking him to go gently.

"I call him Luca because that is his name, human. He says your name is Cat?"

"Yes... wait, how did you know that? He told you? How? And weren't you a wolf just a minute ago?" She fired off one question after another, obviously scared, yet very curious. He saw now how her name could be Cat, for she was full of curiosity.

"He speaks to me, as I am speaking to you now, just in our heads. He cannot speak to you, as you are human, and we are not." Telling secrets to humans was a novel experience; he usually dealt with the ones who already knew, from long-standing covert association with their race.

Kane looked at the human male who was waking up, blinking groggily. He shook his head and saw Kane standing a few feet away, and awareness came back to his eyes. The human female went to his side, running her hands over his face, worried. He watched them together, and saw how Luca could call them mates.

A solid warmth rested on Kane's leg, and he looked down at the beautiful gray wolf leaning on him, staring up at him out of the most incredible silver eyes he'd ever seen. He ran his hand over Luca's face, and wondered again at the twists Fate and the Great Mother laid out before them, only to have their paths collide again, and in this strange, unforeseen way. He tugged affectionately on one of his ears, and Luca twisted his head, catching his wrist gently in his long teeth, growling. Kane grinned, and rubbed Luca's head, before pulling him tightly to his side, holding his long lost wolf, never happier in his life. His heart felt free, light, the long-carried weight of grief and guilt gone at last. Each breath of air, every beat of his heart was spreading the joy through his entire being, and it was with an effort he focused past his rioting emotions to the situation at hand.

He looked for a place to sit down, and grabbed the other chair, pulling it away from the table and sitting. Luca sat on the floor beside him, leaning his bulk on Kane's side. He put his arm around Luca's neck, and held him. Luca wormed his silky head under his shoulder, and Kane indulged him, pulling him in even closer.

"So, we have some things to discuss. First of all, my name is Kane, and I must thank you both for the return of my wolf. We thought Luca lost forever these last fifteen years."

The human male sat up straighter, and held his mate's hand. He gazed thoughtfully at Luca, and the way Kane was holding him. He met the human's eyes, and they stared at each other for a long moment. He sensed strength, and an unwavering dedication in the human male sitting across the table from him. He saw now how Luca could call him an alpha, for if he was wolfkin, he would be one for certain. This human loved his little wolf, and it showed.

"Luca?" the human male asked, looking not at Kane, but the gray wolf he held. The little shaman nodded, as a human would, and Kane smiled, thinking it adorable, rubbing his ears. "We've called him Ghost, since he could disappear and reappear like one, never staying where we put him. He can get past any door or lock, almost as if he went through the walls. Just like a ghost."

The human smiled at his little wolf, and Luca—Ghost, panted, showing white teeth, tongue lolling to the side. He was laughing, and he seemed proud. Kane looked back to the humans, and thought about what to do with them. The love and affection were obvious between the gray shaman and the humans, and he would do nothing to harm Luca, so that meant he must carefully consider the best way to handle the humans. He could not send them away, as they knew too much, but he also could not kill them, which was be customary in this situation, when humans in non-government, no-need-to-know positions found out about wolfkin. Very rarely were regular humans allowed to live once they knew the secret of the wolfkin society's existence.

"Tell me how you came to have Luca," Kane asked, trying to stay polite. Though if they stole his little wolf as a child or had anything to do with what happened that fateful day in Baxter, then he would risk his little wolf's ire and kill the humans. He knew some of it from Luca's thoughts, from the burst of rapid-fire memories that inundated him when Luca first let him in his mind. He wanted answers from the humans who kept his long-lost wolf for nearly fifteen years, and for their sake he hoped they were good ones.

"We found him by the river here in Baxter, almost fifteen years ago, while researching claims that gray wolves had returned to central Maine," Glen replied, and he sighed, staring at Luca, his face full of sorrow, and regret. "We thought him a lost pup, domesticated because he was not afraid of us and didn't act like a wild thing. We run a wolf sanctuary up in New Brunswick, and took him home with us. That's where we raised him, and that was a unique experience, for certain. I didn't know... we didn't know that he could... you know... become a man."

Glen pointed at Kane, referencing his transformation from wolf-form to human. That was an explanation for another time, he wanted to know why they were back now, and not sooner. Nearly fifteen years in Canada, and then now, this winter, they'd decided to bring Luca home?

"What brought you here?" Kane asked, running his hand over Luca's head, over and over, the lovely gray wolf humming happily, eyes closed, leaning into his touch.

"We didn't know Ghost... ummm, Luca—was sentient, we thought he was a dire wolf, a type of wolf long thought extinct the last few thousand years." The female, Cat, spoke up, excited, her green eyes dancing as she spoke, hands flying about. "I sent a DNA sample to another research lab to confirm my suspicions, and we had a meeting with the scientists a few days ago to discuss my theory."

Cat's eyes became haunted, and he smelled fear on her. She put a hand on her mate's shoulder, as if seeking comfort.

"What happened?" Kane demanded, and Luca shivered at his side. He ran his hand over his head, reassuring his little wolf, and he settled down.

"Two men from the other lab came, and two conservation officers from the local outpost. We were discussing my theory... when..." She choked up, a hand over her mouth, tears running from her eyes.

"One of the men from the other lab killed the two officers, shot them in cold blood. Then they tried to kill us, but Ghost stopped them," the human male said, and Kane felt his heart freeze. "They tried to get Ghost, drugged him in fact, but he got back up somehow, and chased them off with that fire trick, the same one he used out front."

He stilled, dread filling his heart at the thought that his enemies would have such a long reach, that they would travel over national boundaries and try to take a lone wolf, killing in the process. It was unlikely this was a different group than the one they were currently dealing with, as the Canadian government was firmly under control of the Greater Clans of North America, so it probably wasn't an endorsed abduction attempt. It must be the traitors, and if it wasn't, he was still going to take zero chances with his returned wolf's safety.

He stood swiftly, startling the humans and Luca. He sent Luca a wordless apology through the link they shared, and went to the door. He'd get the rest of the details later, right now he had his little wolf and his human packmates to protect.

"Burke! Sophia!" His lieutenant and first beta got up from the snow where they were resting patiently with the others, and ran to the porch. "Sophia, I need you to help the humans pack up, then drive back with them in their truck to the park center. Burke, alert Andromeda that we're bringing guests back, and have her set a cabin aside for the humans. I need Shaman River waiting for me back at Andromeda's cabin."

Kane, who is the shaman? You know him, don't you? Burke asked him, gold eyes curious.

"We both know him, Burke. The shaman is Luca." He smiled as Burke stepped back in shock, eyes wide. "Tell Andromeda we're on our way back. Sophia, now please." He waved to his beta, and she promptly Changed, becoming a naked woman kneeling in the snow. She raced up the steps, past Luca and into the cabin, and Kane grinned at the startled exclamations from the humans at having a naked woman suddenly in their midst.

Burke was in shock, sitting back on his haunches in the snow, and Kane walked down the steps, Luca following him. He put a reassuring hand on Burke's head, and turned to Luca who was so close to his side there wasn't space for air between them.

"Burke, this is Luca, whom the humans named Ghost. Luca, this is Burke, my best friend and lieutenant." Luca reached out a timid nose, and Burke succeeded in recovering enough to politely sniff back. It was a quick greeting, as both wolves eyed each other with some trepidation, poor Burke utterly at a loss going by his rapidly flicking ears and wide eyes.

"I need the rest of you to help Sophia get the humans safely back to the park center. I want them and their belongings on the way in the next few minutes," Kane addressed the other wolves, and they promptly got up, and headed for the cabin, Changing as they reached the porch.

"Burke!" he snapped his fingers in the other alpha's face, as his lieutenant couldn't stop staring at Luca. Burke was obviously still shaken. The Speaker shook his head, ears flapping, and finally seemed to pull himself together. He saw Burke's golden eyes go blank as he reached out with his mind, contacting Andromeda.

GHOST STARED up at Kane, as the alpha calmly and swiftly took over, and he felt like a great weight was lifted off his shoulders. He trusted Kane, he trusted him like he'd never trusted anyone before, and he knew that the alpha would keep him, and his humans, safe.

"You and I, my little wolf, will return to the park center now. Shaman River will be waiting." He tilted his head in question, and Kane smiled at him, one of his large and powerful hands cupping his muzzle. "The shaman will show you the way back to your human form."

Kane stripped off the borrowed pants, and threw them up onto the porch, once again naked. Ghost watched eagerly as Kane knelt beside him, and the Change took the alpha. It wasn't as fast as the first time, as if he sensed that Ghost wanted to watch the process.

Black fur sprouted in a wave from his back as his spine bowed, and his skull lengthened, a muzzle parting his lips, fangs filling his mouth, human molars disappearing. The rest of the transformation was a sickening blur of human flesh being swallowed by wolf limbs and claws, black fur covering every inch. It was unnerving, and not pretty to watch, and he felt Kane's gentle amusement at his reaction in the back of his head. If that was what it was like, he wasn't too sure he wanted to find his human form again. That whole process looked very uncomfortable.

The big black alpha stood over him and licked his face, and he sighed happily, leaning into the sweet-smelling caresses. Kane rumbled at him, and a huge paw went around his neck, and he found himself once again under the bigger wolf, Kane surrounding him, protecting him. He snuggled in deeper, the scent of warm fur and an undefinable smell that reminded him of safety and comfort filled his senses. The black wolf grumbled at him, and he wormed his way under Kane completely, the alpha so large he was surrounded totally by him, even his tail. It was a tight fit under the other wolf, but Kane immediately sent him a rush of approval, satisfied to have him where he was. He was happy to be there, and he looked past Kane's front legs to see the alpha named Burke watching them out of the corner of one golden eye. He stared back, and Burke made him want to laugh as he acted like he hadn't been watching, idly gazing at a random snowflake as it fell past his black nose.

Ghost turned his head back to the cabin when the female called Sophia walked out leading Glen and Cat, the other wolves, now in their human forms, carrying their gear and bags. The humans gaped at the scorched earth in a wide arc cut through the snow, but Sophia urged them on. The last wolf out turned off the power, and a burst of white smoke from the chimney said that the fire was out in the hearth. Sophia led the humans to Glen's truck, and Ghost huffed in amusement as the naked, tiny woman held out her hands for the keys. Glen hesitated, but she arched a brow at him and snapped her fingers, and he handed them over. Sophia got behind the wheel, and the humans got in as well, their gear thrown in the back of the truck. A couple of the wolves regained their four-legged shapes, and jumped in the back, as the female beta turned the truck around and drove off. The rest of the wolves followed the truck as it disappeared into the trees, and he whined, worried.

Your humans are safer now than they have ever been. You'll see them soon. We must go, my little wolf. Kane's words eased his fears, and Burke was up, heading back across the clearing in the direction of the park's inner reaches. Kane waited until Burke was out of sight, then slowly stepped away, letting Ghost free. He felt adrift, cold and lonely without that great weight above him, and he whined.

Kane nudged him gently, and then turned away, and Ghost sat for a moment, confused.

It's time to go home, little wolf. Are you coming?

He yipped in agreement, and chased after the midnight black wolf.

THE NIGHT WAS total and all-encompassing under the cover of the trees. Ghost called on his double-vision, and the red star that was Kane bloomed on his horizon, as brilliant as the sun every morning. He had to work hard to catch up, and every time he did, Kane would dip away, making a swift change in direction, and Ghost would try to match him, heart racing. He was playing!

Kane laughed softly in his head, and sent him a teasing glance over his shoulder, the slim line of white around the outer edge of his eyes and the flash of his fangs the only relief in the inky black of his body. He flowed through the shadows as if he were one of them, and it was only the muffled crunch of the snow under his paws that told Ghost the alpha was real, and not a dream. He remembered the dream he'd had as he and his humans traveled south, and he was overcome with an urge to say something, anything, to the wolf with whom he ran.

**I dreamt that you found me, the day I fell in the river.*

*That you found me, and kept me safe, instead of the humans.** He hadn't meant to say that, exactly, and he flinched, thinking he sounded like a silly cub. Kane stopped, and waited for him to catch up, panting in the harsh cold night air, their breath frosting as they exhaled.

Forgive me, little wolf. I searched, but I could not find you. I failed you. Kane dropped his forehead to Ghost's, their panting breath joining, combining. They were in a deep shadow, a foot from a sharp and clean line of moonlight that cut through the pine boughs. Kane was as black as the shadow in which they stood, and if Ghost didn't have his double-vision, he would be impossible to see.

He saw an image of Kane running along the river, exhausted, drenched, body aching, searching for him as a cub, the day the human pulled him off the rocks into the water. He felt the other wolf's despair, his guilt at failing, and the steadfast belief that Ghost—Luca, wasn't dead, even when everyone said he must be.

I'm here now, he told the alpha, who gave him that deep happy growl again, and it radiated out from his great chest, and up and through Ghost's head where Kane was pressed to him.

Yes, you are, my little wolf. And I will never lose you again.

Kane slowly pulled away, and they ran now side by side. Kane kept his pace slower for the sake of his shorter strides, and he relaxed, finding it hard to believe he was really going home, that they'd found each other at last.

They took their time, and Ghost was able to see better in the darkness as they came upon what was a well-tended road that wove through the trees, the moon shining down from a cloudless sky. Their shadows were perfectly defined, and the air was so cold that every breath frosted, ice crystalizing on their noses and eye lashes. Sound echoed strangely, reaching far, yet the pressure of the extreme chill falling from the sky made his ears want to pop at every snap of ice under their paws. Kane led the way, trotting down the road, and Ghost could see in the brilliant moonlight a multitude of tracks, from wolves of varying sizes. Their scents ranged from days to minutes old, the one named Burke ahead of them somewhere, his scent the strongest.

Eventually they came to what Ghost assumed was the center of the park, and his nose was swamped by the scents of wolves. He saw none of them, and he was looking. They passed cabins, some of them occupied, lights on inside, the murmur of televisions and the char of fires burning away in hearths on the faint wind. He sensed eyes on them, but saw no one at all. He speculated that it was the presence of the huge alpha running beside him that kept the other wolves away, and Ghost figured he would be intimidating. Ghost bumped the big wolf lightly with his shoulder, and Kane gave him a toothy grin. He wasn't afraid of Kane, and felt nothing but affection and joy from the alpha.

Kane took him on a path that wound up through the trees and trimmed open spaces, and he paused for a moment as they passed a large stone and wood building that rested on a small plateau on the side of the hill. A harsh jolt went through his nerves, recognizing the council house where his grandfather had told stories the night before the humans attacked. He jumped when a cold nose touched his, and he followed after Kane as he continued up the hill.

The path was icy, but their claws dug in, and they made the top of the hill without mishap. At the top was a huge two story log cabin, every side covered in tall single-pane windows that overlooked the mountains and valley. Lights shined brightly from within, beckoning to them, revealing honey-colored wooden walls on the interior that made the lights seem brighter. There was a wraparound porch on the ground floor, and smaller wooden balconies were placed at even intervals on the second floor. It was taller than most two story buildings, and Ghost had the fleeting impression he'd seen this building before, and he somehow knew the ground floor of the log cabin had high vaulted ceilings, and the second floor was a maze of rooms.

Kane paced towards the front door, and it opened. A slim figure dressed in a light gray slip of cloth stepped out on the porch, and Ghost stumbled to a halt in the front yard. His double-vision was still up, and he inhaled in wonder. She was magnificent, the star of light that burned in her core a true sun, gold and white, the flames burning as brightly as the real sun during a midsummer noon. Her eyes seemed to pierce his heart and see into every crevice of his soul. She gave him a smile that rivaled her star, and he dropped his head, suddenly shy, his bravery reduced by her power.

"Come, Luca, lost son of Black Pine, and be welcome home at last," she called softly to him, her voice accented strangely, and it was deeper than he would expect from a female. She carried power in her heart, and he couldn't find it in him to resist her call. Ghost looked back up, and blinked, his double-vision finally receding enough for him to look at her without her inner star blinding him. He walked the last few steps to the porch stairs and up, and she held the door wide for him, her smile unwavering. He stared up at her as he passed through, and her presence was so magnetic that he had to fight to look away.

Kane was waiting for him, already a man again, dressed in a white robe. The woman closed the door behind him, and he entered a large room off the entrance, a fire roaring in a massive stone hearth. It was sparsely decorated, the space vast and uncluttered, a thick cream colored rug underfoot and two long dark leather couches off to either side. He went to Kane, and sat at his feet, needing the comfort from the alpha's presence. Kane stroked his face, and he sighed, leaning on his thighs. He was nervous, and afraid of what would happen when the other wolves learned he was incapable of Changing. Wolves in the wild who couldn't conform to a pack were chased off or killed, and while he knew the wolfkin weren't animals, they also weren't human either.

"Luca?" he looked up at the sound of his old name, and finally saw the other wolf in the room. He looked so like the woman who had welcomed him that they must be related. They stood side by side, the new wolf and the female, and the male gave him a hesitant smile. Ghost thumped his tail in nervous acknowledgement.

The new male slowly approached him, and sat on the couch closest. Ghost watched him warily, but Kane was relaxed and unafraid, his presence in the back of his mind encouraging.

“I am Shaman River, and I am very happy to see you again, Luca. I was once Gray Shadow’s apprentice, a very long time ago.” At the mention of his grandfather’s name, and the connection this wolf claimed to him helped Ghost more. “Kane tells me you got lost in your wolf-form. I can help you find your way back, if you’ll let me.”

How? he didn’t meant to be rude, but it came out that way, and he flinched, expecting a rebuttal, but the shaman merely smiled at him kindly. He remembered little of his old life, but the respect due a shaman was one lesson he learned early.

“If you were a beta or an alpha, all we would need is an adult alpha with the Voice to order you to find your human form again, but since you are a shaman,” and River grinned widely at him, as if he were pleased by the fact, “the Voice will not work on you. So I will try to show you the way back, if you would share with me what happened during your first Change. It’s rare for a shaman to get lost in the Change, even on his first try, but I think your experience may have been out of the ordinary. Let me help you.”

Ghost hesitated, meeting the shaman’s eyes for a long moment, while Kane’s strong fingers massaged the base of his skull and the nape of his neck. He decided he would try to trust this shaman, thinking if he was once a student of Gray Shadow, he might be more understanding than someone who wasn't.

Grandpa Shadow showed me how, beside the river, he whispered, and both Kane and River reacted, with surprise.

"Your grandfather showed you how?" River asked, confusion marring his pale features, and he sensed an equal amount of confusion from Kane. "You did not Change at puberty?"

Before he...before he died, he showed me how to find my wolf. He took me to the cave, the wolf-den, the dark and quiet place where my wolf spirit slept. He showed me how to wake him... and we... I... Changed. I think I was dying, and Grandpa Shadow did it so I would live. He pulled up the distant memory, of traveling through the dark place deep in his own spirit, of the wolf-den buried so deeply inside he wondered how he could ever find his way back there. He gave the memory to Kane and River, and he felt their wonder at what he showed them. **Is that not....isn't that how it always happens?**

River just stared at him, the shaman at a loss for words. Ghost got nervous, whining, and looked up at Kane. His alpha cupped his muzzle, and ran his thumbs over his eyes, soothing him, making hushing noises. He was suddenly very afraid, the reaction of the shaman telling him that his first Change was far from normal. That whatever his grandfather taught him beside the river that long ago morning was not how their kind usually found their wolves.

"That's what he was doing....." the shaman whispered, his face a mask of stark disbelief, and awe. "He spirit-walked as he lay dying, and went looking for you. He showed you how to find your wolf spirit, and that's the power draw I sensed when I tried to summon him back..."

Ghost made the leap, aided by the presence of the alpha in the back of his mind. Gray Shadow died because he used his magic to show him how to find his wolf-form, consuming energy that he could have used to heal himself. In Kane's mind was an image of Gray Shadow in wolf-form laying on a stone bier, wolfkin layering stacks of logs and branches around him. He realized with a start that he was seeing Kane's memory of Gray Shadow's funeral. He could see with alarming clarity the gaping hole in the great shaman's chest, made by the shotgun the human had threatened them with by the river.

Why would they spare the effort to help him? He'd cost them the greatest shaman the clans had ever known, and he was no fitting legacy for his grandfather's sacrifice. He couldn't even Change back! His grandfather was gone, and he would be a constant reminder of the Clans' loss.

"Luca!" He was too scared to respond, and he collapsed to the floor, afraid he would be broken forever. What use was there for a broken wolf, among these perfect creatures, who moved from one form to the other with practiced ease? Kane would regret finding him, and send him away.

He shivered, and found he was cold, his heart racing impossibly fast in his chest. A layer of strange disconnect rippled through his mind, and he was panting, his vision blurring.

"He's having a panic attack." Someone was speaking but he couldn't be sure who it was. "We need to snap him out of it."

"The Voice won't work on him! River, you're a healer, do something!"

His sight was narrowing down, and he gasped, trying to breathe. He felt like something was sitting on him, choking off his air.

"I'm trying, but his magic is keeping me out. Luca, breathe, it's okay, we'll help you!"

He was going under, the river from his past suddenly tugging at him, dragging at him, suffocating him.

"Kane." He heard through the water, muffled, but powerful. Not the males, but the female, near and coming closer. "You can reach him. Do what you did before, with Gabe."

"The Voice won't work on him!"

"You don't need to use the Voice on him, youngling, you are bound to him at a level past the reach of that gift! You sense it, so use it!"

"What?"

"You are already inside his head and his soul where you need to be! Call him, go to him, and do it now!"

Luca was almost gone, his lungs burning. His vision went from gray to black at the edges, and he was ready to give up when a warm rush of red fire swept across his eyes. It came out from the back of his mind, and it burned as it went, but didn't hurt. The fire consumed the fear, the crippling terror that choked him, and the waters receded, his vision brightening with each sweep of flame. It circled around him, buffering his mind, and he reached out to it. He felt something catch him, and the heat of the connection poured into him. He breathed at last, sucking air into his starving lungs, and his legs kicked feebly. Strong hands were on his legs, holding him gently, and there was something propping him up, supporting his head and neck.

He blinked his eyes, finding them dry, and he was finally able to see again. He was sprawled on the floor across Kane's lap, River kneeling at his side, with the female standing over them. Kane was deep in his mind, and Ghost clung to him, afraid to let go. Kane sent him a wave of reassurance, wordlessly promising to keep him safe.

He relaxed, totally limp, and he felt the ache of his body, every muscle and limb complaining. He was starving, and he idly thought that he hadn't eaten all day long, not since dawn, and it must be well past midnight now. He heard Kane chuckle, the big man's arms shaking gently as they tightened around his shoulders. His stomach grumbled, voicing its own complaints, and the other wolves smiled down at him.

"I think some food is in order before we go any further," the female said, and she reached down, touching the shaman on the shoulder. "Come with me, little brother, and help me gather some food for our lost cub."

Luca thumped his tail weakly in thanks as the two pale

wolves left the room. Kane shifted under him, and he tried to roll to his stomach, but the bigger wolf refused to let him go. The alpha moved them both, so they lay stretched out in front of the fire, Kane wrapped around him protectively.

It was weird, laying on the floor with another wolf, one in human form, but the big hand rubbing along his side in long sweeps did a lot to soothe his nerves.

HE HUGGED his little wolf to him, though he wasn't so little in his current form. They were about the same length with Kane a man, and he propped his head on one arm while he slowly stroked his free hand down the gray wolf's side. Powerful muscles rippled under his hand, Luca's coat thick and soft, and the long guard hairs on his shoulders and along his spine a marvelous silver color, darker at the tips. His ears were sharply pointed, and soft to the touch, and he tugged gently on one, making the wolf he held grumble, happiness coloring his thoughts.

I keep calling you Luca, but in your head, you think of yourself as Ghost. Do you wish me not to call you Luca? he asked the wolf in his arms, and he waited, watching the colors of Luca's thoughts mill about inside his mind, and Kane realized he was finding it hard to separate where he ended and the other wolf began.

I do not feel like Luca. I haven't in a long time. Kane

pondered the response, and rested his chin on the gray wolf's shoulder.

How do you mean, little wolf?

* I don't remember how it feels to wear clothing, or how to say my own name, or how to laugh. I was raised with wild wolves, and I can tell you how to act around them, how to be a member of their world, their pack... but how to be a boy again? How to wear my human form? It is a distant dream, one I fear will never come true.*

You are not alone anymore, little wolf.

I am broken, Kane.

Shush! You are not broken. We will fix this, and I am here. I will never leave your side, I promise.

His little wolf was silent for a time, his thoughts subdued, obviously thinking hard. Kane was about to speak again when footsteps sounded behind them. Kane smelled blood and fresh meat, and suddenly a wide platter of steaks appeared next to them on the floor. Andromeda smiled at them both, and ran a slim hand over the little wolf's face, and he felt the shiver that ran through him at her touch.

"Eat, and sleep. River and I will wake you both in the morning, and with the Great Mother's help, we shall tackle this task anew with the dawn." She stood, and pulled a throw pillow from one of the couches, and a blanket, and she handed both to Kane. He sat up, and his little wolf waited for her to leave the room before he sank his teeth into the New York sirloin steak.

Kane chuckled as the wolf practically inhaled the steak, before attacking another one on the platter, barely chewing. There were several steaks on the platter, and over half were gone before the gray wolf slowed, and peeked shyly at him from the corner of his beautiful silver eyes. Kane smiled widely when his little wolf nudged the platter to him, silently offering to share. He was touched by the sweet gesture, and he laughed softly when the other wolf daintily picked up a prime piece of meat the size of his palm, and offered it to him.

"Thank you, little wolf." He took the proffered filet, and ripped into it with his teeth, those liquid silver eyes watching him carefully as they ate. He stared back, and sent his little wolf all the admiration and affection he was feeling, every shred of joyous relief that he was alive, and home, and now *his*. He didn't know where that certainty came from, as it was oddly autocratic of him, but this little wolf was his now, and he would fight to the death to keep him.

Silver eyes glittered in wild joy, and Kane felt an echo of returned sentiment along their link.

Kane chewed on the cool meat, and he smiled when he finally got his answer.

Call me Ghost.

** I shall, my little wolf, if it makes you happy.**

** I am happier than I have been in a long time, Kane.**

GHOST RELAXED, stomach full and heart content. For now, at least. Kane was sleeping, curled along his back, but sleep was beyond him for now. He stared into the fire, the embers a deep red and orange, glowing amongst the cooling ash, Kane's even breaths keeping time with his own.

His thoughts kept spinning back to what the female said before she left.

The Great Mother's help? Who was she, and why did he feel like he already knew? He remembered his grandfather speaking to him at bedtime, tales of times long ago and far away, and of a woman, beautiful in grace and power, who protected her children from the horrors of a long winter's night. She who made the shamans, and guided her favored children from the path of war and genocide.

Ghost sighed, and let his eyes drift shut. He sent his thoughts spinning out into the darkness of his spirit, the warmth of his inner star a beacon to guide him back, and he turned his mind to the infinite reaches just beyond the edge of his awareness. The answer to his question was out there, he could feel the pull on him, as if he stood under the empty night sky and still could tell where the new moon hid in the darkness.

There was a sound, faint and tantalizing...the words were indistinguishable, and he wanted to know who the whisperer was, and what she was saying.

Sleep came to his body, muscles loose and his heart slow. His mind and spirit coalesced, and he found himself standing on the limits of a vista he'd never seen before.

DREAM-WALKER

"I DON'T think Kane noticed it happening," Sophia said as she passed him the whiskey bottle, half gone already. Burke took a deep swig, and wiped his mouth with the back of his hand.

"I'd agree with that." He sighed loudly, and tipped his head back, staring at the unlit ceiling above them, the exposed rafters dusty. He idly thought about how often they must be cleaned, trying not to focus on the fact that he'd seen the impossible happen earlier that night. He hadn't recognized it at first, but it took Sophia pointing it out for him to see the signs.

"How old are you, Sophia?" he asked, the alcohol playing with his caution, and he took another drink, so he didn't sober up too fast.

"Old enough to smack you into the next century for asking me that," she growled, and kicked him with a dainty bare foot. They were both sprawled out on the couch in the cabin Burke was sharing with Kane. The Heir was wrapped up with his long lost cub, and Burke wasn't expecting him to come back anytime soon.

"Have you seen....." he belched, and covered his mouth, mumbling apologies before taking another drink, "have you seen a soulbond between two males before?"

She went still, and pulled her feet away from him where they were resting on his thigh. He rolled his head to see her sitting up, wrapping her arms around her knees, her dark eyes and hair blending with the shadows. They hadn't turned on the lights when they came in after making sure the humans were secure in the empty cabin next door, and the shadows made it easier to talk, to think about things he'd never thought possible.

Sophia bit her lip, and sighed, her shoulders drooping, and she flopped back on the armrest of the couch. He poked her hip with the bottle, and she took it, taking a couple of swallows before handing it back. He chuckled, impressed, and waited, staring at the golden liquid swirling in the glass bottle.

"It was about a hundred years ago." He jumped, her voice raw from the liquor, and he waited for her to continue. "Males pairing unofficially with males happens all the time, as you know." He snorted, and nodded, thinking about the years-long affair he'd had with Kane.....the affair that had ended around the time the Heir first met the youngest grandson of the two most powerful wolves in the combined Northern Clans.

Sophia put her feet back in his lap, and he rubbed them, thinking it was a good thing the cold rarely bothered their kind, since she was barefoot and the heat wasn't on in the cabin. She spoke again, after giving him an appreciative moan when he used his thumbs on the ball of her foot.

"I was visiting my mother back in the Old Country, and

there was a territory dispute between two neighboring lesser Clans. It got bloody, with a dozen deaths on each side of the conflict, and the humans were noticing the carnage. The Greater Clans over there were about to eradicate both clans to control the violence when it happened."

"When what happened?" he asked after she stopped speaking.

"The first beta and son of one of the Clan Leaders involved in the conflict tried to ambush and kill the Alpha and his Heir of the opposing Clan, and it almost worked. The Alpha and his Heir were the last surviving wolves of the pack that got ambushed, barricaded in a farmhouse out in the middle of nowhere, when the first beta of the other Clan broke down the doors. The trapped Alpha didn't have the Voice, and his Heir was young, only seventeen at the time, and his abilities weren't fully developed. They should have died, but then it happened."

"What?" Burke asked, hanging on every word, easily seeing the scene she painted in his head, the blood and violence and chaos.

"The first beta knocked out the Alpha, and raised his sword to kill him, when the Heir threw himself over his Alpha to protect him. Apparently, from what I was told, all it took was one look in each other's eyes, and a feud that had been raging for nearly a century was over. The beta dropped his sword, let the Alpha and Heir live, and the two new lovers, the young Heir and first beta, they became the first soulbonded pair of either Clan."

“How could it be over? So two wolves fell in love at first sight? That wouldn’t make the other wolves stop fighting.”

Sophia sat up and glared at him. He shrugged, and she kicked him again, this time in the side. “Don’t you remember your history lessons?”

“What do you mean? Kane is the history buff, not me. I know there are two types of bonds between wolves, mating and soul. Soul’s the rarest, maybe one out of a million pairings are soulbonds. So what?”

“Our histories tell us that a soulbond is a gift directly from the Great Mother, and is sacred above all things. To interfere in a soulbonded pairing is a violation of Her Gift, and will incur our Great Mother’s wrath. To continue feuding would put the first beta and the Heir in jeopardy, and neither of the lovers were willing to leave their homes. So they stopped fighting.”

“So because of an old legend about our Goddess making soul pairings a sacred gift, a century-long clan feud was over?” Burke asked, incredulous. “Seriously?”

Sophia sat up all the way, and took the bottle from him, putting it on the floor. She gave him such a stern and exasperated look that he swallowed nervously, seeing the unspoken threat to wallop him in her eyes. “You are banned from drinking, Burke. It makes you stupid. When we confronted Luca at the cabin, and he used his gifts, why did we stop attacking him? Why did we all automatically believe he wasn’t one of the traitors, even though he was trespassing, and in league with unknown humans?”

"That's easy! He's a shaman, and a shaman answers to the ...." Burke blinked, and trailed off, the alcohol burning off faster as his metabolism caught up to the massive amount of whiskey he'd consumed.

"A shaman answers directly to the Great Mother, from whom their Gifts originate, and they cannot act in violation of Her Will." Sophia finished for him, smug. He could hear the capital letters in her voice as she spoke. "So if you can believe that Luca is innocent of treason and conspiracy to commit murder simply because he is a shaman, then why can't you believe that a soulbonded pairing is a blessing directly from our Goddess?"

"Huh."

"The great Speaker of Black Pine says, 'huh'. Very eloquent." She rolled her eyes at him, and he grabbed one of her feet, tickling her. She gasped, and swatted him in the shoulder. He grimaced, and let her go. "Remember when I said Luca was going to be trouble, back at the cabin?"

"Yeah, what did you mean?"

"If we're right, and Kane and Luca are soulbonded, then we have a serious problem."

The alcohol was burning out of his system fast, and he sat up, staring hard at the beta. He had a feeling where this was going, and his heart began to race with dread.

"The ancient alphas were stripped of half their powers, and then those gifts were given to the first shamans by the

Great Mother. She then made it so only males could be shamans, ensuring no alpha could create a mating bond with a female shaman, and have an alpha regain control of the spirit gifts. And we assumed.... we assumed that because only the Goddess can create a soulbond, we needn't worry about an alpha and shaman coming together in that fashion, because the Goddess wouldn't allow it."

"Shit." He swore sharply, and got up from the couch, pacing.

"Shit sums it up pretty well."

"Wolves share their Gifts across a regular mating bond, but it's not reliable, and the wolves involved can shut it down if they want, or a Shaman can break a forced pairing. A soulbonded pair? That's almost always reliable when it comes to a power exchange, and since they're bonded at the soul, they can't keep the other half of the pairing out," he said, almost to himself, low enough Sophia had to lean forward to hear him.

Burke stopped pacing, fists clenched, as if he were ready to fight off unseen enemies that meant his best friend harm. And they would come. Once the truth was out about the bond between Luca and Kane, they would come, from every corner of the globe, to either strike down the perceived violation of their laws, or to try and exploit it. The repercussions of the soulbond could destroy the balance of power, and everything they held dear.

An Alpha soulbonded to a Shaman was anathema, contrary to their histories and their Laws, and he was afraid the sacred blessing that such a union usually conveyed on the soul-pair wouldn't be enough to keep everyone safe.

THE SNOW crunched underfoot, the moon high overhead in an ink black sky, and the trees moved in an icy wind that should have left him cold, but didn't. Stars were small and seemed far away, bare pinpricks of light that wavered in the dark sky. He was standing in a clearing, the virgin expanse of white a perfect circle around what looked like a broken tree stump, weathered by countless years of exposure to the elements, about three feet tall, and just as wide, the surface of it smooth and flat.

He walked, and the snow cracked like gunshots under his bare feet as he made his way to the stump. There was something shimmering on it, and when he got close enough, he saw it was a length of cloth. It shone like liquid moonlight, and he was gazing down at it, bemused, when a slim and elegant hand entered his view, and delicately picked it up.

He raised his eyes to see a woman, naked and lithe, wrap herself in the mooncloth. It left her arms and shoulders bare but for a strip around her throat, and the hem stopped just above her knees. She was tall for a woman, with skin as white as the snow upon which they stood, her limbs smooth and soft looking. She should have appeared washed out, considering the lack of color, but she shone with health and vitality. She had a head of thick, long black hair that hung in a silky fall to her hips. Her lips were curved and plump, a soft pink that matched the light blush on her high cheekbones.

She tied the mooncloth at her waist, and gave him a smile as bright and gentle as the light that fell over them. Her eyes were a dark blue, and they sparkled, and as she moved, her skin shimmered as if was covered in frost, or silver dust. She sat on the wide surface of the tree stump, and patted the open space next to her.

"Come sit with me, Shaman." Her voice was deep, flowing like maple syrup left out in the cold, sweet and heavy.

He joined her on the stump, and she sighed happily, leaning her shoulder on his. She smelled like snow and warm blood, reminding him of a fresh kill after a long hunt. He breathed in deep, every nerve coming alive. She gave him a quick smile as she looked at him out of the corner of her depthless eyes, and he couldn't stop the smile that stretched his lips in return.

"I love full moons, don't you?" she asked him as they leaned companionably on each other. She was warm, and he should have been colder than he was, considering he was naked as she had been only a minute before.

He gazed up to the moon in all its glory, filling the sky, its light so bright and inescapable that he could see clearly all the way across the small field. If not for the silver quality of the light and the stars winking in the royal blue sky, it could have been high noon in summer.

"I never really noticed the moon, truthfully." His own voice startled him, and he jumped a little. He didn't even recognize the sound, as it was deeper than he recalled, and smoother. His words were accent-less, unlike most of the other wolves he'd encountered earlier that night. At least he thought it was the same night; this place was rather timeless. "Aside from whether or not it was bright enough to hunt by."

"A wild wolf rarely notices things outside of what's necessary for survival," she said, and he saw that her breath didn't frost the air as his did. He blew out a lungful of air, and smiled as it frosted in a cloud before disappearing. She laughed softly at him, and waved a slim hand. A shower of light fell on them, and glittered on their shoulders and arms like raindrops. He touched one with a fingertip, and it disintegrated on contact. She laughed softly, and spoke again. "Tell me, my Shaman, what do you think of the moon now?"

He lifted his head, and went back to looking at the silver orb that was so close he felt like he should be able to reach out and touch it. He saw the dark valleys and craters on its surface, and the smooth untouched expanses, looking both hard and unforgiving as it did soft and welcoming.

"An accurate description, Shaman," she said, and he realized that she plucked the thoughts effortlessly from his head. She laughed gaily, and nudged him with her shoulder. "So I did, so I did. None of my wolves can hide their thoughts from me."

"Why would they try?" he asked her, thinking he had no reason to hide anything from her. She was no frail creature to hide from unpleasant or embarrassing things, and she was strong enough she could shoulder the weight of all their worries, and continue on, unfazed.

"Because many of my wolves are ashamed, or scared, or hurt, and instead of asking for my help, they hide from me, and each other. They hide the weaknesses that make them cruel, they hide the hurts that make them ashamed, and they hide their true natures and their own inner truths because they fear my disapproval. Many of my children would be happier if they only trusted me, and asked for my help."

"Why wouldn't they ask?" It seemed simple to him. She was willing to help, wanted to help, and it made perfect sense to ask. The worst she could do was say no, right? She didn't seem the vengeful type to him, to punish someone for asking for something they shouldn't.

"Some don't believe, or they fear my wrath. And some," she turned to him then, her face stern, and he blinked in surprise, "...some of them don't realize they should ask for help."

"Me?" he asked, wondering what he needed from her. He was alive, and no longer alone. To ask for more seemed selfish, somehow. He was too small a worry for her to bother with, considering the needs of a whole species weighed against his troubles.

She growled then, a sound so purely lupine that he couldn't help but smile at the incongruous combination of that dangerous noise coming from such a fair and beautiful face.

"You are stubborn, aren't you?" She laughed, and took one of his hands in hers.

He stared down at their joined hands, and it took a moment for him to realize why it felt so odd. She was holding his hand—his wholly *human* hand, free of claws and fur. Their joined hands rested on his bare *human knee*. He gasped, and looked down. His feet were bare in the snow, human toes curling as he stared. His chest was bare, hairless and well-defined, as was his stomach. His legs were strong, and lean, not an ounce of baby weight on him. His last memory of his human self was that of a little boy, and it did not match the grown and very adult body he wore now.

"Oh!" he gasped, and gazed in wonder at his free hand, lifting it in front of his face, watching as his unmarred and slim fingers bent and curled, how his wrist moved, the muscles flexing in his forearm.

She laughed gently, and grabbed his hand, pulling his attention back to her. She smiled at him, her pink lips shining and smooth, and she leaned over, kissing his cheek. He smiled at the touch of her kiss on his human face, and he couldn't recall ever feeling this happy. Aside from the moment he reunited with Kane, he was happier than he'd ever been in his life.

She sat back, and smiled at him. "Well?"

"Can you help me find my way back to my human form? Please?" he asked, remembering the manners his mother taught him just in time, not wanting to offend.

"I don't need to."

"You don't?" he was confused, and she squeezed his hands. Her grip was powerful, far stronger than her delicate hands should be capable.

"You sought me out, in your dreams. You came here, to this place," she waved her finger, indicating the snow-bound meadow where they sat, "in your human form already. You hold the key to regaining what you've lost."

"I do? How?" She smiled at him, endlessly patient, and he felt foolish, obviously missing her point.

"Tell me how you've felt, since the day you found your wolf. What emotions were always present?"

He sat and thought about it, watching as she played with his fingers, a move so silly for a being such as her that it somehow relaxed him. He remembered with remarkable clarity every day of his life, from the moment Glen and Cat took him away, to the moment he looked up into Kane's eyes as an adult.

"Frustration, grief, and loneliness. I love Glen and Cat, but I've been very lonely for a long time."

"Were you happy?"

He didn't even have to think about it. "No. I was reasonably content, but I wouldn't say I was really happy."

"What else was missing?"

This took him longer, and he looked up at the moon. He sighed, frustrated, but he had to say it. "Hope was missing, I think. I was so frustrated, so lonely, that I gave up."

Tears were falling, freezing on his cheeks, and he looked back down at the creature beside him as she wiped the icy drops away. Her fingers were warm, and gentle, and she gave him a small nod of approval.

He exhaled, and then pulled in a deep breath, thinking. "I've been holding myself back, haven't I?"

"Yes, you have." She hugged his arm, and rested her head on his shoulder. Her hair was soft on his jaw, and he breathed in the scent of her. Blood and snow, and clean fur. "Keep going, you're really close."

"I lost Grandpa Shadow after he showed me how to find my wolf." She hummed as he spoke, and he took that as a sign to keep speaking. "He showed me something that I shouldn't have been able to do, not so young, and in that manner. I knew he was surprised, and tried to hide it. He wasn't expecting it to work, but it did. I did it because I believed in him, but then he left, and I couldn't Change back. I thought it was because he wasn't around anymore to show me."

"He was inordinately proud of you, just so you know. Bragged about you for a long time," she told him, and he laughed, imagining his grandfather doing just that. She poked his side to keep him talking, and he caught her hand, holding it so she wouldn't keep tickling him. He was ticklish, who knew?

"So... when I tried to Change back, and couldn't, I got frustrated. If I had just taken my time, and not been afraid or so worried, I think I would have managed it. Cat and Glen found me, and took me away. I was afraid, and lonely, and frustrated. While I knew they wouldn't hurt a wolf cub, I was afraid as I grew older that they would hurt me if they knew what I was. That they wouldn't want me anymore if they knew I was wolfkin, and they were all I had," he paused, surprised by his own thoughts, of the words coming out of him. He hadn't been able to think this clearly in years. He was seeing things that made sense now, but hadn't while he was a wolf. "And the longer I spent in wolf-form, the less I remained in touch with my human emotions and ability to reason. So I stayed a wolf at first to hide, waiting perhaps for Kane to find me, not understanding he wouldn't be able to, and I got even more frustrated and lost what hope I had left. And because I was more wolf than man at that point, I didn't realize what I had done to myself."

He looked back at his past, regret and bitter disappointment welling up. He felt the knowledge bite at him, and he pushed it back, refusing to give in to the cycle. He traced those hurtful emotions to their genesis, and cut them out, letting the emotions float away into nothing as he repeated his conclusion, not at all surprised anymore by what he'd discovered.

"I stayed a wolf because I gave up. As a wolf, at least I had a place, no matter how badly I fit in it. I gave up—not just in finding my humanity again, but finding my family, my home. I gave up on my future. I did this to myself."

She smiled at him, pride shining in her eyes. She stood, and he mourned the loss of her unshakeable presence at his side, even as she cupped his face in both hands. The moon crowned her shoulders and head, and he was embraced by her shadow. Her eyes were glowing, the deep blue of a twilight sky, the horizon an endless amalgamation of darkness and light.

"And that, my love, that right there is why you are a shaman. You can see yourself, know yourself, with a clarity and an honesty that you can then use in your life and duties. I am very proud of you." She bent down, and kissed his forehead. "Tell me what you have now, my shaman, which will make the difference in finding your human half."

"I have happiness and hope. I have every reason to become a man now." He smiled, and felt free, lighter, as if he could do anything. "I haven't tried to find my human form at all since I came home. I just assumed I couldn't do it. Maybe I should have tried instead of having a fit, huh?"

She laughed with him, still holding his face, and her smile was the whole world, more beautiful than the moon showering light down on the meadow.

"I think that would have been wise, my shaman. But never despair, you have reasons aplenty to try now, the best of them the love that is waiting for you. Return to your soulmate with my blessings." She pulled back, or maybe he did, the shadows dimming the light of the meadow, her eyes becoming the night sky as she faded from his sight.

"I have a task or two for you when you get back, after you learn to walk as a man. Listen, just listen, and you'll know what to do. And my love, if you have need of me, all you have to do is ask."

"GHOST! WAKE up!" a voice called to him, and he stirred, wanting to stay in the welcoming place of his dreams. He heard a faint feminine laugh in his ears, and it pushed him to wakefulness.

He saw the fire in front of him, reduced now to fading embers, and felt the heat and weight of an arm wrapped around his ribs, under his front legs. He felt safe and cared for, the red starlight of the man who held him burning brightly in the back of his mind. He was at peace, and no longer weighed down by frustration or despair. He felt nothing but a sense of belonging and joy. He was home.

"Are you okay, little wolf? You were so deeply asleep I was afraid your heart wasn't beating," Kane whispered in his ear, his big hand running down his side, fingers digging through his fur coat. He remembered the winter meadow, and the woman who was there, her smile full of encouragement and pride.

I am fine, he whispered back, and sent Kane a rush of happiness, and he felt the alpha's heart jump wildly in response. **Let me up, I want to try something.**

"Try what?" Kane asked, but he sat up and backed away.

Ghost retreated from the room, down into his mind, and further, to the place his spirit shone as a star. He closed his eyes, heart full of hope and an overflowing sense of rightness. He reached, confident, and grasped at the magic that rested in the heart of his inner star, his magic burning silver and pure white. He pulled and called, and it answered. Magic came roaring out from his center, filling every inch of his being. A charge raced over his body, from the tip of his nose to his toes, every hair standing on end.

He opened his eyes in time to see the fireplace disappear in a cloud of white and silver smoke. He breathed in, and the stars that glowed in the vast expanse of his spirit spilled out from under his skin, and as they passed through him, he disintegrated just as the drops of light had in the meadow of the moon. He was pure energy, a hundred million infinite stars of life and will.

He was surrounded by magic; he was magic. He remembered the body he'd had in the Goddess's meadow, and it formed at his wish around his inner star, bones and muscles and organs and then skin, and felt the brush of human hair on his shoulders as it grew from his head. Hands lifted in the cloud, silver lightning arcing from fingertip to fingertip, and the tiny stars in the cloud flashed in perfect time with the lightning.

He heard cries and whispers of alarm outside the cloud, voices raised in confusion as he focused on the lights. He was fine, but could not spare the concentration to soothe anyone's worry. He must finish this first.

At last he was whole and he called the magic home. The infinite collection of little stars rushed in and the cloud of silver and white dust pushed against the surface of his hairless skin, and passed through the top layer, illuminating him from within before flashing once, and then disappearing.

He sat up straight, and stared at his hands in the red glow from the dying fire. The shadows in the room were shifting, racing swiftly, and the light from the embers were eclipsed as the sun rose, its brilliant yellow light crashing through the wide windows of the room, throwing his new body in crystal clear relief. His skin was burnished gold in the fiery light, his shadow spreading out over the floor, the silhouette of a man.

He put his hands on the floor, watching as his fingers flexed on the warming wood, and pushed, uncurling his legs from under him as he rose to a crouch. He trembled, but his legs held. He pushed up with his feet and legs, straightening his back as he went, and he rose and rose, feeling somehow too tall, as if he would hit his head any second. He sucked in a deep breath, hands coming to his torso as he inhaled, feeling the motion of his very human body going through the simple actions of living. He exhaled, watching his abdomen flex, and then pulled in a new breath, excitement rushing over him, escaping his first laugh in nearly fifteen years.

He jumped, startled by the sound, but that only made him laugh more, and tears ran down his cheeks. He was happy, exhilarated, and he lifted his hands to his face to feel the tears. They were intercepted on their way by two hands that made his look small. They were hands roughened by use and hard work. His were smooth and untouched by life, unlined, free of blemish.

"Glorious."

An awed, deep voice spoke to him, and those big hands pulled him forward a tiny step. He looked up at last, into dark eyes, eyes full of wonder and an emotion Ghost was unable to name. He saw Kane anew, from human eyes, and it was as if he were seeing him for the very first time. Where the wolf saw strength and power and ability, the man he now was saw the handsome features and attractive body of his alpha.

Dark hair, shoulder length, pushed back behind ears framed a face that was by even his limited definition, handsome. High cheekbones, a wide forehead, strong jaw and tanned skin combined to make a man who was, while not beautiful, striking instead. He caught the eye and held it; he was impossible not to see, not to notice, not to recognize as Power.

Kane was tall, or at least taller than he was, and he tipped his head back to get a good look. His alpha smiled down at him, eyes still full of wonder and awe.

"Kane," he gasped, and heard his own voice as he had in the meadow of his dream. His first word as a man was his mate's name, and he grinned wide, pleased that for the rest of his life, he could hold that piece of his history close to his heart.

He stepped nearer to Kane, and pressed his whole body to the man in front of him.

Hands held him tightly, and the skin on skin contact was electrifying. He put his hands on the firm chest of his alpha, and ran them up, over smooth skin and hard muscle. Kane gasped, and wrapped his sturdy arms securely around him, and his hips collided with the other man's thighs. Kane was taller than him, tall enough he felt the heat of the alpha's groin on his bare stomach, and he groaned, wanting to get closer.

Kane dropped his head, and rubbed his jaw over his, and they breathed in each other's scent. The alpha buried his face in the hair behind his ear, and his breath tickled his neck. He giggled, and tried to get away, but Kane held him tighter, his big arms lifting him off his feet. Kane growled softly, and gently bit his neck, and his giggles turned to a gasp.

A gasp that wasn't his made Kane lift his head, a rueful smile on his lush lips. Kane smiled at him, and pressed a kiss to his temple before pulling back enough to gently put him back on his feet, then bend down to grab a white robe from the floor. It was roomy enough he wrapped it around the both of them at the waist, and used the sash to hold it up. He moved them a bit so he could see the rest of the room.

Shaman River was in the doorway, his pale sister at his side, and easily a dozen other wolves behind them in the hallway, staring wide-eyed. River was grinning, but his face was covered in a red blush, and Andromeda was busy covering the eyes of a young beta female, who was trying her best to peek past her hands.

"Sorry about that, got a little carried away," Kane told the other wolves, laughing.

SHE SAID YOU'D BE SHIRTLESS

THE STRANGE wolves left eventually, most of them so alike the female called Andromeda that Ghost couldn't tell some of them apart. They must be her cubs, or litter mates. Their whispers and stares made him slightly nervous, but the powerful female beta shooed them off, and they went, melting away into the depths of the big house.

Shaman River disappeared, but quickly came back with clothing. He gave Ghost a pair of soft cotton pants that he cinched tight over his hips with the drawstring, and he kicked his feet out in delight, enjoying the sensation of the cloth on his skin.

"The guest bathroom down the hall has clean towels and new toiletry kits, and I'll send a beta for your own clothes. I'll give our new wolf some of my clothing to wear until we can get him outfitted, we should be about the same size. Breakfast in the kitchen when you're done," River told Kane, smiling, and he pointed down the hall, in the direction Ghost assumed the bathroom would be.

"Thank you Shaman, we'll make it quick."

Using a bathroom....I don't remember the last time I used one at all!

Kane was in the robe, and held out his hand, which Ghost took without thought. Kane gave him a sweet smile, and tugged him near, under his arm snug along his side. He buried his nose in Kane's muscled chest, and inhaled the scent of skin and male. His hands wandered on their own, around Kane's trim waist and hips, and the alpha laughed as he slid them down, over the firm swell of his rear.

"Careful, my little wolf. We should save that for later," Kane whispered in his ear, and River threw his hands up and left the room, leaving them alone. "When we're alone."

"We're alone now," Ghost said, and he laughed, unable to restrain his joy that he *could* laugh. Kane shook his head, and chuckled too.

"Still a flirt, I see," Kane said, and pulled away, but keeping his big hand wrapped around Ghost's smaller. The alpha tugged, and Ghost followed, watching as his feet moved all on their own, his legs following, and then he was walking, as if he'd spent the last fifteen years doing nothing else. Well, he had, just on four legs, not two, and he marveled that he was able to keep his balance and stay upright.

"So, my little wolf, how does a shower sound?" Kane asked as he led him down the hall, and Ghost held tightly to his hand, nervous.

"It sounds wonderful." He dipped his head, and realized that he smelled. Not badly, since he smelled of wolf, snow, and damp things, but he didn't think it was acceptable to smell this *strongly*. "I can't recall the last time I had a bath that wasn't involuntary, or a result of rainfall."

Kane sent him a wry smile tinged with sympathy as he stopped at a door in the hall, turning the handle and pushing it open. The bathroom was huge, with a double vanity sink, a sunken marble tub, and a shower stall that was enclosed completely in glass. There were two toilets, off to the side, discreetly tucked between two large ferns in golden pots. The room was lit by skylights in the ceiling, and a large window that overlooked a portion of the valley where the majority of cabins sat.

He tilted his head, confused momentarily, confused as to how he knew that the tub was made of marble, or that the double vanity was anything other than a fancy sink. He felt a rush of amusement that wasn't his, and then he smiled, recognizing Kane in the back of his mind, supplying him with a steady stream of new words, new concepts, things he would have learned just by living indoors full time instead of spending his life on four legs and in the woods of the sanctuary.

Kane was at the shower, the stall door open, adjusting the setting in the wall. Water poured from a rain spout that hung from the ceiling, pooling on the stone tiles, vanishing quickly down a drain in the center of the stall.

"Hop in, little wolf," Kane said, and Ghost eagerly stepped up, pausing when the alpha's big hand came to rest on his arm. "Pants off first."

Ghost looked down and chuckled, feeling embarrassed. "Ahhhh, okay. First lesson as a man—don't shower with clothes on." He tugged on the drawstring, and the cotton pants dropped, where they puddled at his feet. He saw Kane's eyes glow, and his body heated in response. He waited, trapped, his feet unwilling to move as Kane's eyes trailed down over his body, seeming to see every inch of him, sparing no part of his nakedness.

The hand on his arm tightened, and Ghost thought for a moment the alpha was going to pull him close and do...something. Kane instead gently pushed him into the shower stall, and Ghost gasped as the water rained down over his head. It was warm and he was soaked instantly, the sensation of the water flowing over his skin highly distracting, and he sputtered as it got in his eyes and mouth.

"Don't inhale it, little wolf!" A hand tugged him to the side, and Kane was under the spray with him, closing the stall door behind him. The scent of crushed pine needles and citrus rose up as Kane wet a bar of soap, and Ghost groaned in delight as those big hands started to run over his torso. He fell back against the cool tiles, and rolled his hips forward, as Kane's hands spread the soap over his stomach and waist.

His head was tilted back by a long finger on his chin just as another hand reached his groin, and he gasped. The small sound was captured by firm lips over his, and a wet tongue slid over his lips and into his mouth as soapy fingers gripped the swelling flesh between his legs. The fingers on his chin gripped his jaw, and his mouth fell open further, Kane's tongue sweeping in, exploring, a rumbling growl rising from the alpha when he responded hesitantly. He touched his tongue to Kane's, awed by the sensations he was feeling, and he rose up on his toes as a firm hand stroked his now rigid length.

He shook, and luckily his hands fell on the alpha's shoulders, or he would have spilled to the stone tiles. He realized his eyes were closed, but couldn't find the will to open them, and his hands rose from Kane's shoulders up his solid neck, and buried his fingers in wet silky hair, the strands clinging to his skin. He tugged, and Kane's mouth changed angles, his tongue taking now instead of exploring, and he could do nothing but accept the pleasant invasion, little growls of pleasure humming in his chest.

The hand stroking him moved slowly, grip tight enough it was almost painful, and he whimpered softly when Kane squeezed the base, and he swelled even more. Kane gasped, and pulled his mouth away, and Ghost opened his eyes as he pushed forward, chasing the sweet taste of his alpha, but he saw the flinch on the other wolf's face, and paused.

"Claws, little wolf," Kane growled, his dark eyes glowing like pieces of the midnight sky, and Ghost realized his nails were no longer blunt and smooth, but pointed and sharp, the tips pricking Kane's scalp. He loosened his grip, and Kane gave him a smile that made his blood roar in his ears seconds before a long arm wrapped around his waist, lifting him off the floor. He jumped, and snaked both legs around the alpha's hips, his groin right over the other man's. He groaned, head falling back, the feeling of Kane's hard and hot organ throbbing against his own making him shudder, and move. He was mindless, lost, overrun by a burning heat that made his heart knock against his ribs and his limbs tingle like he was caught in a lightning storm.

He twisted, moaning softly, as lips nipped and kissed their way down his neck, latching on the skin between his neck and shoulder. Sharp suction and the bite of teeth made him cry out, the sound a thin gasp of air as his body shuddered hard in Kane's arms. He sobbed, his rigid length pulsing, a sweet ache deep in his groin beating in time with his heart, and wet heat pooled between them. His head fell on Kane's shoulder as the alpha growled savagely, and the bigger wolf jerked hard against him, pressing his back to the hard tiles of the shower stall.

He smelled a rich, heady scent, and a bloom of scorching hot heat washed over his groin, hotter than the water that ran over their shoulders. His head dropped to the alpha's shoulder, and he licked the wet skin under his lips. Kane shuddered, hands gripping his backside, keeping him close. Their hearts beat hard in their chests, no space between them, and Ghost traced his fingers over the broad shoulders and muscled back left open to his explorations, his breathing finally calming, his heart still beating fast, just not as hard.

"I meant this to be a quick shower, but you're a temptation I wasn't counting on, little wolf," Kane whispered in his ear. He was slowly lowered down, and he found his legs not wanting to hold him upright. Kane held him around the waist, and Ghost gave him a grateful smile. "That was quicker than I usually like."

"What...what do you mean?" he asked, trying to find the

words to speak, blinking slow. All he wanted now was to crawl up in a warm, dark corner with Kane surrounding him, and sleep.

Kane smiled, and carefully pulled back, letting the water fall between them again, rinsing away evidence of the last few minutes. Ghost hummed curiously, running a finger through the white fluid on Kane's lower abdomen before the water cleaned it off, and he brought it to his mouth. The scent was a deep musk, purely male, and he licked it, making the bigger wolf gasp out a groan as he watched. It tasted like bitter salt and black walnuts, the kind that fell from the trees around the sanctuary building in the autumn.

"That! That is what I mean. All temptation, and you haven't a clue what you're doing to me," Kane moaned, and reached down to stroke his cock as it began to stiffen again. "Stop it, little wolf, or we'll miss breakfast, and I'm starving."

Ghost pulled his finger out of his mouth, and gave Kane a small smile. He wasn't too certain what exactly he was doing to bother his alpha, but he felt Kane's arousal in the back of his mind, and knew the last few minutes counted as some version of sex thanks to the constant flow of information the alpha was giving him. He wanted to do it again, too. Kane dodged his reaching hands, and he found himself under the water, the alpha scrubbing his back and rear, which made him groan, and he sighed in delighted frustration when the bigger man went further down, washing his legs instead of focusing on where he wanted him to.

Kane maneuvered him out of the way, and cleaned himself just as fast, before turning off the water and opening the stall door. Ghost admired the long limbs and hard muscles as he moved, and smiled, thinking his first day as a man was going wonderfully. He couldn't think of anything to make it better, until his stomach grumbled. Kane laughed, and when he stepped out, attacked him with a towel. He grumbled at the impersonal attention, wishing Kane would take his time, but the alpha gave him a look that said he knew exactly what he was thinking, and made sure to stay out of reach.

"Clothing, little wolf." Kane handed him a pair of denim pants and cotton socks from a pile of clothing on the counter nearest the door. River must have put it there while they were occupied in the shower. He stared at the socks and the jeans, and realized he had a more pressing need to take care of instead of clothes. He dropped them on the floor, and spun around, looking for the toilet.

He remembered how that worked, and strode over, even recalling to raise the seat. Living with Cat and Glen the last several years had taught him some things about being a man, after all. He even remembered to put the seat down once he was done, too.

"Well, I don't have to worry about you being shy. Or house-trained." Kane told him with a chuckle, fully dressed, in dark jeans, thick gray socks, and a long-sleeved tee that was as dark as his fur in wolf-form. Ghost finished, and it took him a moment, but he figured out how to flush. He walked past Kane, knowing the bigger male was watching him move, wondering what he meant by being shy. The housetraining part he understood, and gave his alpha a quick glance, thinking the wolfkin was too large to knock on his butt.

Kane gave him a quirky smile as Ghost washed his hands and dried them on the fluffy white towels hanging on the wall. He found the clothes he'd dropped, and it took him a moment, but he figured out how the socks went on, and then the pants. Kane handed him a shirt much like the one he was wearing, but when he put it on, the sensation of the shirt around his neck and shoulders made him squirm. He grumbled, and yanked the shirt back off, putting it carefully on the counter.

Kane raised a brow in question, and Ghost shrugged, making himself blink at the odd sensation of that purely human movement.

"I don't like things around my neck. Cat tried that a lot when I was a cub." Kane's face darkened for a second, but the anger quickly left him. He reached for the door and opened it, waving for Ghost to go first. He went to walk past the alpha, but he saw movement, and stopped midstride.

It was a mirror. He knew what they were, hard not to, as Cat had plenty. He remembered them from his childhood home, and he'd seen his reflection plenty of times over the years. But he'd seen himself as a wolf, not a man, and he backed up fast, beyond startled by what he was seeing.

"Is that...is that me?" he asked, pointing at the young male he saw in the glass.

"Yes, that's you," Kane said gently, as if sensing how unnerved he was. Ghost watched in the silvered glass as the tall, dark-haired alpha put a hand on the shoulder of the shorter male, and he tilted his head, seeing himself move in the mirror at the same time.

Of all the things he'd pined for over the years, knowing what he'd look like as an adult had never once crossed his mind. He would never have been able to guess, really, as he barely recalled what his parents looked like, and his grandfathers featured prominently in his memories as wolves, and not in their human-forms.

He was shorter than Kane by quite a bit, the top of his head coming to rest an inch or so under the alpha's chin, and he was definitely not as wide in the shoulders. He was slim, lean, his skin a pale gold and smooth. And he was all muscle. There was no part of him given over to the softness of youth, not like the lazy summer interns that used to work at the sanctuary. He had no hair on his body from what he recalled in the shower, but for a fine light brown dusting on his groin, and the hair on his head was a light brown, similar in color to the warm golden walls of the cabin. His face was lean as well, with high cheekbones, and a straight, slim nose, and eyebrows that matched his hair. He leaned in, and saw thick eyelashes that framed his eyes. His mouth was not too wide or too small, and his jaw was set in a way that said he was far more stubborn than he gave himself credit for.

He put a hand up, and ran it over his hair, tugging on the wet shoulder-length strands. Kane chuckled and leaned back on the doorframe, and he saw the alpha smile at him in the mirror.

"Your hair used to be blonde when you were a kid, and your eyes were a dark brown. Not anymore, though." Kane put a hand under his chin, and tilted his face. His eyes flashed in the lights over the mirror, silver-white and brilliant. A part of him wondered why that was, because he thought wolfkin eyes darkened and dulled in their human forms, only becoming ***more*** when they called on the wilder sides of their nature. He blinked, and his eyes stayed the same. He shrugged, and gave Kane a smile in the mirror, enjoying the feel of Kane's hand on his flesh.

"Ready to eat, my little wolf?"

He nodded as Kane took his hand, and he turned his back on the young man in the mirror, the scent of bacon and maple syrup calling to him. He heard the sound of many voices speaking, the clink of silverware, and he was nearly giddy at the prospect of using a knife and fork again.

ANDROMEDA STOPPED him in the hall before they entered the kitchen, numerous wolves milling back and forth in the large space, carrying plates and utensils, platters of food. Kane felt a humming in the air, a residual power leakage of some kind from the Clan Leader. She was deeply affected by something, and the way her gaze lit on Ghost where he peered with innocent curiosity at a dimmer switch next to the doorway told Kane that her thoughts were focused on the newly restored shaman.

The touch of her mind confirmed his suspicions.

We must talk, you and me. Later, she whispered in his mind, carefully, her thoughts withheld from Ghost's silvery-white presence in the back of his mind.

About how he managed to Change like that? Kane replied, one eye on Ghost as he spoke, but the younger wolfkin was too busy playing with the switch, illuminating the hallway before sending it back into shadow.

That, and something else. I sense something... she trailed off, when Ghost grew bored with the dimmer switch and snuggled up to Kane's side, peering up at him with his liquid-silver eyes. Kane's heart jumped, and he smiled down at his little wolf, pleased by the way he fit so perfectly under his arm.

Doesn't matter right now. He wants a kiss, alpha. We will talk later, Andromeda chuckled, her mindvoice pulling away, and she stepped into the kitchen, her actual voice ordering the chaos as she disappeared from sight.

Kane leaned down, and touched his lips to Ghost's, his innocent and eager response enough to make his cock harden to half-mast. He was sweet and responsive, wholly uninhibited, and Kane groaned as he pulled away, not wanting a full raging hard-on to accompany his breakfast.

KANE LED his little wolf into the kitchen, and through it to the morning room, where over a dozen wolves were eating breakfast at the long oak table. Andromeda sat at the head of the table, and there were two empty seats beside her, thankfully side by side and not across from each other. He didn't want to make someone move so he could sit beside his little wolf.

He took the seat beside Burke, and put Ghost on his left, between him and Andromeda, the safest place in the room. His little wolf stared at the chair he pulled out for him, and Kane caught a flash of uncertainty from the shaman before he looked up, saw everyone staring at him, and he sat hurriedly. Kane pushed his chair in, making him jump just a little, and he put a hand on his bare shoulder, rubbing it to soothe him. He sat down, and watched in amusement as Ghost picked up the silverware, a piece at a time, staring at it happily and picking at the tines of the fork to make them hum. He ran a finger over the fine porcelain plate, and got wide-eyed at the tall glass next to it.

Kane grinned, and reached for a platter of breakfast sausage and bacon, piling the meat high on Ghost's plate, before reaching for the serving bowl full of scrambled eggs, adding a healthy wolfkin-sized portion to that as well. Ghost was whip-lean and no inch of him carried any fat, aside from his delectable rear, and he wanted his little wolf to eat up. He was fit, but almost too lean. It was very obvious he'd gotten most of his sustenance over the years by hunting for it himself. Kane didn't even want to think about the humans feeding Ghost kibble.

Next he grabbed the pitcher of orange juice, and filled up his glass and Ghost's, before tending to his own breakfast. He saw Burke smirking at him, and he stole a piece of bacon off his friend's plate, giving him a wink. Burke growled good-naturedly, and Kane turned his attention to his plate. He picked up his fork, and watched as Ghost mimicked his actions. He was relearning how to use a fork, and what the napkin was for, and Ghost would look around the table at the others eating, before using his own utensils. Kane thought it was one of the sweetest thing he'd seen in years, and the way Burke was snickering over his own food told Kane he wasn't being subtle in how he felt.

"Why aren't you wearing a shirt?"

Kane looked up at the little voice that asked, and held his breath. The little Suarez female cub, the girl found in the back room of the Worcester apartment, was standing in the doorway, half in and half out. She was still bruised and beaten, her healing abilities slower pre-Change, and her hair was hiding parts of her face. She wore one of Andromeda's seamless gray wraps, which covered her short body far more than it did the White Wolf. Kane held very still, afraid to move lest he scare her, and knew everyone in the room was doing the same. She carried the scent of fear and pain on her, but her eyes, a light green, were locked on Ghost, and they held a gleam of curiosity.

"She said you wouldn't be wearing a shirt," the cub spoke again, calm as could be, but somehow seeming proud of her observation that Ghost was wearing only pants and socks.

Kane was too afraid of speaking to ask who 'she' was.

"Who said?" Andromeda asked instead, gently. The little cub gave the pale wolf a quick glance, and sent her eyes back to Ghost, not answering.

Ghost was chewing on some bacon, and he looked around at everyone staring at him, then looked down, as if noticing that he was, indeed, shirtless. Ghost swallowed the bacon, and said calmly, as if it were the most natural thing in the world for her to ask, "I just learned how to put clothes on this morning, and the shirt feels too tight around my neck, like I'm choking."

The little cub cocked her head at him, and took a step into the room, letting go of the doorway.

"You didn't wear clothes before?" She seemed to think Ghost was playing with her, little brow wrinkling.

"I spent the last fifteen years as a wolf, and I didn't wear clothes." Ghost grabbed another piece of bacon, biting it in half, before holding the rest of it out to the girl. Kane bit back a warning, afraid the girl would shy away. Andromeda raised a single finger, subtle and slow, and he stilled.

The girl gave Ghost a look he couldn't translate, but she stepped into the room, and went straight to Ghost's side. She took the bacon, and chewed on it, staring at Ghost in a very peculiar manner.

"I can't find my wolf yet. It's why I'm still hurt," she said, as if she had to explain why she was injured. Her little face had a sad cast to it, and Kane wanted to howl in rage that such a precious thing as she had to suffer.

"We all find our wolves when we're ready. Don't end up like me, I found mine too early and got stuck," Ghost told her, sharing his bacon piece by piece, everyone in the room still watching, totally silent. The cub hadn't been seen by anyone but the shaman and Andromeda since the rescue, supposedly too traumatized to come out of the suite given to the Suarez wolves. For her to be out now, and speaking to a stranger, was a miracle.

"That was silly," she said in all seriousness, and Kane smiled. She sounded like a mother beta scolding a cub for touching a hot burner.

"Yes, it was, but I was hurt and alone, and I had to do it, or I would die. Why are you hurt?" Ghost asked, and Kane stiffened, about to warn his little wolf. He was going to get up and tug Ghost out of the room, but the little cub just took another piece of bacon from Ghost's hand and bit off the end.

"Bad humans hurt me. See?" She held out one arm, and showed her wrist to Ghost, where the dark purple and blues of slowly healing bruises littered her golden skin. River had managed to heal the worst of the cuts and contusions, but he couldn't spare the energy on the lesser injuries, saving his limited healing abilities for the larger hurts.

Ghost took her tiny hand in his, as she picked the bacon off his plate with her other, and Kane held his breath, waiting for the tears and screaming. Yet she did neither, and Kane jolted as a warm breeze rushed over the meal, fluttering napkins and moving hair, and he looked up to see surprise cross River's face, where he sat across the table. The breeze smelled like warm summer nights, and pine trees, and it blew gently over them, pulling in from all corners of the room. It was soft enough it didn't knock anything over, but strong enough to really feel it. Kane saw in the corners of his eyes a faint shimmer in the air, as if the light was bending through tiny prisms hanging suspended around the room.

"Can you do my other arm?"

Kane looked back to the cub, and bit back a cussword at the blemish free expanse on her arm, the same one Ghost was holding. She offered her other wrist, and Ghost took it, and the breeze rose again, faster, and Kane held his breath as he watched the evil looking bruises on her thin arms fade, to a blue, then greenish brown, then a pale yellow, then vanish all together in a matter of seconds.

Ghost dropped her arm, then put a hand on her face, lightly cupping her cheek. The breeze rose again, harder, faster, now a soft wind, and it spun through the room, lifting the cub's black hair off and away from her face, revealing the dark bruises that marred her features. Gasps and exclamations of surprise rose from around the table as the wind threatened to knock over glasses, but no one said a word, all of them watching in astonishment.

The bruises faded away as she stared into Ghost's eyes, and she glowed. Her eyes, her skin, shining softly through the cotton dress she wore. She blinked, and Ghost dropped his hand. The glow under her skin faded, and the luster of youth remained unblemished. Her face, her neck, every inch of her that wasn't covered by cloth was free of injury. Kane had a feeling if they were to check, every inch of her would be healed, without injury or scar. Perfect.

She smiled at Ghost, who turned back to the table, picking up his orange juice and taking a sip. He groaned in approval, closing his eyes as he swallowed, turned to the cub, offering her his glass.

"Orange juice? It's really good."

She took his glass in both hands, and took a tiny sip, then nodded once, handing back the glass.

"It's really good. Can I have some more bacon?"

Ghost grabbed the serving platter and dropped it on the corner of the table next to his seat. He sat back in his chair, and the little cub, as calm as anything, hopped up in his lap and ate the bacon.

GHOST CHEWED, loving the taste of the greasy bacon exploding on his tongue. Somehow it tasted better eating it as a man, and he gave up using his fork in favor of his hands. The little cub wasn't using utensils either, so he figured it was acceptable. He scooped his eggs up with his toast, and made happy growls as he chewed. She giggled, feeling them where she was leaning back on his chest. She grabbed his orange juice, and it almost slipped, and he steadied it for her as she drank. She sighed loudly once she was done, and he picked up the pitcher, refilling his glass.

She sat in his lap, eating half his breakfast, but he didn't mind. This was his first experience with cubs, and he liked her solid weight on his leg. It made him feel like he was home, and he thought about sleeping in a pile with his siblings as a cub. He wondered where they were, if they were alive, but he didn't want to ask that in front of the cub. She seemed okay now, but she was sad, and really good at hiding it, and he didn't want to make her sadder. There was a wound he couldn't heal, hidden behind the light green gems of her eyes.

"What's your name?" she asked him, and he swallowed his toast before answering.

"I was born Luca, but I go by Ghost now."

"Is that cuz you're a shaman? Momma said that shamans had funny names."

"I go by Ghost because that's the name my human alpha gave me."

"Humans are mean," she told him with a tiny frown, tilting her head back to look at him.

"I haven't met many. Most of the humans I've met were either boring or mean, but mine are nice. They raised me."

"You have humans? Weird." Kane made a choking sound, coughing into his hand, but he quickly silenced himself when Ghost gave him a questioning look. She went back to eating off his plate, and he grabbed a muffin, blueberry by the scent, and gave it to her when she ran out of bacon. She smiled at him, and nibbled on it, making little growly noises just like he did. She wasn't far away from finding her wolf if she could make those noises. He wondered for a second how he knew that, but he just shrugged and went back to eating.

"My name is Sarah," she tilted her head back again, far enough to see his face, and she almost fell off his lap. His hand came up automatically, and he steadied her on his leg. Talking to her was easy, and he found the words he wanted coming back to him with each exchange.

"That's a nice name."

"I guess. Momma gave it to me. Everyone is staring at us."

Ghost looked up from his plate, and she was right, everyone was indeed staring at them. There were more wolves in the doorway, and everyone at the table was staring at him and the cub on his knee. He shrugged because he could and it felt wonderful to do something so human. He grabbed another muffin, breaking it in half, giving her one piece as he chewed on the other.

"Probably because I'm not wearing a shirt."

He heard Kane snort with laughter, and he looked at his alpha, who was staring at him with a wide smile on his face, dark eyes glowing. He smiled back, and leaned over, careful not to tip Sarah off his knee, and kissed Kane on the cheek before sitting back.

Andromeda made a weird motion with her hand, and the wolves in the doorway scattered, while the wolves at the table slowly stopped staring at him and Sarah, returning their attentions to their own plates. He looked around at the other wolves, noticing that only half of them were pale like the powerful female beta. The others were dark, and he saw the female from last night across the table from him, sitting next to the other shaman. He thought her name was Sophia, but wasn't sure. Her wolfkin form was black and dark brown, he recalled. She was eating, and watching him, her expression cool yet without a harsh edge, as if she were reserving judgment. Burke, the brown wolf, was on the other side of Kane, and his attention was split between the Heir and his plate. There was another alpha at the table, a large wolf with sad and haunted eyes, sitting down at the opposite corner. The alpha looked familiar, it was there in the way his head tilted to the side as he gazed back down the length of the table at Ghost. He felt like saying this alpha's name, it hovered on the tip of his tongue, but he couldn't make the name cohesive enough to speak. He just couldn't place the alpha's name. He probably hadn't been introduced yet and got his name from an overheard conversation. Ghost nodded to the alpha and went back to looking at the other wolves.

He met River's eyes, the shaman watching him carefully, eyes and thoughts guarded. His light blue eyes glittered, and Ghost felt like the shaman was staring into his very spirit, sifting through the parts of him that made him who he was. He pushed back at the sensation, and River blinked, breaking eye contact and picking up his glass. The weird feeling went away, and Ghost eyed the shaman warily before returning his attention to his now empty plate.

Sarah had his glass, the orange juice obviously hers now, and he reached out for Kane's glass, drinking from that instead. His alpha gave him a fake glare and faint grumble, his eyes twinkling.

KANE SAT beside Ghost, watching as he went on with eating breakfast like he hadn't just performed a major piece of magic. The cub sat in his lap as if they were best friends, talking away about everyday things. Burke nudged his arm, and he leaned back in his seat, turning to his lieutenant.

He's a man less than an hour and you indulge in shower sex? Burke said, and he choked back a growl, anger rising at what the Speaker was implying. He was about to grab Burke by the throat and throw him out of the room, right up until he saw his eyes. Burke was laughing at him, and he curled his lip at the other alpha, going to grab his glass, but found Ghost had finished his juice.

You can't be cranky. You just had kinky shower sex. He's really cute.

Mine!

Easy, brother. I would never try to poach on a soulbond, I don't feel like getting struck by lightning, Burke assured him, chewing slowly on a piece of toast, sitting back casually in his chair.

Kane felt like he was just struck by the aforementioned lightning, his eyes widening as he realized what Burke was referring to. Burke was watching him, and started to cough, choking on his toast at the look on his face.

Kane fell back in his seat, jaw slack, and turned his head slowly, and stared. Just stared. At the young wolf beside him--every motion of his gorgeous body enchanting, every tilt of his head adorable and erotic, the way he watched the other wolves in the room, all of it the most wonderful thing Kane had ever seen. Even the way he held the cub on his knee made Kane's heart melt, and the power he could summon as easily as he chewed on a piece of bacon was sexy as hell.

He was soulbonded. As soon as Burke opened his mind to the knowledge, he saw it. The link, the connection between them, a mix of red and silver-white light that glowed with a subtle flame in the not-space of their souls. It shifted in and out of his sight, as if he was trying to see something that wasn't wholly real and occupying the same place as he was in the world. He breathed in, and tried again, and suddenly he saw it, he saw *everything*.

He saw an orb of light, glowing like a star in the night sky, burning with an intense and intimidating silver-white fury, in the center of Ghost's body. It spun out thin lines of light, pulsing against the inside of his skin, and he looked down, and saw a cord of the same light that burned Ghost's heart coiling out, and it was connected to *him!*

He looked further down, and saw a star, this time dark crimson, burning in his own chest, the color of the setting sun after a day of storms. His was just as big as Ghost's star, but its color was so radically different he knew it must be because he was an alpha, and Ghost a shaman. A line of dark red, a wicked and dangerous-looking shade, spun out from his core, and met in the space between them, where it joined with Ghost's light. Pulses of red traveled down the cord to Ghost, and pulses of silver-white traveled into him, and where the two shades mixed was a vibrant hue of rose red and silver.

Kane put out a hand blindly, and grabbed Burke's wrist, and he pulled the other alpha's mind into his. Burke was surprised, but entered willingly, and Kane let him see through his eyes. He felt Burke's arm stiffen as he looked, and Kane knew he was seeing exactly what he was.

Oh, Great Mother, you're using Ghost's Spiritsight! You're seeing the soulbond with his gift! Burke whispered in his mind, and Kane had nothing to say. He couldn't think of anything to say at all, so flummoxed was he, that all he did was sit in his chair and watch.

He gathered his wits, and made a conscious effort to relax, and slowly the Spiritsight faded. The world returned to normal, and Ghost saw him staring, and gave him a sweet smile, his silver eyes glowing with what he knew was the power of the soulbond between them. He gave Ghost a smile, and his little wolf went back to talking to the cub, who was still on his lap, chattering away as if her life hadn't been hell the previous week.

He sensed Burke sigh in the back of his mind, and Kane felt like he was about to be attacked on all sides. It was as if he was exposed, raw, vulnerable, and all because he got his little wolf back, just in time for him to be in more danger than he'd ever been in before.

I am an alpha, Burke, and I am soulbonded to a shaman. I just used Ghost's Spiritsight, and it was easy. I conjured it up as if I was the shaman, with years of training behind me. Oh Great Mother, we are screwed.

Yeah, I'd say you're fucked pretty well. So far only Sophia and I know for sure, and maybe River. I know Andromeda knows for certain, she's too crafty and old not to recognize the connection. I don't think the other wolves who saw the reunion last night picked up on anything other than a long-lost cub coming home, so we might be okay. Cool it on the lovey-dovey shit around everyone else just to be safe.

How do I tell him?

He's Gray Shadow's grandson, Kane. He probably knows already that you're soulbonded. I think he might've known it the second he saw you last night. He may not know that every fanatical wolfkin out there is going to want you two either dead, separated, or worshipped like the evil wolfkin-kings of old, so you may need to explain that part to him. Burke paused, then put a hand on his shoulder, and squeezed, long fingers digging in, as if he was afraid to let go. **Or maybe our people will see the soulbond, and treasure it as the blessing it truly is, and no one will freak out. Maybe.**

Kane let his head fall back, and he stared at the ceiling, thinking about how much he wished it was acceptable to drink alcohol with breakfast.

WHEN SHE SPEAKS

GHOST FELT the draw on his power, and tilted his head, hearing a soft buzzing sound. It was Kane and Burke, speaking to each other mind to mind. He looked down, and blinked his double-vision up, and saw a steady stream of his silver-white light running from his star to Kane's red. Kane was using his gift, the one that let him see the life-energy of living creatures.

He blinked it away, and sat back in his chair, thinking. He focused on Kane's presence in the back of his mind, and with a single push of power, he knew he could listen in to the conversation his soulmate was having with Burke. He didn't need to, though. He could guess, and he had no reason to be so rude. Kane dropped the power drag on his gift, and Ghost knew he'd stopped using the... what was the word? Kane was thinking it... the Spiritsight.

Kane only used it for a few seconds, before letting it go, and he didn't mind. The sensation was like having someone tug on his arm or hand, much like Sarah was as she imperiously sought his attention, and pointed to another muffin. He gave it to her, thinking.

"I'm gonna go give the muffin to my brother," she said, and slipped off his leg to the floor. He gave her a smile, happy that he could erase her hurts. The burning hint of silver was gone from her body, the miniscule particles expelled through her skin, the wind carrying it away, where it couldn't hurt anyone else, through the open window in the kitchen.

When he first took her hand, he'd felt a sense of waiting, nearly impatience, his power rising in him almost as if it had a mind of its own. All it took was a second to see what was going on, and just like he had in the woods with his tracks, he'd found the portion of his mind controlling his gifts, and taken over, accelerating the healing process a thousand-fold, every bruise fading away as he expelled the silver from of her body.

Sarah took his hand, and she smiled at him as she tugged. He didn't even think to say no, and got up, letting her lead him from the room. He licked his fingers, getting the last bit of bacon grease as she pulled him forward. He heard the scrap of chairs over the wood floor as several wolves got up, and the footfalls of many feet as he followed the cub. She was strong for one so little, and he grinned, feeling the new strength in her grip as she took him to the front of the house, to the stairs. She would find her wolf-form very soon, it was there in the way she moved, and how her green eyes glittered just the littlest amount.

He ran with her, careful not to stride on her smaller feet as they made the front entrance. He thought he perceived a murmur of sound, and looked around, out the front windows of the log cabin, but saw nothing, no other wolfkin. No one was in the large room with the fireplace, either. The other wolves were following them, and he cast a glance back, but none of them were speaking, just staring at him in a manner he couldn't decipher. The cool brush of another wolf's mental touch was absent, so whatever it was he was hearing was coming from somewhere... a swell of soft hissing, as if hastily hushed, found his ears, the whisperer seeming to be at his shoulder. He wanted to turn and look, but the faint sound of laughter, the rain of ice drops cascading over stone, silenced his curiosity.

He knew that laugh.

She is here.

Sarah bolted up the stairs, still holding his hand, and he followed, enjoying the stretch of his legs, and the way his body moved with a fluid grace around the turn on the landing. They reached the second floor in a soft blur of speed, and he laughed, catching up to her easily, so they jogged lightly side by side. Sarah took him to the end of one of the halls, and she was about to drop his hand to open the door when he flicked at the handle with a smidgen of mental effort, and it opened, swinging wide. She giggled, and pulled him in the room.

"Gabe, I found the shaman! The strange one the pretty lady told me about!" Sarah all but yelled as she tugged him over the threshold, into the midst of several wolves. He stopped, the scent of pain and fear thick in the room. None of it was overpowering, and he got undertones of surprise and nerves, and a sly burning scent that fled as he tried to focus on it, disappearing quickly under the others. There were six wolves in the room, a boy the same age as Sarah, several youths, and a slightly older female who wouldn't meet his eyes. And they all bore injuries much like Sarah had when she came down to find him. She'd known he was there, and she'd come right to him.

"Sarah! Please stop this nonsense about the pretty lady already, it was just a dream!" He looked at Ghost, and gaped a moment before turning back to the cub. "You can't drag shamans around like that!" A young alpha stood up from a small loveseat and ran over to them, reaching out to grab Sarah. He halted, and stared, his face going slack with surprise as his eyes traveled over her unblemished skin.

"What? How?" he raggedly exclaimed, arms dropping. Sarah giggled, and let go of Ghost's hand, running around the young alpha, heading straight for the younger cub where he sat on one of the couches. She hopped up next to him, and handed him the muffin, whispering in his ear as she stared at Ghost.

"Hi," Ghost said to the other young wolf with a small half-smile, and the alpha pulled himself together enough to really take a longer look at Ghost. This alpha was bruised as well, and Ghost was confused. He was grown, fully joined with his wolf spirit, but he wasn't healing. He was covered in bruises too, a spectacular one blooming on his left cheekbone, blackening his eye and part of his cheek down to his jaw.

"Oh! I'm sorry about Sarah, she said she was going to the bathroom and never came back. I was about to go find her...." The alpha shook his head, still mightily confused. Ghost gave him a full smile to reassure, and breathed deep, his nose twitching as he got a hint of a sharp burning sensation in his nose.

Silver.

He held the scent of silver in his nose, his thoughts besieged by worry at the amount of poison he was sensing, and felt a rush of cold and damp air flow up his back, over his shoulders. It was as if he were outside, snow under his bare feet, the scent of frozen things and slumbering trees surrounding him. It took the bitter pang of silver to get him to focus again, and he realized the whispers were back. Saying something to him, conveying a sense of urgency, of purpose, flowing into his body and mind. He returned his thoughts to the wounded wolves in the room, and the alpha still gazing at him in confusion.

They weren't healing because they had silver in their bodies. Like Sarah had, just in higher quantities.

"Why haven't you pushed out the silver?" Ghost asked curiously, and stepped to the young alpha, who stared down at him, about half a head taller than he was. He leaned in, just a little, and breathed in again, this time through his mouth. Saliva burst on his tongue, and he felt a faint burning down his throat. He swallowed, and it went away, and he dropped back on his heels.

"The silver? What?" the young alpha asked, and he finally caught up, shaking his head. "I can't do that, I'm not strong enough."

'I have a task or two for you when you get back, after you learn to walk as a man. All you have to do is listen, and you'll know what to do."

Her words came back to him, as if she was there at his shoulder, and he was in her snow-covered meadow. She is here with me.

He was listening. *She* was speaking to him.

"Yes, you are," Ghost told him, half his mind listening to that prodding inner *something* that made him reach out, and the other half of his mind flipping the switch on his Spiritsight.

He saw a glimmer, a dark metallic sheen, flowing with the alpha's blood through his body, pooling in the bruises, the ones on his skin, and the ones deeper, in his muscles, and some along his ribs and near his hips. It was slowly, very slowly, being forced out, his organs trying to filter it, but it would take forever at the pace it was going.

"I'm not... what are you doing?" the alpha asked nervously as Ghost moved right up into his space, inches apart, and he raised his hands, palms up, and waited. "Shaman River said no shaman could expel silver in such a quantity. What are you...?"

"I've done it before. Can I show you?" Ghost asked quietly, thinking of when that male doctor had stabbed him with a needle back at the sanctuary, filling his veins with silver and poison, and how he'd forced it back out with his inner light. With Sarah, he'd pulled the silver out for her and healed her wounds, but this young alpha was grown, and could do what needed to be done himself. He just needed to be shown how. Once the silver was out, he'd heal as fast as Ghost did.

The alpha, he thought Sarah called him Gabe, sucked in a deep breath of air, and carefully put his hands in Ghost's, eyes wide with nerves and stress.

Watch me. See through me. Ghost pulled on his Spiritsight, and reached out with his mind, gently pulling the alpha—his name was Gabe—into his mind, and let him see what he was seeing. He felt Gabe's alarm, and an almost overwhelming awe. His mind relaxed quickly, and Ghost sensed a simple and pure thread of trust running through his thoughts. He trusted Ghost simply because he was a shaman, and that trust made Ghost's heart hurt, a soft pang he felt to his very core.

Shaman he may be, but it was her guidance, her prompting, that lead him to what must be done. Ghost listened, and the knowledge came with her whispers.

The star that burned in Gabe was a light red and blue orb that flared sporadically, and it was dimmer, duller, than the stars that burned in the healthy wolves behind Ghost. With his Spiritsight up, he could see the constellations of the small crowd that was in the hall, the three brightest stars his soulmate, the other shaman, and the female clan leader. The other stars weren't important, and after a quick mental scan of his surroundings, his focus returned unerring to the injured alpha.

The silver traces in Gabe were lines of gray clouds that marred the perfect finish of a magnificent sunset. It ebbed and flowed on the wind of his pulse, covering the flares of light that tried to fight its way out from under the staining.

Watch me, he whispered again, and he reached, as he had with his own starlight that very morning when he called on his magic. He reached past the silver lines, with hands that were a scorching source of pure energy, and touched the dull star in the center of the injured wolf. He gave this time instead of pulling power from it; he had an endless flow of energy around them from which to draw. He could see the magic in the air they breathed, in the sunlight that poured warm and heavy through the large windows, in the other wolves cowering on the couches, their own marred starlight aching to be freed.

Silver cannot abide the light of your star, he whispered to the mind sharing space with his, and he felt Gabe's wonder and trepidation. He gently batted the fear and nerves away, and as the red and blue star gained strength from his inner star, he sent out flicks of light, twisted strands of red, blue, and silver, arcing over the surface of the alpha's star. With each lightning fast flick of light, the silver backed away, moving like particles of dust in a stream of clear water, collecting in the low and hidden places of the alpha's body.

Ghost let the silver collect, showing Gabe how to force the spread-out poison to come together, as it was in every muscle, nerve, and bone, and as stubborn to remove as ice collected on damp fur in the depths of a winter night. As the silver pooled, he guided Gabe's light, corralling the poison in his stomach. He was forcing it through tissue, through organs, particles so fine they clung to the small, magic-producing sparks that Kane's influence within his mind was saying were things called cells. Gabe moaned, feeling the poison moving through him, hurting and relieving aches at the same time. The silver raced ahead of the lights, and Ghost gave Gabe a mental shove, a gentle one, but forceful enough the alpha was taking over from him before he realized what was happening. He still gave Gabe energy, but the alpha had the gist of it now, and finally he chased all the remaining silver to his stomach.

Here he could not do to the alpha as he'd done to Sarah; the silver in the young male's body was too concentrated, compared to the relatively minor amount of poison left in the cub. With Sarah he'd chased it out of her body through her skin to be lifted away as dust—here, the poison must be expelled in a larger volume, and quickly.

"I need a bowl, something, now," he murmured, eyes shut, hands still clasping the other wolf's, his breathing slow and measured. He felt weightless; as bodiless as he had during his dramatic return to human-form, in the white and silver cloud. Footsteps came to his side, moving fast, and he let go with his left hand to reach out for what must be a bowl of some kind, hard and weighty and cool. There was a bit of dust on it, and it smelled like this room, so maybe a silly piece left out for looks on a table.

He sensed the contractions building in Gabe's abdomen a second before the first sickening moan spilled past his lips in warning, and Ghost opened his eyes and stepped to the side in time to let the alpha vomit into the bowl. He held Gabe's hand in his right as he caught the heavy, foul smelling liquid that reeked of burning flesh in the bowl he held with his left.

Kane grabbed Gabe's other arm, helping him stay upright

as he moaned again, stomach rolling, and Ghost closed his eyes one last time, sending more energy into the young alpha as he spit into the bowl. The silver was gone, his magic and Gabe's light forcing the last remaining dredges out as he spit again.

Ghost kneeled quickly, depositing the bowl on the floor, and stood, putting his left hand over Gabe's heart. He pulled power to himself first, from the light pouring warm over his back as the morning sun rose closer to noon, then gave it to Gabe filtered with intent through his star to the alpha's. Gabe needed energy, and his body would do everything else on its own, without guidance.

He had more than enough magic to give away, and he heard the whispering again in his ear, but it came from nowhere in this room. Soft satisfaction rumbled through him as he heard a hint of a laugh, pleased and proud. He was still listening, and he would for as long as she spoke to him.

Gabe stood taller, his shaking muscles regaining their control, and Ghost smiled as the bruising on his cheek and the injuries he could sense on the alpha's body healed themselves. A heartbeat, then two, and almost on the third beat—Gabe was healed, restored. His body was perfection, and Ghost felt a pang of sadness that he could not heal the hurts the alpha carried on his soul. He would help, but he did not know how to ease them. Maybe someday he would learn.

Ghost let Gabe go, and moved away, the whispering back. He cocked his head, listening, and followed the subtle nudging on his mind, looking to the wolves past Gabe. Kane was speaking to Gabe, lifting the younger alpha's shirt to see his unmarked skin, both of them casting glances at the bowl. Ghost couldn't hear their words, as they were buried under a rising hum of whispers, and he stepped around the alphas toward the couch.

Sarah beamed up at him from where she was practically bouncing in excitement next to the other cub, whom he guessed to be her brother. Ghost felt the nudging again, and he listened. He knelt on the floor in front of the couch, and the cub stared at him while he fussed with the muffin, uneaten. Ghost said nothing, just gave the cub a small smile, and he put out his hand. This little one was about twelve or so, but small, seeming younger. He was close to his wolf too, from the way the gold light from the windows caught on the reflective surface that came and went in his moss green eyes.

Sarah poked him with her elbow when he flushed, and looked down at his hands, not looking up at Ghost. He gave his sister a glare, and she poked him harder, before leaning into him and whispering in his ear. He was shy and annoyed, but he looked up. Ghost waited, patient, the humming of whispers quieter, softer, and pausing somehow along with him.

A small hand crept over a slim leg, and hovered a second before slipping into Ghost's grip.

KANE WAS at a loss for words. Ghost was doing a work of

magic so grand and complex Kane had never seen anything like it, and he was doing it without training or effort. River was at his side now, both of them checking Gabe over for injuries. The acrid scent of silver and burnt flesh rose from the glass bowl he'd handed Ghost, thankfully in time to collect the expelled poison.

River appeared to be as shocked as he was, both wolves and the newly restored youngster looking at each other askance. Kane realized he couldn't see Ghost, and stepped back from examining Gabe in time to see Ghost use his gifts again, this time on the youngest cub, the sorely abused boy from the bedroom at the apartment.

Kane tried to breathe past his surprise, and found himself walking to stand behind Ghost just as the cub glowed as his sister had done downstairs. Behind them, Kane heard a whoosh of soft scraping, and felt the rise of chilled air. He glanced over to see a window opening on its own. The cub glowed, brighter, the little one gasping, and the warm wind was back, rushing around Kane and Ghost, milling over the cub, then racing away. It ruffled hair on wolves and their clothing as it flowed to the window, and the pane slowly closed itself as the wind died.

He looked back in time to see the cub's injuries fade away exactly as his sister's had, the cub smiling for the first time in days as Ghost patted his tiny hand, then let him go.

Kane reached down just as Ghost turned his head and saw him, and he reached up a hand. Kane helped him to his feet, and he gasped, feeling the subtle thrum of power under the shaman's skin. Ghost smiled up at him, those tempting lips of his curved into a smile. Kane was helpless to resist, and dipped down, tasting him. Sweet and lush, Kane licked his plump lower lip, his shaman smiling as he kissed him back.

Kane slowed his kiss, mindful for once that they had an audience. He plucked another quick kiss from the succulent lips he wanted to taste forever, and squeezed Ghost's hand. He got a return squeeze, and he was immensely pleased by such a small gesture. He eased back, and Ghost tugged him along as he walked from the couch, to the loveseat nearby.

"Will you let me help?" Ghost spoke, not to him, but to the shy beta mother who huddled on the cushions, too terrified to look up at them. She shook her head, and Ghost sat on the coffee table in front of the seat. He held Kane's hand, in fact refused to let it go, even when he would have moved back, so as not to frighten her further.

The cubs, now healed, wormed their way past Kane, and jumped up on the loveseat with the beta. They snuggled up to her sides, and she held them close, eyes shut as she breathed in the scents from their inky black hair. She seemed to gain strength from them, and relaxed the slightest amount. She was as battered as any of them, but her spirit was especially fragile. They were all wounded in their hearts and souls by their experiences, but she seemed to have suffered the most, each memory a harsh and constant remembrance played out in her eyes.

"The pretty lady said he'd help. Remember?" The tiny female cub whispered to the older female, and she stiffened and shook her head. Kane was again left wondering who 'she' was, who this person was who was telling them about Ghost. Did they mean Andromeda?

He looked back towards the doorway, where Andromeda now stood alone, the door closed at her back. She met his eyes, and shook her head in a brief negative. It wasn't her then, telling the Suarez wolves they'd find a healer in Ghost. He returned his attention to Ghost, where everyone was watching. The young shaman was unperturbed by the attention, oblivious, his focus on the injured beta.

"She wants me to help you. If you cannot trust me, can you trust her?" Ghost asked softly, leaning forward the smallest degree. He still held Kane's hand, and carefully reached out with his free hand. She stared at his hand, and seemed to be frozen, not even blinking.

"I can hear her. She spoke to you as well, in your dreams. She spoke to all of you, all you need to do is listen. She wants what is best for you, if you'll trust her," Ghost whispered, and she sobbed once, hard, eyes watering. "Listen. She is speaking to you."

Kane found himself stilling, chin down, as he listened as well. At first he heard nothing, other than everyone's breathing and the combined heartbeats in the room. When it started, he lifted a hand and tugged on his ear, unsettled. It felt like someone was standing over his shoulder, and trying to get his attention. He took a quick look, feeling foolish for doing it, and got a glimpse of River's expression as well. The older shaman was standing at the window now, the one Ghost opened, and his face said he was experiencing something odd as well. He didn't appear to be disturbed, not like Kane. He looked like he was hearing news that he couldn't figure out how to handle, whether to be happy and pleased, or angry and disappointed.

Ghost was still on the table, hand out, infinitely patient. Waiting. The sensation rose again, and Kane wanted to step away, to move, but Ghost's grip on his hand was iron-tight. The young shaman, his soulmate, was in the back of his mind, and Kane, while constantly accustomed to having his wolves in his mind, found that Ghost's presence was one far more powerful than he was used to. The hand in his squeezed tighter, and the whispering rose and fell in waves, a susurration of half-heard words that danced through the quiet.

When she moved at last, Kane was startled from his trance, trying to listen to the unseen whisperer. Ghost began to work his magic on the beta mother, and Kane let himself blend with Ghost deeper, their connection richer, more complete. Ghost's presence in his mind rose as well, and Kane sucked in a deep breath, and on the exhale, found his vision usurped by the shaman's Spiritsight. The physical world dropped away, and Kane was in Ghost's head, seeing as he saw, hearing his thoughts.

Kane's knees went weak and his breath caught in his chest when he realized just what, or rather who, was talking to Ghost.

All shamans answered to the Great Mother. In the early years of their kind, according to legends, the shamans would literally speak to Her, the Great Mother, in actual face-to-face conversations, in the land of spirits. Their history was full of tales where a shaman would seek her out, and gain the knowledge or boon to avert disaster or save lives. Such tales were naught but stories, and Kane, like many generations before his, saw the Great Mother as a distant but benevolent spirit, a being less concerned with the individual trials of the wolfkin, and more focused on their species as a whole. Many wolfkin didn't believe at all, and Kane was in the minority that he trusted the shamans solely on the belief that they were shamans by her grace. As she chose the First Shamans, so she chose every shaman born thereafter. Many wolfkin saw the shaman's powers and gifts as a result of bloodlines and chance, and trusted to the ancient teachings and codes of conduct instilled in the new shamans during their apprenticeship to guide their behavior, not some obscure deity.

Yet now, in this moment, the quiet faith Kane had nurtured in his heart grew to a joyous swell of ecstatic joy and overwhelming relief. Their Goddess, the Great Mother, the Wolf of the Northern Star and the creator of their kind, was here, now, and Kane could hear her.

She spoke now, to his soulbonded mate, and worked through him. She blessed the shaman, and him, and every wolf in this room by her presence, and Kane felt for the first time in a very long time that the future had more in store for him and his people than strife and conflict. There was love, and healing, and there was more to come.

He closed his eyes, holding back his tears, and gripped Ghost's hand as the shaman healed the injured wolves one by one, his strength unfailing and beautiful to behold. Kane stood quietly beside his mate, his long lost wolf, and silently thanked his Goddess.

THE FAMILY WE CHOOSE

"WHERE IS he, Glen?" Cat asked as she paced, arms folded over her chest, staring hard at the door.

Glen pushed off the wall where he'd been watching Cat pace, and walked over to her, wrapping his arms around her and stilling her anxious movements. She stiffened, but he held tight, and she sighed, relaxing. Her head dropped to his shoulder, and Glen pressed a kiss to her red hair over a delicate ear.

"They're his people, Cat. They won't hurt him. You saw Ghost last night with that big guy yourself, right? Ghost looked happy, practically sat in that guy's lap."

"Guy? Guy? He turned into a wolf, Glen! A wolf! I saw it!" Cat whispered harshly into his shirt, and Glen hugged her, trying to calm her down. "Werewolves! Are we going insane, or are we surrounded by werewolves?"

"Certainly looked like werewolves to me, so I don't think we're both going insane. We might die of hunger, but I don't think we're going insane," Glen murmured, eyeing the door. It hadn't opened since the naked woman and her shape-changing cohorts had unceremoniously packed them up and carted them off through the woods, depositing them in the well-furbished but locked cabin.

It was morning, and nearing noon from the sun. Their cell phones had been taken away, and his camera equipment as well. Thankfully he still had his e-reader, so they'd watched movies after their one and only attempt to get out of the small cabin had been greeted with deep-throated growls and eyes that glittered in the dark outside the front door.

"What are they going to do with us?" Cat asked, hushed, shivering.

"Well, I'm not sure, but I'm thinking I'm hungry. And I could use some aspirin for my head. Let's go for a walk," Glen grinned, and stepped away from Cat, grabbing her hand and their jackets.

"Glen! They're out there!" Cat hissed, trying to pull him back from the door. Glen just gave Cat her jacket and shrugged on his own, and walked to the door. He flung it open, golden light spilling in the cabin over the threshold, the snow blinding. He held a hand up to shield his eyes from the glare, and blinked rapidly, eyes tearing.

"Mr. Mitchell, Dr. Medeiros, are you ready for lunch?"

Glen stiffened at the melodious voice that came out from the light, the words lilting with an accent that wasn't one he was familiar with, and he'd spent years around the world hearing all sorts. He lowered his hand, and tried to peer out through the light.

His eyes adjusted, the figure on the bottom step of the cabin porch coming into focus. A woman stood on the bottom step, a slim wisp of a thing with thick waves of golden white hair to match the sunlight and snow behind her. She smiled, her cheeks fair and blushed with the faintest of pink, and her eyes were the bright blue of the sky above.

"Oohhh," Cat sighed from his shoulder, as entranced as he was by the vision smiling up at them.

She was wearing a thin dress, the cotton a light gray that contrasted with the gold and white light that filled the mountainside. Somehow the dove gray drew the eye far better than the brightness around them, and his heart thumped hard in his chest as she smiled again, a smile that was somehow sweet and slightly predatory. He could get no grasp on her age, the dress and her body suggesting youth, but the way she stood, and the way she tilted her head, even the dangerous and beautiful smile, all of which said the woman in front of them was far older than she seemed.

And she wasn't human.

She stood barefoot in the ice and snow, the wind chill below freezing, in a dress suitable for high summer, and she looked perfectly comfortable.

"Glen? May I call you that? And Catherine? Although Ghost tells me you go by Cat. Delightful name, it suits you."

"Oh! Yes, Cat... Cat is fine, thank you. Who... who are you?" Cat stammered, and she slid her hand in Glen's. He was still trying to find his tongue, and could only give her a tremulous smile in return.

"My name is Andromeda." She took a step away from the

porch, and waved a graceful hand towards the path. “The young wolf you named Ghost is waiting to see you. Shall we go?”

She didn’t wait for them, merely turned in a smooth motion and walked down the path. Glen and Cat turned to each other, thinking for a second, then shut the door firmly behind them as they hurried after the mysterious werewolf woman.

“AREN’T YOU tired?” Kane asked him, and Ghost shook his head once, leaning into his mate’s side, enjoying the heat that poured off the bigger man.

“No, I am fine. Hungry. Is there more bacon? Sarah ate all mine.” Ghost walked back into the kitchen, his nose leading him to the stove. He sniffed, and he could smell bacon, but the pans were gone and the sink empty. Someone must have done dishes while he was upstairs healing the Suarez wolves.

He spun, and stared at the fridge, and the door opened with a hiss on its own. Kane laughed and he spared his mate a glance as he hunted among the plastic containers on the shelves inside, hand darting out when he got the scent of beef. Kane was leaning on the doorway, long legs crossed at the ankle, thick arms crossed over his hard chest. Ghost paused in opening the container, eyes trailing over the handsome man who was smiling back at him, a wicked gleam in his dark eyes.

He grinned back, and stepped away from the fridge, letting it close with a mental nudge. Kane laughed again, a rich deep sound that sent tingles all over his body and heated his loins.

"Put that back, youngling, I'll be making lunch soon. And look at you, using magic like a trained shaman. Don't let River see you showing off, he tends to see the less fun side of things," Andromeda said as she strode into the room, and pried the plastic tub out of his hands. He whined, and mourned the loss of a snack as she put it back in the fridge, firmly shutting the door. "And your humans are here, they're in the foyer." Andromeda pointed to the front of the house, and Ghost forgot the beef.

Ghost ran from the room, eager to see his humans. Kane was on his heels, the big man silent on his feet despite his size. Ghost was happy to have him there, as he was suddenly nervous to have his humans see him in his new form.

Glen and Cat were hanging up their coats in the foyer on a tall coatrack, toeing off their boots. Cat saw him first, and her eyes breezed right past him as if she didn't see him, settling on Kane instead. Glen turned and saw them too, and Ghost saw him recognize Kane as well. Glen gave the alpha a brisk nod, and both humans looked around the foyer, as if they didn't see who they wanted.

"Where's Ghost? Is he okay?" Cat asked, speaking to Kane. Glen said nothing, but Ghost watched as his gaze kept coming back to rest on him, staying longer each time.

"Ghost is fine. He's better than fine, actually," Kane replied from behind Ghost, “He was eager to see how you were both fairing this morning. We need to talk as well.”

Ghost walked slowly to his humans, even more nervous now than he was a few moments ago. Glen was watching him, and Ghost took the few steps needed to bring himself next to the man who’d been his alpha for most of his life. Ghost smiled, hands shaking, and found tears pricking at his eyes. Glen peered down at him with a questioning expression, the cut on his face and the bruises from being hit by the human killer mottled and dark. It hurt Ghost to see the injury, in a way it hadn’t bothered him as a wolf. Now as a man he felt something, a sharp ache that weighed him down.

“I tried to stop him,” Ghost whispered, and made a vague motion with his hand towards the wound. “I’m sorry.”

“What are you talking about? Who are you? How could you stop who?” Cat asked, looking at him and Glen. Ghost didn’t answer, just shook his head and rubbed at the tears on his face. She turned to Kane, and spoke, “What’s he talking about?”

Ghost was trying to figure out how to explain, lost for words, and Kane’s presence in the back of his mind was faint, not as prevalent, and he suspected his mate was at a loss for words himself. He could hear him trying to speak to Cat, but didn’t pay attention to what was being said. He was looking down at his feet, face hot, feeling uncomfortable. How could he tell his humans he was no longer a wolf because he’d had a dream with his Goddess and she told him he already knew how to become a man again, after fourteen years of mentally and emotionally imprisoning himself?

"Ghost?" he looked up, shocked, Glen's whisper faint and full of something he couldn't identify.

Ghost exhaled, the sound escaping like a sob, and met Glen's eyes. His human, the man who helped raise him, was more a father to him than the distant memory of his own sire, whom Ghost wasn't even sure was still alive. A new part of him, the clear, logical side of his human mind said he should be asking about his blood family, but the two humans with him now took precedence. Glen and Cat were his family. He loved them, and he was so afraid they wouldn't be able to love the man like they'd loved the wolf. He nodded, head jerking, and Glen's eyes lit up, full of wonder and awe, and Ghost could hear his heart pick up its pace and beat harder. Glen was excited, and Ghost breathed in his scent, and couldn't find a trace of fear or stress. Just the scent of happiness, if happiness could smell like anything—it smelled like how his human alpha did right now.

Big arms came up, and carefully wrapped around him, tugging him to a broad chest. Glen was by no means as big or as strong as Kane, but to Ghost it didn't matter. His human was hugging him. Ghost sobbed, and buried his face in Glen's chest, and hugged him back.

"Hey, buddy," Glen said, choking up himself, big hands rubbing his back as Ghost cried.

"FEEL LIKE talking now?" Kane asked, kissing his temple, and he put a heavy arm around his shoulders, hugging him to his side.

"Yes, I'm fine. No more tears." Ghost smiled at Glen, his human alpha sitting on the opposite couch next to Cat. She was holding her mate's hand, and she couldn't seem to stop staring at him. Ghost gave her a smile, and she smiled back, still a bit frazzled and in shock, but happy. Both his humans were happy, and Ghost was amazed and overjoyed that they were taking it so well. He kept waiting for them to start freaking out and trying to run away. They were both handling everything far too well, and Ghost was half afraid he was going to wake up in the wolf run at the sanctuary, the last few days a mere dream.

Andromeda and River were standing at the windows that looked out the front of the cabin and were silent, just watching, there to witness.

"So, start from the beginning, the morning the two men came for Ghost," Kane instructed, speaking to the humans.

"Sure... but I thought it was Luca?" Cat asked, her brow knit in confusion.

"Luca was my name as a child. I haven't been Luca in almost fifteen years. Ghost is fine for now." Ghost gave Cat a smile, and she bit her lip, but nodded in agreement.

"How old are you?" Glen asked out of the blue, and Ghost stared for a moment, wondering the same. He thought he was nearly twenty, but couldn't be sure. If he could reliably remember what came after thirteen he might know for certain.

"Ghost will be twenty years old in early summer," River said quietly from his spot by the window, confirming Ghost's thought. He smiled at the shaman, and Glen nodded, his eyes lighting on Kane's arm where it was draped over Ghost's shoulders.

"And how old are you?" Glen asked Kane, a touch sharp. Ghost tilted his head, eyeing his mate as Kane's mouth tightened as if fighting back a frown, but he answered anyway.

"I am forty-four years old. Very young for our kind," Kane supplied, and his tone made it clear that was the end to the digression.

Cat sent him a questioning look, but he just waved it off and motioned for her to start talking. She obviously wanted to ask what old was if forty-four was young, but she heroically restrained herself. Glen had his deep thinking expression on his face, and his eyes never strayed far from where Kane held Ghost on the couch.

"Well, I'd sent the DNA and pictures to Dr. Harmon at the conservatory headquarters. He's a wolf biologist who specializes in endangered subspecies, and he said he wanted to help after I sent the first few questions I had his way." Cat started to explain, reaching for her cup of tea on the coffee table. She took a sip, and made a happy face, clearly loving the taste. She put the cup down after taking another sip, and continued, "He emailed me, and said he could make it out for a visit, and that he would be bringing his colleague to go over my theory.

About Ghost being a dire wolf, but...guess that's wrong now." She frowned, and Glen patted her knee.

"You weren't really wrong, Cat." It felt weird to actually be able to say her name, to speak to her directly. It felt so odd. Her expression was confused, and Ghost smiled at her. "We were fashioned after the ancient dire wolf, that's what our Great Mother did to our human ancestors. Gave them the form of their greatest fears, so that they might live."

River groaned and covered his face, and Kane started to shake, laughing silently, and Cat just looked even more confused. "What?" Ghost looked around, but couldn't figure out what he'd said that was so funny. Kane patted his shoulder and gave him an indulgent sweet smile.

"Theology lesson later, young one," Andromeda said with faint smile, and then spoke directly to the human female. "Please continue."

Cat bore a faint frown, not understanding, but she shrugged and started again.

"Dr. Harmon shows up like he planned, and he's got this man with him and two conservation officers with him. What was that man's name, Glen? The man who, you know," she gestured to the cut on Glen's face, her own face whiter than it usually was, "the guy with the gun?"

"I don't remember, I kinda blacked out a few times. Started with an R, I think," Glen said, rubbing the side of his head, wincing.

"Remus," Ghost said absently, remembering how the male doctor kept screaming the killer's name. "It was Remus."

A terrifying growl ripped through the air, and Ghost held his breath, eyes instinctively searching for the danger in the room. His eyes landed on Andromeda and River, and Ghost pressed himself back into the couch cushions, the pale woman and her brother suddenly more frightening than any human with a gun. Andromeda's eyes were glowing, vibrant shards of fiery blue sky, and her hair was moving in a nonexistent wind. River was at her side, hands clenched, and Ghost could sense a strange and powerful magic move in the space between the siblings.

Kane was just as angry, from the change in his scent. Ghost could fell the rage building in the alpha, a red wave that frothed and boiled under the surface of their connection. He would have been scared at the level of anger being displayed in the room if he wasn't so certain it was directed at someone else. Glen and Cat sat very still and silent on the couch, holding hands, eyes dancing between wolfkin in varying states of ire.

"Who is Remus, Kane?" Ghost asked quietly, watching the play of thoughts over his mate's face. Kane was holding back his mind, the red fire still in the back of Ghost's head, just not as bright, restraining his emotions.

"Show me what he looked like, little wolf," Kane growled, and Ghost sucked in a sharp breath at the intensity on his mate's face. Kane put a hand on his cheek, and Ghost nodded, immediately opening his mind completely to his mate, showing him an image of the man who had tried to kill his humans and himself.

"Simon Remus," his mate snarled, lips twisted in hatred. "That man is Simon Remus, CEO of Remus Acquisitions. His older brother, Sebastien, was the man responsible for the death of Gray Shadow and your family."

"I NEED TO call Caius," Kane said, standing fast, keeping Ghost tight to his side. His little wolf made a noise that was almost a squeak, and he kissed his soft hair in apology at the rough move. "But first, we need to act on this." Burke and Gerald were both in the house, Sophia with a team patrolling the borders of the park.

"Burke! Gerald!" Kane shouted, the scraping of wooden chairs on the floor signaling they heard him. He turned to the living room door as his Speaker and newest alpha of his team walked in fast from the kitchen, Burke eating a sandwich of corned beef, brows lifted in query.

"Burke, I need our team alerted along with the Red Fern wolves. Simon Remus and Remus Acquisitions are involved with the attack on Ghost and his humans earlier in the week. Full border patrols, twelve hour rotations. Alert Sophia, now." Burke nodded quickly, and spun on a booted heel, finishing his sandwich in a single bite and heading for the front door. Kane looked at Gerald, who was watching Ghost with an odd expression on his face. The lesser alpha appeared to be in pain, and there was yearning, an emptiness in the way he gazed at his nephew that urged Kane to speak.

"Ghost," Kane murmured, and tilted his head down so he could smile gently at his little shaman. "Gerald is an alpha of Black Pine, Caius' youngest son. He is also your mother's brother. Gerald is your uncle, little wolf."

Ghost peered up at him, his lovely silver eyes wide, mouth parting in a small 'O'. Ghost clutched at him, fingers gripping at the waistband of his pants, before he carefully flicked his gorgeous eyes to the startled alpha still standing in the doorway.

"Gerald, this is Ghost. You knew him once as Luca, your sister Marla's youngest child," Kane said softly to the lesser alpha, who drew in a breath he could hear from several feet away. The scent of surprise and mild stress swirled in the air before it dissipated and a subtle thrumming of excited joy filled the space between them all.

Gerald was staring at Ghost, his face equally shocked as pained; Kane saw sadness and grief warring with a startled happiness. The lesser alpha was speechless, and Ghost huddled at his side for a brief moment before Kane could literally feel the small shaman summon his courage and move. The emotions traveling through their link were chaotic and messy, and Kane mentally stepped back, letting Ghost feel what he would without exterior influence.

Ghost moved from Kane's side, and took a few hesitant

steps towards the lesser alpha. Gerald stood motionless, eyes moving over Ghost as if he couldn't be certain of what, of whom, he was seeing.

With a swift and harsh breath, Gerald broke free from his shock and gave Ghost a small nod, a shaking hand wiping at his eyes as he went to meet the shaman halfway. Kane watched, cautious, because Gerald wasn't the most emotionally available or stable wolfkin, and his temper was harsh even among the few wolves with whom he shared speaking terms. Kane was ready to intercede, but he doubted it would be necessary. Kane may not have been close to Gray Shadow's family, nor with Caius' children, but there was one thing he remembered clearly—the love the sons of Caius bore for their only sister, Marla. She had been the vibrant and generous heart of the two families, binding them together far more securely than the friendship between Gray Shadow and Caius ever had.

"Uncle?" Ghost asked, tilting his head, looking up at the tall alpha.

"I..." Gerald swallowed, and tried again, voice cracking with unshed tears. "I heard the others talking earlier. Heard them call you Luca... Marla, your mom, she was my little sister. I loved her more than anyone in my long life, and you... you look just like her. I wasn't sure, but you look just like her..." Gerald exhaled, face splotchy, eyes red, valiantly trying to hold back his tears. "Boy, you drowned. We thought you dead. Father... Father said you were dead."

"I'm sorry," Ghost whispered, his eyes clear and dry, demeanor calm, but his voice and scent gave him away. He was struggling, too. Kane could feel it in the bonds between them. “I got lost.”

“Not your fault, boy. By the Goddess, you even sound like your momma,” Gerald ground out, tears spilling finally. He let them fall, and Kane made to go to his side to help him calm down, but Ghost beat him to it. Ghost gave Gerald a sad smile, and without any hesitation, stepped to his uncle and held him tight. Gerald paused, but then his arms were up, one hand buried in Ghost’s silky hair, pressing his nephew to his shoulder, clutching Ghost to him as if he feared the younger wolf would be torn away again and lost forever.

Kane smiled, relieved and inwardly cheered. Gerald may be redeemable after all. Having Ghost back in their lives would help close some of the wounds of their pasts.

“GERALD, STAY with Ghost,” he heard his soulmate say, and Ghost peeked past his uncle’s burly shoulder to see Kane gesture to Andromeda as he walked to the door. “I’m going to alert Caius to what’s happening, so you stay with him. He goes nowhere alone, understood?”

“Yes, Alpha,” Gerald rasped as he continued to hold Ghost tightly to his chest. Ghost felt the words rumble under his chin, and he snuggled in deeper to his uncle’s chest. His scent was vaguely familiar, and there was a sensory echo, as if this wasn’t the first time his uncle had hugged him, and he was remembering it even as he learned how it felt anew.

Kane gave him a sweet smile and a mental brush full of a poignant joy as he led Andromeda from the room, River on their heels. He could hear Glen and Cat on the couch behind him, whispering to each other quietly. Ghost sighed, and rested on the older wolf's chest, enjoying the sensation of hugging. It was different, and easier to handle. Receiving hugs while in wolf form felt differently, and while he liked being hugged by Cat and Glen, yet with no one but Kane had he felt comfortable remaining in the embrace. Now he was human, and the hug felt amazing. It was free of nerves and the itch to back away and remove the arms from around his neck.

"You okay, boy?" his uncle asked, and Ghost nodded, squeezing hard. Gerald chuckled, and pulled back just a small amount, peering down at him. Ghost smiled up at him, and his smile grew as his uncle grinned at him in return. "By the Goddess, you are her image. Your momma was a beautiful woman, and she would have been overjoyed to know one of her cubs took after her."

"She would? Did none of my siblings grow up looking like her?" Ghost asked, wildly curious. Here he was presented with family, and every question he had unanswered may be settled by the unexpected gift of his uncle.

"How much do you know, boy?" his uncle asked, brow furrowed.

"What do you mean?"

"Has anyone told you about your momma, your father?

Your brothers and sisters?"

Ghost sucked in a cleansing breath, and shook his head once, as Gerald scowled down at him. "No one's told you about our family? What's your boyfriend been doing all morning?"

"I… well. I had a task to complete this morning, and I only just learned to talk and walk… and now he seems to think this human Remus is a threat…"

"C'mon, sit down," Gerald rumbled, and he broke their hug, towing Ghost back to the couch. His uncle glared at Glen and Cat, obviously not happy having the humans in the room. He didn't say anything though, and Ghost gave his humans a quick smile, trying to reassure them.

"I've got no nice way of saying this, so I'm just gonna be blunt. Two of your sisters, Holly and Isla, along with your brother Misha, died with your momma when Remus Acquisitions tried to kidnap your grandpa and your family. Marla got shot and died from overexposure to silver, while your sisters and brother, being so small, died from an overdose of the same silver aerosol that kept your momma from Changing," Gerald said simply, eyes hard, sitting on the couch facing him, and Ghost tried to process what he was told.

"I barely…. part of me knows those names, but I can't remember their faces," Ghost fell back on the couch seat, and he tried to think. He couldn't, his mind filled with images of riding wolf back, his grandfather tearing through the summer forest, his shoulder on fire from a wound. "I can't even remember what Mom looked like, not really."

“Just a whelp when you went in the river, I’m not surprised,” Gerald said, and Ghost perked up when he caught the edge of a strange lilt in the older wolf’s voice. The accent was pleasing and brought up the hint of warm hugs and cuddles in front of a television, the aroma of beer and chicken wings. Something about football. The accent was subtle, and different, not at all similar to how Kane or Glen spoke. “Fifteen years is nothing to our kind, but that doesn’t matter when it’s nearly your whole lifespan.”

“Who... How many are...” He couldn’t understand how to ask, and the red starlight of Kane’s presence in his mind was dimmer, his mate’s focus somewhere else, so the usual mental support of vocabulary and fluid thoughts he got from his mate was stilted.

“How many are left?” Gerald said, sorting out what he wanted to ask. He nodded, eyes wide, biting his lower lip as he waited for an answer.

“Your older siblings and cousins made it, along with a couple of your younger aunts and uncles on your daddy’s side. They’re all grown now, and spread around the territory, or apprenticing in other clans. Ezekiel, your cousin, is a shaman as well, and is in Russia on the last year of his apprenticeship. He’ll be coming home this summer during the gathering.”

Ghost cheered at that thought, even though he couldn’t recall his cousin at all. Not even a glimmer of a face, or even saying the name. His frustration must have shown on his face, because his uncle put a large hand on his shoulder and squeezed. “It’s okay, boy. Don’t be upset if none of it’s coming back. Got years ahead of you to know your family again. And you weren't all that close to Zeke anyway, seeing as he was so much older than you when you got lost."

Ghost sensed a lessening of tension in his uncle's frame, as if the alpha grew easier with speaking the longer he sat next to Ghost. Something about the way he sat, and looked at Ghost, eye contact fleeting but sure, and the pained yet pleased expression on Gerald's face told Ghost that his uncle rarely communicated with anyone as freely as he was now.

"And.... and my father?" Ghost asked, afraid to know the answer. His parents had been soulbound; the death of one usually meant the death of the other. This, more than anything from his past, he remembered with powerful clarity.

"Well... that's a hard question to answer."

"What do you mean?"

"Your father is alive, but I can't tell you more than that."

"Can't? Why not?" Ghost leaned in, needing to know. He had Glen; he had Kane; and he had now his uncle, but his father, the memory of Josiah, pulled at his heart like nothing else. Gray Shadow was gone, and so was his mother, but his father lived, and the little boy buried in his heart still wanted his daddy. He felt foolish for this need, one that was growing stronger and harder to control the more he experienced grief as a human.

"Your father got shot, three times by silver. The shamans managed to get most of it out, but he was severely poisoned by the bullets. He taxed everything that day, trying to heal, taking care of your surviving family, and then the funerals of your momma and siblings... He even tried to find you through the bloodlines, but he couldn't sense you. I'm not surprised though; Josiah lost his soulmate that day. I've never seen a wolfkin disintegrate like that before. Josiah was always a strong wolf; man could've been an alpha if he'd had even a hint of command or the Voice. But that day, that day he was destroyed."

"No..." Ghost groaned, and he could see it. Less than a day bound to Kane, and Ghost knew that if he was to lose his mate, he would be broken beyond repair, and it would take the meadow Goddess herself to keep him in this world, and not follow Kane into Death.

"He held it together for a couple of days. Got your grandpa's affairs settled, then he disappeared. Your other siblings were all seventeen or older, and they were set on their own paths. He just disappeared out from under our noses. We know through the bloodlines to his other children that he's alive, but that's it. No one, not even my father, knows where Josiah is now."

"SIR, I have news you need to hear, urgently," Kane said as soon as Caius answered his cell. He sat in what must be Andromeda's private study, if the elegant yet comfortable décor and the Clan Leader's heady scent over everything was a clue. He swiped his cell on to speakerphone, and set it on Andromeda's golden maple writing desk.

"What is it, Kane? Heromindes is set to arrive any moment with the human captives, I don't have time for this." Caius was impatient, and Kane feared his Alpha would hang up before he could tell him what was going on. He didn't think Caius deserved to find out the grandson he gave up for dead was alive via text message.

"You'd do well to heed your Heir, Caius," Andromeda spoke, her Old World accent coming through strong as she growled at the cell. River was by the door, and the shaman gave a thin smile at the sound of his sister's growl.

There was a beat of silence, then the sound of a cautious breath could be heard. The White Wolf made everyone nervous, alpha or not; including Caius. There was a reason she was unchallenged for Red Fern these last fifty years.

"Andromeda, what a pleasure. I trust you are well?"

"As I always am, Caius. Enough pleasantries; Kane has news," Andromeda admonished Caius, and Kane coughed into his hand. She gave him a tiny quirk of her pink lips and nodded at the cellphone.

"Speak up, then, I only have a few minutes," Caius snapped, and the echoing boom of the Clan Leader storming through a door could be heard clearly over the line. "What is it, Kane?"

"A few days ago, humans attempted to kidnap a lone

wolfkin in New Brunswick. Luckily, the wolfkin was a shaman, and was able to escape the humans." Kane would not mention Glen or Cat at this time; Caius was not so forgiving of their secret being revealed as Kane was, and the Clan leader had yet to learn that Luca, that Ghost, was alive. "The shaman in question escaped here to Baxter, and is currently here in Red Fern. I have seen the shaman's memories, and I can confirm that the man who attacked him was Simon Remus."

The roar that ripped through the line was enough to make the cell's speakers crackle and spit, the volume too much. Rage and anger and the unspoken promise of spilled blood hung in the air, and Kane was reminded for the first time in years why Caius McLennan was Clan Leader. He was a vicious and dangerous creature who was ruthless in the extreme, willing to do anything to keep his people as a whole safe, no matter the collateral damage.

Kane and Andromeda held still, even though they were miles away and safe. River had a hand on the doorknob, as if he was about to leave the room if Caius started yelling. They dared not make a sound, as they listened to the clan leader of Black Pine struggle to control his rage. Ragged breathing eventually cooled, and Kane risked speaking after a few minutes of wordless waiting.

"Sir?"

A faint growl came through, but it wasn't an order to stay silent.

"Sir, the shaman who escaped from Remus... Sir, the shaman who escaped Remus is your grandson Luca," Kane said softly, keeping all emotion from his voice. "Luca is alive, Sir."

"Not possible," Caius bit out immediately, words strangled, voice dry and cracked. "Your hope and guilt deludes you, Kane, as it has these last several years. My youngest grandchild is dead."

Same damn argument, same damn stubbornness. Caius treated hope like a disease. The second Gray Shadow died, it was as if the future became something to be abided, not enjoyed.

"He speaks true, Caius. The shaman is indeed Luca, grown and fully realized in his powers," Andromeda confirmed, steady and calm. "Your grandchild lives, my old friend. Luca is alive, and he's come home."

Where the silence before was charged with the threat of violence, the quiet now over the cell was heavy, weighted by an unspoken pain and the tiniest, faintest hints of a bitten off breath. A moment, no more, then Caius spoke.

"Kane," Caius said over the line, his name clipped and hard.

"Sir?"

"Send my grandchild home to me, now," Caius ordered. "Have Burke bring Luca to me without delay, I want to see him with my own eyes."

Kane was ordered to stay here in Red Fern and protect the Suarez wolves, but they were healed now, physically at least, and Red Fern was equipped to guard them if Ghost must leave for Augusta. No one would take his mate from him, not even his Alpha's orders, and Kane would take him instead of his Speaker.

"Sir, I will bring him to you instead, we can be there tonight if you wish..."

"No!" Caius interrupted. "You must stay there and protect the Suarez wolves. I'll not explain to Heromindes that I pulled my Heir from guarding his bloodkin to play escort for my long lost grandchild. Stay and do your duty—Burke is powerful enough to bring Luca safely home to me."

"No, Sir—," Kane tried to speak up, refusing to countenance his soulmate traveling to Augusta without him. Being parted from Ghost, just the thought of it, sent a lance of pain across his heart and mind, and he tried to control his unreasoning fear that if Ghost left, he'd never see him again.

"Don't refuse my orders, whelp, I'll not stand for it! Disobey me again I will have you beaten bloody for insubordination!" Caius shouted through the phone. It was a hollow threat, but the anger behind it was not. Caius could no more defeat Kane than the humans sitting in the front room of the cabin. Kane didn't want Black Pine, not for a long time, if ever, but he would not lose on purpose to avoid his duty... so that meant Caius must lose.

"Caius!" Andromeda growled, "Remember where your heir is and whose company he keeps! You will speak to no one in such a manner in my presence!"

Silence.

Kane sighed, and was about to speak, to explain as best he could to his Alpha that Luca, now Ghost, was his soulmate, and that they couldn't bear to be parted, not now, not ever. He had no idea how Caius would take it; whether religion and Law were about to fight for Caius' reaction. Elation that his grandson was home and blessed with a soulbond, or horrified that an alpha was soulbonded to a shaman?

Andromeda made a sharp motion with a graceful hand, gesturing for Kane to stay quiet, as if she knew what he meant to say. He closed his jaw shut with a snap, and she nodded in approval. River shifted on his feet, but stayed silent as well, eyes intent on his sibling.

"Now, my brother, I know you wish for Luca to come home to you. Thinking him dead and gone these last several years was a burden of grief you never should have carried, and for Fate's cruel treatment of you both I am dearly sorry. But Luca cannot leave Red Fern, not in his current state," Andromeda said calmly in the direction of the cell, resting a slim hip on the edge of her desk and folding her hands neatly in her lap. She spoke to Caius as no one else could, as an equal and yet an old, respected friend. "If you wish to come here, my brother, then I will look for you gladly. It has been a long time since you visited me."

"What state is Luca in? Was he injured by Remus?" Caius growled. "What's wrong with him?"

"He is untrained in his abilities, Caius. He escaped Remus

by instinct and pure power, not skill. He is currently under the watchful eye of my brother River, and he needs to stay here until he has better control." Andromeda paused for a second, eyes darting to River where he still stood by the door. "Taking an untrained shaman with full access to his powers out of Baxter into the human world could be a disaster."

Caius made no reply for several moments, and Kane hoped he was thinking clearly, without emotion clouding his logic. Andromeda hadn't lied, not really; Ghost was untrained, and so far he had no issue using his powers where humans could see. He didn't believe Ghost was out of control or a threat, not to innocents, at least. All Ghost needed right now was instruction to not reveal his magic and abilities to humans who didn't already know about him and their people. Though Ghost was adaptable and smart; he probably already knew to be cautious. Letting Caius assume the worst of Ghost's control might mean the Alpha would let Ghost remain here in Baxter, with Kane.

And he didn't doubt for a second that River was watching Ghost already. The shaman couldn't take his eyes off Ghost whenever they were in the same room.

"Fine," Caius snapped. "I will think about how to best handle Remus, and you will do nothing but guard the Suarez wolves and my grandson. I will deal with Heromindes and the human prisoners, then once I have the names of the wolfkin traitors, I will come to Baxter. I will see Luca for myself, Kane. For your sake, he better be who you say he is, or I will not forgive your lapse in judgment."

"He is, Sir. I will be expecting you soon, then."

"And Kane?"

"Sir?"

"The day will come when you will not have the White Wolf to hide behind, or my grief to restrain me. I will not tolerate insubordination from you again. This is your second strike."

"Understood, Sir," Kane growled, and for the first time in a very long time he let a hint of challenge enter his words. He would not fight Caius out of greedy need to lead Black Pine; but to stay alive and whole for Ghost's sake, Kane would fight the world. Even if the end result was leading it.

Kane leaned on the desk, hands in his pockets, distantly aware his stomach was demanding food. Wolfkin ate a lot, and it took something major to pull them away from their food. Sex usually trumped food. Thinking of sex brought Ghost to mind, and he fought off his body's reaction. It helped he was in the beginning stages of a foul mood. He rubbed his face, trying to dispel the bad feeling left hanging over his spirit. Andromeda was watching him, but he hadn't anything to say about the call with Caius.

"You're not bothered," Andromeda said out of nowhere, one pale brow raised in question. He frowned, unable to understand her non sequitor. She saw his expression and chuckled, "His transformation this morning. It didn't bother you? Ghost was able to pull off a trick that hasn't been seen since the wolves of Red Fang were born."

"He's perfect, completely glorious. Of course he didn't bother me. I don't know how he did it, since I couldn't understand half of what I was seeing in his mind through our bond when he woke up from that dream of his. I'm confused, and concerned, but Ghost's power and abilities don't bother me at all."

"You're aware, then," she said, tilting her head to one side, her unblinking regard settled on his face.

"Aware of what?" he asked tiredly. He wanted to see Ghost. Hold his firm, slim body, bury his nose in the golden-reddish brown hair behind his ear and breathe him in, blocking out the rest of the world.

"That Ghost is your soulbonded mate." So plainly spoken, and so calmly too. He couldn't hear how she felt about that. She was a Clan Leader, one tasked with upholding the Laws and traditions of their people, and her brother was a shaman. Hard to say how she would react to a bond between an alpha and a shaman.

"Yes, he is," Kane said, and he closed his eyes in relief as the weight of carrying that worry inside seemed to fall from his shoulders. He opened his eyes, and gave Andromeda a measured perusal, trying to catch a glimpse of how she felt.

"Do you know what you're going to do?" she asked, the faintest of growls in her lilting voice.

"I have hopes, but nothing concrete. No one knows beyond the few of us here. Burke, and Sophia since he can't keep his mouth shut around her and she's too damn smart not to notice. River for certain, considering the not so subtle stares he's been throwing my way all day long. You, and obviously Ghost and myself," Kane paused, and went back to rubbing his face.

"What are *you* going to do, Andromeda?" he asked in turn, dropping his hands, trying not to give in to his rising stress levels. "A shaman and an alphaare bonded in your territory. Every history we have says that's sacrilege. You're the Clan Leader. So what are you going to do about this?"

Andromeda gazed back at him, her cool blue eyes remote, her expression closed off and undecipherable.

"It's not up to me, alpha, to interfere with the will of our Great Mother. I know better," she finally answered, a small smile twitching her lips. Her eyes were still cool, the blue as sharp as shards of shattered ice. "But be aware, if I discover you are abusing your access to Ghost's shamanic powers, you won't have time to incur our Mother's wrath—you'll be dealing with mine."

IN THE hall outside the Clan Leader's study, a small, thin blonde beta hovered, listening through the crack between the slightly ajar doors. She leaned in as close as she dared, and gasped when the Alpha Caius spoke the name of her lover's long dead nephew.

Luca, son of Josiah, the youngest and last grandchild of Gray Shadow and Caius McLennan, was supposed to be dead, drowned the day of the tragedy almost fifteen years prior. She had followed Roman from Red Fern to Black Pine that fateful summer, and spent the long years since in and out of his bed and affections. So she knew, better than most, how much he would want to know about his nephew. She also knew, because she was there that fateful day, that Caius had never expected his grandchild to be found alive, and had given him up for dead.

He was alive. And a shaman. Another of Gray Shadow's heirs was a shaman, and in the state, within reach. Her lover would want to know. He needed to be told.

She heard the Clan Leader shout, and jumped back from the door, scurrying down the hall to the stairs, and she ran up to the second floor.

The beta slipped through the half-open door of the now vacant room of Roman McLennan, exiled son of Caius. She could still smell her lover, his scent everywhere, filling her senses with his presence. He was days gone now, but she missed him dearly. He had left, without a word to her, no promises to send for her once he found a new Clan, but she had hope what she would tell him might change his mind, make him remember why he chose her the most above all his other lovers.

She pulled out her cellphone, and dialed, hoping he would answer. It rang and rang, and she bit back a nervous giggle when he answered after what felt like the thousandth ring.

"Roman? It's Claire... I'm sorry, please don't hang up... Roman, your nephew? The dead one? The other one, the one who drowned! He's alive..."

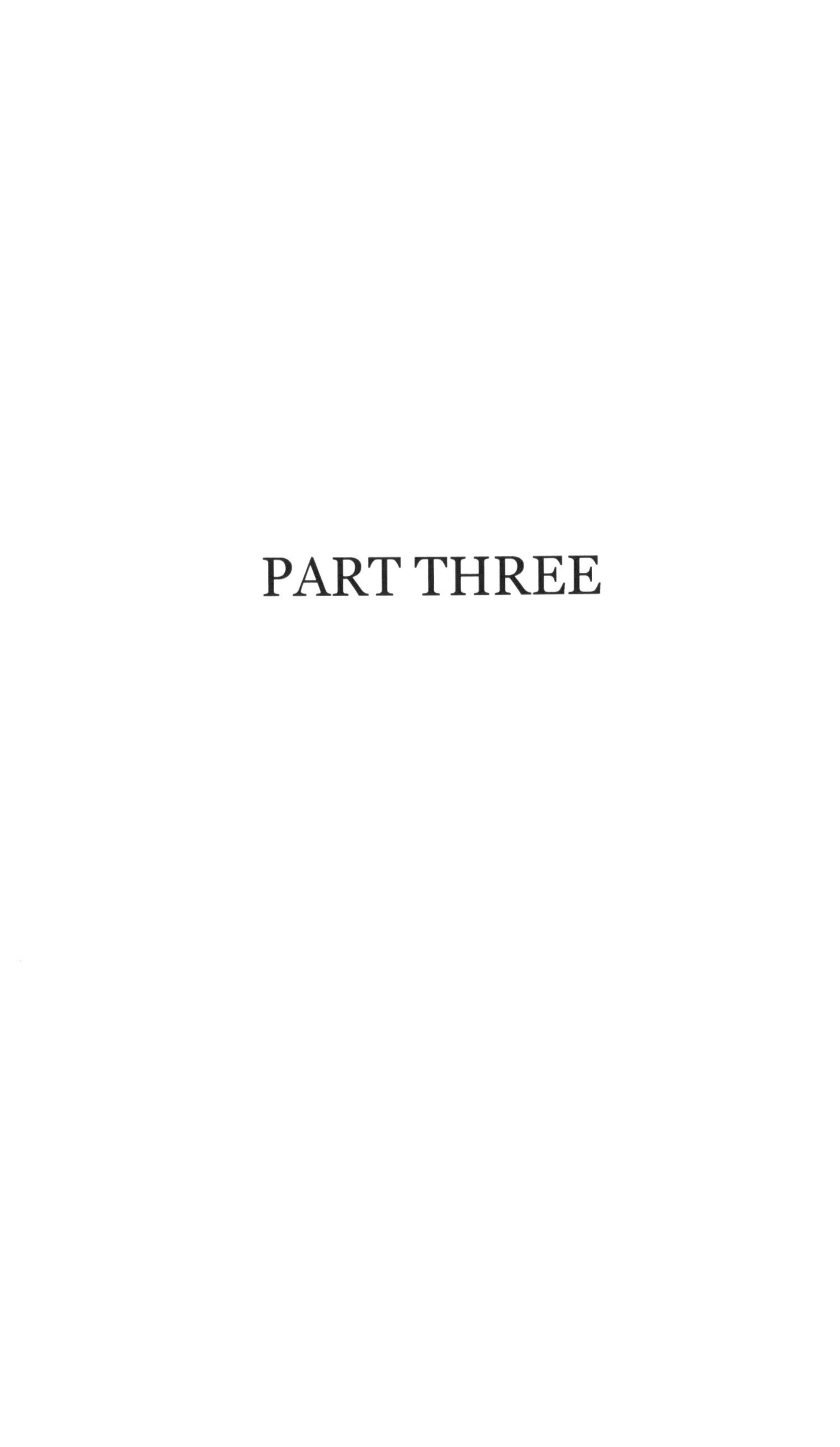

PART THREE

THE TIES THAT BIND

"PATROLS AROUND the clock. Doubled, no one goes anywhere alone. Restrict all cubs to their homes and the inner core of the park center. I need the food stores and our water supplies monitored at all times, and everyone is to check in with their head of family or their masters if they are apprenticed. Speaker Burke," Andromeda gestured to the greater alpha where he stood beside her, "will be in the pack links. If anything happens, no matter how seemingly small or meaningless, if it makes you nervous, contact him, myself, or Alpha Kane. Any questions?"

The mess hall was packed with people. Every member of Red Fern not on active patrol and all the members of Black Pine not on guard duty as well. It was late in the afternoon, the day after Ghost regained his human form and revealed Simon Remus's involvement in Ghost's attempted kidnapping, and Andromeda and Kane had gathered the clan for a meeting. After healing the Suarez wolves, Ghost had made it another couple of hours trying to explain the last fifteen years of his life, but he fell asleep mid-sentence and woke the next morning, hours later, in Kane's arms in a guest room of Andromeda's cabin. His exhaustion had been swift and extreme, coming over him quickly, and he'd not been prepared for the lack of energy that came after using his gifts. Breakfast that morning had chased him out of bed and his mate's arms, and his appetite was almost bottomless, only stopping when Andromeda flat out refused to cook any more bacon. Kane told him it was common, but in a way that left Ghost with the impression that Ghost wasn't experiencing the symptoms in the same way as other shamans. Especially with the way Shaman River was watching him, his cerulean eyes tracking every move Ghost made.

Ghost spent the morning recounting again and again his side of what happened when the interlopers attacked the sanctuary, mostly at River's insistence. For some reason the older shaman was having trouble understanding how Ghost was able to conjure the spirit-fire, and without engulfing the building in an inferno on his first attempt. Telling River he remembered Gray Shadow using the spirit-fire the day of the ambush and then conjuring it without thinking about whether or not he should be capable of the spell apparently wasn't sufficient explanation for the older shaman.

The myriad scents and the subtle thunder of dozens of hearts broke him from his memeories, and he looked out over the mess hall. There were so many wolfkin that Ghost's head spun, his senses overwhelmed by the scents and sounds of so many of his people in one place. He slipped his hand into Kane's, and his alpha pulled him in close to his side, tucking him under his arm.

Ghost watched the crowd. A sea of blonde hair and lithe bodies with gem colored eyes filled the space, and the random and few darker colors of Kane's wolves and what Ghost assumed were out-Clan mates occasionally showed through the throng. Surely Andromeda wasn't the founding mother of Red Fern—not all of the wolves present were her litter, were they? Most of the wolves looked similar, alike to a degree that spoke of multiple births and several twin pairs. Was she the mother of them all?

"Smart observation, little wolf," Kane whispered in his ear, hearing his thoughts through their link, "she is the founding mother of this current incarnation of Red Fern. Most of the wolves here are her descendants."

"I want things to remain as normal as possible, but please take these precautions seriously, my children. I don't want a repeat of what happened the last time we took our safety for granted," Andromeda said gently, her quiet voice reaching the far corners of the mess hall. Her wolves, from the rare elders to the suckling cubs, gazed back at their Clan Leader with nothing short of iron-clad faith and adoration. "I've called many of our brothers and sisters back to Red Fern to increase our numbers for safety's sake. The only wolves allowed back in the park are those vouched for by Black Pine, and our kin."

They are all related by blood? What about inbreeding? Ghost asked, giving up trying to speak as wolves milled around them, many of them heading for their Clan Leader, vying for her attention. He kept his thoughts to Kane alone, so they wouldn't be overheard. Sharing Kane's thoughts, his knowledge helped Ghost put words to the near instinctual worry he felt at the thought of a too small breeding pool.

Inbreeding was something Cat and Glen tried to prevent with the sanctuary wolves, especially since there was a small population in an enclosed space. Ghost shivered, very thankful he escaped the castration planned for some of the subadult wolves coming of age in the sanctuary. The Canadian government kept trying to tell Cat how to manage her pack, and she put off their orders for years until the last season. The sanctuary wolves were safely out of reach of man now, too, and he hoped they flourished in their freedom.

They all look for mates in other clans, usually at gatherings. There are no alphas here, and none dare migrate here either, so political pairings don't happen. Red Fern wolves mate for love. Andromeda allows refugees, ill-fit wolves in other packs and clans to petition for sanctuary and most requests are granted, so there's an influx of fresh blood every few years. Kane chuckled in the space of their link, and Ghost followed his attention to Red Fern's leader. **Andromeda's sire is where the coloration comes from, and even several generations later, it still breeds true.* * Andromeda was speaking to several wolfkin, their fair heads nodding in agreement as she gave them instructions and settled nerves.

Ghost absorbed Kane's reply, and he unconsciously nuzzled deeper into the alpha's embrace, breathing in his scent. It was a delicious and heady mixture of fresh-cut sweet wood, pine, coffee, and soap from their shower. Thinking of wolves mating for love, and then their shower that morning, stirred Ghost's blood, his body heating. The dull roar of many voices and the vibration of dozens of feet coming up through the soles of Ghost's borrowed boots receded until nothing existed for him except his mate.

He laid his hands flat on Kane's stomach and side, feeling rock-hard muscles under his thin shirt, heat radiating through the fabric. Kane was speaking over Ghost's head to someone, but he wasn't interested in who it was, or their words. He put his nose on the smooth, soft cotton, and pulled in deep, smelling the winter air caught in the threads and his mate's scent underneath, knocking his thoughts astray. There was so much to learn and do and think and simply be, and Ghost wanted none of it right that moment. All he wanted was to keep on existing in his mate's space, feeling him, smelling him, listening to the rumble of his words as he spoke.

Ghost ran his hands down Kane's sides, to his hips, nostrils flaring as he pulled his heady scent in deeper, until it felt like his mate was wound around his very bones, twined with the fibers of his very being. Red starlight pulsed, grew brighter, flooding his vision, his eyes floating shut as he leaned into Kane, everything falling away but for the other wolfkin's heat.

Time passed without meaning. He'd never felt like this before. Was it because he was a human man now? The female wolves of the sanctuary never appealed to him when he was in wolf-form, nor did the scrawny males, the submissives of the female alpha's pack. Perhaps his dual nature, both wolf and man, had kept him from having an interest in such things until he was back among his own kind.

Kane was everywhere. His heat, his scent, his taste. Ghost came back to the surface momentarily, as his tongue traced the dips and hollows of Kane's collar bone, revealed by the open neckline of his shirt. Salty, and yet sweet. He wanted more. A voice came to him through the haze, trying to calm the storm of heat and need, but he didn't want to hear it. He growled softly, teeth bared against his mate's soft skin, nipping and tasting.

"Kane, take Ghost to your cabin," an accented voice said, laced with humor. It came as if from a great distance, muffled. Ghosts sighed, lathing his tongue over a hard ridge of muscle, standing on his toes, fingers curled tightly in the fabric of Kane's shirt.

"What's gotten in to him? I'm not complaining, but he growls every time I try and get him to calm down." Kane was speaking. Why was he speaking to someone, and not touching him?

Ghost whined, and pressed closer, wanting to crawl inside his mate and roll in him, surround himself in every facet of his mate. He was falling deeper, every thump of his heart rocking him under his body's response to his mate. His thoughts were thinning, becoming less complete, Kane's sharing of thoughts and ideas, behaviors–it was becoming less important. He wanted something. Needed something, and soon.

"Your bond is getting stronger, deeper. Whether you knew it or not, you've had nearly fifteen years of adjusting to the bond. Whereas Ghost was a little boy, then a wolf, when the bond first began, so it never had time to grow in him as it did in you....the bond is hitting him hard, making up for lost time. The two of you need to cement your connection. Get him alone, now."

"Well, shit," Kane swore, grabbing at Ghost's hands. He growled again, trying to get closer, not wanting to be denied. "I'll ask how you know that later."

Big arms picked him up. Ecstatic, Ghost whimpered, and roped his legs around Kane's waist, and he buried his hands in his long dark hair, the silken strands flowing through his fingers like water. He ran his mouth slowly over Kane's high cheekbones, to his ear, nipping at the soft lobe. There was a rough hitch in Kane's breathing, and there was a change in his scent, a fiery and spicy taste of which he wanted more.

Kane was walking. Carrying him, to somewhere. He didn't care. All he cared about was the strength in the muscles under his hands, against his body, the way his skin tasted and smelled and felt. Chill air and the scent of pine greeted him, light filtering through his eyelids. He blinked, and lifted his head from Kane's neck. He saw a hillside covered in snow, a thin path cutting through the trees behind them as Kane took them down a new path.

"There you are, little wolf. Can you hold on for me? Just another few minutes?" Kane asked him huskily, his long strides devouring the ground as he walked along the path.

"What happened?" Ghost gasped softly, and he tightened his arms and legs around Kane's torso. He felt different. Head lighter, skin tingling, heart thrumming. And he was hard, his cock aching where it was pressed to Kane's stomach.

"Can you tell me? I don't mind at all that you want me, little wolf, but in the middle of a Clan-wide meeting was perhaps not the best place to... you know." Kane didn't sound upset, he sounded amused, and yet strained. "My cabin's right here, just hold on, I'm going to open the door."

KANE WOULD have dropped Ghost if the shaman wasn't clinging so tightly to his torso, nuzzling and nibbling his collarbone with his sharp white teeth, distracting him as he barely managed to open the front door. Kane kicked the door shut, the sound loud in the empty cabin. Arms full of horny wolfkin, Kane strode for the bedroom, shouldering it open, and he was too impatient to care that it slammed shut behind them.

Ghost was whimpering, and Kane's neck around the open neckline of his shirt felt like he had a field of love bites from his eager mate's attention. Kane grinned as he bent over, depositing Ghost on his back on the bedspread. Ghost clawed at Kane's clothes, biting his lips, his silver eyes burning like captured moonlight, glowing in the dim winter light trying to come through the shades over the window. He made a small keening cry, lifting his hips invitingly, his eyes burning brighter and brighter. His pale pink lips parted as he cried out, and Kane wanted to bend over and bite them, suck on the soft flesh. Dip inside and taste his mate. Yet getting rid of clothes was important. Nothing really fun could happen clothed.

"Easy, my mate," Kane whispered, and he put his hands on his own waistband, standing over Ghost, watching as his mate showed his need with every twitch of his body and whimper escaping past his lips. “Take your clothes off, little wolf.”

Ghost moved in a blur as Kane unbuckled his belt and pants, kicking off his boots and socks. Ripping fabric and discarded clothing fell off the bed in all directions, and then Ghost was naked, crouching on the bedspread, eyes wilder, lips parted as he panted, inch-long claws growing from his fingertips. Kane saw the flash of elongated eye teeth, as Ghost crouched lower and crawled on his hands and knees to the edge of the bed, face mere inches from Kane’s partially exposed groin. Ghost closed his eyes, briefly obscuring Kane’s view of his glowing orbs, and he breathed in deeply, sucking in Kane’s scent. Kane’s cock was hard, flushed red and leaking precum from the hard tip, tenting his boxer briefs.

Kane shucked his underwear, and yanked his shirt over his head. He tossed aside the last of his clothing, and just in time, as a wet, hot tongue flicked out past pink lips, and swiped over the head of Kane’s hard, aching shaft. Kane’s hands were buried in Ghost’s silken locks before he could think, and Kane lost all thought and plans of taking things slowly as Ghost growled, opening his mouth and sucking Kane’s cock past his lips.

He groaned, shocked and pleased, surprised Ghost knew what to do, that his little wolf knew precisely how to move his tongue, to suck hard, to swallow around the broad head of his cock.

A chuckle rippled through his mind. Silver-white overtones of lust and amusement, as Ghost peered up at him out of wild eyes. **I see what you like, my mate. Your mind, my* *mind. Your taste makes me ache. I want more.**

How Ghost could think, much less communicate past his lust was a mystery. Kane growled, and he snapped his hips forward, Ghost's clawed fingers digging into his thighs, meeting him halfway. Taking it easy, going slow, easing Ghost into a sexual relationship was a moot point; his little wolf was in charge, and Kane followed his lead. Ghost swallowed hard and repeatedly around Kane's cock, the head in his throat, his shaman reading his thoughts, seeing what he liked best and putting it to devastating use.

The smell of hot blood tickled his senses. Ghost's claws had dug deep enough to make him bleed. His arousal ramped up, his cock swelling, as Ghost sucked hard, and Kane gave in to the urge to fuck the talented mouth of his little wolf. Ghost's eyes flared white, and Kane could feel the wild lust of the other wolfkin as Kane ravaged his mouth, thrusting in and out fast, saliva dripping from Ghost's chin, his eyes tearing up, cheeks flushed red. Kane dug his own growing claws into Ghost's scalp, holding him in an unbreakable grip as his hips moved faster, each thrust sharper, taking his cock to the back of his little wolf's throat.

"I'm going to come, little wolf," Kane snarled, nearly breathless, sweat forming on his forehead and running down his spine as he thrust. "Tell me now if you don't want it."

Mine! Taking Ghost's claim as understanding, Kane thrust faster, his lips curling in a soundless snarl at the sight of his aching hard cock coated in saliva stretching his mate's mouth wide.

It was impossible but Ghost sucked harder. The increase in pressure was the breaking point; Kane threw his head back and howled, hips stilling as he came. His spine erupted in a storm of fantastic bolts of pleasurable release, he lost feeling in his extremities, and his thoughts collapsed under the weight of the waves of pleasure swamping his mind. Pleasure rolled through him, and as it poured through the connection of their mind-link, Kane could see, could feel, an answering wave from his little wolf.

Ghost's release flowed into him, a river of silver and white pleasure, filling him up. If emotions could have flavor, it tasted of spicy sugar and cinnamon, heady as mulled wine. He growled, wanting more of the sensations that flowed in a never-ending loop between them.

It was a miracle he was still on his feet, considering he couldn't feel his legs. Or much of anything except the heat of his mate leaning his shoulder on his hip. Warm puffs of moist breath floated over his overheated flesh, and he finally found the ability to move his head, looking down at Ghost.

His lover peered back up at him, his face pressed to Kane's lower abdomen, not far from his groin. Ghost's lips were glistening, parted as he panted. His eyes still glowed, but it was now dimmer, a hint of light compared to the solar flare when his passions were higher. Kane cupped Ghost's silky smooth cheek, brushing his thumb over his swollen lips. Ghost had come on the bed, staining portions of the blue quilt, the musky scent a delicious addition to the scent of lust filling the room.

"I like the way you taste," Ghost exhaled, voice raspy. "Am

I supposed to be this tired?"

Kane laughed, somehow finding the strength. He leaned down, and picked Ghost upright with hands under his arms, lifting him to his feet. Ghost grumbled at being moved, but came willingly enough, curling into Kane's chest and nuzzling his skin.

GHOST LICKED his mate's skin, tasting sweat and spicy arousal. He leaned his weight on Kane, knowing his mate would keep him upright. Their naked skin rubbed together, and his spent cock twitched with renewed life. Feeling Kane's pleasure through their link made his own explode in a startling burst of musky liquid, leaving him weak and boneless. He'd shot his seed all over himself and the bed, and the taste of Kane's hot fluid still coated his tongue. He licked the firm skin of his alpha's chest, mixing the tastes, and Kane moaned, the vibrations buzzing under his tongue.

"Alpha," Ghost whispered, licking again. The power that shone brightly in his mind, the power that was Kane's connection to his soul and spirit, was deeper, more interwoven with his own. Where the colors had been easier to define before as alpha and shaman, they now blended, changing, connecting on more levels, with tendrils thoroughly twining together.

"My little wolf, my shaman," Kane responded, dipping his head, nuzzling his temple, breathing in his scent behind his ear. Ghost shivered, and pressed himself fully to Kane's muscular frame.

"Mate," Ghost rasped. He breathed slowly, trying to still his heart, realizing he could now think, his focus no longer narrowed to his mate. He lifted his head, and peered around him, taking in the wooden log walls, the big bed and the white and blue quilts. He scented his alpha's presence in the room, and saw a collection of black duffel bags in one corner. He breathed in through his nose, and caught a hint of ozone and sulfur, something akin to smoke.

Ghost furrowed his brow, and sent a wordless query to his mate along their link.

"My tactical gear is in there," Kane murmured, nuzzling in his hair. "My guns, and vest. That's what you smell."

"Tactical gear?" Ghost asked, leaning into Kane's caresses. His eyes wanted to shut, suddenly heavy. His heart skipped a beat when a warm tongue licked behind his ear, teeth nibbling on the sensitive flesh there.

"I fight in human and wolf-form. When we breach buildings, I go human most of the time. Managing hallways and stairwells and fire-doors as a four hundred pound quadruped isn't easy. My wolf-form is too big a target for anyone with half-way decent aim to miss in most urban settings. In rural areas and forests, I go in wolf-form."

"Oohhh, I... I see," Ghost sighed, his head falling back on his shoulders. He didn't, not at all, as his tenuous grip on his thoughts once again let go. A new tension was rising inside, and he shivered. His cock was taking an interest in the very masculine body still pressed to his own, and the hands wandering over his torso weren't helping.

"Get on the bed, little wolf," Kane ordered him softly. Ghost tried to nod and comply, but all he managed was a graceless scramble backwards onto the mattress. Hands pressed on the quilt, and he dragged himself a foot or two before Kane's weight fell on him, lean hips spreading his legs.

Lips latched to his and a tongue slipped inside, exploring every crevice, filling his mouth with the intoxicating flavor of his alpha. Hands found his wrists and lifted them above his head, pressing them to the soft quilt, and the growl that purred from the man on top of him told him to keep his hands there. His heart racing, his mouth occupied by Kane's, his hands out of the way, Ghost lifted his legs and wrapped them around Kane's naked hips. He whined when a thick and hot piece of hard flesh rubbed against his own. Kane growled again, and a big hand tugged at his hair, pulling his head back as Kane nipped down his throat. Teeth that felt sharper than a human's blunt ones marked his flesh, and Ghost lifted his hips in response. His claws tore through the quilt, cloth shredding as he fought the need to put his hands on his mate.

When a clawed hand wrapped itself around his cock, Ghost lost the fight and his hands flew down to land of the bigger man's shoulders. He kneaded the firm muscles as Kane wrapped his lips around one of his nipples and sucked. A swift current of pleasure ran from his chest down to his cock, making it jump where it lay pressed between their abdomens. Kane growled in satisfaction, and kissed his way to the other one, latching on and driving Ghost wild. The sharp zips of pleasure amped his arousal, and he couldn't control the whines and whimpers of need escaping past his lips. Kane's heftier frame kept him pressed to the mattress, and he wanted to be closer.

"More," he whined. He didn't know exactly what he wanted but he *knew* that there was more to feel, experience. Kane's thoughts were hard for him to touch as his need grew, so he couldn't see what he was supposed to do. His claws scraped at Kane's shoulders, leaving red trails in his tanned skin, not quite deep enough to draw blood. Dark hair fell from Kane's head, the ends teasing his skin as the strands trailed over his chest and stomach. A wet tongue traced the lines of his abdomen, licking into the dips and curves of muscles as his alpha headed south.

"I'll give you what you need," came the heated whisper just before Kane returned the favor and sucked him deep. Lips touched his body as Kane swallowed him down, and Ghost lifted his head and cried out in disbelief at how it felt. Wet, tight, hot. Too much.

His mouth dropped open on a thin howl when Kane pulled back, sucking hard, his hands lifting and spreading Ghost's knees. Hands held his hips still as Kane devoured him, his tongue lapping at the head of his cock, dipping into the slit. A hand found its way to his tender sac, and it gently tugged, pushing back the building pressure at the base of his spine. His skin was on fire, every nerve alive, his teeth now dropped to fangs as he panted. He couldn't stop watching. In and out, over and over, Kane sank down on his shaft, soaking him with saliva, dexterous tongue stroking and licking.

The sound of shredding cloth filled the air. Ghost howled, spine arching, feet trying to kick at the bed, looking for traction. Kane pulled off, and fingers gripped the base of his shaft, squeezing hard for a moment. Ghost collapsed back to the bed, breathing fast and hard, whimpering past his elongated canines. His alpha looked up at him, and smiled, his grin feral, the tips of his fangs glinting in the dull winter light. He put both hands on Ghost's hips, and Ghost found himself suddenly on his stomach, face full of ripped and torn bedding, his shoulders resting on the bed. Those same hands lifted his ass in the air, knees nudging his legs apart so to hold himself up.

It was a vulnerable position, and Ghost whined in the back of his throat, abruptly worried. He didn't know what was about to happen, he just knew something was, and he couldn't hold back the sudden onset of nervous tension tightening his muscles.

"Sshhh, little wolf," Kane murmured in his ear as he leaned over Ghost, pressing his whole body along Ghost's hips and back. He felt the burning hot thickness nestling into his crease, and his hips pushed back at the heat, needing to be closer, even as he quavered inside. "Let me back in, baby."

Kane kissed his neck, licking behind his ear, big arms wrapping around his chest, holding him close. Ghost relaxed as Kane nuzzled him, the occasional nip of sharp teeth giving him shivers. The other wolfkin's words made little sense until the red wave of Kane's consciousness seeped into his own. Kane felt his nerves, his fear, and showed Ghost without words how he felt.....what he wanted. Ghost's whole body quaked as he saw a vision of Kane on top of him, looking down at where their bodies were joined in a way Ghost never knew was possible, thrusting in and out....Kane wanted him, and badly. So badly he shook and burned, at war with his very nature to dominate and seize what he wanted.

But he wouldn't. Ghost sensed under his desire to take an equally strong desire to protect. The alpha in him wanted to make Ghost submit, to accept his dominance and his body's invasion as Kane took him. The other part...the part that was all Kane, the kind and patient man who cared for his people.... the other half of his soul wanted Ghost to want him just as much, and was willing to wait for Ghost to say yes. Kane felt his fear and tried to ease it, giving him the choice of whether or not they kept going.

KANE TRIED not to let Ghost know how close he was to losing control and just taking his mate, fucking him into the mattress. His little shaman was understandably nervous, and their passion hadn't left them much time to talk, to express exactly what was going to happen. His cock was so hard he felt like he would blow at the tiniest movement, but he couldn't keep his hips from rotating the slightest amount, sliding his cock over the place he wanted to be buried balls deep.

Mind to mind, he saw Ghost's nerves. His little shaman was untouched....in every way. It was hard to remember he'd been stuck in wolf-form for almost his whole life. He took to humanity like he'd been raised in the clans, only hints in the way he talked and moved that spoke of the novelty he experienced with his human body.

Ghost whimpered, and pushed his ass back against Kane as he continued to pant. Ghost's arousal was extreme, and the scent of sex and need filled every breath he took. Kane held Ghost tighter, covering his smaller body with his much bigger one, and his weight and arms had the desired effect of calming the younger wolfkin. Showing Ghost exactly what he wanted, and how, seemed to startle his young mate, but not scare him. As Ghost took in the images Kane gave him, his body eased, the tension flowing from his lithe muscles.

Kane kissed his perfect shell of an ear, nipping at the small lobe. Ghost inhaled and lifted his hips in entreaty. He sensed the shaman's curiosity, his desire rising now that he knew what to expect. Golden brown hair with hints of red fell across the torn bedspread, and Ghost's silver eyes were beginning to glow again. The silver fires within cast lights of their own, and tiny waves of silver-white light danced over the blue portions of the damaged quilt. His head was turned enough for Kane to bend further and give him a gentle kiss on the lips, sipping lightly as Ghost sighed in enjoyment, beginning to move under Kane. The shaman's tiny movements were enticing and sweet, and Kane groaned as his restraint rapidly evaporated.

"Please, mate," Ghost whispered as he lifted his hips again, rocking his ass back against Kane's groin. Kane groaned louder this time, and when Ghost's words registered, he slowly sat up, keeping his hips flush to Ghost's perfect ass. "I want you. Give me what you showed me."

Kane growled, and he fought back his body's need to Change and mount the smaller wolfkin under him. He wanted so badly, the desire so intense, that maintaining control was nearly impossible. Until he felt along their bond Ghost's trust in him, his faith. Ghost believed that Kane would not hurt him, would take care of him.

Pulling away from his mate in that moment was the hardest thing he'd ever done. Kane left Ghost whimpering his need into the quilts, and scrambled for the edge of the bed. Kane reached out, nearly falling from the bed as he snagged his personal travel bag from the stack of duffels. He yanked it back to him, his claws ripping fabric as his impatience destroyed the zipper. He found his toiletry kit, and the tube of lube inside. He didn't often masturbate, his desire dimmed the last few years, so the tube was almost full. He grabbed it and returned to his mate, who was still as he left him, perfect, toned ass in the air, shoulders dropped to the bed, silver eyes watching him.

"Glorious and perfect," Kane vowed, getting back behind his mate. Taking Ghost this way soothed his baser nature, and would ease the ache of the younger wolfkin's first time. They may heal faster than humans and could tolerate more damage, but losing his virginity would still sting unless Kane took the time to do this right. He refused to hurt Ghost. Every cell of his being and atom of spirit refused to rush this, and risk hurting his mate.

Tube in one hand, he held up the other. His claws were out, his fingers longer now, partially transformed due to his emotional and physical state. He would do Ghost serious harm if he tried to prep him like this, so he focused on his fingers. It was difficult to calm himself enough to relax the minute muscles responsible for initiating the Change. Ghost whined in impatience, and he leaned his weight into his mate, sending wordless reassurances along their link. Ghost grumbled, but he subsided, joyously pliant and submissive enough to make Kane's cock jump eagerly, precum leaking from the flushed tip.

Eventually his claws receded, and he opened the lube and poured a thick dollop onto his fingertips. Ghost was watching through his eyes, and whined, bucking his hips. Kane moaned, but went about prepping his mate as thoroughly and quickly as he could. As he put a fingertip to the blissfully tight guardian muscle, he pulled Ghost's mind to his, the shaman submitting without qualm. He buffered Ghost from further fears, and he groaned in delight along with his mate when Ghost experienced the faintest of burning sensations as Kane pushed one finger past the second knuckle. Kane rarely bottomed, even when he was having sex on a regular basis, and he found that experiencing Ghost's first time as he added a second finger to the first made his own hole clench in sympathy, setting off an ache inside. His cock throbbed harder as he carefully moved his fingers in and out of Ghost's body, his little shaman whimpering pleas for more, both vocally and mentally.

Soon he added a third, and Ghost was bucking up every time he withdrew, chasing his hand and the sensations he set off inside. He held Ghost still, and curled his fingers, teasing around the small gland inside. Ghost howled again, a thin reedy cry that was full of want and need, and he canted his hips, silently begging for Kane to do it again. Kane obliged, and he grinned as Ghost cried out when he pegged his gland. His muscles were relaxed, though still tight, and Kane bit at his lip, wanting nothing more than to sink his cock into that welcoming heat.

GHOST WANTED more. Lots more.

"Do it!" Ghost cried out, arching his hips even more, spine curving. Kane had three thick finger in his ass, every other dip of the digits lighting up his nervous system with fire as he hit a certain spot. It burned, and he ached inside, and his heart was thumping so hard he felt like the poor organ was trying to escape his chest. Clawed hands scrabbled at the quilts, ripping a new layer to shreds, and his toes dug into the bed as well, claws protruding as his feet began the transition.

Part of him had enough sense to rein himself in, refusing to ruin this moment with his mate by turning back to his wolf-form. His claws remained but his transition halted.

Kane's fingers leaving his body made him gasp in dismay, and he whined until he felt a hard heat prodding at his entrance. He froze, and delved back into Kane's mind, peering through his eyes. Kane welcomed him, red starlight writhing like flames around his consciousness. He was inside Kane as surely as he was still in his own body, and he felt Kane's hands on his hips from both sides. Felt Kane's cock pushing at his entrance, felt it as if he were Kane, and when the big, broad head popped in past the tight guardian muscle, they both gasped together. Ghost watched as Kane watched, and when the head of his thick shaft was fully engulfed by Ghost's body, his eyes drifted shut, and he resisted the urge to fight of the invasion. He was full, too full, and his body wanted to bear down and force the throbbing heat out. It hurt, the deeper Kane went, and he must be huge, because it felt like there was no end to him, or the rising tension inside.

"Bear down, the pain will ease," Kane growled through clenched teeth, hands digging claws into Ghost's hips. He wanted to, but he was afraid Kane would leave, and not try again. "You won't force me out, little wolf."

Kane was in his mind, too. Hearing his fears, his worries as he had them. Ghost gave up all pretense of thought and obeyed, bearing down on the hot flesh splitting him open. Kane continued to sink into him, his inexorable thrust opening him inch by inch. When he pushed back, his body opened up even more, and Kane slid to the hilt with one smooth motion. Ghost jerked, sucking a quick breath, and held it as Kane stopped moving, holding very still. Big hands rubbed over his flanks, soothing and spreading heat. He could feel Kane's sac where it was pressed flush to his ass, and the man's thighs supported his own. They were joined, in all ways, and Ghost could feel the alpha's desire to move, to take him fast and hard.

The pain was duller now, replaced by a twitchy need. He moved, a slight hiccup of his hips, and Kane hissed through his teeth at the movement. The thick cock in his ass moved over that special spot....and Ghost melted. The pain evaporated, like it was never there at all, and in its place was a building heat. Kane must have felt it too, as he gripped Ghost's hips so tightly he couldn't move, and began to withdraw. He pulled back, the ridges and veins along the length of his shaft slipping over that spot, and Ghost lost all control over his body as mind-numbing pleasure swept over him. Constant pressure on the spot rolled through him in waves, and he whined loudly.

Kane stopped just before he left Ghost's body completely, stretching his hole from the inside, nudging at the guardian muscles, making Ghost squirm. Kane began to push back in, faster than his first thrust in, and Ghost opened his mouth on a silent howl when the hard head pegged his gland again, straight on, barely pausing before the thick cock was buried to the hilt.

Kane wanted to ride him fast and hard, so connected were they mind and body Ghost could feel his mate's desires and wishes. Yet Kane refused, taking them at a slow, deep, and thorough pace that left no part of Ghost's ass untouched by the rock-hard cock spearing him over and over. Kane's care of him, even in this moment, left Ghost feeling treasured, cared for...wanted.

Time stopped. All that existed was the sway of their bodies, the passage of winter light over Ghost's skin, the baited breaths and clutching hands as Kane moved inside of him. He went so deep that Ghost knew it should hurt, but there was no place for pain in what they did. Kane was so wide, his girth so thick, that Ghost knew he would bear the mark of his body forever, the shadow of this moment held in muscle memory.

His knees were digging into the bed, his claws were latched onto the quilts, his toes curled in the fabric. Ghost buried his face in the quilt, a hint of silver light playing under his lids as he closed his eyes. His hips were canted at an angle he would never be able to keep if it weren't for the hands holding him, giving Kane perfect access to his body. His alpha took it, took him, and made his possession thorough and clear. Through their link he felt Kane's arousal, how much he loved the soft satiny-grip of the hundreds of smooth muscles he thrust through.

When it happened, it shocked them both. One moment Ghost was floating in an ocean of pleasure, rocked by every thrust and drag of Kane's body, feeding his arousal back to Kane through their link. He was Kane, and Kane was him—they were one. Kane felt his claiming as if he were Ghost, and Ghost felt the tight hot grip of his ass as Kane sank into him with each roll of his hips. So when their orgasm hit, they were so deep and complete in their connection that it was impossible to tell who came first, and dragged the other over into bliss.

Heat, everywhere heat. Red flames and silver wisps of smoke, flashing bursts of light that burned for a heartbeat before dying, only to be reborn. A cry rose from the embers, coiling through spent muscles and over slick skin.

Wet heat, scorching hot, pumped into his body. Kane shuddered and roared, pushing so deep Ghost howled in response, pulling his face free from the shredded quilts, eyes blind and glowing. A rumble split the air, and the bed shook under them, the windows creaking in complaint. The walls trembled, and the pile of duffel bags toppled, the contents clanking as they hit the floor. A loud thump and a chorus of rattling noises filled the cabin, and neither of them reacted when the floorboards began to shake.

As quickly as it started, the phenomenon stopped, and quiet descended.

Kane collapsed, groaning, his full length pushing Ghost flat to the bed. The bigger wolfkin was shaking, and Ghost gasped for air under his weight. Warm liquid seeped from around the semi-hard cock still buried inside of him. He squirmed at the discomfort, and both of them moaned when Kane slipped free. He moved slightly to the side, and Ghost was able to breathe. Firm lips brushed over his forehead, nose, and cheeks. Ghost smiled, as Kane kissed his way across his face, finally settling on his lips. Soft nips and licks teased him into smiling wider, and Ghost blinked past sweat and tangled strands of his hair to see Kane smiling back at him between kisses.

"You okay?" Kane asked softly. Ghost gave a happy hum, and when Kane licked his lower lip, he dived in and sucked his tongue into his mouth. Kane returned his kiss, both of them exploring and tasting each other, sweat and their own flavors mixing.

"Just perfect," Ghost said with a smile when the kiss broke, and he dropped his head to the bed. Kane rolled to his side, and pulled Ghost with him. He tucked his head under Kane's chin, and their legs tangled together as he snuggled closer.

A door opened in the front of the cabin, and the floor creaked as someone entered the building.

UNEXPECTED GIFTS

BURKE STEPPED into the cabin, and the scent of sweat and sex assaulted his sensitive nose. The noises had quieted down a few minutes prior, and his eyes went wide as he took in the destruction.

"Is it clear?" Sophia whispered from behind him, and she peered around his shoulder. "Whoa!"

"Yeah...," Burke nodded, mouth agape as he stepped further into the cabin, taking in the toppled furniture, the pictures knocked off the walls, the open cabinets in the kitchen, the broken china on the floor. A log support beam in the ceiling was cracked in two, one half hanging low in the living room, and dust from the seams between logs coated the walls and floorboards.

Sophia followed him in, stepping around the debris on the floor, one small hand clutching at his sleeve as she jumped over what was once a framed picture. Glass littered the floor, and she grumbled about cleaning as they took in the chaos.

"What happened?" Burke asked, and he shook his head at himself. He knew what happened, he just couldn't believe it.

"I think we both know what happened." Sophia smirked at

him, and he bit off a laugh at the sound of a mattress creaking in the rear of the cabin.

Sophia jumped over a pile of glass and shattered frames, and bounced onto the couch, then over the back. The crunch on her boots was loud in the relative quiet, and Burke rolled his eyes at her antics, but he followed her all the same, not wanting to risk a shard of glass cutting through his boots. Blood was a pain in the ass to clean up.

They peeked down the hall, and saw movement in the light under the door to Kane's room. They would have risked a mind touch, but when Burke had tried earlier, he'd retreated as fast as he could, the emotions and thoughts that occupied the Heir of a highly personal nature, and he'd backed out before he was noticed. Hopefully.

"Guess they aren't having any trouble with the bond, huh?" Burke said wryly, and Sophia smacked him, even as she giggled. She was centuries old, and giggling. "Think they're done?"

"Well, the ground stopped shaking and the moaning stopped, so maybe."

The door opened, and a naked Kane scowled at them. Burke snapped his mouth shut, and Sophia's giggles fled fast. Both of them straightened, and kept their eyes low, in the area of his knees. Kane growled, the rumble of it drifting down the hall to where they stood.

It was an angry sound, a wolf defending his mate kind of sound.

**Maybe we should have risked another mind call,* Sophia said nervously, and Burke sent back a wordless agreement as Kane continued to growl at them.

"Hi Burke!" came a cheerful greeting, and the growl cut off. "Hi Sophia!"

Burke risked a look up, and Ghost smiled at him, naked and appearing thoroughly ravished. His body was lean and lithe, supple youthful lines and gorgeous skin shiny with sweat. Ghost was perfection, and Burke pulled a quick breath in through his teeth, a small hiss of surprise. Kane snarled as Burke took an eyeful of his naked mate, and Burke promptly dropped his eyes and made himself stand as still as possible. Interfering in a mating, and one so new, was suicide, especially with an alpha with the Voice. Kane didn't need fangs or claws to kill; he could drop them both with a thought, and in his current state, he might. Ghost was naked, a normal state for a wolfkin, but he was also fresh from his lover's bed, and Burke was another alpha, and far too close to Kane's soul-bonded mate...

"Stop growling at them," Ghost said, and there was a crack of sound, followed by the smell of ozone. Kane let out what could only be called a yelp, and Burke looked up to see the Heir rubbing his shoulder and glowering at the shaman.

"Did you just zap me?" Kane asked incredulously, staring down at Ghost, brow lowered.

"I don't know what 'zap' means. No growling," Ghost scolded his mate, and Burke choked back a snort and a laugh at the expression on Kane's face.

"Fine," Kane bit off, teeth clenched. "Why are you here?" he asked them, stepping back in his room and leaving the door open. Burke eyed the door warily, but Ghost's smile and cheerful wave gave him courage to walk down the hall...slowly. Just in case.

"Maybe some clothing would be a good idea?" Sophia said wryly, smiling at Ghost. The young shaman looked down at himself, and then back up at where they stood at the door. He shrugged, obviously not understanding Sophia's reasoning, and he turned back into the room, gifting Burke with a marvelous view of his pert ass. Ghost was sleekly muscled, a sculpture worthy of an old master, not an ounce of miscellaneous or wasted flesh on his body.

"Why are you here?" Kane asked impatiently from where he stood by the duffels, digging through his bags in search of clothing. He pulled out a dark tee and tossed it to Ghost, who made a face at it before pulling it over his head and down his lean torso. Kane tossed a pair of dark sweats, and he eyed Ghost until he pulled them on as well before he went back for something to wear himself.

"Well, we—," Burke paused as Sophia nudged him hard in the side with her elbow, "ouch! Fine, *I* was somehow nominated by a very concerned shaman with a melanin deficiency and a scowl to see if, and I quote, 'everyone is still alive' in here after a minor earthquake shook the park center."

"Oh, that was an earthquake?" Ghost asked excitedly, sitting on the edge of the bed with a bounce and tilting his head at Burke, that innocent smile on his face gaining a devilish glint.

"Uh, yeah bud, that was an earthquake. Sent River into a tizzy and Andromeda into a laughing fit. Half the cabins have broken windows and everything fell from the walls. Most of Red Fern is at Andromeda's place, freaking out."

Ghost just grinned wider, teeth pearly white and perfect.

"And Sophia?" Kane asked, dressing without hurry, buttoning his jeans and glaring.

"Came to watch me get torn to shreds?" Burke mumbled, and Sophia pinched his side under his arm, hard. "Ouch! Dammit woman, he won't have any part of me left to kill by the time you're through with me!"

She gave him a wide eyed stare and slow blinked at him, making him growl. Ghost started to giggle and he fell back on the bed, rolling around as he laughed. His obvious delight made both Burke and Sophia smile in joy at the sound. Burke made a happy grumble in his chest, the young wolfkin's emotions contagious, and Sophia took a step closer to Ghost, her pretty features lit up with appreciation.

"Children," Kane warned, one brow raised as he took in Ghost's giggles and their reactions to his mate.

Burke shrugged, and gave his best friend and alpha a smile. "Supper's done, too. Andromeda said come and get it, and she's not making more if there's nothing left by the time you get there. Hurry up, I'm starving."

GERALD'S CELL rang, and he pulled it from his jacket pocket. He eyed the small crowd outside the cabin with disfavor, and paced away from the porch where half of Red Fern was congregated. The shaking earth earlier sent most of the younger generations running to their Clan Leader, frightened out of their wits. Not Gerald, though. He knew the signs of a young shaman losing control of his powers. He'd finished his meal, ignoring the gimlet stares of the formidable beta, then found himself at a loss while the Speaker and Sophia went to fetch his nephew and the Heir.

"Hello?" There'd been no name on the Caller ID, and no one but Clan had this number.

"Little brother," Roman purred over the line, and Gerald stopped in his tracks, free hand curling to a fist.

"What do you want, Roman?" he snapped, wishing he'd ditched his cell after Father gave him to Kane. Roman was the cause of so many problems that Gerald regretted not hanging up immediately.

"Can't I be concerned, checking up on my little brother's welfare?" Roman said, and Gerald grimaced at the hypocrisy. It was because of Roman and his scheming that Gerald had no place in his father's home and left reliant on Kane's mercy for a place in the world. Gerald wasn't a fool. He knew why Caius sent him away. It was either send him away and let another wolf kill him, or slay his own son and deal with the fallout to his reputation.

"Maybe if you've ever shown concern for me before, I might believe it. What do you want?"

Roman growled quietly over the line, but he answered with an affected calm.

"I heard from Father that Marla's son was alive. Luca is back. Is it true?" Roman said, impatient as always, yet there was an edge to his voice that resonated with Gerald. It sounded like hope.

Gerald bit his lip, and looked up at the graying skies, the sun almost set. His little sister's face flashed before him, her long red-brown hair and bright smile now her son's. For all the discord in their relationship, the one thing the sons of Caius shared was the love for their only sister.

"Yes, brother. It's true. Luca is alive."

"Thank the Goddess," Roman breathed. "Where was he? What happened? Why didn't he come home sooner?"

Gerald pulled the cell away from his ear, and stared at it like it was a snake about to bite him. Roman's voice was full of concern, an emotion Gerald could barely recall his brother expressing more than a handful of times over the last two centuries. It took Roman calling his name for him to shake himself out of his stupor and bring the cell back to his ear.

"What happened?" Roman demanded, sounding more like himself, a touch of derision returning to his words.

"Nothing. Look, Luca's fine. More than fine. There was some problems up north over the border, but he handled it and escaped. He's here at Red Fern."

"Escaped?"

Gerald sighed, eyeing the trail, wishing to see Kane and his group returning so he'd have an excuse to get off the phone. He hated the infernal contraption, and talking to Roman was never pleasant, even when he was going out of his way to be marginally cordial. Roman may be exiled, but that didn't mean he couldn't talk to his older brother, and this conversation was actually going sort of well. For them, at least. Usually Roman just ordered him around or ignored him.

"Yeah. He was at a wolf sanctuary or something up there in Canada, and some humans tried to kidnap him, almost got him. He pulled a witchy trick and got away," Gerald explained, using the Old World term for a shaman using his gifts, "and now he's here."

"Luca is a shaman?" Roman said, almost breathless. "This is all amazing."

"Yup. Looks exactly like Gray Shadow, too. In his wolf-form, I mean. Otherwise, he looks just like Marla. Even sounds like her."

"That's...that's just great," Gerald could hear Roman breath in deep, and hold it. Even Roman had loved Marla, her loss hitting his older brother hard. "What is Father going to do? How did he know Luca was home?"

"Kane told him. Father ordered Kane to send Burke back with Luca to Augusta," Gerald said, still watching the trail, thinking this was the most normal conversation he'd ever had with his brother. Though mentioning the Heir probably wasn't the best idea, considering that Kane had soundly beaten Roman in a Challenge not too long ago.

"I can't see Luca if he goes back to Augusta. Do you think Burke would bring him to see me before taking him to Father? I'm not that far away, the detour shouldn't take long. I'd risk Father's wrath to see Marla's son, but I don't want to end up on the wrong side of an Alpha Challenge," Roman said casually, probably hiding how afraid he was of their father's temper. Caius may have lost some of his edge in the last several years, but he was still a formidable Clan Leader, and was sure to punish Roman for breaking his exile if he saw him in Black Pine territory. Gerald frowned, wondering why Roman was still in Black Pine territory. He'd stayed in the hall outside his father's study long enough to hear Roman get banished from their Clan.

"Kane refused to let Luca leave with Burke. Andromeda backed him against Father," Gerald said, and he saw movement on the trail. His new alpha and his nephew were coming down the path, Luca jumping over the iciest steps, laughing as Kane presumably scolded him for being reckless. Luca—No, *Ghost*—just smiled, and gravitated back to Kane's side like they were magnets. "Kane doesn't want Luca outta his sights after what happened with the humans."

"Kane defied Father?" Roman asked eagerly. Gerald grimaced again, a bad taste in his mouth.

"Don't get your hopes up, Roman. Kane's smarter than that. He isn't going to Challenge Father over a long-lost cub, no matter how much he cares about him," Gerald stated, and Kane and his group were almost upon him where he stood in front of the cabin. "Look, I gotta go. If you want to see our nephew, he's here in Baxter. I'd call and ask Andromeda for permission, don't just show up. You're not her favorite person."

Gerald hung up, not waiting to see if Roman had an answer to that. He really hoped Andromeda said *No* if Roman asked to come into her territory, not that he expected Roman to ask. Last time those two were in the same vicinity, Roman Challenged the White Wolf for Red Fern, and lost. Roman spent the last fifty years avoiding the White Wolf after his embarrassing loss, going so far as to leave any space she entered, even at the last gathering here.

Kane hailed him as they approached, and Ghost sprinted over the remaining distance, a sweet grin on his fresh face. Gerald found a rare smile on his own lips in response, and it grew into a wide grin of his own as Ghost barreled into his side, hugging him. His excitement was contagious, and Gerald chuckled.

"Uncle! Did you feel the earthquake?" Ghost asked, leaning back in the circle of his arms, silver eyes bright and glittering. He smelled like Kane, and Gerald felt his brows raise up as he deciphered exactly what type of scent was clinging to his nephew. Kane wasn't wasting any time staking his claim to Ghost.

"Hey, pup. I think everyone felt the earthquake. Doesn't happen often here in New England, but we get one or two every few years. Think we might get aftershocks?" He teased Ghost, ruffling his hair like he really was still a cub, and the young shaman dodged his hand, mock growling.

Ghost shook his head, his hair falling haphazardly. "I don't know what an aftershock is, but as long as Kane doesn't make me crazy with sex again, I think I can keep from breaking the park."

Gerald choked, coughing into his hand, and he let Kane tug Ghost away from him as he walked by. Burke and Sophia brought up the rear, and Burke gave him a small grin, obviously having overheard Ghost's statement.

"No promises, little wolf," Kane said as they walked up the path to the porch, the Red Fern wolves parting like a sea of blonde waves. "More sex is the answer, not less. You'll learn control soon enough."

GHOST FROWNED down at the hand gripping his elbow. River refused to let go, and pulled him away from the counter where he'd been sniffing out some more meat. He sent Kane a glance where he sat talking to Andromeda, but Kane didn't look his way before River moved them both out into the hallway.

"What?" Ghost asked, tugging hard enough to dislodge his arm from River's grip.

"You! That was you, wasn't it. What were you thinking?" River said, his whisper harsh, eyes flashing.

"What are you talking about?" Ghost replied, not bothering to lower his voice. He glared at River, and the weird mental pressure from earlier that morning was back. It was River, and whatever he was doing made Ghost uncomfortable. River's blue eyes seemed to darken in color, from cerulean to twilight in seconds. Ghost shook his head, pushing back with his mind at the odd sensation emanating from the other shaman.

"Do you mean the earthquake? I didn't mean to do that," Ghost growled, taking a step away from River, hands clenching to fists, his feet taking a combative stance instinctively. "Kane said it was because we were having sex, and that he would help me control it."

A wind moved down the hall, and blew in Ghost's face. River's blonde hair lifted slightly, the ends moving over his shoulders. River's eyes went black, and Ghost saw the wilder side of the shaman.

"Help you control them? Has he already? Has he used your gifts?" River demanded, stepping into Ghost's space. "Has your mate used your abilities?"

Ghost glared, but answered, not understanding what the problem was or why River was so upset. Kane had accessed his Spirit-sight at breakfast, and their connection was growing stronger by the minute, so it was bound to happen again. Not that he minded. Kane taking advantage of their bond wasn't even a thought, let alone a possibility. "Yes, but—"

"By the Goddess! I was afraid this might happen," River snapped, and reached again for Ghost's arm, his slim hand a steel band above his elbow. River started to pull him down the hall, away from the dining room and Kane. Leaving his mate was out of the question, and Ghost snapped.

He didn't know how it happened. One second, River was pulling him down the hall by his arm, and the next, there was a resounding bang in the hall as River's back hit the wood paneling. Ghost gaped as River moaned and slid to the floor, and the sound of chairs scraping over the floor and voices raised in concern met his ears. Ghost stared at his own hand, which was raised up, palm out and facing where River had been standing. He curled his fingers in and pulled his hand to his chest just as Andromeda and Kane seemed to materialize at his side.

Andromeda knelt at her brother's side, and Kane was there, wrapping him securely in his big arms.

"Are you okay, little wolf?" Kane asked, concern in his voice, powerful hands running over his body, as if checking for injury. "What was that noise?"

Ghost opened his mouth to answer, but Andromeda beat him to it.

“That was my idiot brother not using his head,” she snarled, even though her hands were gentle as she helped River to his feet. The other shaman wore a shocked expression, eyes dazed and their normal light blue color again. He groaned, and put a hand to the back of his head, pulling it back and checking his fingers for blood. There was a small dent in the wood wall, and Ghost’s stomach roiled in dismay. He’d somehow thrown River off of him and into the wall, and he didn’t know how he’d done it. He’d hurt a shaman.

“I just wanted him to let go,” Ghost whispered, “I’m sorry.” He said the last part to River, who was suffering under Andromeda’s fingers as she parted his hair, looking for injury.

“Don’t apologize, youngling,” she scolded, though not unkindly. “If you hadn’t knocked some sense into him, She would have, and he’d have more than a bump for his trouble.”

“I’ll speak with you later,” she murmured to her brother, who shook off her hand and nodded. River didn’t look at Ghost or Kane, keeping his eyes down at the floor, one hand on the back of his head. “Kane, perhaps you and Ghost should retire for the evening.”

“Good idea,” Kane agreed, though he didn’t look like he wanted to leave, eyes glowing as he stared at the older shaman. He hugged Ghost to his side. “C’mon, little wolf.”

Ghost nodded, and tucked his hands under his arms, afraid to touch anything or anyone. Kane put a big hand on his shoulder, and guided him away from River. Ghost was confused, and he couldn’t figure out what just happened.

Little wolf? Kane whispered in his mind, the red starlight ebbing and flowing through his thoughts. **Can you tell me what happened?**

I don't know, Ghost whined as they stepped outside into the night air. He saw a shadow following them, and looked over his shoulder. Gerald was at their heels, and then Sophia and Burke followed out the door. His uncle gave him a small smile, the barest glimmer of motion in the darkness. Ghost relaxed a little, feeling safer somehow.

He opened his mind to Kane, not having the words. He played the few seconds in the hall over for Kane, and felt his mate's anger and confusion as well at what transpired.

I will speak to River tomorrow, Kane reassured him. **He is fine, little wolf. He is wolfkin. Getting thrown into a wall is a matter of a few painful moments, nothing more.**

** I hurt a shaman!** he cried in his mind, ducking his head as they walked along the nearly invisible path, the moon hidden behind trees as it slowly rose over the horizon.

Shamans are not perfect, Ghost. They are as flawed as any wolfkin. Just because they follow Her will doesn't mean they can't mess up, Kane told him, words quiet in the night, pulling him against his side as they passed under snow-clad trees, their boots crunching on the icy path. The others were just as loud, the snap and crack of breaking ice loud in the vast silence of the night.

They walked for a few minutes in easy companionship, the mental buzzing of the others behind him telling Ghost that two of them, if not all three, were speaking to each other. Kane was quiet, eyes alert and his mind sharp despite the late hour. Dinner at Andromeda's had run long, the wolfkin taking the evening as a chance to talk and catch up. Gerald had been silent for most of the night, the tension he seemed to carry with him easing as the hour progressed. Sophia and Burke spent most of the evening teasing each other, their comments speaking of a lifetime of friendship. Ghost spent his time eating, enjoying the fact he was eating human-style food and not needing to worry about Cat yelling at him, or at Glen for slipping it to him under the table. Even sitting at a table was a treat. Andromeda and River ruled over the dinner crowd like monarchs, and what seemed to be the White Wolf's immediate family hovering around her and her sibling. River patiently listened to every wolfkin that spoke to him, and offered advice or teasing comments depending on the topic. Every once and a while his cerulean eyes would land on Ghost where he sat beside his mate, staring before the other shaman would tear his gaze away. Andromeda was a force of nature, and every blonde haired wolfkin in that grand cabin orbited around her every move like moths following a flame. The dynamics were subtle, but powerful. She was a Clan Leader in truth, her gender and class irrelevant in the face of her authority.

They passed the cabin where Cat and Glen slept, the lights out inside. Ghost caught their scents as they walked by, hours old, telling him that his human packmates were in for the night and had been for a while now. He smiled, glad they were here with him, and able to know him as he really was, and not just a semi-tamed pet. They left the humans' cabin behind, and turned the bend on the trail, Kane's cabin just ahead. The others followed, none of them taking the branching paths for other cabins, so they must be all staying in the same one. Ghost mentally shrugged, not bothered. Just the thought made him feel more settled, at ease. He had a picture flash through his mind, of wolves piled together in a cave, snoring and limp with sleep, warm and content.

Pack. He had a pack again. He had a real home, and it started with the wolfkin man next to him. Ghost peered up at his mate, who gifted him with a smile and a one-armed hug.

Their cabin loomed out of the darkness, unlit and as dark as the previous one. There was no difference from the outside, but as they got close to the door, Ghost saw a dark line along the front door, a darker shadow in the black. His shoulders tightened, and something told him to hold still. He froze on the path, and the others almost ran into him from behind.

"Stop," he said, his voice shocking in the near absolute silence of the night. "The door."

Burke walked around him, and Sophia around Kane, and Gerald moved closer to their backs, the three lesser ranked wolves moving to keep Ghost in the middle. He resisted as Kane tried to move in front of him, and narrowed his gaze at the front of the cabin. There was something wrong.

"I can see something," Sophia said, and made to take the last few steps to the front stoop. Ghost's heart leapt in his chest, and a cry of warning came out before she made a full step. She froze, looking over her shoulder at him. Kane made to move forward, and Ghost snagged his arm, pulling his much bigger mate back to his side.

"No! Stop!" Ghost ordered, terrified. There was a hissing whisper on the subtle wind, and Ghost struggled to focus the niggling fear past the distraction.

Something was very wrong, and it was the black odd-shaped shadow resting on the stoop in front of the door. Not even their eyes could penetrate the black, as the stars' dim light was shining brightest at the rear of the building, and the waxing moon wasn't high enough yet to be of much help. None of them had flashlights, and Gerald was the first to pull his cell out. He tapped the screen a few times, and sharp light exploded from his cell. It lit the path ahead and part of the stoop, but couldn't reach the black object to show what it was. There was a glimmer of something bright, long and thin, before Gerald moved the cell, trying to illuminate the object from a better angle.

"Burke," Kane started to say, and the Speaker moved forward. Ghost wanted to scream, every instinct telling him that Burke was in horrible danger. A sharp snap shot out as Burke stepped up, and Ghost's heart stopped.

"NO!" Ghost screamed, hands coming up, throwing off Kane's restraining grip. Burke finished his first step up just as Ghost reached out with his mind, and yanked the greater alpha off his feet and through the air backwards.

A deafening roar and a blinding light eradicated the peaceful quiet. Scorching heat poured in a massive wave, and the blast rocketed across the front lawn. Ghost screamed, and his hands felt the inferno as it fought against his power. Time slowed. Kane was trying to reach for him; Sophia was crouching, hands up in a futile attempt to protect herself; Gerald's cry of alarm was paused in his throat. Ghost pulled as hard as he could on Burke, and the Speaker raced the fire wave, flying past Ghost in a blur.

The fire raged and his ears were assaulted by the explosion. He stood against it. How or why would be answered after he beat the savage energy that eddied around the wall of solid air he'd raised the nanosecond Burke was behind him. Eternity happened in the space of a single instant, and Ghost held the wall forever. Red and orange flames licked at his hands, but could not reach past him to the wolves he shielded.

Finally, after what felt like a lifetime, the fire died away, no longer eating at him. His panting breaths were loud, and his ears rang. He was tired, never more exhausted in this minute than any other moment in his whole life, including the fateful day he fell in the river. His hands blazed with agony, and sweat started to drip down his temples. He shivered, and straightened as best he could, somehow having fallen into a half-crouch as he fought back the shockwave and flames. Smoke rose from his jacket sleeves, thin wisps, and more smoke billowed out from the remains of the front of the cabin.

A groan broke his shock. He cried out, and spun, looking down and frantically searching through the smoke for his mate. Kane was just a step behind him, Gerald next to him. Ghost sobbed in relief, and knelt at his side, trying to touch

Kane's face and whimpering in pain as his hands tried to follow his commands. Gerald was sitting up, and the lesser alpha crawled to a small bundle of limbs nearby. Ghost managed to cradle Kane's head and shoulders in his lap just as Gerald picked up a coughing Sophia and dropped her in his lap, both of them sitting on the slush-covered earth. She tried to shrug him off, but he won the battle, and she fell limp on his wide chest, her dark gem-like eyes blinking slowly as she gazed around the fire-lit front yard.

Shouts rose from the woods, and Ghost spared the rescuers a single glance before he returned his attention to his mate. Kane was breathing, and appeared untouched. Ghost shivered again, and reached for Kane with his mind, searching for his red starlight. It glowed low, the waving patterns slow and languid. Ghost prodded at the starlight with his own, brightening it, and Kane opened his eyes just as Ghost ran out of energy.

"Kane?" he sobbed, crying, tears running down his face, burning thin lines of pain down his cheeks. The skin on his face felt tight and dry, and he figured he was burnt there as well. Not as bad as his hands, but enough for tears to sting. "Kane, please be okay."

"Sshhh, little wolf," Kane whispered, eyes closing briefly in what must be pain before he lifted a hand, and wiped at a tear. "I'm fine, my love. Let me up, let me look at you."

Ghost had no strength to argue. Kane sat up, moving with some stiffness, but he appeared to be unhurt. He clutched at Ghost, pulling him to his chest just as a pack of wolfkin breached the clearing, many of them in wolf-form, others still human. Cat and Glen came running with them, pulling on coats as they exited the tree line.

A wraith flowed over the debris, a terrifying creature that glowed with its own light, purest white and it moved with a deadly grace that caught Ghost's attention even through his pain and exhaustion. Pain made him cry out, and he lost sight of the illuminous being when Kane made apologetic sounds as he tried to examine Ghost's hands.

"Ghost! Oh God, sweetie, no!" Cat cried as she ran to him, falling to her knees in the melting snow, her gentle hands grabbing his wrists as he tried to pull them back to his chest. "No, baby, keep them away from your clothes, you've been burned. Don't move."

"Get Shaman River!" Kane shouted, and Ghost whimpered at the volume. "Shit, love, I'm sorry. Sshhh, you'll be fine in no time. Wolfkin, remember? You'll be just fine." Kane crooned to him, nonsense sounds as Cat held up his arms.

Glen peered down at him, worried, eyes tight and mouth pinched. Ghost tried to give him a smile, but it fell flat. Glen relaxed at his attempt anyway, and gave him a quick nod.

"Burke," Ghost gasped. "Find Burke, please."

Glen's eyes widened, and he nodded again, gaze lifting to search the clearing. He disappeared after a second, two blonde wolfkin following him.

"Kane? Goddess, his hands!" Sophia crawled across the ground to their side, collapsing next to Cat, her already pale face ashen now even in the light from the flames. “Kane, his hands!”

“Sophia.” Kane spoke her name, calm and in control. She shivered, and dragged her eyes up to his. “Sophia, are you well?”

She blinked. Again, then pulled in a steadying breath and relaxed. She nodded, and leaned back on her heels, Gerald standing over her protectively, one big hand on her shoulder. She didn’t shrug him off, instead relaxing even more at his touch.

“I’m... shaken. Fine, boss,” she said, and then rubbed at her face fast before dropping her hands. “I’ll help them find Burke.”

“Good,” Kane said simply, and Gerald helped the beta to her feet, both of them moving with care, stiff and sore, but functional.

It was getting harder to keep his eyes open. He wanted to stay awake, to get up and find Burke. He wasn’t sure if he’d pulled Burke to safety in time, and he didn’t know how far he’d thrown him to make sure he escaped the blast. Ghost tried to look past Cat, but Kane’s hands on his shoulders and Cat’s grip on his wrists held him still. He should be strong enough to dislodge her, but he couldn’t, and frowned. His hands weren’t responding, and the cold ground and freezing air actually bothered him, seeping into his bones. He shivered, and couldn’t fight off the cold.

“He’s going into shock,” someone said over his head, and

Kane pulled his back against his chest.

Ghost lost his hold on reality then, the last thing he felt before the black was Kane's arms.

PLAN FOR THE WORST

KANE HELD Ghost, his mate, unconscious. The scene was chaotic, wolves running around or standing in shock, a few of them wrangling with the fire. Glen, Gerald and Sophia were searching for Burke, and Kane bit back his worry.

He couldn't reach Burke mentally, his best friend's quicksilver mind a blank absence from its usual place. Burke could be unconscious, hurt, or....Kane shook his head, refusing to countenance that Burke was dead. They survived the bomb, surely Burke did as well....

He looked up from Ghost's face in time to see a cream-colored wolf break the tree line, running full out for them. River transformed at a full run, sliding to a stop in the snow on his knees, reaching for Ghost around the human woman.

"He's in shock, third-degree burns, and power-drained." River stated, blue eyes vacant, staring at Ghost as his hands held the young shaman's head. "What happened?"

Kane assumed River's question was directed at him, and he answered just as a great white shadow moved in his periphery. The White Wolf stood over them, her shadow covering them, her mouth open to reveal dagger-like fangs and a blood-red tongue tasting the air. Her glacial eyes burned with a fire that made Kane hold very still and speak with a calm he truly didn't feel.

"There was a bomb on the front stoop. Ghost tried to warn us, but we didn't listen. It exploded...and Ghost did something. Burke set off the trip-wire, but he wasn't caught in the blast. Then...I don't know how, but Ghost held back the blast wave and the flames. Some of the wave hit us, and threw us all back...I must have been knocked out. I got some images from our link before he passed out. Whatever Ghost did, he shielded us from the majority of the explosion."

"Power-drain is the biggest worry. He can fall into a coma if he doesn't get his levels restored, and he won't be able to heal his injuries." River let go of Ghost's head, and turned his attention to the angry red burns and blisters forming on Ghost's hands. "I don't have the strength to heal such a condition and his burns, but thankfully we have another option, so it won't be up to just me."

River stood, and gestured to some human-form wolfkin nearby. "Help them back to Andromeda's; I'll treat him there"

Kane made to protest, but the subtle shift of the White Wolf in the snow made him rethink. Kane stood, and lifted Ghost in his arms.

I will hunt the ones responsible, a thought whispered past his mental shields, and Kane nodded to the White Wolf as he carried his mate to safety.

HIS HEAD really hurt. And his ribs. And every inch of his body.

Burke coughed, ribs screaming, and rolled to his side, or at least he tried. Whatever he was laying on moved and creaked, and he shuddered in pain. Crushed pine and smoke met his nose, and he sneezed, groaning as his ribs complained even more.

"Hey now, don't move. Easy buddy," a soothing voice reached his ears, and Burke blinked teary eyes, trying to see who was talking. He cautiously moved his head, and saw naught but starry skies and the rising moon.

"Wha...what's going on?" Burke asked his unseen companion, and tried to remember, well, anything. Leaving Andromeda's, walking back to the cabin....then nothing.

"I'll tell you, but you gotta stay really still, okay? Your friend is climbing up to get you, but you need to stay still," the invisible man warned, and Burke frowned, really confused. "You were in an explosion. Somehow you ended up getting blasted into a pine tree. You're about twenty feet up, and we don't want you to fall, so hold very still."

"Huh," Burke murmured, staring at the stars. That explained the weightless feeling. He was in a tree. "I've never been blown up before."

He heard laughter as his eyes rolled back in his head, the stars fading.

"ALL YOU need to do is open the link as wide as you can," River reiterated, cutting away Ghost's clothing as Kane sat on the side of the bed beside the unconscious shaman. "Power flows between you already, a near constant exchange. Just let it happen, and his body will pull what it needs from yours."

"I understand," Kane nodded, and sank down to his side, careful not to touch his mate's badly burned hands as he curled around him. He put his forehead to Ghost's temple, smelling smoke and sweat, and his mate's own unique scent. Kane closed his eyes, and breathed, trying to calm his nerves.

Finding the connection between them was easy. It was everywhere, his thoughts encapsulated by Ghost's presence in his mind. Even unconscious, his little shaman was present, his starlight restrained and fitful, but there. Kane knocked down all his mental walls, and breathed through the sudden vulnerability of his open mind to the wolfkin nearby. Kane could hear the far off murmur of many minds, but turned his focus away from them and gave it all to Ghost. He was fully recovered now from the explosion, and his strength was now his mate's.

A river of crimson energy flowed from his center, where the red and black star burned. His spirit, visible and realized in a way he'd never thought about before mating with Ghost. He followed the energy, and it twisted through his being until the color began to change, lighten, rivulets of silver and white energy twisting through the crimson. This was where he joined with Ghost. Their spirits becoming one, every heartbeat drawing them closer to being one soul. Kane never knew he was incomplete until he found contentment and joy in Ghost's embrace. Here, in the vast nether of their spirits, Kane hovered at the place where he ended and Ghost began. He drew in his will, and pulled on the crimson power of his star. It answered, and roared down the river of light towards Ghost's spirit, spilling over the edge of an abyss, to a tiny speck of light that fitfully burned in the distance.

Kane floated in the heavenly spaces, sending every atom of energy he possessed to his mate's star, a far-off glimmer that grew brighter as the stars swirled in the heavens above.

"Kane," a whisper broke through the quiet, echoing. He ignored it, and concentrated on keeping the flow of energy constant. The silver-white star was again vibrant, flares of brilliant light shooting off into the abyss, a tumult of energy that spun tendrils out to him, through him, into him.

The echo returned, his name spoken over and over, gentle chiding calls that irritated and soothed in a confusion that finally broke through his concentration. He was pulled from that heavenly place, and back to reality. Kane gasped, and his whole body jerked on the mattress, eyes opening to meet lovely silver orbs full of emotion.

"Ghost," he sighed, and he cupped the sweet face of his

mate, kissing his pink lips. Ghost sighed in his mouth, opening for him, tongues mating in a languid dance. Kane pulled back, but only enough to look down, and see the fresh skin flushed with a healthy glow on Ghost's healed hands.

Kane tilted his head to see River sitting on the other side of Ghost, looking exhausted but satisfied. The older shaman nodded, blue eyes quiet as he gazed at Ghost. Kane's mate whined and curled into a ball on his side, burrowing under Kane and breathing out a long sigh of exhaustion.

"Get some sleep, both of you." River slipped off the bed, and turned off the lamp before heading for the door.

"Wait," Kane whispered, River pausing at the doorway, one hand on the knob. "Burke?"

River looked back at him, eyes flashing in the light from the hall. "Burke is alive and well. Minor injuries. Go to sleep."

The door snicked shut behind him, and Kane sighed, muscles going limp as he curled around Ghost and held him tight.

SOPHIA PUNCHED the wall. She snarled at the pain radiating up her wrist, and went to strike again. A big hand grabbed her wrist, and she spun, lashing out with her other hand, claws out and ready to slash whoever dared touch her.

Gerald dodged her strike, but kept his grip on her wrist,

tugging her to his chest and wrapping both arms around her, effectively keeping her from hitting him. She brought her knee up, enraged, ready to lay him out, but he twisted, and the blow landed on his thigh instead of his groin. He grimaced, but held her fast.

"Stop, woman," he growled. "Save your anger for the enemy, and spare the walls...and my hide!"

"Enemy? What enemy?! We could be surrounded by traitors, but we don't know who they are!" she cried, frustrated and angry. "Waiting on reports like this is killing our chances of finding them."

Her fear after the bombing had morphed to rage, but after rescuing Burke from the tree, there was nothing to do but wait for word on Ghost and Kane's condition. The soul-bonded mates were with the shaman, and the White Wolf was hunting, searching for the person or persons who planted the bomb that nearly killed them all.

With Burke unconscious, and Andromeda gone, Sophia was left in charge, the Black Pine wolves waiting in the large living room of the Clan Leader's cabin, waiting on word of everyone's condition. Every able-bodied beta was out patrolling the park, circling back to report at the cabin as they finished their sweeps before returning to patrol another section. With Burke out of commission and Andromeda busy, Sophia was left handicapped by her class. As a beta, she could be many things, warrior to mother, but she was horrible at speaking mind to mind, and with more than a couple of wolves in a link, she got lost. Here was where Burke was invaluable; he could hold several simultaneous conversations at once with multiple wolfkin, and not drop a link or confuse the threads. She was no Speaker, so the wolves on patrol either had to stay in human form and use cells or radios, or return to the park center and communicate one on one with Sophia.

"Let me help you," Gerald said softly. She frowned, and looked up at him, his swarthy face flushed with a red hue. "I am no Speaker, but I can help."

"What?" she was so confused she didn't notice when he'd stopped restraining her, and the embrace changed to holding. She rested on his chest, hands on his hard pecs, and her eyes went wide as she finally understood what he was offering. All alphas, lesser and greater, had the gift of command, to varying degrees. Gerald's reach was substantially longer than her own, even if he was a lesser alpha. "By the Goddess, can you?"

She surrendered pride and went with necessity. Gerald nodded, his eyes locked on hers for a long moment before he let her go and strode for the front door where the next wave of runners were coming. With Gerald handling long-distance communication, she could focus on the rest of Red Fern. She let him deal with the wolfkin in their four-legged forms, and she grabbed the radio from where it hung from her waistband when it squawked with a new update. She took down the all clear and noted the border section, and then watched the alpha through the front windows, wondering if the explosion had finally knocked some sense into the older wolfkin.

Gerald, son of Caius, and Kane's newest wolf, may not be the greater alpha Fate demanded of him, but a lesser alpha was better than no alpha.

"Sophia," a faint voice called, and she looked up to see River coming carefully down the stairs, moving like he'd been in the blast instead of his patients. She hurried to join him as he made the ground floor, and his expression was all she needed. She exhaled, and her stress levels dropped a few notches.

She opened her mouth to ask, but River held up a hand and beat her to it. "Burke is awake, and asking for you. First door on the left at the top of the stairs. Be quiet, Kane and Luca... sorry, Kane and Ghost are sleeping next door. They need their rest, so don't be long."

"Thank you, Shaman," she replied, giving him a respectful nod before she took the stairs three at a time.

She felt his eyes on her as she went up, and she couldn't shake the feeling that he wasn't as happy as she was about the astounding luck of her team mates.

TREASONOUS ACTS

"DO WE know if any targets were killed?" Simon asked, tightening the straps to his tactical vest, eyes on the illuminated map projected on the wall of the situation room. His temporary base of operations was located at a closed campground on Katahdin Lake, southwest of Baxter State Park.

"Our source says there were some injuries, sir, but no fatalities," the tech answered, his headset chirping and his face pale from perennial lack of sunlight and nerves. "The shaman was present, sir."

"Our spy was able to plant the bomb inside the cabin?" Which was the plan, to take out the Speaker and the Heir's First Beta, reducing the monster's chances of mounting an effective defense when his teams breached the park's borders. Roman was convinced that Kane was too strong to fight directly, and needed to be defeated by grief instead of brute force. Killing his wolves one by one would leave the Heir vulnerable to grief, and perhaps his control of the Voice would diminish enough for him to be rendered unconscious. The source said the Heir and the long lost shaman slept the night before in the Clan Leader's cabin, so logic said they should be there again that night. Killing the shaman and the Heir now wasn't the plan. "Was the shaman one of the ones injured?"

"No information, sir. We lost contact with the beta after the bombing. Source said the wolves in question returned sooner than expected and the placement wasn't on target. No contact since then," the tech answered, clicking away at his keyboard, studiously avoiding making eye contact with Simon.

"Fuck," Simon muttered, not liking the idea of going in blind. They needed their spy in place feeding them information so this wasn't a repeat of Sebastien's blunder fifteen years prior. Sebastien messed up in letting his insider wolves leave the park prior to the ambush at the gates—if they'd stayed, then perhaps Remus Acquisitions would have their multi-billion dollar military contract producing super-soldiers. "That's what I get for sending an amateur in to do a professional's job."

Not that he had much choice, since the park was shut tighter than St Pete's Gates to a sinner. Simon pursed his lips and whistled, the shrill sound making most of the technicians in the make-shift control room jump. Though nothing made the humans more nervous than the sound that came a heartbeat later, a deep, low rumble of a growl that swept through the room. If he wasn't so impatient he would have regretted the folly of whistling for Roman like he were a family pet, but he was past the point of caution.

A shadow passed through the projector beam, blocking the map as the beast that was Roman stalked around the tables and desks, head down, eyes glittering in the light from a dozen monitors. Quick flashes of shiny teeth reflected as the beast dropped his lower jaw, heavy bellowing pants loud in the closed space. Simon swallowed, doing his best not to let his hands shake. Roman, a deeper shadow in the artificial lights, appeared and disappeared, and Simon peered into the darkness, about to order the lights turned on and damn his view of the map.

Hot breath misted the back of his shoulder, and a ripping noise made him jump. "Turn on the fucking lights!" Simon shouted. The lights clicked on, revealing the nightmare wolfishly grinning at him with unholy glee. He swore, backing away from the demon dog that tossed his head in a canine equivalent of laughter and spit out a black shred of his sleeve.

"Not funny, asshole," Simon snarled, and sent a lethal glare at the techs as some struggled not to laugh. A few snickers escaped, but he didn't want to take his eyes off the werewolf long enough to reprimand anyone. They were all worthless anyway.

Where the shaman in New Brunswick had been a big, intimidating creature with devilish silver eyes and snow white teeth, this monster was truly frightening.

A shaggy, thick coat in deep browns and blacks in a subtle brindle pattern covered the massive frame of the werewolf, his eyes black pools of liquid shadows that seemed to glow even in the overhead lights. Standing, they were nearly the same height, the wolf's head coming to the center of his torso, and the animal's powerful frame was a few hundred pounds of densely packed muscles. A thick neck and massive skull dominated by giant jaws and large eyes attached to the equally huge chest and shoulders of the beast showed very clearly the hunter that almost killed off mankind at the dawn of civilization. Claws that retracted like a cat's gauged at the floor as Roman paced in front of him, eventually turning his back to Simon, thwacking him hard on the hip with a huge bushy tail. He could damn near count each bone in the appendage from the force of the blow, and Simon gritted his teeth to hold back his indignant cry.

There was a mass exodus in the make-shift command room once the noise akin to the snapping of wet wood rose from the now sitting beast. A whole body shudder rippled under the fur, a second before a wave of flesh rose through the dark strands, raw and angry looking before it changed, melting into blemish free human skin. Limbs contorted and bent, snapping and straightening. The skull's transformation was the thing of horror movies, the transition rough and incredibly painful looking, and when teeth receded back into the warping jaw Simon almost lost his supper. Simon knew that the more powerful of the wolves, the greater alphas, made the Change in a swift and almost graceful transition, but the lesser wolves struggled. It seemed the lower the wolf's power-ranking, the harsher the Change.

He'd heard from the other wolves on his payroll that some betas could transform in seconds, as smoothly as a one of the ancient Greater Clan Leaders, but he'd yet to see proof. Betas and lesser alphas were the magic runts of the werewolf society, the shamans and greater alphas holding all the true power. Simon had yet to get access to a greater alpha of enough power to influence a large number of wolves, and his attempts to capture a shaman were all fruitless, the closest he and his team had come being the gray one in Canada. If he'd known the werewolf was a shaman and not just a lone and vulnerable beta, Simon would not have risked trying to take him. Shamans were dangerous and crafty, always slipping away before his traps could snare them. Simon's belief in the shaman's magic had been nearly non-existent right up until one chased him through a house with a wall of conjured fire and scorching hot air.

The only shaman DNA they had was a corrupted sample from Gray Shadow's body, taken hours after his death as he was prepared to be burned on a pyre. Roman had stolen the blood, and due to the increased vigilance after Sebastien's failed abduction attempts, Roman wasn't able to get the blood out to him in time to keep most of the sample viable. It wasn't until Roman was sent to retrieve Sebastien for retribution that Simon got the sample, and by then it was almost too late. It was contaminated by silver, and the minute strands of DNA they recovered were enough to prove they needed more.

A very naked and sweaty Roman stood at last, his muscular frame covered in hard muscles and flushed skin. Simon tore his eyes off the beast's ass, still astonished at how human he appeared when he was anything but. Simon wasn't gay, not even a little, but he was well aware that the werewolf was an envious specimen of masculinity, despite his nasty personality. Whenever they were in the same space, Simon was incredibly aware of the creature, as if his senses refused to forget there was an apex predator nearby. At least, that's what he hoped it was, and not the constant reminders of the creature's physical perfection and casual disregard for clothing.

Roman turned and Simon saw his smirk, as if the werewolf knew he'd been looking. The naked creature stalked him, cock long and intimidating even flaccid, swinging slightly with each step, and Simon could smell musky male heat and the sweat that misted hot smooth skin as Roman towered over him. His stomach quivered, and sweat pooled at the base of his spine. He wanted to touch the smooth flesh exposed to his gaze, the desire sudden and unexpected, and incredibly disturbing. Roman's scent filled his nose, and it was so powerful he could almost taste the werewolf's skin under his tongue.

"See something you like?" Roman growled, and Simon made a concentrated effort not to look down, the beast so close now that he could feel the intense heat emanating from his groin. Simon frantically shook his head, and Roman grinned, an evil twist of his lips that flashed a hint of fangs. "Be careful, human. Your scent betrays you. I may ignore your words and slack my lust in your tight ass. I haven't had a man's ass in years. Ever been fucked?"

"Back off, you animal," Simon tried to demand, but it came out a breathy whisper. Roman leaned down just a slight amount, and sniffed at Simon's neck. Simon was horrified that his limp cock twitched, and he held his breath. Somehow he was pressed back against the table behind him, hands desperately grasping at the edge of the table, Roman leaning over him. The creature's body heat rolled over Simon, and black spots danced in his eyes.

Roman's mouth opened on his neck, and he felt dagger-sharp fangs scrap over his skin. Roman nuzzled down under his collar, and Simon gasped, sucking in air and forcing himself to stay still. He felt Roman's hard cock pressing eagerly against his stomach, and Simon was about to risk pushing the beast away when Roman struck.

Simon's cry was strangled as fangs sank into his shoulder where it met his neck, under his collar. White-hot pain lanced the muscles as Roman sank in deep, huge arms wrapped around his body, thighs spreading his legs, taking him off his feet, forcing him back over the table. He struggled, but Roman growled with a mouthful of flesh, hot blood spilling past his lips. Simon froze, instinctively holding still as the predator marked him. Roman didn't tear into him, but that didn't mean he wouldn't.

Roman growled in satisfaction, sucking, rubbing his hard cock over Simon's abdomen, making him whimper in fear and pain. And confusion. His cock was thickening in his pants, pressing against the zipper, hardening at the pain caused by the strong suction on his neck. Roman was drinking his blood, lapping at his flesh with his fangs buried deep. Simon was aroused, even as his heart drummed with panic and his head went dizzy.

Abruptly Roman released him, throwing his head back, lips covered in Simon's blood. Trails of hot liquid ran down Simon's chest under his shirt, and Roman lifted a hand, ripping his shirt to bare the wound. His tactical vest was ripped from his chest, landing on the floor with a thunk. Simon struggled, but Roman held him easily with one arm, the free hand sliding down over his chest and stomach. A hard hand grabbed his throbbing cock through his pants, squeezing hard, making him cry out, hips jerking. Roman's grip hurt, and he squeezed a few more times, making Simon writhe in his arms in an attempt to escape. It may have hurt, but his cock responded to the stimulus, growing harder, aching with need while Roman's rough touch made him whimper. He'd never let anyone touch him like this, and his body was going up in flames as Roman took what he wanted.

Roman licked his lips, and Simon shuddered at the dark eyes glowing above him that shifted from human to animal. Roman's hand was working him faster, claws out, and Simon looked down when he felt cool air on his groin. Roman had sliced through his pants and underwear, exposing his groin. A big hand capped with claws stripped his cock, fast and hard, the pain and pleasure indistinguishable. His balls drew up close to his body, and he jerked as his orgasm was dragged from him, white ropes of hot liquid coating Roman's hand and spilling over their thighs.

Roman's hand abruptly left him, claws flashing again as his belt was slashed and his pants dropped to the floor. Fear crawled out of his stomach, and he scratched at the werewolf's arms. "No! Dammit, let me go!"

Roman snarled, fangs fully dropped, eyes wild. "I've got nothing from our arrangement but scorn and near misses. I was promised power, but you've given me nothing but hollow, useless words. I'll take what I want now, and you can let me, or I'll reduce you to ribbons as I fuck you into submission."

"I don't want it," Simon said, half lying, not giving permission but not denying Roman's claim to his body. He saw an image of Roman bending him over, rabid with frenzied need, and his hole clenched in aching need and fear. He didn't want this animal, he couldn't. He refused, but his body had other ideas. There was no way his cock was thickening again, responding to the thought of being mounted by this monster, but it was, and Roman knew it. Roman chuckled, a deep evil sound that made liquid heat pool in Simon's gut. "I hate you."

"The feeling is mutual," Roman growled past his fangs, and claws flashed in the lights, tugging and ripping off his clothing. His boots were reduced to rubber bits and his socks weren't spared either, the small pile of cloth scraps and tactical gear pooling at his feet. He was naked in seconds, Roman plastered to his body, marking him with his scent and nudging at his stomach with his huge cock. Simon was by no means a small man, but this creature outweighed him and outclassed him in power, and was manhandling him like a ragdoll.

He found himself thrown over a hard shoulder, upside down, Roman's arm around his knees and the other on his ass. Clawed fingers dipped into his crease as Roman carried him from the room, and Simon tried to evade the invading digits. A thick finger speared his hole, and the dry burn made him cry out and buck his hips. The finger wiggled deeper, and hit his prostate. Simon cried out, the pain and pleasure surreal. He was afraid to move, afraid the clawed finger in his ass would lacerate and tear his vulnerable flesh. He'd never touched himself there, never thought to do it. He wasn't gay, he only ever slept with women, but this brutal creature was working his body with practiced ease and making him respond.

He saw the walls in quick glimpses, Roman's finger thrusting in his sore hole distracting him. He was suddenly dumped on a bed, and Roman was on top of him, ruthlessly spreading his legs and lifting them over his shoulders. His ass was exposed and he tried to slip his legs off the werewolf's shoulders, but the thick cock nudging at his tight hole made him freeze. Roman grinned, a feral light in his eyes, and he thrust once, just enough to bounce the hard, broad head of his cock off the virgin entrance to Simon's body. Simon winced, and his hands gripped the blankets under him. Stopping Roman was out of the question now, and he knew it, but he couldn't relax, or stop the fear coursing through him.

Roman breathed in deep, as if scenting his fear and liking the taste of it on his tongue. Hands ran down his sides to his hips, pushing Simon's ass harder against the thick shaft throbbing at his hole. Simon tried to buck him off, but all he did was push the cock head harder against his virgin hole, and he backed off, going limp. Roman chuckled, and Simon hated him fiercely in that minute, even as his own cock pulsed with renewed vigor. His body wanted this, and badly, and Simon felt his fear begin to sour with anger. His body was betraying him, and he had no control.

Roman leaned down, tongue longer than it should be, and the werewolf licked up a thin trail of blood from Simon's chest, lapping at his nipple. Simon jerked again, and his cock dripped with early ejaculate, the clear liquid pooling on his abs. Roman nipped, tasting his flesh, occasionally pressing his cock to Simon's hole, making him wince and his hips buck in response.

Roman reached out a hand, claws sharp and dangerous, and scored at the dresser next to the bed, claws latching onto the drawer and pulling it open. The drawer landed with a thud on the bed, smacking Simon on the shoulder, and Roman rifled through the contents. He came up with a tube of lube, and Simon's tight hole clenched as reality set in. Roman was going to fuck him. The werewolf threw the drawer off the bed and the wood cracked when it hit the floor, everything spilling.

The werewolf ignored Simon's nerves, and Simon watched, eyes wide, as he dribbled lube on his thick cock, before squeezing a generous glob over Simon's untried hole. A heavy claw pressed to his entrance, and Simon winced, afraid the werewolf would slice him open before he even fucked him. Roman used more care than he was expecting, expertly sliding his clawed finger into his ass, spreading the thick lube inside his tight channel. In and out, Roman prepped him, somehow not cutting him, thick digit sliding with ease in his virgin ass.

"Tight, and hot," Roman growled, panting through his teeth. "Going to own your ass. Make you my beta bitch."

"I'll get you back for this," Simon gritted when another finger filled his hole, two digits spreading him. It hurt, and yet it pulled pleasure from him, liquid heat seeping through his muscles. The wolf made certain to tag his prostate, seeming to enjoy the way he gasped each time. "Our arrangement is over."

"No," Roman snarled, pulling his fingers away and lining up his cock. "I own you now. We're doing this my way from now on."

Simon screamed as Roman thrust in all the way to the hilt. Roman withdrew, and thrust back in, rutting hard from the start. Simon cried, gasping at the ruthless pace, the pain at the invasion strong. He clawed at the bedding, and tried to kick, but strong arms held him down. He couldn't control his sobs, Roman riding him deep and fast. Tears ran down his cheeks, and his whole lower body tensed with the wrenching pain, the thick cock owning his ass with dominating ease, the lube letting Roman take him without resistance.

Roman's pace was demanding, and Simon gave up, his body going limp under the powerful thrusts. The werewolf's hands gripped his thighs, fucking into him, stretching his hole wide, the broad head opening his channel more with each and every thrust in and out. Roman grunted as he rutted, bottoming out each time, somehow finding his way deeper into Simon's body. Simon's ass relaxed around the invading shaft, and he sobbed at a startling pleasure when the thick flesh spearing him rubbed over that small gland. His own dick, which went soft when the pain started, was regaining some interest in the proceedings, and Simon watched in horror and denial as he grew hard. Roman growled, and a clawed hand fell to his cock, stroking him in time to the beast's hips.

The pain was still present, but not as intense. Roman rode him hard, the noises coming from his fanged mouth animalistic and raw, and Simon couldn't hold back his gasping cries. Pleasure was rising in his gut, and Simon gave up fighting his arousal. Roman must have felt his capitulation, as his hips sped up, spearing him faster, his ass taking everything Roman gave him, sucking his huge cock deeper inside. Simon's head lolled on the bed, eyes rolling back in his head when each thrust in rubbed over his prostate, his cock dripping and leaking, and Roman's hand stripping him with a painful grip of which he couldn't get enough.

Finally Roman's hand fell away, and the pace of his hips lost that even rhythm. Simon moaned as the cock in his ass swelled, growing impossibly harder, Roman fucking into him like he was trying to crawl inside his body. Simon opened his mouth to demand the werewolf withdraw before he came, but all that escaped was needy cries. The cock owning his ass was constantly applying pressure to his prostate, and he couldn't summon the control to speak. He lay pliant to the beast dominating him, and he knew Roman was very close when his eyes flashed with feral satisfaction and his breathing hitched.

The explosion of cum in his ass filled him up deep, Roman buried to the hilt. Jet after jet of hot semen bathed his sore flesh, and Simon came as well, his thin cry bouncing off the walls with Roman's roar. Simon's ass clamped down on Roman's thick cock, and the werewolf fucked him through it with short and rough thrusts before stilling with a moan. Simon's whole body seized up as his orgasm hit him with the force of a freight train. His seed splashed over his abdomen, and Roman jerked above him, still experiencing his own powerful climax. Simon lost himself to his own orgasm, cock spurting still, Roman filling him with an impossible amount of hot semen, which was dripping from his sore ass and down his crack.

Roman collapsed on him, his weight pressing him down into the mattress. Simon sobbed, still feeling his own climax, stricken by the strength of his response to the beast who was still shooting random jets of cum into him. His ass hurt, from hole to the deep place inside where Roman was still coming in him. The pleasure no longer masked the effects of the rough mating, though the wet heat of all that cum soothed as it spread through his abused ass.

Simon gasped as Roman withdrew, rolling to his back, hands falling to his sweat-dampened abdomen, cock still hard and glistening with seed and lube. A warm rush of seed slipped from Simon's ass, and he squirmed at the discomfort. His ass flinched at the movement, and he stilled, trying not to aggravate his well-fucked hole.

The beast beside him chuckled, and reached for him again.

ROMAN YAWNED in satisfaction. Simon was lying beside him, obviously in some discomfort and reeking of Roman's seed. He should have done this years ago. The brash and confident human was nothing now but a twitchy little bitch, with tear stains on his cheeks and a deliciously tight hole built for fucking. Roman's cock, still hard, throbbed as he remembered how spectacular Simon's virgin ass felt clamped around him, and he reached for the human. Simon flinched, but Roman ignored his reaction. Simon was his now, marked and mated, and he was not letting Simon ruin his plans. Simon was as useless as his late brother. Fucking him into submission was the perfect answer.

He grabbed Simon's hips and lifted the feebly struggling human over his cock, which was hungrily pointing straight up. Seed dripped from Simon's hole, still wet with lube and red from his recent fucking. Simon cried out, hands trying to free his hips from Roman's grip, but he was weak compared to wolfkin strength. Roman grunted as he lowered the human, his cock slipping back into that hot channel with remarkable ease. He was slick with lube and cum, and still very tight, despite Roman not sparing him just minutes earlier.

He sat Simon on his cock, firmly planted balls deep and pulled his hands away. Simon made to scramble off him, but Roman pushed his hips up, making the human wince and still. He was remarkably easy to train, his stubbornness defeated by the cock buried in his hot little hole. Roman felt satisfaction grip him when he glimpsed the bite mark on Simon's shoulder, still bleeding. It was going to leave a nasty scar for certain. Wolfkin bit during sex, but they never marked their mates like werewolves did in human stories. The bites always healed, and the mating bond was easy to sense on a spiritual and mental level when encountering a mated wolfkin if one knew where to look. Wolfkin took human lovers in secret, the relationships never officially condoned, but it happened often enough that it wasn't uncommon. The bite mark was a clear indication to another wolfkin that the human in question was claimed, and off limits. Breeding was impossible, but the sex was fantastic, the humans responding on a primal level to the animal spirit in the wolfkin. The wolfkin got off on dominating the weaker humans, who were naturally submissive and brought out the wolfkin's urges to claim and fuck. Humans turned into little sluts for their wolfkin masters, even if they hated the wolfkin in question. Simon was a perfect example of the influence wolfkin could hold in sway over a human lover.

"Fuck yourself on me," Roman ordered. Simon stared at him, panting. "Do it, or I take you outside in the snow and mount you in front of the other fangless worms."

"You wouldn't," Simon moaned. He moved anyway, lifting himself up a scant inch and then flinching as he dropped himself down. Roman moaned, drinking in the conflicted expressions on Simon's face and the sensation of his cock sliding in the hottest ass he'd ever fucked. "I hate you so much."

"Good. Now fuck yourself harder, bitch. Make it hurt. I want you feeling my cock for days." Roman loved the way Simon glared at him, but he obeyed, riding Roman's cock, taking himself hard and fast.

Roman relaxed, thinking about the best way to get to his nephew before Caius got to Red Fern. Simon was whimpering and driving his ass down hard on Roman's cock, forcing himself to take the thick shaft to the hilt again and again, conflicting desires on his flushed face. The human's cock was trying to get hard, and Roman idly grabbed the limp flesh, stroking it until it grew thick and long in his hand. Simon's hot hole gripped him as the human obeyed beautifully, and Roman gave up trying to plan in favor of training Simon how to please his new master.

ANDROMEDA HUNTED. The scent she followed from the cabin was familiar, floating over the snow as she ran. It pooled over her tongue, filling her nose, the other wolfkin's scent full of rancid fear and desperation. Guilt added a tang to it, and her heart hurt beneath her determination to catch her wayward wolf.

The traitor was one of her own.

The moon was low on the horizon, dawn lighting the eastern edges of the forest when she caught up to the struggling beta. The slim female fought through the heavy snow, and she whined when she caught sight of Andromeda on her heels. Her struggles were for naught.

Andromeda rammed into her side, lifting her high in the air, the small beta twisting and crying out in fear. She fell to the snow in a crumpled heap, and lay still, eyes wide.

Andromeda shifted, and delicately picked her way through the crumbling snow crust to her beta's side. She knew this wolf well, having carried her beneath her heart over a century ago, naming her as she took her first breath. She remembered her tiny cries, the day she found her wolf, her first howl, her first hunt. She remembered the day her daughter left, foolishly following after an unworthy lesser alpha of Black Pine.

Andromeda's heart broke, a thin crack in her implacable

demeanor.

Children were her greatest joy, and her fiercest sorrow.

“Change, my daughter,” Andromeda bade her beta, who obeyed promptly. She sighed, heart heavy with regret and grief. “Claire, my child, what have you done?”

“Forgive me, Mother,” Claire sobbed as she Changed, huddled in the snow, tears freezing on her cheeks. “I’m so sorry.”

Claire broke down, sobbing, as Andromeda stroked her pale golden hair, silver in the moon’s dying light. “Tell me all, my daughter. Tell me everything.”

Dawn broke over the forest as Claire confessed, and Andromeda’s heart turned to stone even as the sun warmed her flesh.

HOPE FOR THE BEST

GHOST CRAWLED out from under Kane's arm, his mate slumbering, limbs strewn over the bed. The big wolfkin took up the entire bed, and kept Ghost under his arm the whole night. He smiled, and tiptoed to the bathroom.

He relieved himself and washed up, leaving the bathroom to see Kane still asleep. His stomach rumbled, and he sniffed, not smelling bacon. Andromeda must not be cooking breakfast. Dawn was still breaking over the trees, so maybe it was too early. He frowned, and tried to recall the last few hours.

He smelled smoke and sweat and the leftover bitterness of stress and worry.....the cabin!

Ghost sprinted from the bedroom, following his nose, and he burst into the room next to his, jumping to the bed. He landed at Burke's feet, the Speaker asleep with Sophia on the pillow next to his, both wolfkin exhausted and reeking of smoke and stress. Burke jerked awake, and sat up, a bemused expression on his face as Ghost ran his hands over his naked torso, looking for injuries.

"What the hell?" Sophia muttered, hair astray as she sat up, blinking. Burke shrugged, and Ghost made a distressed sound in his throat when he found the residual bruising on

Burke's ribs.

"Hey, bud, whatchya doing?" Burke asked him, trying to stop his hands, wincing when Ghost pressed lightly over the still broken bone.

"I'm sorry," Ghost whispered softly to the Speaker. He pulled from that heavenly expanse in his center, spindling out light to the fractured bones under his fingers. Burke would heal soon enough on his own, but his hurts were Ghost's fault. He wasn't fast enough, didn't warn them in time. He hurtled Burke through the air like a toy, and his mate's dearest friend was hurt now because of his actions.

Burke's skin glowed under his hands, and he could see with his Spirit-sight the bones knitting together. The bruises faded away.

"Sorry? Pup, you saved my life," Burke said, incredulous. "I didn't even get singed, when I should have been nothing but pink mist. I should've known better, especially with you warning us like that. We all know better than to ignore a shaman's warning. Don't be sorry."

The door slammed open and hit the wall with a brutal crash, bouncing back fast. Burke and Sophia jumped as Kane strode into the room, snarling. He wore only a pair of loose sweatpants, chest and feet bare. Ghost smiled at his mate, who glowered at the sight of his hands on Burke's sleekly muscled chest. The glow receded, and Ghost lifted his hands away, turning to Sophia. She held up her hands and shook her head, warily eyeing Kane who stalked to the side of the bed and pulled Ghost up and into his arms.

"I woke up and you were gone, and I find you in bed with my best friend," Kane grumbled, nipping at Ghost's neck. Ghost frowned, not understanding the problem, and he snuggled in close, wrapping his legs around Kane's hips. "Naked, and in his bed."

"Sophia is here, too," Ghost replied, licking his lips and staring at Kane's mouth, wanting to taste it. Sophia groaned and slapped at Burke when he snorted out a laugh. "Burke was hurt. It was my fault, so I fixed him."

Kane glared at Burke, who sat back against the headboard, shaking his head. "I told him it wasn't his fault, but he's stubborn like his mate." Kane rolled his eyes, which made Ghost smile. He nibbled along his mate's strong jaw, licking the firm flesh. Kane exhaled, and his hands wandered down to his bare ass.

"Fuck, Kane, watch where you're putting your hands in mixed company," Burke grumbled, and a blush rose over his cheekbones, his dark eyes going gold as he gazed at where Kane's hands were resting. Kane growled, and spun on his heel, putting his back to the room and blocking Burke's view.

"Get dressed, and meet us downstairs. Andromeda has the traitor, and is on her way back. I need a moment with my mate," Kane ordered his wolves over his shoulder, and he carried Ghost from the room. He could hear Burke swearing, Sophia saying something about him hogging the blankets, and letting his eyes wander where they shouldn't.

Kane carried him back to the room they slept in the night before, kicking the door shut. Kane tried to put Ghost down, but he held on, and with a mental push, toppled them both to the bed. Kane settled between his legs, and Ghost ran his hands over the firm muscles of his mate's back, relishing in the feel of his smooth skin and warm strength. Kane growled, a gentle rumble that made Ghost give a breathy laugh, tilting his head to let Kane at his neck.

Kane pulled his head away after laying a wet kiss to his neck, dark eyes lit up from within. “We need to get dressed.”

Ghost sighed, knowing his mate was right. He wanted to stay here, under Kane's body, secure and safe, the world just the two of them. Yet he couldn't, they couldn't. Kane was the Heir, and they could not ignore their duties. There were things to do, and his mate had wolves to protect.

They got dressed, more of Shaman River's clothing appearing mysteriously for Ghost to wear, since he had none of his own. Kane had clothing in the hall next to the door, a small duffel bag that must have survived the explosion, presumably Sophia taking care of her alpha while they slept. He felt a brief pang of guilt when he pulled the soft sweater over his head, but if River was leaving him clothing and healing his hurts then the other shaman must not be that mad at him for throwing him in the wall. He frowned as he sat on the bed, staring down at the heavy brown leather boots next to his sock-covered feet. Kane was waiting by the door, doing something with his cellphone, dark head down and fingers flying.

Ghost thought about what happened the night before,

backing through his memories from when the bomb exploded, all the way to the altercation in the hallway with River. He was unaccustomed to thinking thusly, to concerning himself with important matters in his human form. Wolf was easy; eat, sleep, hunt, play. No responsibilities, and no need to apologize. He threw a shaman into a wall with his mind, and now his mate was about to deal with a traitor. His life was so much simpler when he just had to exist as an over-large pet wolf. Confusion clouded his thoughts, and he realized he'd been staring down at his borrowed boots for long minutes. He pushed his feet into them one at a time, the long thin laces hanging from his fingers.

Fingers, hands. Feet. Days old as a man, his skin smooth as an infant's, untouched by life and time. The laces twirled around his fingers, moving in a wind that came as he stirred the power that lay quiet just under his skin. It had always been there, his power. His use of it over the last several years was instinctual and sporadic. Until he burned Remus and the weakling doctor at the sanctuary he'd never used it with true intent, with purpose. Opening locks and doors was idle thought expressing itself as action.

He had no true control. Last night was proof enough. The whisper that carried the warning to his ears had been a faint annoyance, his mate and packmates distracting him just enough that the words weren't clear until it was too late. He may have saved his new packmates lives, but if he'd given coherent warning in time, then he wouldn't have tossed Burke like a chew toy and risked the life of his mate and his wolves. River would never have been hurt if Ghost was trained.

Throwing someone head first into a wall was not the reasonable response of a grown man to being tugged on his arm. And especially not to a shaman.

Finding his humanity brought with it the need for control, and responsibility. He was a shaman, and reactionary behavior and unschooled gifts were not the way to go on as a man.

Ghost sat up, the laces falling from his fingers, curling in the soft wind that flowed over the floor. He narrowed his eyes, and breathed evenly, focusing. His will bent the wind, and the laces moved, invisible fingers guiding them along the riveted hooks, lacing up the boots. He recognized the wind for what it was, his ability affecting the physical world, a bleed over side effect. He banished the wind as the laces tied, a neat bow like he'd seen Glen tie on his own boots hundreds of times over the years.

"You are glorious, little wolf," Kane sat on his heels at his feet, big hands resting on his knees, their warmth and inherent strength soothing Ghost's melancholy. "What makes you so sad?"

"I have power," Ghost said, holding up his hand, calling to the celestial river of energy he could feel brewing and writhing beneath his skin. His hand glowed, a glimmer and sheen of silver white light that winked in time with his heartbeat. "I have power, and no training. I know what Andromeda told Grandpa Caius, I saw it in your mind when you came back to me after calling him. Am I dangerous?"

"We are wolfkin. We are all of us a danger." Kane put a

hand to his cheek, thumb rubbing his skin. He sighed and leaned into the touch, needing it. Wanting more. "Never be afraid of what you are, or what you can do. I have the power to destroy any of our people with a careless word and thought. I can break the strongest of wolves with my jaws. But if I fear my power, then I can't control it, and I will end up hurting someone. I will never be happy that I carry the Voice, but I will not fear it. True control comes from embracing your powers and gifts, and letting go of fear and guilt."

Ghost tried to nod, but for all of Kane's faith in him, his mate couldn't remove the doubt in his heart. Ghost dispelled the lights, and sighed again.

Kane stood, and gently tugged him to his feet. Ghost went into his arms, snuggling close, chin on his alpha's chest, looking up into his dark eyes. Kane gave him a sweet smile, gazing down at him as if he were the greatest treasure, precious and rare. Ghost smiled in return, helpless to resist the blatant affection in the older wolf's eyes.

"I am not afraid that you will lose control, or hurt someone innocent. Even betas have power, and gifts to control. We all do. We are none of us perfect, my little wolf, and we all learn to live with who and what we are. You will too, and I somehow think you'll gain control of your abilities far faster than any shaman the clans have ever seen."

"Hope for the best?" Ghost said softly, repeating a phrase Cat was fond of saying. It usually accompanied Glen's warning of 'plan for the worst'. He was moved by Kane's faith in him, and he hoped to do his mate proud.

"Yes, little wolf," Kane affirmed, and graced his forehead with a chaste kiss. Kane gently led him to the door, and Ghost felt a shimmer of power rush over his skin. "She's here, let's go."

Andromeda was back. Her anger rolled over the cabin, and Ghost pulled up his Spirit-sight in time to see through the walls as a golden-white star gained the front yard, burning to his eyes like a supernova.

The White Wolf was not happy.

KANE SILENTLY called his wolves to the front porch. Gerald was there, exhausted and yet resolute, and he let Kane and Ghost take his place at the railing as Andromeda led a small cream-colored female beta to the middle of the snowy yard. Kane put a hand on Gerald's shoulder and gave the lesser alpha a brisk nod in thanks for his vigil through the night before giving his full attention to the White Wolf. Sophia and Burke came out as well and stood at their backs, followed by the remaining members of the Black Pine wolves.

The White Wolf Changed in the barest of seconds, her brother there immediately to offer her a cotton dress, this one white and pristine as the snow in which she stood. River paused when he noticed the small beta, and he shook his head, turning his back on the beta and walking to the porch. The shaman must know the traitor, given her coloring and his reaction. He disappeared among the crowd, though Kane knew he wouldn't go far.

Kane was about to speak when the door opened one more time, and his brows went up in surprise when Gabriel Suarez stepped out, making his way through the assembled wolfkin to stand beside Ghost. This was Gabe's first foray into public since his kidnapping and torture, and Kane gave him a nod, trying to show how proud he was of the youngling that he would brave everyone's eyes and the whispers that followed him.

Ghost surprised Gabe in turn, grabbing the young alpha's hand with his free one, before turning to the scene in the yard. Gabe looked down at the small shaman, but said nothing, the tightness around his haunted moss-green eyes fading a bit.

"Shift, my daughter," Andromeda ordered the beta, and Kane stiffened. Daughter?

Her voice held an edge to it that made everyone present stand straighter in response. The White Wolf's power was inescapable and ruthless. The cream-colored beta hung her head low, nose touching the snow, and she Changed, the transformation slow and typically awkward for a weaker beta.

Kane growled when the beta gained her human-form. She sniffled, wiping a small hand over her face, tears pouring from her eyes as Claire lifted her head, formerly of Red Fern, a current wolf belonging to Black Pine. She was one of the betas that hung around the alphas and first betas that lived in Caius' Clan House in Augusta. She also spent the majority of her time with one wolf, hanging on his every word and depressingly in love with him, even though everyone knew he was never faithful or returned her affections.

Gerald swore where he stood at Kane's shoulder, obviously making the same intuitive leap as Kane. He scented nothing from Gerald but anger and frustration, the sour tang of deceit and fear absent. At least one son of Caius was honest, and free of treason.

"Talk, my child," Andromeda ordered the beta, who nodded even as she choked back a sob, thin and small in the cold wind on the mountain, naked, on her knees in the snow.

"I am Claire," she sniffled, her words garbled by tears but clear enough to their sensitive ears. "I was born to Red Fern, my mother Andromeda, but I moved to Black Pine to follow my lover fifteen years ago. I was the one who placed the bomb on the steps of the Heir's cabin, at my lover's request, to kill the Speaker and the Heir's First Beta."

"Why?" Andromeda said casually, as if asking if anyone wanted more tea. Kane admired her iron control, even though she must be beyond angered.

"Because Kane is impossible to beat in combat. His Voice is useless if he cannot control it, and the hope was that grief and anger would render that Gift impotent enough to take out the Heir."

"Tell them who your lover is, my daughter," Andromeda said, words like stones, each flung with harsh precision, Claire flinching with every syllable. "Tell them the name of the great traitor."

Kane knew. Gerald knew. Sophia and Burke knew, as did the wolves of Black Pine standing behind him on the porch. The wolves of Red Fern were coming, filling the edges of the yard, silently watching one of their own confess her sins. The second Claire revealed herself, they all knew. Growls and snarls of rage rose in the wind, and Claire quaked in terror, tears falling faster. She looked to her mother, as if pleading for a reprieve, but there was none in the Clan Leader's expression. Gone was Andromeda, beta mother of many cubs. The White Wolf, Clan Leader of Red Fern, was resolute, and Claire's eyes spilled a river of tears in total defeat before speaking the name.

"My lover is Roman, son of Caius, and he is the traitor the Heir and his wolves have been hunting the last fifteen years."

GHOST, GABE, Sophia, Burke and Gerald were all that remained in the front yard, the remaining wolves sent to patrol the borders and post sentries among thc cabins. Claire shivered in the breeze, still kneeling, Andromeda behind her. River was gone, somewhere nearby, but heavily affected by his niece's betrayal and unable to join them. The older shaman's absence worried Ghost, part of him wanting to find the wolfkin and help him, but River's face left little doubt of how unwelcome his gesture of comfort would be taken.

Ghost still held Gabe's hand, a few feet from where Kane

stood over Claire as she answered his questions.

“Where is Roman?”

“I do not know for certain, Alpha. Mother called us home, and I used that to meet him without anyone noticing. I met him just outside the border, and took the package he gave me. He told me where to put it, and how to arm it. I was supposed to kill your First Beta and the Speaker.”

“Why?”

“Because he can’t defeat you in a Challenge, you’re too strong. You defeated him twice in combat, and that was without using the Voice.”

“So killing Sophia and Burke would gain him what?” Kane demanded, growling. Claire ducked her head, tears now dry. Defeat and despair was in every word, every line of her body.

“He reasoned that if the First Beta and your best friend were both dead, then you would be crippled by grief, and easily restrained,” Claire admitted.

“That is the stupidest thing he’s ever thought of,” Gerald scoffed, shaking his head and turning away, kicking at the snow under his boots. Kane snarled, and Gerald quieted.

“Restrained? Not dead?” Kane asked.

Claire nodded, and Ghost was as confused as Kane appeared to be. Why not try to kill Kane?

“Yes, Alpha,” Claire whispered, head ducked, as if expecting a blow. This beta was nothing like her mother. She was meek and beaten, starved for affection and weak-willed. "All I know is he wants you and..."

"And?" Kane snarled, impatient.

"A shaman named Luca," she gasped out, eyes on the snow under her snow-scraped knees. She purposely did not look at Ghost, and she kept her face averted. "The one long lost, thought drowned in Baxter's river fifteen years ago."

Ghost felt Kane's fear through their link, and he sent reassurance along the river of light that wove between their spirits. The Heir did not visibly react, maintaining his control. Kane breathed easier, but he sensed the greater alpha's hyper-alert state.

"Why?" Kane asked, and Ghost paid attention. The easy answer was power of course, but the how was truly relevant. Power and gifts were only transferrable along a mate bond, and could be blocked, and forced mating bonds could be broken by any shaman. Soulbonds where the power exchange was reliable and dependable would be the best way to gain another wolfkin's abilities, but they only occurred at the discretion of the Great Mother. How Roman planned to gain power was the true mystery here. Unless the humans developed a means to steal gifts...

"Power, Alpha," Claire said, lifting her head at last. Her eyes were bruised from crying, skin flushed and her lips turning blue. "He wants your powers, always has. He hates you so much, and cannot abide shamans for the gifts he feels rightly belong to alphas."

"He would never be able to gain what he wants from me, and from Luca," Kane said, trying to reason out Roman's motivations. "Our abilities don't work like that, they can't be stolen. Each gift belongs to the wolfkin in which it was born."

"Is he working with Remus? We know the older brother tried to kidnap Gray Shadow and Luca, and Gray Shadow's family. Was Roman the wolf responsible for the ambush fifteen years ago?" Burke said, turning on Claire directly.

"Yes...," Claire stammered, and the tears returned. "I was there that night, the night before the ambush, and told Roman about Gray Shadow's plans to leave at dawn with his family. He told Sebastien Remus, who then tried to capture them the next morning."

"You were the beta at the council house," Kane breathed in realization, anger swelling so fast Ghost could taste the rage coming off his mate. The Heir's whole body seemed to vibrate, and his shoulders tensed, fingers curling to claws. Foreseeing Claire was about to die a brutal death, Ghost stepped up to his mate and placed his hand on the Heir's shoulder, pulling at the vicious anger inside his mate, clearing his thoughts. Kane shuddered, and carefully looked over his shoulder at Ghost, his eyes wild, fangs descending, but that was all Ghost would allow. He didn't know how he did it, but he restrained his mate's impending Change.

Claire may yet die for treason, but not like this. Not at Kane's hands in a rage. Ghost would never let Kane kill in anger, his actions, no matter how justifiable, haunting his mate all their long lives.

Burke jerked on his feet, a small movement that Ghost saw only because the Speaker was nearest to Kane and in his line of sight. Wondering what happened to startle Burke, Ghost released his mental hold on his mate and met Burke's eyes. Kane returned his attention to Claire after taking a deep breath, his anger under control. Kane sent him a wordless thanks along their link, and Ghost squeezed his shoulder, still watching Burke. The Speaker was staring at him, brows raised, mouth slightly agape.

Burke? Ghost asked, making sure to keep his query private, so as not to distract his mate.

Burke shut his mouth with a snap, and shook his head once, clearly telling Ghost not to ask. Ghost frowned, but nodded, knowing this wasn't the time. He would ask later what happened to disturb the Speaker so much.

"Burke," Kane said, his voice a low rumble, slightly warped with his fangs elongated.

"Alpha?" Burke replied formally, cautious. Kane was still on the edge, though fully in control.

"Contact the Clan Leader, please," Kane ordered, "tell him everything. Call until he answers, the Clan Leader of Ashland is there and he may ignore you." Burke nodded once before walking a few feet away and pulling out his cellphone, presumably to call Caius. Ghost wanted to listen to Burke's call, wanting to hear his grandfather's voice, but Kane needed him too much right now for him to split his focus. Kane stared down at Claire, clearly thinking.

"Alpha Kane?" Ghost dropped his hand, and they all turned to Gabe, the young alpha of Ashland nervously shifting on his feet, vibrant green eyes flickering over the assembled wolves, landing the most often on the traitor at their feet.

"Yes, youngling?" Kane replied, his fangs slowly disappearing as he calmed, though his eyes showed his wilder side.

"May I speak to the traitor?" the young alpha swallowed loudly, nervous, and he was still gripping Ghost's hand in a tight hold. He was shaky, and uncomfortable with all their eyes on him, but his shoulders were back, and his head up, eyes clear.

Kane waved his hand, stepping back, leaving Claire to Gabe. Gabe squeezed Ghost's hand before dropping it, and walking the few steps to stand over Claire. She peered up at him, clearly confused, not knowing who he was. Gabe shifted once more on his feet, biting at his lip, golden skin flushed in the winds that were growing steadily harsher on the mountaintop.

"Do you know who I am?" Gabe asked, voice cracking a little. His hands curled to fists at his sides, shoulders stiffening.

"No," Claire said, shaking. She was becoming petulant, her behavior showing that she saw the young wolfkin as no threat whatsoever. Gabe was an alpha, but he carried the scent of pain and fear on him, and though his head was up, he flinched when the bigger wolves moved. Claire could sense this, even in her weakened state.

"My name is Gabriel Suarez. My family was brutally attacked by unknown wolves a few weeks ago. We were taken, raped, beaten and drugged, and over half of my family is still missing. My youngest siblings were brutally abused and allowed to be assaulted by humans. Is Roman McLennan the bastard who did that to us?" Gabe was growling by the end of his words, biting them off as his eyes glowed, a fiery green that spoke of a terrible anger well-hidden under his beautiful features.

Claire paled even further, jaw dropping, crystal blue eyes growing wide with fear. She shook her head, though not in a negative, but in denial. "No! Roman would never do that to cubs, would never allow that to happen! You're lying!"

Gabe snarled, and lunged, faster than a thought. Kane reached for him, but of all the wolves present, Ghost was not expecting it to be Andromeda who stopped Kane from reaching Gabe. The White Wolf pushed Kane back, and kept her hand on his chest as Gabe lifted Claire in the air by her neck, fingers warping to claws. He shook her, once, hard. She scrambled for a grip on his arm, scratching ineffectively until he dropped her back down.

She tried to run, crawling on her hands and knees through the snow. Ghost and Sophia went to grab her, but it wasn't necessary.

"Stop!" the command snapped across the yard, the power behind the single word so formidable it rocked Sophia, Burke and Gerald on their feet. The command rolled over Kane and Ghost, and Andromeda appeared unaffected as well, but the White Wolf and the Heir were clearly startled.

Claire was not so lucky. She froze, collapsing to her stomach in the icy snow.

"Get back here!" Gabe ordered, and even fighting it, Claire reluctantly crawled back to where the young alpha stood, whimpering at his feet. Gabe's eyes were alight, green embers of fury and hurt spurring on his nascent gift.

"Is Roman, son of Caius, the monster who attacked my family? Does he have my father and uncles?" Gabe demanded, putting a boot under her hip and flipping her to her back, her hands up as if to deflect the power of his words. Every time he opened his mouth, the strength behind each command grew.

"Yes!" Claire screamed, hands over her ears. "Yes, he did it! He steals wolves and gives them to Remus!"

"Where is my family!" he shrieked, words warped by fangs and fury.

"I don't know! I never asked, he never told me what he did with them!"

Claire sobbed, but Gabe wasn't done with her.

"Where is Roman? Where is Remus?" he demanded, and she shook her head, crying out. She'd already answered that she didn't know where her lover and his partner were, but Gabe clearly didn't believe her. Ghost didn't blame him for that disbelief, but Gabe was going to do her injury if he didn't rein himself in, and soon.

"Tell me where they are!" Gabe screamed, and Sophia, Burke, and Gerald all fell to their knees in the snow, Andromeda rocking back a few steps under the force of his command. Kane flinched, but held his ground. Gabe was crying too, fists raised, mouth twisted in pain and anger, fangs lowered. His eyes were fully changed, fully wolf now, nothing human left.

"Gabe! Stop! She doesn't know, she cannot answer you if she doesn't know!" Kane shouted, striding to Gabe's side, but the younger alpha shrugged him off and Kane fell back on his ass, surprised. Gabe roared, his pain escaping on that horrible sound, Claire's scream climbing into the frigid mountain air in twisted accompaniment.

Ghost moved, as Claire writhed on the ground, Gabe commanding her to answer him. She was being torn apart under the rising strength of Gabe's raw gift. The young alpha had the Voice, and had no idea, no control. He was wild, lost in the power, his gift without a guiding hand. Ghost reached out, and with a gentle gathering of air particles, zapped Gabe on his temple with a pure bolt of energy. The bolt discharged with a crackle and a burst of light, and Gabe dropped like a stone to the snow.

Ghost knelt at his side, and checked the youngling, satisfied he'd done no permanent damage. Gabe's power was a roiling miasma of grief, pain, fear and a horrible anger that was looping endlessly. Even unconscious Gabe was being tortured alive by his emotions, and Ghost peered deeper. There was something Gabe's mind was fighting, a red thread of foreign thought inserted within his own.

Hands other than his moved over Gabe's supine form. Ghost looked up to see his mate, shaken and stricken. Kane put a hand over his mouth, and dropped his head.

"He's fine, Kane," Ghost murmured. He put his hand on Kane's, and tried to reassure him. "I promise you, I didn't hurt him. I just stopped him. His gift was caught up in his pain, and he couldn't stop."

"I didn't know he had the Voice," Kane gasped, clearly at a loss. "I never would have left him untaught if I'd known. He showed no signs of it, I thought him a regular alpha, unconfirmed in his strengths."

"I don't think he knew, either," Ghost mused. Kane gaped at him, his powerful mate terribly shaken by the abused alpha's actions the last few minutes.

GHOST WAITED until Andromeda was gone, her sobbing daughter in the grip of Black Pine betas, the Clan Leader following behind. He'd heard something about the cellar, and he might have asked what they were talking about if not for his uncle standing nearby, waiting.

"Alpha," and he and Kane both turned to look at Gerald, his uncle pale and sweating, even in the cold.

"What?" Kane said, voice sharp. Gerald flinched, and Ghost gave his mate a glare. Kane made a visible effort to calm down, and nodded to Gerald.

"Kane... Roman called me, right after... right after the earthquake the other day," Gerald said, meaning the day Kane had sex with Ghost and he almost broke the park. "He never calls me, so I should have known then... I am so sorry, I told him Luca... that Ghost was here. I'm the reason we almost died in the explosion."

Ghost tried to speak, to tell his uncle that he was not to blame for Roman's actions, but Kane's hand on his shoulder stopped him.

"Did you know he was the traitor?" Kane asked, eyes glowing.

"No, I swear," Gerald gasped, fear building in his expression.

"Did you know he was killing our kind and working with Remus?"

"No, Alpha." The truth was in Gerald's every word and breath. His uncle was breaking under his guilt, and Ghost whined, wanting Kane to stop and fix it.

"Did you mean to place us in danger, your nephew in danger, by telling Roman that Ghost was here?"

"No! Never," Gerald cried out, and his shoulders shook as he began to sob.

Kane let go of Ghost, and put both hands on the lesser alpha's shoulders, straightening his back. Gerald lifted his head, and the two alphas made eye contact. Gerald winced, but Kane was peaceful, calm. He wasn't angry, and Ghost waited, holding his breath, as Gerald saw what Ghost did in Kane's demeanor. Kane did not blame Gerald for anything, least of all talking to his own brother, a wolfkin whom at the time he didn't suspect of treason and murder.

"The second you became mine, I stopped believing the worst of you," Kane whispered, and Ghost smiled at the wonder on Gerald's face. "I now believe in you, trust you. Your love for your nephew makes me trust you even more, and your misplaced guilt is proof enough there is a decent, good man under all the layers of anger and pain you carry as armor. Gerald, my wolf, I don't blame you at all."

KANE PUSHED off the doorframe, arms crossed as he walked to the downed alpha's bedside. His mother, whose name Kane still didn't know, hovered at his other side, holding her son's hand as he slumbered under the effect of Ghost's knockout spell. The room was in shadows, the noonday sky darkened by a brewing storm that River was calling a blizzard. Red Fern was going in to lockdown, in more ways than one.

"Kane?"

Burke was at the doorway, beckoning. Kane spared Gabe one last look before leaving the room, joining Burke in the hall. He shut the door softly, and looked to his Speaker. Burke had his cell in hand, and gave it to him. "It's Alpha Caius."

Kane answered, holding the cell to his ear and walking a few feet down the hall, not wanting to disturb the Suarez wolves. Burke followed, his eyes gone gold and worried.

“Sir?”

“Is it true?” No need to ask what Caius meant; Burke already told him.

“Yes, Sir. Roman is the traitor. He sold out Gray Shadow to Remus Acquisitions, has been aiding Simon Remus for the last fifteen years in systematically hunting and killing our kind, and is the wolfkin who ordered his lover to blow us all up last night.”

“I sent my betas and the few greater alphas here in town out after Roman. Heromindes is here, and I have to tell him my son is the wolf responsible for the capture and torture of his relatives.” Caius sounded exceedingly unhappy about that prospect. Kane could agree with that, as Heromindes was a formidable alpha, and a Greater Clan Leader. “I expect Ashland to declare a blood feud with Black Pine over this if I can’t turn over my son.”

“Roman is nearby, Sir. He was outside Baxter yesterday morning, and I think he’s still in the vicinity. He wants Ghost, and for some reason me as well.”

“Ghost?” Caius asked, clearly confused. Kane bit back a curse, not wanting to explain why the Clan Leader’s grandson wasn’t going by his birth name. Telling Caius that Luca was raised by humans who thought him a pet and named him after a spiritual apparition wasn’t the best thing to do in the current circumstances.

"That's Luca, Sir. He changed his name a few years ago."

"Odd, but not important. I'll discuss it with my grandson after I arrive. Expect myself and the Ashland Clan Leader by morning."

"Yes, Sir," Kane said, but he was talking to a dial tone. Caius had hung up on him. Kane thought about calling him back and warning him about the weather but he was certain that he would only be hung up on again for his trouble.

"The Big Bad Wolf is coming, then?" Burke said, walking to his side, eyes still glowing. For Burke to show his wilder side like that meant his Speaker was seriously upset.

"Yes, Caius is coming, and Heromindes is as well," Kane confirmed, and Burke echoed his rumble of displeasure. Things were about to get worse, not better. Nothing gummed up the workings of a clan faster than too many greater alphas in a small space, all trying to do things their way. Thank the Goddess for the White Wolf. She would keep the other Clan Leaders in line.

"What's wrong, Burke?" Kane asked, and his best friend gave him a rueful smile, closing his eyes for a heartbeat. When he opened them, they were again a deep, peaceful brown.

"Can't hide anything from you, can I?"

"No, and quit stalling," demanded Kane, wondering what else could go wrong today.

“What happened out there, earlier? With Ghost?”

“Ghost knocked Gabe out...”

“No,” Burke interrupted, shaking his head. “I meant with you, when you lost your temper. What did Ghost do?”

“Ah,” Kane exhaled. Knowing immediately what Burke was referring to. “Don’t worry, my brother. Ghost just helped me regain control, nothing more.”

“He used the Voice on you, didn’t he?” Burke was smart, and knew Kane well. “He used your Gift, ***on you***, and made you pull back on shifting.”

Kane saw no reason to deny it. Burke wouldn’t believe him anyway if he tried to lie.

“Yes, he did,” Kane agreed, smiling faintly as Burke blinked at him in consternation. “He pulled on the Voice, seamlessly and with a subtle grace that I don’t even think I could match. It was beautifully done, and he let me go as easily as he swept me under. It was so flawless I’m convinced Ghost has no idea he used my gift.”

“And that doesn’t bother you at all?” Burke exclaimed, voice getting a bit shrill. “He’s a stripling, an untested and untrained shaman who uses his abilities out of instinct instead of skill. He has access to the most devastating weapon an alpha can possess, and you aren’t even the slightest bit concerned?”

“I’m concerned we may find ourselves in a situation where he may need it, and if that’s the case, I may not be in any condition to help my mate. But am I worried about Ghost using it and hurting someone with the Voice?" Kane started for the stairs, wanting to hold his mate before Caius came howling into Baxter and disturbing their time together. "No, I am not at all afraid of that. Ghost has only ever acted out of self-defense or in the defense of others. His first instinct is to help, not harm."

"I hope you're right, but that doesn't discount accidents, and you know it!" Burke said in a harsh whisper as they walked down the steps, pausing on the landing. Burke grabbed his shirt and tugged him closer. "What if he gets scared, or angry, or hell, he gets ***horny***, and instead of shaking the ground he blasts your brain with your own damn gift?"

"That won't happen, Burke. If you can't trust Ghost not to hurt me, then trust me in knowing my mate best. It may only be a matter of days, but he's so deeply entwined in my mind and soul I know him better than I do myself. We would not be soulbonded without reason. We would not be bonded if we were going to cause harm."

"You're asking me for trust ***and*** faith."

"Yes," Kane said, blunt. He needed Burke to believe in him, and trust Ghost as well. And if Burke could do neither, then to trust their Goddess.

Burke was silent for a minute, his eyes searching Kane's face, looking for answers. Burke must have found what he needed, because his dearest friend soon let go of his shirt and wrapped him in a hard hug, squeezing enough to make his ribs complain.

"I love you too much, I can't help but worry," Burke sighed, pressing his face to Kane's shoulder.

Kane hugged him back, just as tightly, breathing in Burke's scent.

"I love you, too. You're my greatest friend, and I need you. Now more than ever," Kane whispered, eyes burning with tears he refused to shed. Now wasn't the time to start crying.

Once Remus and Roman were defeated, Kane and Ghost had the small matter of a potentially sacrilegious soulbond to survive. The second the Clans as a whole learned about it, chaos would erupt across the globe. They would both need their friends and family to make it through the coming turmoil.

"What worries me most is what Caius will do once he learns that I'm soulbonded to Ghost," he said, murmuring his words into Burke's ear.

"Me too, my brother," Burke whispered back, "me too."

WHEN STORMS CONVERGE

GHOST SAT beside Gabe, both young wolfkin staring out over the view provided by the second floor balcony. The young alpha next to him had his legs dangling over the side of the balcony through the widely spaced railings, and Ghost followed suit, swinging his feet in the rising wind. Boot laces twirled in the twisting wind, and the smell of wet, fresh snow filled the air.

The park was growing darker, black clouds milling overhead while a chilling wind barreled through the valleys and glens where the cabins were nestled. Wolfkin in varied forms were hurrying about, some lugging in bags of supplies to the Clan Leader's cabin, while the Black Pine wolves were standing sentry in their black tactical gear, armed to the teeth.

The traitorous Claire was under guard in one of the smaller rooms, two Black Pine betas making sure she didn't attempt to escape, and that no one attempted to get to her before her fate was decided. While it did not seem she actively participated in the kidnapping and slaying of the dozens of wolfkin victims over the last two decades, she did play a major role in providing Roman and Simon Remus with detailed insider information at crucial times that resulted in the deaths of several wolves. Her refusal to tell her Clan Leader or her own mother about Roman's activities was enough to garner Claire a death sentence, and the enmity of her birth-clan. Andromeda may have ordered her people to stay away from Claire, but Ghost could sense the rising ire and bitter need to avenge the fallen. Wolfkin led long lives, and many wolves in Black Pine territory older than the younglings were acquainted with each other, some friendships spanning a century or more. Claire was the first traitor identified, and while not the leader, she was the one on hand, and her death was a certainty if she was left unguarded.

Ghost cast Gabe a sideways glance as the young alpha shifted, his golden-skinned hands growing white at the knuckles as he worried his fingers together. Ghost leaned a little to the side, and nudged Gabe with his shoulder, earning him a quick, surprised glimpse of moss-green eyes before Gabe looked away. Ghost did it again, and that garnered him a very small smile from the young alpha.

"Why aren't you mad at me?" Gabe asked suddenly, and Ghost turned, pulling his legs back through the railing so he could face Gabe more comfortably.

"Why would I be mad at you?" he replied, carefully watching Gabe's facial expressions.

"You knocked me out when I lost control, and instead of getting a lecture or a beating from the Clan Leader or the Heir when I wake up, I get my mom and a crazy shaman asking me if I'm okay," Gabe said, clearly confused. Ghost assumed he was the crazy shaman, and giggled, grinning.

Gabe gave him a look that said he really did think Ghost insane, and Ghost laughed some more. He settled down after a minute, and gave Gabe a half-hug, the young alpha staying stiff for a minute before relaxing.

"You're hurt, Gabe. Injured in your soul and spirit. You have hurts that I can't heal, but I can help you. That means not punishing you for things over which you have no control. I could tell you had no idea that you had the Voice. You didn't know that the gift was rising in you. So I stopped you, instead of Kane or Andromeda doing it. Their way would have been painful and bloody, on everyone's side. Which meant knocking you out."

"Huh," Gabe exhaled, and went back to watching the activity going on below. "Is it true you spent the last fifteen years as a wolf, and only just learned to Change back?"

"Very true," Ghost confirmed, and leaned toward the railing when he caught sight of Kane and Gerald below in the yard, the two alphas talking. Their words were lost in the winds, but whatever it was, it was serious from both wolfkins' expressions. "More like fourteen years and six months, but then I have trouble counting. Fourteen does come after thirteen, right?"

Gabe laughed at that, and nodded, eyes glinting. His smile stayed longer, and Ghost cheered internally at the sight.

"In fact, this is the longest time I've gone in years without hunting for my own food or going for a run through the woods. I'm feeling itchy," Ghost mused, his whole body suddenly aching to feel the wind in his fur, the snow under his paws, and the cold rush of flying through the trees after prey.

“I haven’t gone on a run in weeks,” Gabe said, looking hopeful. “I wasn’t able to Change because of the silver poisoning, but you took care of that. Think we can go on a run before the storm sets in?”

“Sure,” Ghost said, climbing to his feet. “I hope I don’t get stuck again, that would be really embarrassing.”

“Stuck? How does that happen?” Gabe asked curiously, following Ghost as he led the way back inside, heading for the stairs. They passed two Black Pine betas, and a steady stream of Red Fern betas filling the halls, the sound of many wolves running up and down the stairs loud in the great wooden structure.

“Very long story. Short version is I Changed too early, under bad circumstances, and I had no one to show me how to get back. I eventually gave up and stopped trying,” Ghost said, as Gabe gaped at him, surprise writ on his golden features.

“Stopped trying?” Gabe asked, incredulous. “Why did you stop trying?”

“I was afraid,” he replied. There were multiple betas climbing the stairs with their arms full of supplies. Ghost was too impatient to wait, he wanted to get out of the cabin, and feel the wind. Ghost sprinted down the stairs, Gabe on his heels, and they jumped over the railing at the landing, boots smacking the floor of the foyer. The betas climbing up spared them an amused glance before continuing on their way. He would be so happy to stop wearing clothes for a few hours.

"Afraid of what?" Gabe went to open the front door, but Ghost gave it a mental nudge and it opened with a snick, the wind pouring into the foyer. Gabe missed a step, but regained his stride and followed Ghost out of the cabin. Kane and Gerald looked up at them as they came outside, and Ghost spared the door one last thought as he shut it against the wind.

"I was afraid of lots of things. Afraid I would Change back, and then deal with my humans learning I wasn't an animal. Afraid I wouldn't be able to Change, and that I would be nothing but an animal the rest of my life, cut off from my people and alone. I was just afraid, and so I crippled myself."

"Fear held you back," Gabe said, staring at Ghost with an odd expression on his face.

"Yes it did," Ghost nodded, and they walked down the path to his mate and uncle. Gabe was almost hiding behind Ghost as they approached the two older alphas.

"Thank you for helping Sophia last night," Kane was saying to Gerald, his uncle trying to hide his pleased expression at the Heir's praise. Ghost cheered internally, gladdened to see his uncle slowly losing the gloomy air he carried with him. He didn't know what it was that gave Gerald that sour and unhappy demeanor, but it was quickly fading away by the hour.

"If you need me to help again, just ask," Gerald said, gruff and to the point, valiantly trying to keep the happiness out of his voice. His uncle saw them coming, and wiped the small grin from his lips. Kane was clearly upset by the time Gabe and Ghost got to their side.

"What are you two thinking?" Kane asked, glowering. "He shouldn't be out of the house unattended," Kane pointed at Gabe, who blushed and dropped his head, "and it's not safe for you, little wolf. Roman and Remus want you, and it's not to reminisce over the last fifteen years. Get back in the cabin."

Gabe nodded and went to walk back up the path, but Ghost grabbed his arm and stopped him.

"No," Ghost said, calm. He gave Gerald a smile when his uncle looked like he might choke on his tongue, and then went back to smiling at his mate. Kane was surprised, and then frowned at him. Kane opened his mouth, but Ghost popped up on his toes and kissed him.

Kane pulled him in. Big arms held him, cradled him close, demanding tongue sliding over his own, his mate's scent and taste filling his senses. He put his arms around Kane's neck and kissed him back, quickly learning what his mate liked through their link.

The kiss went on for a few minutes, until the awkward shuffling of the two alphas nearby brought them back to reality. Kane put him down and made to pull him close to his side, but Ghost shook his head and gave his mate a big smile. Kane frowned, and reached for him again.

"Gabe and I are going for a run," Ghost said, taking a step back out of Kane's reach. His mate growled, but subsided when Ghost stayed an arm's length away. "Gabe won't be alone, he'll be with me. His gift cannot hurt me, so I'm the safest person for him to be with anyway. River is too busy dealing with his other duties to watch Gabe. And I need to run. I'm not used to wearing clothes and boots and I want the snow under my paws."

"Little wolf," Kane started, but Ghost rolled his eyes, knowing what Kane was going to say.

"Kane, you can't come with us, you have things to do here. Uncle Gerald can keep an eye on us both," Ghost said with a quick wink to his uncle, privately pleased he could manage the tricky human expression. Gerald looked like he wanted to object, eyeing Kane warily. Kane grumbled about stubborn shamans, but nodded.

"River said the storm will hit in about two hours. You have one hour to stretch your legs, then all three of you are to come back here." Ghost yelped when Kane suddenly grabbed him and pulled him in for a quick plundering of his mouth before setting him back on his feet, dazed. "One hour, little wolf, and then I'm coming after you."

"Yes!" Ghost grinned in victory, and in his excitement, called to his power.

A lightning storm of silver-white mist eclipsed his vision, and his clothing fell to the snow. He thought of the form that felt more like himself than the human one did, the form he wore for years and years, and it answered, his power shaping his reality and forging him anew.

Four paws settled to the earth, and he opened his eyes as he pulled the cloud full of miniature stars and lightning back inside, the power flaring as it was absorbed back under his skin. He sniffed at his boots, thinking he may have been a bit too eager to Change. He shook out his thick fur, and ducked his head, picking up his boots in his teeth.

Laughter and groans met his ears. Kane was shaking his head and laughing so hard he was crying, and Gabe and Gerald were staring at him, as were most of the Red Fern wolves and the Black Pine sentries stationed around the cabin. He wagged his tail, and sprinted for the porch, dropping his boots on the steps and returning for his shirt and pants. His socks had stayed in his boots when he dematerialized during his transition, so thankfully he didn't need to pick those out of the snow, but his shirt and pants were getting wet. He dropped his clothes beside his boots and went back to Kane.

"Little wolf, please don't be scaring the locals like that," Kane said through his laughter, but he bent down and pressed a kiss to the spot between Ghost's eyes. His mate appeared to be proud of him despite his chiding words. "I guess that answered the question about how your transformation will go from now on."

Ghost yipped and danced on his paws, feeling slightly abashed at his eagerness. The Red Fern wolves were still actively staring, the Black Pine guards casting him nervous glances as they returned their attention to their duties. Gabe shook himself out of his shock, and started walking for the tree line, obviously intending to Change in private. Gerald went after him when Kane waved a big hand at him, and Ghost gave his mate one last look before following, claws digging into the thick snow crust.

ROMAN STOOD in front of his wolves, lesser alphas and former first betas, all wolfkin stripped of position in their former packs and clans. Exiles and criminals, and some murderers before they came into his employ. They were his, all for the chance to become more than Nature and Goddess decreed at their births. Twenty wolves, the ragged and bitter dregs of their kind, dangerous and aggressive beasts that delighted in misery and pain, they looked to him for money, power...and the chance for revenge.

Simon leaned against the door behind in, the moon lighting the human clearly, his skin burnished bone-white by the light, but for where the blood leaked past the soaked handkerchief he was pressing to his shoulder. Roman huffed in satisfaction, glad he took the time to bite the fangless worm again before calling in his wolves. Let them see his new place of power, with the human now his bitch. If Simon behaved, he might even let him get dressed.

"We go in, now, tonight," Roman growled, and his wolves, all in their wolf-forms, shifted on massive paws and grumbled, jaws dropping, fangs flashing in the moonlight. A kaleidoscope of gem-colored eyes reflected back the light, all eager for blood. They spent too long hunting the easy pickings of their kind, using the human weapons to incapacitate and kill, and not enough time tearing apart their prey and enemies with fang and claw. "Caius—," he snarled the name to an answering growl from his wolves, "—is coming in the morning. Black Pine's Clan Leader is sure to be bringing reinforcements, and we need to get into Red Fern, get the shaman and the Heir. Before Caius arrives."

"What good will it do to send wolves after a greater alpha with the Voice?" Simon sneered, shivering in the cold, bitter air. After his run in with the gray shaman, Simon was now apparently a believer in the gifts of wolfkin. "You send them after Kane, especially after we tried to blow up his wolves, and he won't bother killing you. He'll just tell you to kill each other."

The wolves in the snow shifted, their attention passing from him to Simon and back. He sent the human male a look that made him snap his mouth shut and send his gaze to the ground. Satisfied Simon was cowed, he returned his attention to the wolves, who had unfortunately all heard the human.

"By not sending wolves after him at all, that's how," Roman scoffed, and threw back his shoulders, lifting his head higher. One greater alpha, while formidable, was not invincible. Kane could be defeated, and not by another wolfkin. "I will be leading the attack on the Clan Bitch's cabin, where our spy said the shaman Luca was staying. Shaman River should be there as well, since that pale-haired pussy never steps far from his sister's shadow."

One of the wolves in the back let out a nasty moan, and the Change rolled through him. A lean, homely man with thin features and a wraith-like cast to his body kneeled in the snow, and hacked at the cold air entering his lungs. Roman growled at this show of disregard for his status, since he'd ordered the wolves who answered to him to all stay in their wolf-forms. The former First Beta of a minor lesser clan from the Midwest laughed, and sent him a twisted smile.

"So we'll die attacking the White Wolf, instead of the great and powerful Kane?"

Roman took a step forward, hands clenched, before he could stop himself. "The White Wolf!" he spat, the words tumbling from his throat as anger pooled in his gut. "She is naught but a haughty bitch who plays at being an alpha. She is a beta, and a fucking female! A she-bitch! Red Fern is a clan of betas, and the only strength there is the borrowed might of Black Pine!"

Roman pulled in a breath, and held it, trying to calm himself. None of the wolves present knew that Andromeda once defeated him in combat over fifty years prior. If he was lucky, she would spend her time either chasing humans at the park border or tearing his wolves apart while he got the shamans, leaving him alone as he escaped with his prizes.

"The humans will attack the perimeter near the gates, and Kane and Black Pine will respond. The humans will keep most of the park residents occupied while we come in from the opposite side, and head for the fancy wood shack the She-Bitch uses as her clan house. River and Luca should be there, since they have the throwaway wolfkin we left behind with the human slavers in Worcester. Simon and his men will overwhelm

Kane and his wolves, and once the Heir is down, they'll retreat with him in tow."

"Attack shamans with fang and claw? This ought to be fun," sneered the thin beta, who snarled back at Roman as he tried to quell the other wolf with glare. "Of course, it's preferable to going up against the Heir or the White Wolf."

"Shamans don't use their gifts to harm wolfkin," Roman said. "I haven't heard of a shaman ever using his abilities against one of his own kind in centuries. By the time Shaman River and the whelp realize we're there, we'll have them hog-tied and halfway back to the border."

Roman ignored the laughing, bleeding human behind him, and called to his wolf-form, losing himself to the Change. He wanted blood. He would have it, even if he had to sacrifice his wolves to do it. Better them than him.

GHOST RAN, tail flagging as he dodged around a tree and poured more speed into his legs. The white rabbit was inches from his muzzle, Gerald and Gabe a few lengths behind him.

Neither alpha was as fast as Ghost, nor as nimble on their feet. Ghost sensed their frustration as he outstripped them at every turn, both alphas' pride twinging as he made that final push and caught the rabbit. One hard shake, and the rabbit stilled in his mouth, spine broken.

He lifted his prize, tail high, as Gerald and Gabe caught up to him. He waved his tail lazily, laughing inside as Gerald grumbled at him. The older alpha was a huge beast, dark and brown in alternating patterns, stocky and heavily muscled. His eyes were dark liquid pools, alight for once with something like happiness, even as he panted from the fierce sprint Ghost put them through. Gabe was leaner, and a solid black, though not as dark as Kane's wolf-form. There were a few streaks of gray on his lower jaw and throat, and his eyes were a brilliant green.

Gabe threw himself to the ground, big body displacing wet snow with a crunch, and Gerald went sniffing nearby among the pines, looking for his own snack.

You are very fast, Gabe said with a cool breeze of thought. *I thought I was fast, but you left me in the dust. You're faster than most alphas.*

Years of running on four feet instead of two? Gerald's disgruntled voice offered, even though he was just out of sight past the pines. Ghost wagged his tail, laughing mentally at his uncle's snarky tone.

Been hunting my own food for years. Never got enough at the sanctuary. Cat always wanted to feed me cold dead cow from the butcher or dog food. I got faster out of necessity.

They starved you? Gerald growled, and the big alpha rambled back out from the pines to stand over his nephew. That wouldn't do. No one needed to be mad at Cat and Glen for thinking him an animal instead of a sentient individual.

No. They just couldn't feed me enough. I ate three times more than the other wolves there. Cat and Glen had trouble buying enough food for the regular wolves, I didn't want to be a burden. I ate a lot deer and rabbit.

You were a pet? said Gabe, curious, his sleek black head tilted to look at Ghost where he ate his rabbit. The meat was succulent and delicious, still hot from the chase.

Kinda. I wasn't treated badly, and other than trying to make me wear a collar when I was a pup, they never tried to restrain me. I always got out, and they stopped once they realized I wouldn't go too far. Had nowhere else to go, since I couldn't remember where I was from or how to get back.

He sensed Gabe was curious, wanting to know more, but the young alpha restrained himself. Ghost nibbled on his rabbit, and nudged the heavily muscled hind section toward the other wolfkin. Gabe eyed him like he was expecting to get bit for even looking at the rabbit remains, but Ghost insisted and Gabe leaned out his muzzle, nipping a leg piece and chewing happily, tail thumping a few times in the snow.

You're too skinny to be sharing your kills, his uncle grumbled, but Ghost gave a semblance of a shrug and watched as Gabe finished the rabbit. Gerald stalked off, mentally grousing about finding another rabbit, but he came back after a minute and stood over Ghost, dutifully keeping watch.

The young alpha needed someone to take care of him for a while. He had the feeling that Gabe was waiting for someone to start yelling at him, to punish him. He was expecting more pain, more fear, even though he was trying to hide it.

Gabe's behavior when around someone other than Ghost was telling. He pretended well, but Ghost saw the flinching, the nerves in the way he stood and moved, the hitching in his breathing and the wariness in his green eyes. Ghost had no experience to know how to handle Gabe's mental and emotional injuries that resulted from his kidnapping and assault. River was dealing with the other Suarez wolves, namely the cubs, but Gabe seemed happiest staying in Ghost's orbit, even though Ghost dropped him with a thought earlier that morning. Gabe had shrugged off his mother's concern and glued himself to Ghost.

So now Ghost was watching an alpha who had as little control over his fledging Voice as Ghost had over his shamanic powers. He wasn't worried at all, even content to have Gabe in his orbit if it meant keeping the wounded wolfkin happy and healthy. If sharing a run and a rabbit made the young alpha cheer up even a little, then Ghost would do so every day.

KANE WOVE his mind through the pack links, combining Red Fern and Black Pine together before tossing the multiple minds to Burke, his Speaker catching the collection of wolfkin minds with envious dexterity. Burke's mind was a beehive of thoughts, lightning quick and impossible to decipher. A near audible buzz of mental energy filled the space around the Speaker. Burke wasn't even at full strength, the hundred or so minds he shepherded now the smallest portion of his capability. They did not know for certain how many minds Burke could coordinate and track at once; there was never an event big enough among their kind that would offer a true glimpse into Burke's full range. The closest they ever got was the ambush at Baxter that fateful morning almost fifteen years ago.

Kane could handle twenty minds with ease, and regularly did so when planning and running ops and missions. He started to struggle around forty. Any more than that and Kane couldn't manage, the collective links collapsing as his mind fought to keep control. To be a Clan Leader he was in the average range when it came to the gift of command. Caius had the benefit of a few century's experience, but his range was no greater than Kane's. Clan Leaders either lucked out and had a Speaker, or relied on the most capable of their lesser alphas to coordinate clan-wide mind links, each lesser alpha handling part of the whole.

Greater alphas tended to avoid contributing, as the highly dominant males could never work well enough together to keep things cohesive. The humans had a saying that Kane was fond of, translating it to work for wolfkin, 'too many alphas, and not enough betas.' Kane was lucky that while Burke was a greater alpha by the merit of his abilities, he lacked the aggressive and territorial urges of many unranked greater alphas. The greater alphas who weren't Leaders, Heirs, or Speakers had no ready position in packs, and kept to themselves, for everyone's sake.

Black Pine was huge. Combined with the lesser clans like Red Fern that pledged allegiance to Caius, the Greater Clan and all its member clans were several thousand strong. When the unavoidable day came that Kane was Clan Leader, he would need Burke. The Speaker's gift of command was extraordinary, and very necessary.

Burke, he whispered to the glimmering and vast expanse that was the Speaker's endless mind, *do you have them all?*

* Yes,* came the serene reply, the chorus of whispers in his friend's mental voice eerie yet reassuring. It was as if a thousand Burkes all saw him, held his mind, a net of hands and thoughts to catch and hear and control everything. If Burke had been born with the Voice along with his exceptional gift of command, he could have ruled the world.

I don't want the world, a single voice whispered, as if Burke were talking to him from his shoulder. *I have my pack, my best friend, and a life worth living. I don't need the world.*

You are far more worthy than me, my friend, Kane said in return, a common thought of his. *Why Caius never chose you to be Heir I'll never know.*

* He was about to,* Burke said, surprising Kane enough that he almost fell out of the collective link, and he barely managed to keep his shields up so their conversation wasn't shared amongst the clan members. *He was about to name me Heir, when his distant cousin in Hartford called, and asked if he would teach her young son how to use the Voice.

*To Caius, an alpha Heir with the Voice in full measure had more worth than a Speaker. Then I was tasked with pup-sitting a young alpha with too much power and a quick temper, who caught my heart in his adorable little paws. The rest, as you know, is history.**

Adorable little paws? Kane mentally sputtered, Burke's mirth pouring through the link. He sent a wordless growl back, but his tail wagged in the snow. **And it wasn't your heart I caught in my paws!**

No flirting, you're mated now, Burke chuckled, the echoes of his many mind voices bleeding through Kane's shields. **Don't make me tell on you. Ghost is scary. He can strike people with lightning!**

Kane could feel Burke's mental laughter through the pack-links, and he rolled his eyes, not so easy in wolf-form. He was on the hill overlooking the park center, the sky murky black and darkening. The clan was setting up an interwoven patrol system, and the easiest way to teach the Red Fern wolves how to use the Black Pine method was through the collective link.

Enough chattering, younglings, a cool and stony voice infiltrated their private link, the White Wolf's presence as overwhelming mentally as she was in the physical world. **My Clan is ready. Begin your lessons, Speaker.**

As the White Wolf bids, Kane said without a trace of sarcasm, the White Wolf's lupine form impossible to see through the trees and snow. She was there, somewhere, presumably directing her people. **Burke, are you ready?** It was an unnecessary question, as Burke was always ready, but the day he took Burke for granted was the day his best friend ripped him a new one.

I am, and I'm bringing the Red Fern wolves in one group at a time, Burke said, and Kane could see in his mind the lights that represented the small packs of Red Fern wolves moving in and out of the bright webbing that held Burke's consciousness.

As each group of wolves were brought in to direct contact with Burke, the Speaker would 'give' them the memory of running patrols in the overlapping, timed patterns that let the Black Pine wolves maintain a close-knit and nearly seamless border for any area they may be holding at any given time. It was a tactic Kane learned over a decade earlier from human military members, adapted for the wolf-form, and it served Kane and his team remarkably well since then. Teaching the long-lived wolfkin new things was always a challenge, since the majority of their people were around the century mark, and took to changes slowly. The most recent generations, the younger wolves, the ones with cells and tablets and e-readers and social media pages took to human innovations and new ways of doing things with an enviable dexterity and little difficulty. He was expecting the younger adults to be leading the way by example, given the chance to shine in front of their parents and elders, and the eagerness he could sense through the links reinforced his expectations.

Kane, secure in the knowledge that Burke had things well in hand, cast his mind out farther, looking for the now familiar silver-white star of his mate. He'd been keeping tabs on the two alphas and his mate since they left, thankful he didn't need to keep an active mental foothold on Ghost. Their soul-bond was deeper than any regular mental connection, serving as both a mate bond and a mind link, the flow of emotions, some thoughts and energy between them constant and ever-deepening. Days into their mating, and Kane was more connected to Ghost than he'd ever thought it was possible to be with another person. Ghost was there in his mind, even now, though not actively present in his higher thoughts. Kane was thankful; not that he would keep things from his mate, but having Ghost constantly in his thoughts would quickly irritate them both.

Kane sent a wordless wave of affection and desire along their bond, and a moment later he got an answer, a twisting river of images, a joyous affection and tenderness and a hint of wild lust, and strangely enough, taste and smells. Coppery blood and the scent of warm rabbit fur tickled his nose, and Kane sneezed, amazed at the breadth and vivid nature of the bond. Ghost let him in with a ready welcome, no words needed between them, and Kane could see his mate sat under the boughs of huge black pines, in a sheltered glen, the scraps of a rabbit between him and the young Ashland alpha. Through Ghost's senses he knew Gerald was nearby, and Ghost obligingly turned his muzzle and let Kane see the lesser alpha standing protectively over the two younger wolves.

Kane was pleased Gerald was taking his role as his mate's protector seriously. Gerald's petulance was gone, Ghost's sudden reappearance in all their lives seeming to reset the lesser alpha's attitude. His surliness was still there, and Gerald had yet to reach out to anyone other than his nephew...and Sophia. His First Beta had told him about Gerald's assistance the night before, in connecting the patrol packs while Kane dealt with Ghost's injuries and Burke was recovering. The beta and lesser alpha appeared to be getting along better now that Gerald stopped hitting on her and Sophia stopped trying to break body parts. Gerald was running on next to no rest, yet wasn't faltering. Kane would spare Gerald if he could, but keeping his mate safe and happy took precedence. Letting Ghost out for a quick run while in the company of two alphas, not to mention protected by his own considerable gifts, was the least he could do for his mate.

Ghost must have caught the edge of his thoughts, as he felt his mate's mental scoffing of Kane's presumption for thinking Ghost needed to be 'let out' with permission for a run.

Not actually a pet, dear mate of mine, Ghost whispered through their bond, and Kane shifted in the snow, slightly uncomfortable. *_Don't need permission to do anything._*

I was being a bit autocratic there, wasn't I? Kane returned, chagrined. *_I'm sorry, my little wolf. I need to work on that._*

I don't know what that means, Ghost grumbled, and Kane's view changed as Ghost turned his head again, his nose twitching as he tracked scents on the icy winds. Even with Gerald standing watch, Ghost's wilder nature kept him at a wary alert, nose and ears and eyes constantly evaluating his surroundings for threats. This cheered Kane despite his uneasiness at having Ghost out of his sight and reach. **Too many words I don't know,** Ghost continued, breaking into his musings. **Can't keep relying on your—education? Knowledge?** Kane felt Ghost seeking the words and inflections he needed even as he complained about doing so, and his mate's frustrations bled clearly through their link, **—to keep me functioning as a thinking...and...articulate?—creature. I should have paid more attention to Cat and Glen growing up.**

You're just perfect the way you are, my little wolf, he said to his mate, sending him a rush of reassurance and pride along their link. Ghost was absorbing so much from him, and Kane kept his mental walls down just for that reason, welcoming Ghost into his mind so that his mate wouldn't feel inadequate in any way for having been raised as a pet of sorts instead of a sentient person needing an education. The small shaman's manner was one of casual confidence, with an innocent obliviousness to social structures, saying what he meant and thought, without filter. It was the wilder side of his spirit, the wolf side, which shaped Ghost's behavior the most, and the little shaman must find dependency and vulnerability irritating.

If you want an education, you can go to school, Kane suggested, thinking of all the younglings, like Gabe, who went to human schools and universities. It was only the very young who were home schooled, since no five year old can resist telling his or her friends about how they can use magic and turn into wolves. **Gabe goes to Boston College, ask him about school. We can forge paperwork and transcripts, and you can get an education in anything you want.**

School? Ghost all but squeaked, a difficult feat mind to mind. Kane flinched, and was about to calm his mate when Ghost abruptly pulled away from their connection.

Worried he'd made Ghost feel bad for not having an education, Kane was thinking up an apology when Ghost suddenly returned, his mind voice sounding off, distracted.

Are there wolves patrolling in this area of the park? his mate asked, his attention drawn outside, away from their conversation.

He heard the crackle of breaking ice under paws and a sudden chorus of deep snarls from the trees surrounding his mate.

Ghost! he screamed through their fading link, just before his shaman dropped their intimate connection. He got a glimpse of sleek shadows pouring through the black pines before he lost Ghost's sight.

Kane! Wolves near the gates are reporting humans approaching, military-style vehicles, heavily armed! Burke said urgently, and Kane was suddenly torn—his mate and his people were both in danger.

Kane jumped to his feet, snow flying, and howled in rage, with voice and mind. His cry shattered the mental dance among the Black Pine Speaker and the Red Fern wolves, and Kane could care less—his mate was in danger, and their enemies were already here.

CARNAGE AND CHAOS

GHOST LEAPT to his feet, Gabe tumbling in frantic surprise as three strange wolves flowed out from the pine trees. Gerald roared in challenge, immediately engaging a wolfkin as the big brute jumped straight at Ghost. They fell to the snow in a flurry of growls and bloody fur.

Ghost could hear Kane calling him through their link, but he was too occupied with the two other wolves who circled him and Gabe. Ghost dropped his head and pulled his lips back in a snarl, Gabe doing the same on his right side, the strangers both ragged wolves of intermediate browns and grays, a harsh mien in their eyes as they snarled back, saliva dripping from their fangs. Malice rolled off them in a veritable wave, and Gabe moved to cover Ghost, trying to put himself between Ghost and the attackers.

Ghost! Kane finally broke through, but Ghost had to ignore him, as both wolves leaped at the same time. Ghost dodged, ducking down, his opponent sailing over him with a frustrated snarl. Ghost spun, putting his back to Gabe, snarls and grunts letting him know Gabe was fighting as well.

Stop, Ghost spoke to his attacker, sending the thought as forcefully as he could. The wolf was mid-leap, and Ghost got a glimpse of harsh shock on his face as he went abruptly limp, falling to the ground in a tangle of limbs and tail. Ghost paused, head tilted, and sniffed the wolf. He had no idea what just happened. The strange wolf was still alive, and unconscious.

A yelp sounded behind him, reminding him he wasn't alone, and Ghost spun back to see Gerald taking on the other foreign wolf, his first opponent laying still in the snow. Gabe and Gerald circled the remaining wolfkin, both alphas bloodied and torn.

Gerald and Gabe charged, and Ghost ran to block the last attacker's retreat. The coward yelped and made to bolt, but Ghost was on him, pinning his bigger body to the ground, Ghost's teeth on his throat. He didn't break the skin, just held him still for the split second it took him to send a snapping electrical charge into the downed wolf. He went limp, much like the first, and the scent of ozone rose as Ghost backed away from the unconscious wolfkin. He snorted, and danced in the snow, looking back the way the attackers came.

GHOST! Kane's mental shout made Ghost jump, and he guiltily remembered his poor mate, who was frantic with worry.

I'm fine, Ghost hurriedly explained to his mate, able now to let Kane back in the forefront of his mind. *_I don't know why we were attacked or who they are, but they are down._* Ghost checked the wolfkin Gerald dispatched, and realized he was dead, neck torn apart. His uncle had made short work of the attacker. *_One is dead, the other two I stopped._*

Kane's relief swept through him, the Heir looking through Ghost's eyes as if to reassure himself Ghost wasn't holding anything back. Ghost snorted again, and he went to check on the two alphas, both big males sniffing at the downed wolfkin, growling low. From the way Gabe and Gerald's ear tips were flicking, Kane or Burke must be talking to them as well, the low buzz of their kind's telepathy fading in and out of Ghost's ability to sense.

Get back to Andromeda's, now! The park is under attack! Kane cried across their link, and Ghost's head shot up, and he was off for the park center before he could tell his paws to move. The urgency in Kane's mind voice was impossible to resist. **Sophia and some Red Fern wolves are coming out to escort you back. Armed humans are at the border near the gates. I'm taking my team to stop them. Remus will not get away with this.**

Be careful, my alpha, Ghost told his mate, paws digging in the snow as he flew through the pines, Gerald and Gabe on his tail. If they made it back in time, they might be able to join Kane and the wolves of Black Pine in their counterattack.

Ghost thanked his many years in wolf-form for his reflexes when a handful of furred bodies burst out from the groundcover, fangs and claws extended to slash his throat—Ghost ducked in time to avoid instant death, but got a furious beta on his back instead.

KANE, WITH Burke close on his heels, tore through the gathering winds, the storm screaming across the mountain tops, both alphas heading for the gates where the initial alarm was raised by the sentries. Most of his tactical team was shifted and a few strides back, minus a few wolves who had been on border patrol when Burke sent out the alarm. Ten wolves, all highly skilled fighters and the strongest betas Black Pine had to offer, howled and snarled, their cries echoing through the dormant trees, the bending road beginning to straighten as they rounded the last curve before the gates.

Kane fought back the rising tide of memories, of the last time he ran for the gates of this park, the summer sky warm and bright, the earth alive… and soaked with the scent of wolfkin and mortal blood. The last time he took a run like this, wolves at his back and danger ahead, he failed to save the clans' greatest shaman, and the wolfkin cub who would one day become his mate was lost to him and their people for many years. This time he would not fail; Simon Remus would follow his brother to the grave, and Roman would again learn the bite of Kane's fangs.

Leave Remus for Caius; Roman was going to die under Kane's fangs. He'd had the chance, at the last Challenge, and Kane howled in frustrated rage as he came to feel twenty years of grief and bitter impotence—for Roman was the wolfkin responsible for the deaths of dozens of their kind, wolfkin all slain for a fruitless ambition to steal goddess-gifted abilities from shamans and alphas. If he'd killed Roman years ago when he'd first Challenged Kane, then countless lives would have been spared. Even killing Roman last week, instead of thinking to assuage Caius' increasing ennui with mercy for his son, Kane could have unwittingly avenged his people and possibly stopped more from dying.

A sharp, loud report of a rifle blasted through the air, and Kane dodged, pushing Burke into the snow bank on the side of the road as the icy gravel splintered inches from his nose. More guns fired, flashes illuminating the shooters who took cover behind black jeeps and big SUVs. The Black Pine wolves scattered, Kane and Burke ducking behind a thick cluster of trees next to the road, bullets spitting little geysers of snow into the air as the shooters followed them into cover. Bullets bit into the dense tree, bits of bark landing on their fur. Kane hunkered down as far as he could, Burke managing to hide better, being almost half Kane's size.

Guess we should have thought this through better, Burke mused, both of them ducking, bullets zinging off the trees they hid behind. **Any plans that don't involve getting shot, oh Fearless Leader?**

Shut it, and keep your head down! Kane snapped, wishing he could see where the humans were. The storm was covering up any sounds they may be making, and the wind wasn't helping any. Thick clouds were releasing giant snowflakes, and the wind was sporadic and undependable. And growing stronger, which meant they couldn't hear or scent the humans ahead of them. Kane couldn't tell if they were still at the vehicles or if some of them were peeling off, waiting to ambush them in the trees. He tried peering around the nearest tree, but a bullet chewing into the bark made him back up in a hurry.

Fuck, Kane growled, Burke sending a wordless agreement back. **The others?** Kane asked his Speaker, and Burke sent him reassurances. His team was blocked off, pinned as they were, and waiting for orders. No one was hit. **Sophia?**

She went for Ghost as you told her, Burke replied, and Kane sensed he was speaking to their beta, the older wolfkin heading out with some Red Fern wolves to escort Ghost back to Andromeda's. Burke sent him an image of Sophia racing through the woods with a handful of cream colored wolves, the storm growing stronger there as well, but she had a good grasp of the young shaman's location, Gerald linked to Burke as well. He had faith his First Beta would get to his mate and help keep Ghost safe.

The hail of bullets paused, the wind screaming, and Kane risked another look. The cloud cover was thick, as was the snowfall, and his nose was useless. His vision and hearing were suffering as well, and Kane could just barely make out the silhouettes of several humans peel off from the vehicles at the gates and head into the woods. Burke saw through his eyes, and both alphas growled. Humans in the woods were usually easy prey; but with their senses dulled by the weather and the humans armed, things just got evened out.

Stay low, stay smart, and stay in pairs! Kane ordered his team, and they sent back their silent agreement. **No mercy. Kill them all. If Remus is here, I will handle him.**

Kane crouched low, and went around the trees, smelling blood and wolfkin ahead as they went. Burke stayed in his shadow, the brown greater alpha a reassuring presence. They'd hunted side by side for decades, and this was familiar territory. Kane thought of his mate, his little shaman, and vowed to finish this once and for all. Ghost must be kept safe.

CLAWS RIPPED at his fur, but Ghost rolled with the attack, throwing the other wolfkin off his back and into the snow. Ghost got to his feet, and was nearly trampled by Gabe and another wolfkin, both bigger wolves snapping and tearing at each other in a flurry of fangs and claws. Blood stained the snow, and Ghost followed the trail, to see his uncle and two other wolves locked in combat, fur bloodied. He spared no thought for himself, and ran forward, barreling into the bigger of the two strangers. He called to the power writhing in the storm-eddied winds, and loosed it when it came to his will.

A brilliant flash and the odor of burnt fur filled his nostrils, and the wolf who'd been seconds from hamstringing his uncle was down. Ghost leapt over his body, and ran to Gerald's side, the lesser alpha still on his feet, blood dripping and running freely from wounds on the back of his neck and shoulders. Both strangers must have attacked him in tandem to cause such damage. Ghost whined, concerned, but Gerald shoved past him with a snarl, his last opponent charging ahead as well.

Gerald bowled him down, and the ragged stranger yelped, thrown to his back and left exposed to Gerald's lethal teeth. Ghost barely had time to step forward before the other wolfkin was dead, throat torn apart, just like the last wolfkin Gerald fought. Ghost was impressed, and then turned to look for the younger alpha.

Gabe was still fighting, one rear paw dragging in the snow, but his head was down and his fangs dripping with his opponent's blood. He was now facing two wolves, the other the wolfkin who'd tried to ambush Ghost. The two older wolves circled the young alpha, looking for a way in past his teeth. Gabe was bigger, but noticeably younger, and less experienced in fights to the death, his hesitancy obvious.

Ghost and Gerald both howled in challenge, and ran to Gabe's side, standing between him and the two remaining wolves. Gabe faltered and almost fell, and Gerald braced his big shoulder for the younger alpha to lean against. Ghost growled a warning, gathering more power, his Spiritsight active and showing him the baleful lights gleaming in the other wolfkin. There were no bright colors or joyful patterns of light; they were muted, dark, and angry.

He could see, with his Spiritsight, more wolves coming through the trees. Dark stars, tainted by hatred and anger filled his line of sight, and they appeared out of the snow and wind like wraiths. Gerald and Gabe growled with eagerness, both alphas willing to fight to the death, their instincts to dominate and defeat roused by battle. The answering chorus from the new wolves was full of bloody thoughts and death.

They were outnumbered, more than Ghost cared to count, and Ghost dropped his head and bared his teeth.

He was not afraid. He was angry. They growled back, and began to lope forward.

Ghost gave up thinking to spare these wolves, while they charged ahead, their malice and intent to harm clear. He pulled, at the place inside that glowed the brightest, and reached out.

Lightning, so bright the trees were illuminated in fine detail, and the clouds above were traced by its glow, burst free. The small space where they stood under the pines was naught but light and fire, and burning flesh.

BURKE! KANE snarled, and lunged through the short space between himself and the human, the shotgun in his hands still smoking from the blast he'd leveled at the Speaker.

The snow was falling hard, so thick Kane was almost blind, but his teeth found the human's shoulder and neck, and he shook hard. Bones cracked and the human male went limp, the gun falling to the snow. Kane dropped the body, and ran to Burke, the brown alpha slowly getting to his feet.

Blood dripped and the rancid odor of silver in wolfkin flesh smacked Kane's senses, and Burke whined. He swayed on his paws, tail drooping. Kane nosed at his neck, and his heart clenched when Burke leaned into his chest, shivering. They were rarely cold, their kind; Burke was injured, and badly. The human had come unseen out of the trees, the wind working against them, and Burke took the brunt of the shotgun blast.

Burke?

I... am fine. Get me to your talented little shaman soon enough, and I won't even have a scar. Burke panted, whining. Kane didn't believe a word, but he wasn't given a chance to say anything, as he heard the sound of booted feet coming their way. The shotgun blast must have alerted the rest of the humans to where they were.

His team was slowly taking out the humans, but Burke wasn't the only injured wolf. Several of his wolves were shot, none dead, but the silver would slow the healing process and leave them vulnerable. Many of the humans were dead, but enough remained to be a threat. Red Fern wolves were still at the park center, protecting the Suarez wolves and the family packs, the youngest and the most vulnerable directly under Andromeda's protection. So far no one had made it that far into the park, but neither Kane nor Andromeda wanted to take the chance that Roman or Remus would have people get through.

Kane gently pushed Burke back down, and stepped over his best friend, head lowered, paws soundless as he stalked through the shadows under the trees. There was a human directly ahead somewhere, he could hear the thump of a heart. Yet he couldn't see where, and was cautious, wary of being shot in the face if he got too close and the human pulling the trigger before he could take him out.

He needed to be able to see, to smell, the wind and snow hindering him to an impossible degree. Kane swallowed a growl, the sound of the human's heart coming closer, steady and even. The human was not afraid, a practiced killer of their kind to be that unaffected in the woods with wolfkin hunting. A soft crack of ice breaking made Kane pause, and he quivered, the need to kill warring with his better judgment.

A yellow light appeared in the snow, and another, a field of light gleaming amongst the falling flakes. Tiny flames glimmered, and Kane breathed out, realizing it was with his mate's Spiritsight that he was seeing the human tactical team. Six lights glowed, spread out ahead of him and to the sides, coming closer. One was within reach, and an easy target with how far Kane could leap. Somehow he knew the human was looking away, and Kane gathered his legs underneath himself, and paused a heartbeat. Then he leapt.

He cleared the space between himself and the human in seconds, driving the smaller male to the ground. A scream was cut off as Kane buried his fangs in the soft skin of his throat and he yanked. Blood fountained out, thick in his mouth, hot over his tongue. Kane shook his head free of the corpse, blood flying, and looked for his next target.

Ahead and to the right. Kane's big paws sank in the snow, the wind covering his approach. The baleful light flickered as this human moved through the trees, heart racing faster than the others. Perhaps some instinct told him he was now the hunted, and vulnerable. Kane didn't even pause; he slinked through the shadows and came up behind the human, moving with effortless strides over the snow and ice. He was tall enough that all he had to do was lean forward, and he crushed with a single bite the arm holding the long gun, metal and bone snapping. The human screamed, falling to his knees, and Kane let go of his arm to snap his jaws around the human's skull and clamp down. Bone shattered and brain matter spilled under the intense pressure he bore down on the human, and the body went limp in his jaws.

Kane spit out the dead human, and with Ghost's Spirit-sight aiding him, he hunted for his next target through the snow and trees.

One by one the humans fell, their blood and screams soothing his wilder side.

Simon Remus was nowhere to be found.

A WET, COOL nose nudged at his face. Ghost winced, and slowly opened his eyes. He saw bare earth and blackened grass, ash and smoke wafting on the breeze.

"He's awake! Ghost, can you get up?" asked Sophia, shooing away the small Red Fern beta who was crouching at his side. The little wolf scampered off, and a naked Sophia knelt beside him.

Ghost climbed to his feet, and realized he was in his human form. He frowned, wondering when that happened, and looked around. Smoke and charred meat filled his nose, and he sneezed. Bodies were burnt past recognition and lay scattered across the ground under the trees, and there wasn't a tree or patch of ground untouched by flame and smoke.

Several Red Fern wolves sniffed at the bodies or huddled together, and they ducked their heads when they saw him looking, afraid to meet his eyes. Ghost lifted a brow at that, and shrugged. Sophia regained his attention by touching his naked shoulder.

"Where are Gabe and Gerald?" he asked, suddenly worried he'd scorched the two alphas he'd been trying to protect, turning to his mate's First Beta. She pointed with her chin, her dark gem–toned eyes glittering. He looked where she indicated and he smiled in relief, glad to see Gabe and Gerald were untouched by the lightning storm.

He ran over the wet earth, the snow melted by the intense heat, squishing under his bare feet. Gerald got up, reverted back to his human form as well, and covered in mud and blood. Gabe was still on the ground, just as naked and bloody. Gabe was pale and shivering, and a Red Fern wolf hovered at his side, licking his shoulder, the younger alpha slow blinking and dazed.

"You okay, pup?" Gerald asked gruffly, and reached out, grabbing both his shoulders and pulling him in close. "What the hell was *that?*"

"I stopped them, Uncle. That's all," Ghost said instead of answering. He wasn't too sure himself, and couldn't think of anything else to say. "Has anyone heard from Kane and his team?"

Ghost could feel a burning rage along his connection to his mate, the greater alpha's full focus and attention on whatever task he was performing. Ghost tried to get through, but his mate was too intent, his anger and bloodlust overpowering, and Ghost gave up after a few tries.

"I lost my connection to Burke a few minutes ago," Sophia answered, worry evident on her timeless face. "I think something happened."

"I can't reach them either," Gerald growled, his dark eyes glowing, his hands tight on Ghost's shoulders.

"Then we go to them," Ghost said, and stepped back in the mud and gore. Gabe tried to stand, but fell back to the damp earth. Ghost hurried to his side, and put a hand on the young alpha's lean chest. He poured power and strength back into Gabe, and the dull haze over his eyes cleared, and his shivering ceased. Gabe inhaled a deep breath, and then nodded in thanks to Ghost. He helped the alpha to his feet, and called to his power again.

He found his wolf-form in less than a thought's time, and waited for the others to Change.

Ghost waited only a few heartbeats, his body vibrating with the need to run, but he would not leave his people behind. They may be capable alphas and beta warriors, but he was the strongest here, and they were his to protect.

But his heart was with Kane... and his alpha was hunting.

KANE GRIPPED the steel door with his bare hands and pulled back, the frame warping until the latch released and the last impediment to Kane getting inside the SUV was gone. He ducked back in time to avoid getting shot in the face, then he leaped inside and knocked aside the gun in the human's hand. He grabbed the weak mortal by the throat and pulled him out of the SUV, the human obviously no mercenary. He was shorter and plump, and smelled of chemicals.

He recalled Ghost's memories of Remus' attack at the wolf sanctuary, and knew this was the human doctor who'd drugged Ghost. His hand tightened on the short man's neck, and it took Burke's whine to still his fingers.

We need him alive, Burke said, mental voice feeble. He was panting in pain on the pavement, blood pooling under him, surrounded by dead humans. The rest of Kane's team swept the woods or tended the injured, those too hurt to move resting in their wolfkin forms not far from Burke. **He can tell us where our kidnapped brethren are, and what Simon Remus was doing to them.**

I know... I just want him dead, I want them all dead, Kane replied, refusing to speak in front of the human. He pulled back his fist, and struck the doctor across the face, knocking him unconscious. He threw the man back inside the SUV, and went around to the driver's side, and removed the keys, tossing them on the hood of the vehicle. All the vehicles were either disabled or the drivers dead, torn apart on the pavement. Kane was covered in blood, and he breathed through the heavy stench of fear that hovered over the park gates.

Kane knelt on the freezing pavement at Burke's side, and pulled the Speaker's head into his lap. Burke sighed, his great form heaving with the effort to keep himself under control. Kane felt Burke's pain, the shotgun blast having torn through fur, skin, muscle and tendons along his side, the silver in the buckshot burning and searing flesh. It was serious, perhaps mortal, and Kane feared Burke would not make it through the injury, not without some crippling or maiming.

I called for River...he is coming once Andromeda says it's safe, Burke whispered, his once boundless and infinite mental voices reduced to a singular thread, weak and thin. He panted, mouth open, his blood still seeping from the long wound along his ribs and flank. His golden eyes were the barest lines in his dark chocolate brown furred face, and Kane gently petted his ears.

The storm was calmer, the snow falling slow, the flakes huge and drifting over them, white dotting Burke's dark coat. His eyes shut, the golden light dimming.

"If River can't help you, then Ghost can," Kane whispered, snow melting on his cheeks, tears pricking his eyes. "Stay awake, don't go to sleep."

I won't... Burke said, so softly. Kane bit his lip, refusing to cry, his team mates nearby watching, silent. They all waited, Kane calling wordlessly to the rest of his team to wait at the gates, and they came, in ones and twos, hunkering down in their wolf-forms and watching him as he held Black Pine's Speaker. Burke's heart still beat, slow and struggling, the poison from the silver coursing through his veins.

"Stay awake," Kane ordered his best friend, unleashing the Voice on Burke for the first time in all their years together, from boyhood friends to lovers to finally brothers. Just a small amount, the power barely tangible, but enough to affect the Speaker. Burke shuddered, but he opened his eyes and his mind came back from the edge of consciousness. "I haven't given you permission to die, dammit."

Can't leave you alone, Burke gasped, the pain brutal now that Kane was forcing him to stay alert and conscious. His heart thundered, offbeat and labored. **And you won't be. You have him, now. You will never be alone again.**

Stay awake! Stay alive! I am ordering you to stay here! Kane hugged Burke to his chest, crying now, not caring if his team saw him or not. Kane was a killer, an alpha, and even he in all his strength could not stop death. The Voice was useless against a failing body and the slow insidious assault of silver. Shaman River wasn't going to make it in time, and the older shaman wasn't as adept as Gray Shadow had been at removing silver from the body... **Ghost! I need you! Please, my mate, I need you!**

*I hear you, my love,** Ghost answered, silver starlight filling his heart and mind. Kane looked up, down the road towards the park, and he could see, in the far distance, a flowing wave of lights glimmering in the trees. A brilliant silver-white star led the way, and Kane knew it was his mate coming to the rescue, the little shaman moving faster than the wolves who struggled to keep pace with him.

Ghost broke through the gloom and snow, shining brighter than the Northern Star, running full out and devouring the distance between them. Burke went limp just as Ghost leaped over the Black Pine wolves, shifting in the air with a glimmer of silver-white power, coming to kneel as a man in front of them. Kane cried out Burke's name, and Ghost put his hands over the Speaker's wounds.

Burning heat and blinding light erupted from under his mate's hands, and Kane was forced to look up. He watched his mate's face, and the serenity and joy there made Kane's tears fall all the faster.

SIMON LOWERED the binoculars, the infrared lenses showing through the snowfall the collection of wolves gathered around the fallen brown beast. Simon's lip curled, and he pulled his jacket tighter around his neck, wincing at the sting from the bite wound Roman had inflicted earlier.

His whole body hurt, and he was thankful for the cold,

since it numbed his body. His ass was sore and his pride dented, the experience of being made Roman's bitch as unpleasant as it was enlightening... and arousing.

Roman was out there somewhere in the woods, his attempt to breach the perimeter of the park as idiotic and uninspired as every other idea the alpha had come up with in the last fifteen years. Simon had seen a horrific flash of light, a blinding, concussive wave along the route Roman was to take with his wolves, and Simon knew that it was a failure. The men Roman had sent to the park gates were dead or taken hostage, and Simon could spare no more time waiting around. Roman was a lost cause, and the involvement of Remus Acquisitions was now made apparent to all parties.

Simon would not be caught unawares, not like Sebastien had been all those years ago. Simon had money, power, and men hired to kill. If Caius McLennan and the other Greater Clan Leaders decided to come for him, Simon was prepared to unleash war across New England.

Damn the consequences.

He would come out of this just fine. In fact, he still had his pets, in his labs, just waiting to fulfill their purpose. If Simon couldn't get from them the secrets of their near immortality and abilities, then he would sell them to those who could get the information. Sending the doctor on the assault, to 'drug the Heir', was one last loose end neatly tied off. The doctor didn't know where Simon held the remaining Suarez wolves, and the lab was being scrubbed this very moment.

Hatred and a sick fury burned in his gut. Let Roman suffer, Simon was cutting his losses. His neck and ass smarted, and Simon swore as he turned back to the waiting SUV, and climbed inside. The mercenary at the wheel pulled a three-point turn and they drove away from Baxter, heading south.

ROMAN CREPT along the side of the cabin, the lights low, voices muted. The rear of the building was dark, and just above his head a balcony door was cracked open. He caught the scent of pain and fear, and knew the Suarez wolves were just overhead. The shamans would be there with their patients. His nephew might be up there. There was no sign of Andromeda anywhere, so the beta bitch must be out dealing with the humans at the gates.

Roman took one last look around the darkened exterior of the cabin, then leapt up, his claws catching the railing. He pulled himself over, and crouched on all fours before creeping across the balcony to the door. He listened, hearing the slow steady beat of hearts, and the sound of someone whispering.

“Shaman River...” the voice cut out, the whisper drowned out by the wind. The storm was still very much present, but not as severe as it had been when the lightning storm eradicated the wolves Roman had sent to attack the cabin. He'd seen them all die a horrible death, and then made his way through the park to the cabin alone.

He stuck his nose in past the open door, the room dark. He couldn't see anyone, and risked entering a few steps more.

The lights flicked on, and a foot connected firmly with his rump, sending him sprawling into the back of a couch. He whirled, teeth bared, and resisted the urge to cower under the glacial stare of the White Bitch. Andromeda slammed shut the balcony door, and her skinny little brat of a brother walked around the couch to stand at her side.

"Always a fool, Roman McLennan," she growled, eyes burning bright. He snarled back at her, teeth bared, and made to leap at the beta bitch, but her hand slapped out and landed across his temple. Everything went dark.

EPILOGUE

Reckoning

THE COMBINED wolfkin of Red Fern and Black Pine gently carried Burke out of the rear of the SUV, the Speaker returned to his human form and resting peacefully. Ghost paced at his side until River met him at the front porch, and Ghost nodded to the older shaman wearily, grateful it was over.

"He'll be fine," River assured him, and Ghost tried to smile, too tired and cold to say anything. He was exhausted, and he swayed, but he stayed, waiting until all the injured wolfkin went past him in to Andromeda's cabin.

Warm, powerful arms came around his waist, and pulled him back to a firm chest. Ghost sighed at the welcome heat, leaning on Kane in thanks.

"You saved him, my mate," Kane leaned down and whispered in his ear, kissing a sensitive spot on his neck. Ghost shivered, though for a different reason. "Thank you, Ghost. You saved so many lives today."

"So did you, my love," Ghost twisted in Kane's arms, and met his mate's dark gaze. "The humans would have killed the families here without hesitation, and they needed to be stopped. The wolfkin at the gates wouldn't have made it if you and your team hadn't gotten there in time to stop the humans."

"Many of our people were hurt," Kane said, frowning, unhappiness clouding the air around them. "This never should have happened. If I'd killed Roman all those years ago..."

"Never blame yourself for this! Never," Ghost snapped. "This is all on Roman and Simon Remus. My uncle turned his back on his people, and Simon Remus is an evil man who will find justice under your fangs. None of this is your fault, and I never want to hear you say anything like that again!"

Kane blinked down at him, and Ghost growled softly under his breath until his alpha gave him a small smile and a nod, leaning down to soothe him with a kiss. Ghost opened his mouth, letting Kane inside, and he found himself wrapping his legs around Kane's lean waist, big hands gripping his ass. He buried his hands in the bigger man's long dark hair, the soft strands delightful to the touch, and the taste of Kane in his mouth made his stomach clench in need.

"Take it somewhere private, younglings," a woman called out, and Ghost lifted his head from Kane's lush lips to see Andromeda and Sophia on the front porch, both female betas smirking at them.

"I'll keep an eye on Burke and the others," Sophia said, laughing.

"And Roman isn't going anywhere," Andromeda said with a deep growl, her blue eyes intense. "Caius will be here in a couple of hours; get some time in now, before explanations must be made to our Clan Leader."

Ghost nodded, as did Kane, and his alpha carried him up the steps of the cabin and inside. Kane took the stairs, ignoring the wolfkin loitering on the steps and in the front foyer. Ghost was naked in an equally naked Kane's arms, and surely the unspoken truth about their relationship was no longer a secret. Whether more than the select few already knew they were more than just lovers, that they were soulbonded mates, was another thing entirely.

Kane took them to the room they'd used before, kicking the door shut and lowering Ghost to the bed on his back. Ghost kept his legs open, and Kane settled between them. Big hands cupped his ass, kneading the flesh, and Ghost all but purred, eager for the touch despite his exhaustion.

"I should let you rest," Kane murmured, placing kisses along his jawline. "You must be tired."

"I want you, my mate," Ghost breathed, tilting his head, lifting his hips, needing more. Wanting it, desperately. "Please, I need you."

"Anything for you," Kane said, and he leaned down, hand searching alongside the bed for his bag. Kane found the lube, and poured some onto his fingers.

Kane gently worked two fingers into Ghost's ass, and he sighed, enjoying the sting. Kane's fingers spread apart, opening Ghost's hole, and he gasped, clutching to his alpha's shoulders and lifting his hips. Kane knelt above him, and Ghost grabbed his knees and pulled them up and apart, trying to watch as Kane's fingers moved in and out of his ass. The brush of his mate's hand over his rear, the heat of his large body so close was too much for Ghost. Exhaustion was dragging at him, and yet his cock wasn't listening to the rest of him. He was hard and he ached, bobbing against his stomach as clear fluid pulsed in sticky streams from the flared head. Kane murmured in appreciation, his other hand coming to grip his hard length in his big hand, fingers expertly stroking. Ghost moaned, and lifted to the touch, his cock growing harder and ass loosening with each wonderful thrust of his mate's fingers.

"Fill me, weigh me down and fill me up," Ghost begged softly, so tired, but needing Kane inside him. He was ready to erupt, waves of tingling nerves flowing out from the base of his spine, out through his hips and legs, to his toes. His fingers dug at the bedding, claws ripping, and he growled, impatient. Kane never hurried, taking his time, stroking and thrusting, fingers curling, touching a spot inside of Ghost that made him snarl in hungry need. "*Now*, mate."

Kane's eyes were dark flames, flickering in the shadows of the bedroom. Every muscle was taut with need and his skin bronzed by sweat, blood still tracing the lean lines of his arms and shoulders. His alpha smiled, fangs dropping, as he twisted his fingers again, and pegged that mysterious spot in Ghost's channel. He cried out, and went limp, legs falling from his grasp as Kane did it again.

"You are never leaving my side again, little shaman," Kane whispered past his fangs, leaning down over him, blocking out any light left in the room. Kane's dark eyes glowed with a light of their own, and Ghost couldn't look away. Kane kissed him, lightly, withdrawing his hand and then reaching for the lube again. "You under me, taking me inside, howling my name... that's where you belong."

Kane held himself above Ghost, who lifted his legs as Kane slicked himself up. His arms found their way around Kane's neck, his alpha positioning himself, holding still for a slow, wet kiss before pushing inside with his long, thick shaft.

Ghost tensed before Kane wordlessly begged him to relax, and Ghost did, Kane slipping inside deeper. The broad head pushed in, widening Ghost's muscles, stretching him, and the sting was just there on the edge of too much, and Ghost curled into Kane as the alpha lowered his full weight down on him. Kane slid in, fully seated now, and Ghost sighed, enjoying the deep ache. The pain was just enough, and the heavy weight of Kane's balls pressing to his ass helped make it plain that his mate was on him, inside him, and weighing him down. Ghost shuddered, enjoying the sensations, Kane's tongue dipping in his mouth, rubbing their tongues together.

Ghost whimpered into Kane's mouth, and his alpha growled, lifting his hips just a little, and then pressing back down. His cock slid out and in, the gentlest of rhythms, barely moving, shifting inside Ghost just enough to put pressure on that special spot that sent lightning shivers through his whole body. Kane's kiss went on forever, the pressure building between them, and Ghost let his mate inside his mind and heart, their spirits combining in a storming riot of colors.

Kane's hips surged, pressing Ghost down, and teeth found his neck, biting. Ghost came, spurting hot seed between them as Kane lost his steady rhythm and rutted hard and deep. Kane growled, a horrible rumble that made Ghost shiver, his orgasm chasing itself across his body in a tangled mess of firing nerves. Ghost howled, his cry shattering the heavy quiet, and the floor shivered with him. Kane filled his ass with wet heat, flooding him, and Ghost held his mate tightly, locking them together mind, body and soul.

"You are glorious, little wolf," Kane sighed in his ear, and Ghost licked his mate's neck, humming happily. Kane was still cumming in him, and the heady scents of sweat and seed filled the room. Ghost held his mate through the last waves of his orgasm, and Kane went limp, his bigger frame holding him down on the bed.

Ghost closed his eyes, fingers tracing the chiselled muscles on Kane's back, enjoying the warmth and weight of his mate. He felt it when Kane slipped into slumber, still hard and buried to the hilt inside his ass, Ghost's legs locked tight around his lean hips.

Ghost let himself follow his mate into sleep, his eyelids closing, heavy as the rest of his body.

ANDROMEDA STALKED down the hall, pausing only briefly outside the bedroom door where Kane and Ghost slumbered, the scent of sex wafting through the air. She smiled, but continued on, glad the younglings were cementing their bond in the face of what was coming. The deeper their connection, the safer they would be.

She took the stairs in a blur, out the front door of her cabin and along the icy path. The storm may be over, but the accumulation on the ground was still treacherous. Andromeda ran through the fresh snow, bare feet sinking only briefly as she ran.

When she reached the cabin she wanted, Andromeda saw a flash of pale skin and red hair in the window, and the door opened before she could even knock. She swept in, the human female closing the door behind her, eyeing Andromeda with a mixture of trepidation and intense curiosity. The human male came out from the restroom, stopping in his path to the kitchen.

“Ma’am,” the human male named Glen said, tilting his head in a show of respect. “Is it over?”

“Yes,” Andromeda said, watching the snow drip off her feet to the floor. She gave the humans a lightning quick grin, but it lacked warmth. “As over as such things can be. Time moves on, and wolves and men all die. Peace is temporary.”

“Ghost is okay?” Cat asked, hand to her mouth, green eyes wide.

“Our young shaman is well, but he may not be for much longer.” Andromeda watched as the humans who’d raised Ghost paled, their heartbeats erratic for a moment as they battled their sudden fear. These humans cared for Ghost, regardless of the fact they'd thought him an animal for the last several years. Their attachment to the cub was dangerous, for them more than Ghost.

"What do you mean?" Cat asked, Glen's eyes tracking every move that Andromeda made. The human male, if born wolfkin, would have made a fine alpha. He was all solid strength, and calm power radiated out from his spirit. He would perhaps handle the coming decision better than his mate.

"Humans are only ever told about our kind as a last resort. I believe humans call it 'need-to-know', and the two Greater Clan Leaders coming in a few short hours will not think you both worthy of knowing our secrets. You must leave, for your sake as well as Ghost's. He cannot survive the coming months if he is worried about your safety, or mourning your deaths."

"Leave? But..." Cat gasped, upset.

"If you stay, I can promise to try to keep you safe, and your involvement with Ghost might protect you, or even place you in greater danger. Caius may think you guilty of kidnapping, and kill you himself. Or he will be swayed by the love his grandchild holds for you, and spare your lives. Yet caution tells me that where Caius may be swayed, Heromindes may not."

"We won't leave," Glen stated, firm, jaw set. "Whatever happens, we won't abandon our cub. He's ours as much as he's yours." His mate nodded, her green eyes full of determination.

"I thought you might say that," Andromeda said, her lips

twitching. She hadn't squared off against Caius in decades, and Heromindes was a mystery to her. Fighting for the humans' right to live in safety would be a battle, and she couldn't wait.

GHOST HELD Kane's hand, standing beside his mate while the two large black vehicles took the last curve of the gravel drive. Burke, Gerald, Sophia and Gabe waited behind them, recovered from their assorted wounds and shifting nervously on their feet, their scents saying that these were going to be a few tense minutes once the Greater Clan Leaders disembarked. Cat and Glen were in their cabin, where they would stay until Ghost and Andromeda made it clear they were under their protection and exempt from the standing kill order on humans who learned the secrets of the wolfkin.

Ghost was nervous, though not as badly as the others. He was going to see Grandpa Caius for the first time in almost fifteen years, and he didn't know how to feel about that. Where Gerald, for all his dour and biting exterior, engendered in Ghost a feeling of familiarity and reassuring comfort, Ghost's memories of Caius McLennan were ones of nerves and wary respect, the greater alpha a stern figure of authority in his few memories from his life as Luca. Ghost had avoided the cellar room where Roman was chained and gagged, and he wanted nothing to do with the uncle who betrayed his own family and killed so many of their people.

Andromeda stood just in front of them, waiting with them for the vehicles to stop and park. She sent them a sharp glance over her shoulder, and said calmly, “Say nothing of your bonding until we have Caius alone. Or your humans, Ghost. Cat and Glen are staying out of sight until later. I don’t know Heromindes well, and I’d rather not find out how his reaction will go at the same time Caius learns of this. Let me sound out Caius before we tell him the happy news.” She gave them both another glance, before turning back to the SUVs and saying, “Stop holding hands, younglings.”

Kane stiffened at his side, and Ghost gripped his mate’s hand tighter. Kane gave him a soft look, and squeezed once before gently unclasping their fingers. Ghost growled, displeased, and he fought to keep the curl in his lip from showing when the vehicles came to a full stop and the doors opened.

A number of wolfkin stepped out, and Heromindes, Clan Leader of Ashland, was easy to pick out; the greater alpha was huge, towering over Caius and even Kane, hair long and braided, and he bore a striking resemblance to Gabe and his family.

Ghost immediately recognized Caius McLennan, the Clan Leader and greater alpha unchanged through the years. Still as large, still as formidable, and the stony reserve on his face was exactly the same. He felt all of a sudden five years old again, and scolded for running in his grandfather’s study, playing tag with his siblings. Ghost shivered, lost in his memory, while the strangers climbed the stone path to where they waited. Kane leaned into his shoulder, snapping him free, and Ghost relaxed, his mate’s presence enough to ground him. Everyone else's nerves were starting to get to him now, and he pushed it aside, recognizing the worry of how his grandfather would react to his soul binding as useless. Whether or not Caius approved was a moot point: his Goddess blessed them, named them soulmates, and that was more than enough for Ghost.

As it should be for every wolfkin.

Ghost was so focused on his thoughts it wasn't until Caius was staring down at him, brows furrowed, that he realized he'd missed the introductions. Kane shifted next to him, and leaned down to whisper in his ear.

"Little one, this is your grandfather, Caius McLennan. Alpha, your grandson Luca, who changed his name to Ghost in his... absence," Kane said, trying to be diplomatic. Ghost sent his mate a wry smile, and before he could restrain himself, kissed Kane on his cheek. Kane blanched, and looked at Caius, but stayed close, letting Ghost lean into his side.

"His absence," Caius grumbled, towering over Ghost, and once he would have been intimidating. Yet Ghost was no longer that tiny cub, cowed by a firm growl. He was a shaman, and mated to a fine alpha. There was no room for fear in his heart, not with Kane's presence there growing stronger by the hour. Andromeda was just past Caius' shoulder, shaking her head and smiling, and he looked back to his grandfathers he kept speaking. "Subtle way of reminding me that you were right, all these years. Right that he lived."

"Hello, Grandpa Caius," Ghost said with a small smile, cutting in, not wanting an argument in what he sensed was a sore subject between both alphas. He was home now. “You look the same.”

“You sound like... you sound like your momma, cub,” Caius replied, paling slightly. “And you look just like her, too.”

“Shaman, Grandfather. Not a cub,” he said gently, softening the rebuke. He would not be treated or seen as a child, and having Caius recognize him as fully grown and a shaman, outside of his influence, was the only way to maintain control when surrounded by greater alphas and clan leaders.

Caius gave a small start, and Ghost heard Gerald snort from where he stood behind them with the others. He collected himself quickly, and eyed Kane and he with something close to disfavor and what smelled bitterly like spite. Caius watched how Ghost leaned into Kane, and Ghost decided that lying, even by omission, was never the best way forward. Humans lied; he was wolfkin, and a shaman. Lying served no one.

Ghost took Kane’s hand, his mate bravely following his lead, pulling him into his strong arms. Caius watched them, eyes wide, and he breathed in deep. Ghost felt a buzzing, a building mental pressure, and knew it came from Caius. He pushed back, and Caius frowned, staring at them both, expression hard.

“Kane...” Caius growled, realization dawning in his eyes. “What have you done, you fool?”

“Grandfather, Kane is my soulbonded mate,” Ghost revealed, and he stood strong against the shocked expression on his grandfather’s face, and the exclamations of disbelief from those watching.

KANE PACED back and forth in front of the door, the big alpha nearly bristling with indignation and anger. Ghost's declaration to Caius, in front of Heromindes and their combined entourage, hadn't gone very well. Kane was listening, as he was, to the arguments happening in the living room of Andromeda's cabin. They were in her study, two greater alphas that Ghost did not know outside in the hall, presumably guarding the door. Though how anyone thought to keep Kane restrained by a single door, or Ghost for that matter, left him amused. Kane had gone willingly when Caius ordered him into the room, and Ghost shrugged, following his mate. The guards were confused as to why a shaman was being detained, but they said nothing when they locked them in here.

"...how do you expect me to *not* say anything to the other Clan Leaders?! This is an abomination of our Laws!" Heromindes yelled, the Clan Leader's opinion hard not to hear at that volume.

"Their bond is Goddess blessed and sacred, you fool!"

Ghost sat up from where he was leaning against the desk, brows raised in surprise. That was Shaman River out there, defending them, in a wholly unexpected move. Kane stopped pacing, his reaction the same as Ghost's.

"Yelling at each other solves nothing," Andromeda said, cool and calm. "Heromindes, this is a soulbond, not a mating bond performed by ceremony. That means our Goddess bound Kane and Ghost, and it is not our place to dispute her actions or to interfere in their bonding."

"He has the Voice. He broke our Laws once already in Worcester when he used it on me outside of a Challenge. Who is to say he didn't do so to the youngling he's taken as his mate?" Heromindes retorted. "I've never seen a soulbond, so for all I know, that is naught but a forced mating bond I can sense between them!"

"No shaman can be affected by the Voice, Hero," Caius said, his voice emotionless. "I know this fact well."

"There is something wrong here, Caius, and it's not just the abomination of an alpha mating with a shaman. It is your son who has been killing and torturing our people, and betraying our kind to humans! And from the information we tortured out of the human captives from the Worcester raid, Roman has been selling the kidnapping 'cast-offs' to sex slavers! Abomination rots in the heart of Black Pine, and how can I trust this wasn't endorsed by the Heir or his wolves? Twenty years to catch a traitor is a bit extreme! So far I put nothing past Black Pine and the laws your wolves seem willing to break. Your grandson may be a shaman, but he is too young to be fully trained, and I see no reason Kane couldn't have used his powers on Luca if he can't utilize his powers correctly."

Ghost grumbled, flashing a hint of fang at that insulting idea. Kane would never do that, never try something so evil.

Kane shook his head, and walked over to Ghost, pulling him along his side, both of them still listening to the argument down the hall. Ghost breathed in Kane's scent, the heat from his long body warming Ghost as they snuggled. He didn't sense any fear or shame from Kane, no worry. Ghost gave himself a tiny smile, gladdened again that he was gifted by such a fine alpha.

"That's enough, Hero," Caius said, some heat returning to his voice. "My son will face a tribunal if that will alleviate some of your worries. We have three clan leaders here now, and I can call in another who will be impartial if that is your wish. Even so, I don't doubt the outcome. Roman will pay for his crimes."

"I should declare a blood feud on Black Pine, for the loss of my wolves and kin! I entrusted my kin to you for safe keeping, and all along they've been under the protection of an alpha who didn't hesitate twice to break our laws, and the White Wolf succors this mockery of a mating. And Shaman River, who I never thought would allow such a thing, just defended it to my face. What has been done to my kin here, while my attention was elsewhere?" Heromindes demanded, his growls heard all the way down the hall.

"Hero, you saw Gabriel yourself. The youngling is well, and much improved, surely the rest of your kin is...," Caius began, but Heromindes cut him off.

"Kane will sit in front of the tribunal as well, for the violation of entering a mating bond with a shaman. That's a crime punishable by death," Heromindes stated. Ghost froze, and

Kane went still beside him. "And I want impartial shamans here to break the forced bond."

Ghost's heart thumped once, hard.

"Kane and Roman face the tribunal for their crimes, or Ashland revokes all bonds of treaty, and we will have a blood feud."

There was a whisper in the silence, Heromindes' declaration stealing everyone's voices. Ghost tried to hear it, but it faded away under the sudden cacophony of voices raised in anger from the other room.

Kane gave Ghost a slow, easy smile and caressed his jaw with a big hand when Ghost turned his head and looked up at his mate. There was no fear, still. Kane was not afraid. Ghost wasn't too sure what the clan leader meant by a tribunal, but he was not worried about the validity of their bond. They were gifted to each other by the Great Mother herself, her words to Ghost in the snowy meadow proof enough for him. Kane was innocent of breaking that Law.

Ghost became lost in Kane's eyes, the dark orbs full of affection, desire, and an emotion Ghost could not name. It burned in his heart too, fiery and pure, and left him feeling invincible.

The whisper returned, teasing Ghost's comprehension, and Kane reacted to it too, both wolfkin tilting their heads. The whisper called to Ghost, and he stepped to the door, pulling a willing Kane along by his hand. Ghost opened the door, and the two greater alphas outside both jumped, peering down at him. Ghost ignored them, and pulled Kane out into the hall. The greater alphas tried to stop them, but Ghost stilled them with a single glance, knowing somehow his eyes burned like silver fire in warning. The whispering led him down the hall, to the living room.

Everyone abruptly stopped yelling, and turned to look. Ghost stood, calm, feeling remarkably centered. Kane was at his side, both of them together, hands clasped.

“Kane has broken no Laws, and I have willingly claimed him as my mate, in front of clan leader and family,” Ghost said, meeting everyone’s eyes equally before landing at last on the Ashland clan leader. Heromindes was glaring, the huge alpha vibrating with insult and anger. “If Kane is to stand in front of the tribunal for giving me the privilege of loving him, then I will stand there with him, always by his side. I will share his fate.”

TO BE CONTINUED

The Wolf Of The Northern Star

The Wolfkin Saga returns in Early 2016

OTHER BOOKS BY SJ HIMES

Saving Silas

Necromancer's Dance (Release Late Winter 2016)

Symbiosis (Spring 2016)

Made in the USA
Lexington, KY
24 September 2018